Kathleen Rowntree grew up in Grimsby,
Lincolnshire, and was educated at Cleethorpes
Girls' Grammar School and Hull University
where she studied music. Her previous novels
are *The Quiet War of Rebecca Sheldon*, *Brief
Shining*, *The Directrix*, *Between Friends*,
Tell Mrs Poole I'm Sorry and *Outside, Looking In*,
and she has contributed to a series of monologues
for BBC2 TV called *Obsessions*. She and her
husband have two sons and they live on the
Oxfordshire/Northamptonshire borders.

Also by Kathleen Rowntree

BETWEEN FRIENDS
THE QUIET WAR OF REBECCA SHELDON
BRIEF SHINING
TELL MRS POOLE I'M SORRY
OUTSIDE, LOOKING IN

and published by Black Swan

LAURIE AND CLAIRE

Kathleen Rowntree

BLACK SWAN

LAURIE AND CLAIRE
A BLACK SWAN BOOK : 0 552 99608 4

Originally published in Great Britain by Doubleday,
a division of Transworld Publishers Ltd

PRINTING HISTORY
Doubleday edition published 1995
Black Swan edition published 1996

Set in 11/12pt Linotype Melior by
Kestrel Data, Exeter

Black Swan Books are published by Transworld Publishers Ltd,
61–63 Uxbridge Road, London W5 5SA,
in Australia by Transworld Publishers (Australia) Pty Ltd,
15–25 Helles Avenue, Moorebank, NSW 2170
and in New Zealand by Transworld Publishers (NZ) Ltd,
3 William Pickering Drive, Albany, Auckland.

Printed and bound in Great Britain by
Cox & Wyman Ltd, Reading, Berkshire.

To Joanna Goldsworthy

'I'm throwing caution to the winds this morning,' he said, tucking into a carton of low-fat yoghurt.

Her eyes slid over and beyond him, became focussed on seemingly empty space three feet behind his chair. Dennis Price was gliding through it, Dennis Price in his Jeeves persona. Imperceptibly, she nodded. At which Dennis Price raised his silver tray and bounced it down on the yoghurt-eater's head; then bowed, nodded, withdrew, and melted in dusty sunlight by the sideboard – where in solid flesh a young waiter lounged, ostensibly keeping an eye on the hotel guests' breakfast requirements, in fact chatting up the new waitress.

'Caution to the winds,' she marvelled, do me a favour! But it was sadness she felt rather than irritation. Not his fault, this decline into hypochondria, into pathological faddiness. Lydia's fault.

Those two at the sideboard were discussing them – she could tell from their covert glances. He was probably filling her in along these lines: 'That couple in the window are regulars – been coming here for years, on and off. Fell walkers, of course, like most of the guests. Wonder how much longer they'll keep it up. Must be getting on, they look pretty decrepit.'

A good few years yet, old son, she mentally retorted; looks can be deceptive – a thought which immediately returned her to Lydia and that moment in her life when 'caution to the winds' had certainly applied to herself. If the waiter knew about that, then he would have something to gossip about. She conjured up herself from his point of view: a slight woman in her late middle years, neat as a pin in straight-cut navy cords and crisp white shirt. 'See her by the window – proper little lady, wouldn't hurt a fly, wouldn't say boo to a goose? Not as innocent as she looks. What she got away with – well, some people call it the worst crime in the book.'

'Do you mind? Pull the other one, Eric.'

Stupid, she scolded herself; what the hell's the matter with you this morning? Hunger was the matter with her. Why didn't the lad stop gossiping and bring her the kipper she'd ordered?

But now she became aware of developments on the opposite side of the table: a stilled hand, spirits drooping, eyes grown anxious. She didn't need to look; she had his every trick, mannerism, hope, fear, strength, weakness, off by heart – and no wonder, she had known him all of her life. Come to think of it, the roots of his besetting anxiety probably lay in their peculiar background. Funny how often these days their minds went back to that time, how so many of their conversations began, 'Remember when we were at Foscote . . . ?'

Hey, the poor darling's waiting, she reminded herself, he's wondering why you don't respond, worried in case you're so out of patience with his health fetishes you've become terminally bored with him. . .

As if she ever could! Putting her head on one side, she delivered at last her belated grin (not a smiley grin, more an ironic moue of the sort she knew he had anticipated).

'There's brave,' she said.

Part One:
THE FOSCOTE EXPERIENCE

Claire, six years old, running through the corridors to
the bathroom, trailing her hand over smooth white-
painted plastered walls, bumping it over thickly
painted matt-white door panels, singing the song
Laurie was singing just now as they came chasing
through the wood in response to Aunt Margaret's call,
'*Laurie and Claire? – tea's ready*', came to a sudden
and silent halt. After a moment sang again, experimentally, the last line of Laurie's song. *Listened* to herself – the noise coming from her mouth, not the tune
running through her head that she intended to sing,
that she imagined she was in fact singing, and heard
– no doubt about it – a horrid monotonous growl.

Suddenly, many things were clear to her. Her
mother's anger, for instance: 'You are doing that
deliberately, Claire? No? Then, please, *silence*!', and
her father's evading eyes; also Uncle Peter's peculiar
habit of detaining her – 'Claire, dear, can you sing this
note I'm playing? No, don't hunch up; relax; listen to
this little tune. Now, breathe in: *you* sing it.' – and she,
in her hurry to be gone, assuming she'd satisfied him,
for ho always sounded satisfied – 'All right, Claire,
good girl, run along. Don't worry, she'll grow out of
it.' – this last to Sabine, Claire's complaining mother
– Claire unable to care less what it was she would grow
out of, merely registering that she was free to go and
find Laurie. Her mother's crossness had never struck
her as surprising or hurtful because Maman got angry
with lots of people for unknowable reasons. She was
an angry sort of person, sometimes screamed at Daddy
or at one of the students. Claire knew it made her

father sad when she failed to make headway with her piano lessons (luckily, she'd been let off these recently because Uncle Peter said so many people trying to teach her had made her muddled and it would be better to let lessons rest for a while); but Daddy soon brightened if she brought him one of her drawings of leaves and flowers with their names printed neatly beneath, or surprised him, as she did last night, by rattling off her six and seven-times tables. Now though, standing in the corridor with her ears on fire, she understood everything. Even difficult times tables like six and seven (actually she knew eight and nine times, too, but was hoarding these to please her father on another occasion) couldn't make up for this one terrible fault: *she couldn't do music.*

From listening to and observing adults, Claire had absorbed this fact: life was conducted in two ways – doing jobs and doing music. Jobs were cutting down trees, knocking down walls, building, sawing, hammering, cleaning, cooking, gardening, even going off in the car for a morning. She herself constituted a job for someone, for she had to be washed, fed, watched over, taken to and from school. Doing jobs was a tiresome necessity. Doing music, the occupation of most people at Foscote in one form or another, was what life was actually for.

'Claire?' (It was one of the students sent to look for her.) 'Have you used the bathroom? Have you washed your hands?'

She blinked through her one-eyed spectacles. (She was made to wear spectacles with the right eyehole blocked out to make her 'lazy' left eye work harder.) She shook her head.

'Hurry up, then. There's chocolate cake.'

In the bathroom she tried swallowing. Her throat felt tight. Even imagining chocolate cake failed to make it work properly. Full of dread, she trudged slowly back through the corridors and down the bare wooden stairs into the enormous kitchen.

They were all here at the long refectory table, Maman and Daddy, Uncle Peter and Aunt Margaret (who were not her real uncle and aunt but Laurie's mother and father), Laurie, and all the other people who were staying at Foscote at the moment – so many that the benches were crammed and Laurie had to squeeze up to let her in. Yes, they were all here, eating heartily: Uncle Peter giving out with his booming laugh, Maman smiling for once and passing bread and butter, someone singing a phrase and tapping the table – *de dum, de dum, dadadada dum*, someone countering – *tetata tetata tum*; now an argument breaking out amid more table thumping, and Laurie next to her nudging her in the ribs while slipping two biscuits into his pocket, one for him, one for her. She couldn't raise her head, not with this knowledge burning, knowledge everyone else had possessed for ages and she had only just stumbled upon: that she was a dunce at the single most important thing in the whole world.

'Did you get anything?' Laurie hissed behind his hand as teatime broke up. But before she could confess her failure to pocket a morsel, he was sent to do his violin practice.

A woman detained him by the door and caught hold of his hands and scrutinized them; pronounced that, as she had suspected from a study of his face at the tea table, he had musician's bones. 'Always sing to yourself as you play, dear boy. Sing every phrase inside your head,' she advised; and Laurie promised he would. 'How is he taking to the violin? I have heard he is already an accomplished pianist.'

'Quite a useful little player for an eight year old,' answered Laurie's father and went on to offer a demonstration.

A sharp pain, like her heart wincing, hit Claire: how awful to have to play for these people! But Laurie appeared unruffled. She ran after and brushed against him; whispered, 'I'll get some apples.' And briefly, covertly, the manner he assumed in the presence of grown-ups was supplanted by one of his awful gargoyle faces. She veered off, chased across the yard into an outbuilding to gloat over it in private.

In here, the part of the pottery where Aunt Margaret's unfired work was stored, where row upon row of grey dead objects waited to be transformed in the furnace, she ran her fingers along the dusty lower shelf, and reflected that 'the everyone' aware of her being a dunce at music must include Laurie. For he was amazingly clever at it, as well as able to know things about people as though their faces were books he could read. But Laurie knowing about her was not dismaying, not like imagining the grown-ups talking about her and shaking their heads and writing her off. Laurie, she recalled, sometimes complained that all the music going on in this place made his head hurt. He said that from the way everyone here behaved you'd think music were the only important thing. (She'd giggled at this, taking it for a piece of naughtiness, for music *was* the most important thing, of course.) Now though, a hopeful notion stole over her: that Laurie scoffed because he truly believed things like climbing trees and building dens, like damming the stream and catching a fish in your hand, like squinting through a magnifying glass at the thousands of hairs on the ditch willow herb, at bright green caterpillars with spots and stripes, at spiders spinning – things she and he did together, really were just as important. Come to think of it, the Laurie doing these sorts of things was the real Laurie, not the Laurie the grown-ups saw (dignified and polite and obediently doing his piano and violin practice), but the Laurie who was funny, sharp, adventurous, rude . . .

'Claire, where are you?'

It was her bath-time. Afterwards she'd be allowed some quiet occupation before settling down at half past six – a stupidly early hour, especially in summer, but her parents had many evening activities to attend to.

At half-past seven, Laurie would tap on her door on his way to bed, which was her signal to get up and dress and sneak along the corridor. Then they'd creep off to one of their hide-outs – one of the attics where they'd hidden books and torches and drawing materials; they might even risk a dash to their den in the woods (the further from the house, the more daring the adventure). Hidden away they would usually eat something and tell one another stories, or make plans, or just read or muse in friendly silence.

'Claire, you bad girl!'

It was Maman sounding cross. 'Coming,' she called in a resigned voice, and trudged out into the open.

ii

Towards the end of the war, Wing Commander Peter Stone and Group Captain Andrew Haddingham, released from active service and working for the War Office, had jointly purchased Foscote Hall. Passionate and accomplished musicians, they had conjured a dream together during unbearable hours waiting for take-off: the purchase was a first step towards its realization. Few of their number had survived. It seemed a fluke to find themselves not only alive, but more or less in one piece (Andrew had lost a leg as a result of crash landing on the right side of the Channel, and Peter had breathing problems). They felt singled out by providence, and having won the jackpot, felt positively obliged to hurl their winnings (the rest of their days) into a glorious venture rather than work-a-day ordinariness.

With their families, they moved into Foscote Hall – Peter with his wife Margaret and their son, four-year-old Lawrence (who, to his father's disgust, had become 'Laurie' during the years spent in his grand-mother's house), Andrew with his French wife Sabine and their two-year-old daughter Claire – and began to establish the Foscote Community and the Foscote

Music Festival (which in time would be affectionately referred to by the *cognoscenti* as simply 'Foscote'). Though equally committed to the project, Peter's force of personality was the vital factor in its growing success. Andrew was constantly in discomfort, and chiefly wanted to practice and perform the violin in the company of other musicians. Peter's health steadily improved, his energy and ambition grew; he organized the rebuilding programme, organized the festival, chivvied and inspired while leading the life of a fully active musician – composing, arranging, conducting. His wife Margaret, a competent cellist, was also a talented potter and thus brought another dimension to the project, eventually founding the stone-coloured ridge-ringed style which characterized Foscote pottery. Andrew's wife Sabine had at first been a doubter. A professional singer before the war and married to a professional violinist, getting involved with amateurs, she feared, might ruin their reputation. ('What reputation?' Andrew asked. 'Chorus singers and pit players are two a penny.') Andrew's disability rather than his arguments persuaded her, for she had been brought up to revere the rejuvenating properties of country air. Soon, she too was caught up in the Foscote experience, teaching voice, singing solo, acquiring a reputation for her ability to interpret the less accessible works of contemporary composers.

For Claire there had always been Foscote. Laurie, on the other hand, could remember living in his grandmother's house. Particularly, he remembered lying amongst the mounds and channels of the feather bed he shared with his mother, and the night he was ousted by a stranger (his father) and put to sleep on a couch. No memories of a former life disturbed Claire. Foscote was her starting point – she, in her mind, always twinned with Laurie, for he and she were the Foscote children. (There were no others; if they possessed children, visiting adults left them at home.) 'Laurie and Claire,' – went up the cry several times a

16

day – 'Laurie and Claire, tea's ready; Laurie and Claire, it's time to come in; Where are you, Laurie and Claire?' Their linked names, ringing through house, courtyard and outbuildings, drifting over meadows, dying in the woods, rising above the constant din of rehearsal, seemed to Claire to describe the natural state of things.

Until she was five years old and sent to the village school, Claire supposed that a Foscote sort of existence was how life went on for everybody; people living more or less communally, some arriving for a month in the summer then moving on, music-making the prime common purpose; people, it was true, engaging in other creative activities such as potting, sculpting, painting, wood carving, spinning, weaving – depending on who was around to provide instruction and what was the latest novel enthusiasm – but always as sidelines to the *raison d'etre*.

The people whose job it was to look after her were various: her mother, Laurie's mother, someone else's mother, one of the students, one of the village helpers. During the summer weeks leading up to the festival, there was a great influx of people, including a dozen or so students and extra village women coming in daily to help with cleaning and cooking. This was the time of the most avid music making, when other activities subsided and the whole place became a throbbing noise bubble – instrumentalists practising in one of the outbuildings or the garden sheds or even in the woods, groups learning their parts in the practice rooms, endless mass rehearsals in the huge performance hall (formerly one of the barns). During the festival proper, several important visitors arrived to rehearse and conduct the orchestra, to sing or play a solo part, or give heart to an instrumental section by taking the lead. Claire could tell how stupendously important these visitors were from the way their names were bandied. (So much so, that some remained lodged in her mind for all time, she could still repeat them as an adult – Julian Storey, Eric Petheridge, Louis

Bratner, Pamela Paul. She understood, then, that these had been the names of Foscote's saints, invoked for the same reasons that Christians call upon the Virgin or St Peter or St Jude, to bring luck, to inspire confidence, to convey authority, or for simple pious pleasure: 'Such a privilege to have played with Louis,', 'Wait till Julian comes; he'll soon sort out the brass section,', 'Were you at Foscote in '53; the year Pamela Paul threw a wobbly; swore the choir was singing flat and no-one had the nerve to point out it was she who was sharp?', 'Thing I like about Eric, he's approachable. And such a wicked sense of humour. Remember last year? We'd been flogging Beethoven Seven all afternoon, then gone at the old Rach Two for hours; nearly nine o'clock before Eric was satisfied – and there we all were, limp and starving, when Eric raps on his stand and yells "And now, ladies and gentlemen, the Mahler!" Had us all fooled for a ghastly moment . . .').

Though the rest of the year belonged to the professional musician (composers needing cheap accommodation and the chance to try out ideas, instrumentalists forming ensembles, singers arriving to learn a score), for the duration of the festival, Foscote belonged to the passionate amateur. People arrived with caravans in tow, pitched tents, or put up for bed and breakfast in the nearby village. The excitement of these festival-goers was such that an uninformed visitor might suspect mass inebriation. And perhaps they were intoxicated – though not as a result of alcoholic consumption (which was rare at Foscote save for those few years during the sixties when there was a vogue for country wine making) but of *joy* – the joy of music lovers, free at last of their working lives in offices, shops, factories, schools; able to live and breathe music for a fortnight. ('A Butlin's for culture vultures,' Laurie would say, years later, of his childhood home; and, shuddering, of the festival-goers: 'Your typical *English* enthusiast. You know –

18

open-neck shirt, socks and sandals; shiny red face, shiny bright eyes; simply bulging with passion – of the non-sexual variety, you understand . . .')

iii

In a first-floor practice room, Laurie sat on his hands at the baby grand and waited for Aunt Sabine's bout of temperament to exhaust itself (sat on his hands in order not to bite his fingernails). Preparations were under way for the festival of 1950, and this afternoon things were going badly. Aunt Sabine had collapsed backwards in the piano's curve. Propped on her elbows with her head thrown back, she alternatively groaned (deeply, sonorously) and wailed (thinly, like a cat). 'Peter, Peter,' she cried to Laurie's father (though *Peetair* was how her accent made the name sound). 'It is 'opeless. I give it up . . .'

Laurie peeked cautiously round. Aunt Sabine's back-stretched body was an arc from which jutted quivering little bumps – her small breasts under the silk blouse, the mound of her throat, her rounded chin and little snub nose. She was considered a beauty, but he could never see why; she resembled, he considered, a petulant Pekingese dog.

'I am *exhausted*,' she wailed. 'No-one understands the stamina required. There is no precedent to guide a first performance; I am the initiator, on my interpretation the work stands or falls. Should I not preserve my strength for such a task? Ouf, but everyday I am bombarded with trivialities, with endless stupid demands. You comprehend, Peter? – the dreariness I endure day after day, the *frustration*?'

Laurie knew as well as his father to what particular frustration Aunt Sabine referred. In a moment she would become more specific. She would begin to speak darkly of 'he' and 'him'. Never naming her husband, it was always perfectly plain that Uncle Andrew was the source of her complaint, the cause of her grimace, her tiredness, her *migraine*.

'My dear girl, you are right,' soothed Peter Stone, turning from the window. 'Too many unnecessary chores – on top of everything else. No wonder you're tired. From now on you shall do nothing but cherish your voice. I'll arrange it. I'll have a word with Margaret; she must organize something. You must lie late in the morning, take breakfast in bed. From now on, darling, you shall be properly pampered.'

She stretched out the hand nearest to him, her arm trailing along the piano, and uncurled her fingers to reveal her palm. 'So – masterful, Peter.'

Thank goodness for that, thought Laurie. Now perhaps they could get on with it.

Laurie (now ten years old) had been detailed to play the piano accompaniment of two rather esoteric songs at their first public performance, songs composed for Sabine Haddingham by a Foscote *habitué*. It was desperate work trying to oblige Aunt Sabine. For one thing, she had a complaining nature and was inclined to get peevish when Laurie misunderstood her or made a mistake. For another, Laurie disliked her voice which he considered shrill – though maybe this was due to the sort of music she favoured, full of endlessly repeated staccato notes, sudden swoops, and dissonance of the voice against the piano which put him in mind of a quarrel in a hen-coop. Furthermore, the strain of producing these sounds resulted in outstandingly ugly facial contortions. He disliked having to look at her. ('Eyes on the singer!' his father would shout, should Laurie seek relief in the sight of the keyboard.)

But hardest of all to bear during these sessions was his father's habit of pressing down on Laurie's shoulders. The paternal weight sent him hot and prickly. He could not remember why or when he had developed ill-feeling towards his father. It had grown surreptitiously, as if from a seed planted inside when he was sleeping, at first causing mere hiccups of discomfort, later sprouting tentacles which blocked his throat and stirred nervy unease in the pit of his stomach. The cause was more what he sensed about his father than any particular incident – that at all costs Peter Stone must have his own way. He was an overbearing man, very tall, very broad; his booming voice dominated the meal table; in a crowd, his balding head rode above others. But more than this physical dominance, Laurie sensed a need to subject even trivial matters to his will, from the programme for the festival to where people were positioned at table. When he was opposed he did not raise his voice or show temper; on the contrary, this was when he softened his tone with reasonableness, gentled his relentless persistence. But there was never a chance he would give in. Overhearing such an encounter, Laurie would feel balked on the opposer's behalf. If possible he would remove himself from earshot; seek out Claire, slip into the wood, filled with a craving for airiness, for lightness of touch, for subtlety. Not that he named those needs, but as he edged from his father's presence, images drew him – Claire running ahead, her body plopping comically from side to side as her heels kicked up behind; light dappling down through the branches, the heavy odour of plants breathing, clumps of fungi in dank hollows, moss covered roots lining the stream bank . . .

Today, for the time being, such escape was out of the question.

Aunt Sabine was in defeatist mood, possibly on the brink of despair – you could never tell with Aunt Sabine. Yesterday, for instance, she'd been ecstatically confident. Guy Lethersage (the composer of these songs) had come to lunch and stayed to hear what they were making of his masterpiece. The run-through went brilliantly, one or two small slips failing to faze them. Guy was thrilled: praised the piano's attack (amazingly vigorous, he'd said, for a ten year old), and Aunt Sabine's two voices – the harsh declamatory one and the appeasing cooing one – which were both spot on, perfect beyond his dreams. In her delight Aunt Sabine became skittish; laughing and teasing, she had gone so far as to run fingers though Laurie's curls, thus demonstrating her agreement with praise for the accompanist. Today, though, had brought total change. She had arrived looking black, sighed, chucked down her score, muffed her entry, sung flat. At a look from his father, Laurie's hands had abandoned the keyboard.

Peter Stone was now making a determined effort to revive her confidence. 'You were magnificent yesterday. Guy was delighted. You can't possibly disappoint him.' He moved closer to her, took her hand in both of his, marshalling his arguments. 'You know, my dear, how thrilled I am that this is a *family* thing – you and Laurie making a special effort for the festival-goers, making them feel privileged to be attending a first performance with the added cachet of it being written specially for you. That's such a compliment, darling, and so thoroughly deserved.' His voice was soft, but it pulsed with determination – and Laurie sensed his father had hit on the clincher: 'You owe it to your marvellous talent, to your unrivalled reputation for tackling new and difficult work . . .'

'Ah, Peter . . .' (And yes, a promising note had entered her voice, one of yielding enjoyment.)

Silence.

That's it, then, Laurie decided. Surely now they'd get on? But the two adults remained speechless with Aunt Sabine's 'Peetair' left hanging in the air. The tension unnerved him. He freed his left hand and inspected the fingernails. The middle one had a tempting bit of growth on it. Knuckles rammed across his mouth, dark brows drawn up under his jutting black curls, he nibbled and gnawed and contemplated the possibility of an early escape. Perhaps, as rest and recuperation had been promised her, Aunt Sabine would want to sample some before re-embarking on the rigours of rehearsal. In which case, could he not casually rise, have a bit of a stretch, then just sort of go?

But it gradually dawned on all three of the tongue-tied that the silence was not quite perfect. A faint rasping disturbed it, like a mouse hesitantly attacking skirting board. It seemed to come from behind the door.

Peter Stone strode towards it, pulled it wide.

Claire was sitting there on the floor with her legs spread open and a sketch pad between, crayoning vigorously. She glanced up as the door opened (for once virtuously wearing her one-eyed spectacles), but continued with her strokes and offered a shy smile.

'What are you doing?' cried her mother.

'Drawing. Waiting for Laurie.'

'She is waiting for Laurie,' repeated Sabine Hadding-ham witheringly. 'Laurie is busy. He is working hard to be a credit to Foscote. While you – you sit on the floor like a baby with a colouring book.'

'It's not a colouring book,' Claire started to explain, but Sabine had swung back to the piano.

'Go along, Claire, and find some useful employment. See if you can be any help to Aunt Margaret,' urged Peter Stone.

Claire clambered to her feet – 'Aw-right,' – scooped her crayons into a tin, departed.

'What are we to do with that one?' wondered her mother. 'Not a scrap of talent, graceless, cross-eyed. You say "family thing", Peter. Well, with Claire, I fear you will be disappointed. I don't understand: her father is gifted, and I – I am her mother!' she marvelled, clapping hands to her chest.

'Sabine my dear, Claire is not cross-eyed, and you mustn't say so – you know how it upsets Andrew. She has a cast – a sluggish eye, which – we have it on the best authority – the glasses will correct.'

'She hardly ever wears them,' Sabine cried scorn-fully. 'It's all very well for you,' – she looked

23

meaningfully at Laurie scowling at her from the piano stool, and nodded – 'you and Margaret are fortunate.'

Laurie bit viciously to the nail's quick until a smart of pain made him thrust the digit under his thigh. Rocking back and forth trying to deaden the soreness, he thought how detestable Aunt Sabine was and how he regretted all the work he'd put in for her – particularly now she had cited his efforts against Claire. It was not even as though these angry sounding compositions by Guy Lethersage were worth the effort. The unbalanced attitude towards music in this place was beginning to put him off.

For some time he'd been trying to impress upon Claire the possibility of music having a more lowly position in the scheme of things than Foscote allowed – purely in her own interest – and the funny thing was, he'd begun to believe it himself. He had been prompted in this by overhearing his father one day expostulate to his mother: 'That child's a growler, and I strongly suspect tone-deaf. I know it's hard for Sabine – she's got the daft idea it's some reflection on herself as a singer – but, you know, these agonizing lessons are a waste of everyone's time. Simply, the girl is cloth-eared.' His father had sounded brutal, as if while talking about her he were at the same time grinding her under his heel.

'Well, never mind,' his mother soothed. 'She's a clever little soul. According to Andrew she's already mastered long division. And do you recall the drawing of celandines she made for my birthday? I thought it acutely observant. Music isn't the be-all and end-all, you know.'

There spoke someone with a second string to her bow, Laurie had thought, experiencing a rush of gratitude towards his mother.

His immediate concern had been to test whether Claire was aware of her disability. He concluded that she was not; she was too carefree, too intent upon the activities which pleased her. But realization must come some day, and he resolved to bolster her against this with a steady undermining of Foscote idolatry. Strangely, two years later (Claire was now eight years old), she still appeared blithely oblivious, and therefore had never been in need of his propaganda. It was he whom it had impressed.

Really though, it was not music itself, but the unattractiveness of these musical zealots from which he longed to dissociate. He was also desperate to avoid those pressing paternal hands. Thinking of these, his hunched position on the piano stool became suddenly intolerable. He sprang up – at which his father and aunt, who were talking in an undertone, broke off and looked round. 'I need to be excused.'

'Oh.' Peter Stone turned to Sabine Haddingham. 'Shall we call it a day? Have a go at it tomorrow when you're rested?'

'So kind, Peter,' she murmured, touching his arm.

Laurie gathered up the score and stowed it in the music cupboard.

'Thank you, Laurie,' Peter Stone boomed after his son before the door closed – recalling the importance to the young of exemplary manners.

Her feet dangling from a high stool, Claire sat at a bench in one of the pottery rooms bending over a flat oval of damp clay which she had previously punched from a round ball. On its surface she was carving a spectacular fish – thorny fins erect, scales like mail, eye of concentric circles, curved tail. It was a laboriously detailed job in which she was thoroughly engrossed, etching, scraping, pricking out. The area around her – bench, floor, the front of her dress – was liberally sprinkled with grey clay bits. Her face was smeared from the dampness caused by her jutting tongue and her hands constantly brushing away trailing hairs. Thus, Laurie discovered her when, hands in pockets, he sauntered in.

'I've been let off,' he said. He watched her working for a few moments. 'Did my mother say you could?'

She nodded.

'Didn't she tell you to put on an overall?'

Claire paused. 'I forgot,' she admitted.

'Forgot your specs, too.'

'No I didn't. I took them off, 'cos I needed to *see*.'

'We could go to the wood.'

'I want to finish my fish first.'

This seemed reasonable, so he drew up a stool and climbed up beside her. At which her face tilted to him sideways, showing her confederate's smile – the iris of her left eye (which was uppermost) not quite able to detach from the magnetic pull of the bridge of her nose. He laughed – he couldn't help it; and her grin transferred very amiably down to her work. Ordinarily, he wouldn't *allow* himself to be amused, it was bad enough coping with the feelings stirred by other people's reactions (comments he had over-heard varied from a mild 'Quaint little thing,' and 'Odd-looking scrap,' to the frank and pitying 'Unprepossessing'); but the particular smile she saved for Laurie was such a badge of happiness and ease, it somehow gave him permission. Of course, her face *was odd:* her laggard left eye, and the alarming close-ness of both eyes to her nose; the way the nose turned up at the tip, the way a smile lengthened her mouth almost to an ear on one side and blunted into a dimple on the other; her dark scrappy hair that Aunt Sabine was forever rearranging in vain attempts to prettify – features such as these made 'oddness' undeniable. But to Laurie's eyes it was a delightful oddness, the odd-ness of a sly and secretive imp. It made him impatient (and sometimes hurt and indignant) that no-one else perceived this.

'That's very good,' he said, as she continued to pick and scrape.

Eventually, satisfied, she made two neat holes near the top of the plaque, then carried it on its supporting

26

board to a tray of objects awaiting the furnace. 'Aunt Margaret will be pleased.'

'Your mother will be furious,' he said, indicating the state of her clothes.

She squinted down her front. 'When it's dry I 'spect it'll brush off.'

'Wash your hands, at least.'

She proceeded to swill them under a tap, and dry them and deposit much of the dirt on a roller towel. 'Come on, Laurie.'

He moved sluggishly, stiffened by hours spent sitting on a piano stool. When he started across the yard she was rounding the corner. Next time he saw her she was already through the gate and running up the sloping path. Her fleetness, despite her funny side-to-side lolloping, always amazed him. 'Wait,' he called. But she ran without pause to the top of the slope. There, by the side of an oak tree, she stopped to look back; then tucked the skirt of her dress in her knicker legs and executed a handstand. 'Slow coach,' she taunted, upside down against the tree.

He broke into a jog-trot and was soon puffing. With every step his bladder jarred; now he really did need to 'be excused'. 'Mind out,' he commanded, arriving several paces short of the oak tree, and unbuttoned his fly. 'Bet I can hit that tree from here.' His confidence (inspired by urgency), prompted him as he took aim to take a boastful step backwards; he found he could send his stream into an arc and still spatter the bark.

Claire (who once thoroughly wetted herself peeing upside down in a vain attempt to produce a spurt) watched in silence. 'I did six cartwheels last term across the playground. No-one else in my class can do six.' And Laurie, she knew, could not manage one, never having been able to summon the necessary abandonment. She raised a pointed toe, lifted her hands with splayed fingers above her head, and spun off – over and over, feet and hands like the points of a star. But the field was tufty, not smooth like playground asphalt; after the fourth cartwheel her foot snagged in the grass and she landed with a thud on her stomach. (Laurie was not alarmed: Claire's body was like India rubber, he'd seen her take fearful-seeming tumbles with no harm done.) When she got her breath and opened her eyes, she found she was nose down in a spongy hummock of a paler green than the surrounding grass and studded with tiny white flowers. 'Hey, look here.' (He joined her.) 'We haven't seen these before – weeny – the stalks are like hairs – quite tough, though. We need the magnifying glass.'

'It's in the den. Come on, we'll bring it on the way back.'

'We might not find this again.'

'I'll count how many paces from the hedge.'

Claire had a passion for tiny plants. She spent hours examining and comparing. Laurie's great love was the wood and he was impatient to be in there. 'Ten paces,' he called, 'from the stem of this blackthorn bush.' Satisfied, she clambered to her feet.

They plunged into the wood, and immediately the light changed – from blatant all-pervasive to slanting, tender, aqueous; and sounds enlarged – twigs snapped, leaves scrunched, birds called with new and startling clarity; in a world of giants, they seemed shrunken in height and importance. Between the entrance to the wood and a watery ditch, the trees had been left to grow and spread their branches unhindered; the shaded earth beneath was bare save for some timid fern clumps and tenacious stems of blackberry. Roots ran like petrified arteries over the hard ground where, in this most accessible part of the wood, Foscote's residents and visitors came to stroll. No-one (save Claire, Laurie and a part-time woodman) ever bothered to leap the ditch into what appeared to be more tangled, wilder territory.

The woodman, Joe, was a nephew and apprentice of Mr Graveny, the head forester of the Manor Estate whose grounds abutted those of Foscote Hall. A stream formed the boundary between the two properties. When Claire and Laurie first ventured as far as the stream and learned to wade barefoot along its pebble bed and swing from side to side on ropes suspended from overhanging branches, Mr Graveny was their enemy. His shouts were intended to warn them of the dangers of flowing water and hidden snares beneath the surface; but they were afraid only of him. One day when they were trespassing on the far side of the stream, Mr Graveny and his terrier cornered them. Claire would have hurled herself into the water rather than remain trapped by *the man*, but Laurie, catching her arm, decided to face it out; he was already confident of his ability to disarm most people in most circumstances. Persevering with Mr Graveny eventually yielded benefit not only to the children (who learned about the why's and how's of tree management, the names of plants and characteristics of their habitat), but also to the Foscote woods, neglected for more than a decade. Laurie persuaded his parents to take the wood seriously, and his protestations certainly stirred the conscience of Margaret Stono whose father's land had included several wooded acres. Her support led to a consultation with Mr Graveny and subsequently to the part-time employment of Joe. Soon, between the stream and the ditch many old trees were felled and young ones coppiced. The wood's centre became a grassy clearing where in spring or summer primroses, wood anemones, bluebells, violets, white shamrock, even orchids bloomed.

One thing Mr Graveny did not know (and neither did Joe so far as they could tell, nor any other human being) was the fact of their cleverly camouflaged den in a tangled and so far unimproved part of the wood. This was sturdily constructed from several wooden pallets they had filched from the building materials left about when Foscote was undergoing expansion. Since then they had carted to the den many of life's necessities – a rug, a torch, a magnifying glass, tins, boxes, rope, string, netting, a knife, pencils, notebook. They were always on the look out for useful articles; after all, they had two dens to furnish, this one in the wood, a second in a disused hayloft.

'When we grow up we'll live in a wood,' Laurie promised. They were sitting on a boat-shaped tree root in the river bank with their bare feet in the stream, he whittling a stick to a sharp point (sore finger, over-bearing father, complaining aunt and other irritants all soothed to triviality by his hands' satisfying activity, by the water's chuckling over pebbles, by Claire beside him).

Claire was half-watching her feet looming like white tendrils under the flowing current, half-watching for fish. 'With a stream,' she amended.

'With a stream, of course.'

'And not have people always coming, making noise.'

'Certainly we won't have that.'

Thinking she spied a roach, she leapt down, but her hands fastened on weeds. A shoal of tiddlers weaved round her knees. Farther upstream, a splash – made by a water-rat perhaps – prompted her to collect her stick from the bank and wade to investigate.

They remained until the air blew chill against their arms. Then, simultaneously and without communication, they pulled on their sandals, gathered up bits and pieces to take to the den – where Laurie remembered to collect the magnifying glass for the return journey.

iv

They had always known that when Laurie was thirteen he would go away to Prestbury, the public school where his father had been educated. When the time was still far off it did not seem momentous that this would happen; after all, they had never attended the same school at the same time; Claire had begun her schooling, as Laurie had, at the church school in the

30

village; but Laurie left, as she arrived, to attend a prep school in the nearby town. During the summer of 1953, however – Claire having passed the eleven plus examination and soon to start at the local grammar school, Laurie preparing to depart for Prestbury – it began to feel momentous indeed. A step away from one another. A parting.

Parcels arrived from a school outfitter. Claire hovered in the doorway as Aunt Margaret opened the long shallow boxes and ticked off the contents as present and correct – several pairs of flannel trousers, shirts, socks, ties, sweaters, games kit, a suit and a blazer. She watched covertly as Laurie checked himself in the looking-glass, tied his tie, pulled down the cuffs. He caught sight of her watching – white-faced, still.

'I'll only be gone during term time. We'll still have the holidays. The terms are quite short,' he told her. He knew these were mere palliatives; knew that by trying on the uniform and lining up treasures to take with him, he was preparing to desert. And it was no salve to his conscience to have no choice in the matter. The fact was, he *wanted* to go to Prestbury – or at least, he was glad to be leaving Foscote. It was just a pity that one leave taking could not be accomplished without the other, for he had no desire to leave Claire. No-one seemed to appreciate this. Aunt Sabine even speculated (in Claire's hearing) that he must be keenly looking forward to getting away from her. But then the adults at Foscote had never understood their closeness and its equality. Because he was the boy and the elder by two years, they supposed that by spending time with her he was doing her a favour. He had heard them say as much – 'Laurie is so good-natured. Most boys of his age wouldn't put up with a small girl forever tagging along.' (A lowered voice was no safeguard when Laurie was around. He could pick up the most distant comments; in fact, someone assuming a confidential tone was like a signal, his ears automatically

31

pricked – he couldn't help it: his ears were like two yawning and insatiable orifices on the sides of his head.) But how contemptuous he had felt at those remarks about Claire. With the exception of his mother, no-one at Foscote ever found much in her to value. Whereas he knew how brave she was – braver and far more daring than he. Also, she was sharp. So he was not surprised when his nonsense about their life continuing largely unchanged earned him her special insolent look – head tipped to one side with only the right eye properly focussed on him (the left seeming to prefer a contrary inward view), the tip of her tongue peeping from the side of her mouth and slowly curling upwards – the look which drove her mother to apoplexy.

Then a form arrived from Prestbury on which 'extras' were to be indicated (extra tuition in subjects outside the normal curriculum). It focussed Laurie's mind. He saw a chance to further detach from the spirit of Foscote. The trouble was, try as he might, it proved impossible to gain his father's attention for long enough to make a stand.

It was time to fill in the form. His mother called him to the kitchen table. 'Right,' said Margaret Stone, looking at the son who so strongly resembled her (the same mass of wiry black hair, the same thick black brows and prominent bones), and licked the tip of her pencil: 'Piano and violin, of course, and your father said you might as well start on the oboe . . .'

'No,' said Laurie, calmly taking the form from her. 'Not violin and not the oboe. I'll continue with the piano – if you think their teaching's likely to be any use. But look, it says here you can do extra science . . .'

Margaret Stone gaped. 'Not violin? What are you talking about? Of course you'll do the violin, and your father thinks . . .'

'Mother, I don't want to be lumbered with endless

music practice at Prestbury; I want time for other things.'

'What other things?'

'Extra science – put that. Put Biology and Botany – we only get lessons in Physics and Chemistry.'

'Have you thought about this, darling? It sounds a bit spur of the moment.'

'Of course I've thought about it.'

Margaret Stone ran a hand through her hair. 'Laurie, you really will have to discuss this with your father.'

'I've been trying to,' Laurie said reasonably. 'But he just keeps saying "Not now".'

It was true. For the past few days Peter Stone had been more heavily engaged than usual. He was either in discussion with one of the musicians currently in residence or with Uncle Andrew or Aunt Sabine, or he was busy rehearsing, or the door of his study at the top of the main staircase was sporting the familiar pretend-jocular notice: DO NOT DISTURB – COMPOSER AT WORK! The reason for the present turmoil was a proposed newspaper article featuring Foscote, to be written by the music critic from a prestigious paper who was due to arrive with a photographer in a few days' time. Peter Stone had composed a modest work for the occasion and was now in the process of revising it to accommodate the available musicians. He had announced at the tea table his intention to involve all members of the two founding families – in however humble a capacity, he had added, beaming with special kindness at Claire. (This was another matter on Laurie's mind. His father had better not make a fool of Claire.)

'Well, he is busy at the moment. Oh dear. I suppose if your mind's made up . . . But your father's not going to like it. He's going to be terribly upset that you've even contemplated giving up the violin.'

He'll be outraged, Laurie thought, he'll say I haven't a right to decide. 'However, I shall give it up,' he declared to his mother. His confident tone made him

33

feel more certain of facing down his father. For some months he'd been working on a more authoritative voice (together with a matching demeanour); it had felt like a wall going up, high and dense, girding him for the battle of wills which he had always known must come one day. Perhaps giving up the violin would trigger the showdown.

'Look, has Uncle Andrew put you off? I know he can be depressing sometimes; his pain is so much worse. Is he an irritable teacher?'

'It has nothing whatever to do with Uncle Andrew. I shall go and see him in a minute and explain . . .'

'For goodness sake don't breathe a word of this to Andrew until your father's had his say. You know, Laurie, I'm certain he'll point out how vital it is to have at least two instruments at your fingertips for a career in music.'

'Who said anything about a career in music?'

Now Margaret Stone *knew* there was something amiss with her son. Perhaps it was the strain of being sent away to boarding school. She spoke gently, coaxingly: 'Laurie, dear, of course you'll have a career in music. You're gifted – your father – everyone says so.' (And what else is there? her tone implied.)

'You know, Mother, music isn't the be-all and end-all,' he said, triumphantly quoting her own words, which she failed to recognize. 'Then what are you going to do, do you suppose?'

A picture leapt into Laurie's mind – a house in a wood, he and Claire setting out from it, tool bags draped from shoulders in the manner of Mr Graveny. He knew better than to utter the word 'forester' – his mother would consider it had plebeian overtones – but could think of no more reassuring occupation that was also connected with trees. Bound to be one, though, which he would discover eventually. 'I'm far too young to say,' he rebuked her. 'How can I know at only thirteen? I expect I'll get plenty of ideas at Prestbury.'

Only thirteen. Margaret Stone mentally shook herself. This was a boy's whim. Laurie was often tricky to deal with, he could fool you into treating him like an adult if you weren't careful. 'Right-oh, darling. I'll talk to your father, when I get the chance.'

'And I'll go and see Uncle Andrew.'

'No, Laurie,' she protested.

But he was already gone.

How Claire's stomach had clenched when Uncle Peter, fixing his determined eyes upon her and pretending to make light of it, said that even she was to have a small role in the coming performance. *For a newspaper.* Now the whole world, not only Foscote, would know she was maimed. ('Maimed' because living amongst people who made music as naturally as they breathed, made her inability to do likewise seem the aural equivalent of a club foot.) What role had he in mind? Could it ever be small enough?

But even Uncle Peter's bombshell failed to rouse her long from the lethargy she had fallen into. In everything she did these past weeks she was an automaton; she was only half there in the fields and woods with Laurie; the shine had gone, it was all dull and tediously hopeless.

'I wonder if you'll get piles of prep? I wonder if you'll play rugger?' she said, trying to turn Laurie's going away to school into an ordinary event instead of a catastrophe. They were sitting on the bank of the stream, their foot dangling in the water. 'I wonder,' she said with false lightness, 'if you'll make a special friend, you know, *a best friend*, and go and stay with him in the holidays?' This was not so much to hear him deny it as to discover whether by stabbing herself in the heart she could wake herself up, feel something. The thought of there being no Laurie at Foscote for weeks on end was so outside her experience she had gone numb trying to envisage it. It was like, she supposed, trying to imagine what it meant to be dead.

'Thank you very much,' retorted Laurie in his quick-fire way and with one of his famous shudders, 'but I dare say I shall get quite enough of my school fellows without extending the pleasure into the holidays.'

They stared at the opposite bank. After a long silence, during which the fact of her existence became even more problematical, Claire laid her head back against the tree-trunk: 'I might invite Moira Davis here one weekend,' she mused. And added – she wasn't sure why: 'I suppose she's sort of my best friend.'

'In that case, I certainly should,' he agreed, deliberately offhand. And thereby equalized the hurt between them.

In the hall, the musicians were gathered for a run-through of the piece they would play for the press tomorrow. All the family members (as Peter Stone liked to describe them) were present – Andrew Haddingham with his violin, Margaret Stone with her cello, Laurie at the piano, Sabine Haddingham ready to sing, Peter to conduct, Claire to ding briefly on a triangle – together with further, currently resident musicians: a second violinist, a viola player, a flautist, a horn player. Seated informally to listen were several visitors to Foscote. Claire's father had prepared her well, had shrewdly coaxed her to regard her role as more of an arithmetical exercise than a musical one, and in the safety of their living-room with only Andrew beside her humming and tapping, she found she was perfectly able to count the beats to her entrance and make accurately timed strikes. But now, having clambered on to the stage to take up the position indicated by Uncle Peter, the thorough-going musicality of the proceedings overcame her. As Uncle Peter brought down his baton, and bows attacked strings, and her mother's chest took a preparatory heave, she could only feel embarrassment. No good Aunt Margaret smiling, her father winking or Laurie leering like a goblin round the side of the piano: they couldn't help her take stock of the swirling noise around her, nor quieten the blood-rush in her ears. The noise being featureless, how was she ever to make out the beat she was supposed to count? What a fool she was standing here, uselessly holding out a triangle – which seemed to swing and assume looming proportions, to glint spitefully, drawing fatal attention to its hapless holder.

When the piano rested (her signal, Claire remembered, to start counting and watch Uncle Peter's baton) her heart lurched – *one-two-three-four, one-two-three-four*, she gabbled to herself as the triangle wobbled and her eyes darted from baton to triangle, baton to triangle, baton. . .

The baton stopped dead, impaled her between the eyes; at last fell away to rap out a furious jig on the music stand. 'Andrew?' roared Peter Stone, 'I thought Claire understood what she has to do. Dear, dear. Look, everyone, shall we . . . ?'

Voices now, rapid discussion, and it was all about *her*. But they know perfectly well I'm no good, she thought indignantly. They know, yet they insisted; I didn't want to, I was *made*. There were no more thoughts, just cold rising anger. She dropped the triangle, dropped the beater: but scarcely heard the resulting clatter. For her feet had leapt the platform and were covering the hall, and now carried her in a flash through the doorway.

She couldn't do music, but she could certainly run.

A hubbub broke out in the hall – several offers to take over the triangle part, Peter's protestations that he had only written it in to accommodate Claire, Margaret reproaching Peter, Andrew taken with a fit of coughing, Sabine's voice rising like a descant to bewail her daughter's humiliating inadequacies – all brought to an abrupt end by the resonant crash of the piano lid closing. Laurie then rose and, walking not running, took the way of Claire two minutes earlier.

'Stay where you are! (Whatever has come over these children today?) Lawrence, I am addressing you, sir . . .'

His father's tone frightened him, but he still wouldn't run. But nor would he pause. A thud behind him made him correctly suspect that his father had bounded from the stage. And still he plodded towards the door.

'STOP,' yelled Peter Stone as if to a deserting squaddie, and clapped an arresting hand on Laurie's shoulder. 'Come with me,' he commanded more quietly, mindful of his audience, and frogmarched his son out of the hall, round to the front of the house and up the stairs to his private study. 'You will wait in here until I can deal with you,' he declared ominously, withdrawing the key from the inside of the door. He then stepped outside, closed and locked the door and pocketed the key, took a deep breath, then set off towards his neglected guests and colleagues in the hall.

Where was Laurie?

After running from the rehearsal, Claire had cut straight across the courtyard into the pottery and up the stairs into the display area (where Aunt Margaret's best pots were set out on shelves for customers' inspection). Practised climbing took her over the shelves, through a trapdoor in the ceiling, and thus into the disused hayloft. Here she waited. Laurie must know where she'd be. He might consider the den in the woods, but surely he would check in here first. By now the rehearsal should be finished. It was probably teatime. Perhaps he had decided to fill his pockets for her at the table and *then* come up. Yes, that must be it – and a good job, too, thought Claire as her stomach suddenly yawned and she realized she was famished.

Taking care to make no sound, she eased the lid from an old cake tin. Inside, her hand recognized some battered biscuits; she retrieved one and held it to the ghostly light from the grill in the wall. It was a

38

digestive biscuit: good. Cross-legged on the floor, taking nibbling bites with her front teeth, she pretended to be one of the mice whose rustles and scuttles now and then shivered the silence. She felt utterly safe. As long as she remained in the hayloft, facing the consequences of her desertion could be postponed. For no-one save she and Laurie even knew of the hayloft's existence.

Well, William did, of course. It was he who had told them where the *steps going nowhere* led. 'Steps going nowhere,' she and Laurie had marvelled, standing in the paddock behind the barn, gazing at a series of broken stone steps rising up the barn wall. *Steps going nowhere* – it had seemed a delicious mystery. 'Nah,' scoffed William (an ancient gardener, whiskery and knobbly, who had worked the Foscote land since he was a lad in the last century). 'Not going *nowhere*; they be the steps to the hayloft. See where they lead? – you can just make out where the door's been filled in. That's where they brought the wagons – piled high with hay they was – and the man on the top of the hay forked it in through the door. Nah, not going *nowhere*; going to the hayloft! Funny to think of it all closed up. Only mice in there now. And house martins, I shouldn't wonder . . .'

Claire was disappointed; *steps going nowhere* deserved a more magical explanation. But Laurie ran into the barn. (It was not the barn which had been turned into a concert hall but the barn used mainly as a storage area. It was full of old furniture – settees and easy chairs, folding tables and tents. When it was wet during the festival, people ate their meals in here and at night spread out their sleeping-bags.) High in the barn's gable end, Laurie spied a barred aperture. 'That's where the hayloft will be,' he declared. 'Behind those bars.'

But it was Claire who discovered a way in. One day, watching an electrician install special lighting in Aunt Margaret's display area, she observed cable being pulled through a trapdoor in the ceiling. 'Through the roof space,' explained the workman. *Roof space* – and this side of the pottery adjoined the barn. As soon as the work was finished, she climbed carefully over the shelves and raised the trapdoor, wriggled through, then felt her way along the beams in the direction of the barn. She met no dividing wall; the beams ended abruptly in space where a dim light gleamed. When her eyes adjusted, she found she was peering down into a small room.

When she came to collect him, Laurie was reluctant to climb the shelves; he dreaded kicking over one of his mother's prize pots. But Claire insisted – 'Come on, it'll be worth it. You'll have an enormous surprise.' So he wriggled after her. 'Down there,' she said at last. 'See what it is?' He knelt beside her. A ghost room, was his first thought, a ghost room suspended and hidden from view, existing in a half-light. Then he understood. 'You've found the hayloft.'

They suspended a rope down to provide access, and gradually furnished the little room to exactly reflect their idea of comfort. It was their all-weather den and almost instantly accessible. In here they could shut out Foscote.

Still Laurie didn't come. Claire searched for a reason. Perhaps he was in trouble. Uncle Peter and Maman were bound to be furious with her; perhaps – as had happened before – Laurie had spoken up for her and earned a punishment. Perhaps even now Uncle Peter was ordering him to do extra piano practice. She had better go and investigate.

Tea was over, it seemed. Aunt Margaret and her helpers were clearing the kitchen table. Claire, creeping in cautiously at the scullery door, avoided the kitchen and slipped noiselessly along the corridor, pausing briefly in the pantry to stuff cake into the pockets of her gingham frock. She sped up the back stairs and went along the landing to the Haddinghams' apartment. The door of the sitting-room was ajar. She considered stealing past to her own room – but recriminations had to be faced sooner or later; and besides, she wanted to discover Laurie's whereabouts. With trepidation, she pushed the door wide.

Smooth as a cat, Sabine Haddingham moved from her chair, over the floor, and pounced; with one hand gripped her daughter's elbow, with the other dealt four sharp slaps to her legs.

'Steady on!' cried Andrew Haddingham, wincing in his armchair.

'She is a wicked girl. Not only does she ruin Peter's rehearsal, but her stupid, babyish behaviour brings trouble to Laurie. I suppose he imagined he was being gallant, going after you. And now he will be whipped.'

'Beaten,' Andrew loftily corrected his French wife. 'We don't whip boys in this country. Dogs are whipped.'

But to Claire's ears, 'beaten' sounded worse – more forceful, more brutal. 'But why? Who'll . . . beat him?'

'His father will,' said her mother placidly.

'Because he disobeyed orders and left his post,' further enlarged the former public schoolboy and ex-officer. 'It'll be a taste of what he can expect at Prestbury if he doesn't knuckle down.'

'Where is he? I want to see him.'

'Of course you can't. You've caused him enough trouble for one day. He's locked in his father's study.'

'You know,' said Andrew Haddingham to his wife, 'the boy shouldn't be kept in suspense for ever. It's been nearly three hours. Peter ought to get it over with.'

'Peter is saying goodbye to the Emmersons who can't stay for supper.'

'Mm. And Claire missed her tea. A glass of milk and a slice of cake wouldn't come amiss. You were pretty vigorous, Sabine.'

'I don't want anything,' Claire sobbed.

'Then you can go to bed,' her mother answered. 'It's the best place for cry-babies.'

In his father's study, Laurie was pacing the floor. Every worn bit of rug and every good bit, every grain and every nick in the polished oak boards were nightmarishly familiar. He paced bent forward from the waist, his hands clasped over an aching bladder. Oh, how he needed a pee! Sometimes he paused and crossed his legs and jigged gently on the spot, sometimes the pain eased off and he could sit comfortably for a while in his father's chair. Once or twice he thought he was going to wet himself. But he *would not*. Imagine confronting his father with wet trousers! He could just picture the contempt in those pale eyes as they fixed on the mark – mark of a coward, the Wing Commander would assume.

He froze; from his bending position and from under his brows, stared at the door knob – which, faintly rattling, turned, righted, turned again.

'Laurie,' hissed Claire. 'Laurie, I've come to get you out, but the key's not in the lock.'

His tension subsided. He was suddenly overwhelmed by weariness. Putting his lips to the keyhole, he whispered with emphasis, 'Go away, please.'

'But Laurie,' came back urgently on hot breath, 'you've *got* to come out. Uncle Peter's going to beat you.' (Laurie had assumed this to be the case; even so, he flinched at the words.) 'Don't worry, I'm going to get something,' she promised cryptically.

'Please don't,' he countered – but too late; she had sped already from the door. He groaned aloud. She would make matters worse. But Claire was unswayable. The disapproval she encountered had never daunted her. If she were in his shoes, she wouldn't even have got this far; frogmarched from the hall with an arresting hand on her shoulder, she would have twisted, bitten, kicked herself free. Whereas it had never occurred to him to try. He had fallen in meekly

42

– the fear and shame of what was about to happen clear on his face for all to see. Perhaps – oh God, he could hardly think for his throbbing bladder – perhaps part of him had even secretly relished the drama.

He dropped on to his knees, sank his forehead to the floor. Finding some relief in this new position, he let out his breath and blanked his mind; tried to make the most of the temporary respite.

In the room next to the study (which was the Stones' bedroom) Claire was busily rifling the dressing-table drawer. She had often seen Aunt Margaret use a metal nail-file with a hooked end to remove clay from under her fingernails. Before she could lay hands on this likely implement, a door slammed in the hall below and footsteps started smartly upstairs. She shut the drawer, and as a precaution shot under the bed.

It was well that she did, for instead of pausing outside the study door, the footsteps continued. They were coming in here. Through the counterpane fringe, she observed the approach of two shiny black shoes – undoubtedly Uncle Peter's. They went swiftly by the bed. She heard a cupboard door open, then the sound of rummaging . . . Then, *whoosh* – the noise sent her heart to her throat. Then the shoes came back into view, marched by, and turned out of the room in the direction of the study.

A moment's blank delay, and she understood: Uncle Peter had come in here to retrieve a stick and now he had gone to beat Laurie with it. The whooshing noise had been a practice stroke. And yes, she could hear a key being turned, a barked command, now a door closing.

She scrambled out of her hiding place, tore to the study, thrust open the door – at the very moment of Uncle Peter's cane striking Laurie's bottom (which was uppermost – he was bending over, clasping his calves). Without pause, like a miniature battering ram, she butted her head into Uncle Peter's stomach. Her force

43

and his surprise combined to send him off balance. But Claire was more nimble: as Uncle Peter staggered backwards, she whirled and grabbed Laurie's arm, jerked him towards the door.

There was no time to think. Caught up by her urgency, he simply ran for it.

As soon as they gained the pottery, Laurie dashed to the lavatory. It was a basic wc, built into a cupboard beside the giant sink. Claire went to a grimy window and stood on tiptoe to keep watch. No sign of life outside. Perhaps she had better follow Laurie's example, for another chance might not come for hours (although – she giggled weakly – there were always Aunt Margaret's pots). 'Me too,' she whispered when he returned. As she left him he reflected that 'me too' were her first words since those she had hissed through the study keyhole; everything – flying into the room, head-butting his father, seizing his arm, dragging him off – had been executed without a sound escaping her. His reflections were suddenly halted by the sight, across the dusk-covered courtyard, of someone emerging from a lighted doorway; then another and another, until a group formed. 'Hurry!' he hissed. She returned almost at once, and joined him at the window. 'They're wondering where to search,' he whispered. Without more ado they climbed the stairs into the display area and over the shelves to reach the trapdoor; pulled themselves into the roof space, then let the door down behind them.

The hayloft, deprived even of secondary daylight, lay in dense shadow. Claire shook out the rugs, patted cushions, and produced the cake she had taken from the pantry. Laurie stood and pondered. He kept one hand in his pocket but bent the fingers of the other over his mouth – not permitting his teeth to nibble, but tantalizing them.

'Sit down,' she urged. 'Have some of this. And there's some lemonade left in the bottle.' They sat and ate. Neither spoke. They ate and drank and listened.

Soon, below in the barn, a door opened, and a light came on. 'Laurie and Claire?' – their names floated, rounded and bouncy, among the rafters. Murmuring followed, then footsteps and the sound of furniture being moved. Claire crept forward on her knees to the rim of the aperture. She saw, far below, the top of Aunt Margaret's head and of one of the visitor's moving between rows of furniture, then their backs as they bent down to look under things and pull furniture out of their way. Eventually, Aunt Margaret straightened. 'They're not in here,' she said, and went to the door where the other searcher soon joined her. Then the light went out, and the door banged.

When they had finished the cake, Claire lay down on the rug. Beside her, Laurie sat hugging his knees. They listened to faint voices coming from the other side of the loft, the pottery side. Soon these dwindled, and there was only a thick dark all-pervading hush. Now and again came the sounds of small creatures, but unassumingly, gently, like an aspect of silence.

Claire was breathing evenly. Laurie concluded she was asleep, exhausted by her derring-do. He lay back and crooked an arm under his head, thinking of her mercy-dash, grinning at the memory. She was a courageous little tyke; determined to let no-one get the better of her. He wished he were as resolute; but he wasn't and rather suspected he never would be. Why? Staring into the darkness, pushing the fingers of his free hand through holes in the rug, he struggled to find an answer.

He was like, he decided, a pottery mask his mother had made of the man who faces two ways. Janus. Because, about almost everything – even about what had happened this afternoon – he seemed always to have conflicting wishes. For instance, when Claire burst into the study to save him, he was certainly relieved to escape further blows; but on another level, deeper, darker, he would have preferred the beating to continue. (And not merely to have got the punishment out of the way – oh the hideous embarrassment of facing his father tomorrow!). The truth was, as the blow had fallen, with the shock and pain had come a thrill of secret glee – the triumph of knowing he had been right to despise his father, of having goaded him into betraying his true colours. His weak position had lent him a kind of power, he reflected, and experimentally rocked on his bruised buttocks, pressed them against the hard floor, to discover whether, by reawakening the pain, he could revive the thrill.

His activity disturbed Claire. She opened her eyes, stared into the dark, and for the first time pondered what the morning would bring. 'Laurie,' she whispered harshly. 'Ought we to run away?'

'Of course not.'

'But Laurie . . . ?' – she sat up, leaned over him – 'he might beat you again, even harder.'

'Don't worry. We'll sneak out early and see Mother. She's pretty reasonable; I expect she'll speak up for us. In any case, they'll probably be so relieved to see us and not have their interview with the newspaper ruined, they'll just let the matter drop.'

'So they should, they're in the wrong. They shouldn't have made me play the triangle.' She paused for a moment, then added shyly, 'Because, actually, I'm no good at music.' It was the first time she had admitted this aloud.

'I know you aren't,' he said. 'But it doesn't matter a toss. Stop thinking about it. Go to sleep.'

She lay back, pulling the edge of the rug over her. 'Have you got enough cover, Laurie?' she asked sleepily some moments later. But never heard his reply.

They woke early – 'Laurie, you awake?'

'Mm . . .' – and lay blinking at the shadowy rafters. Eventually, Laurie decided it was time to move.

'We'll go down and wait in the pottery till we see Mother in the scullery.'

They clambered stiffly to their feet, stretched, and straightened the rug. Claire went to the rope and started to climb. But Laurie reached out and caught her ankle. 'I say,' he said, taking a last look round at the hayloft, 'you won't bring any of your friends in here while I'm away at Prestbury? I mean, this is *our* place, isn't it? Just yours and mine.'

'No, I won't,' said Claire, peering down. 'We're the only ones who must ever know about it.'

'Good. That's all right, then. I'll be looking forward to coming back, you know.'

'So'll I be looking forward,' she declared, and hauled herself deftly up the rope.

v

Two years later, after Saturday breakfast one morning in spring, Uncle Peter detained Claire. He wanted to give her some news, he said. Sabine Haddingham also remained, her eyes fixed attentively on Peter Stone. Claire drew no special significance from this, her mother always paid exaggerated respect to Uncle Peter's sayings and doings, though she did sense her mother already knew what was coming and stayed to ensure her co-operation. When it emerged merely that they were expecting a special visitor, Claire felt a yawn coming on (visitors were hardly news); she hid her stretching mouth in the crook of her elbow which lay, studded with toast crumbs, on the uncleared breakfast table.

'Don't slouch like that! Attend when your uncle is speaking!'

Uncle Peter waited patiently for her to raise her head, then carried on. And it began to dawn on Claire that the special visitor was not an adult but a girl of her own age. She began to take notice.

'Jeanette is English, having been born in Surrey. But

she has spent most of her young life in the United States. In fact her father was, um, *is* an American – I fear poor Jeanette has been most unfortunate in her father.' Peter Stone sent a look to Sabine who gave an appropriate sigh. 'And now her mother is gravely ill. So you see, Claire, I'm depending on you to be particularly kind to her, to make her feel at home. You'll be able to help her out at the grammar school, too. She will be at a loss for a while, torn away from her American school, where, I believe, she was ideally happy. So many things here will be strange to her, that she's bound to feel shy. And desperately worried about her poor mother, of course.' (Such a catalogue of things for which this Jeanette must be pitied that Claire already felt ill-disposed. Uncle Peter's next words clinched her ill feeling.) 'I'm sure Laurie will wish you to take a kindly interest. Jeanette's mother,' he explained, 'is my sister, so you see, Jeanette is Laurie's first cousin.'

Uncle Peter tended always to employ an official tone. But his voice pronouncing kinship between the newcomer and Laurie sounded more portentous than usual. It occurred to Claire that her own link to Laurie was comparatively tenuous, and only the result of the accident of their fathers' friendship. This girl, on the other hand, was bound to Laurie by blood. She had an official claim on him to which a name could be put: *first cousin*. She, Claire, was merely Laurie's friend (the word seemed hopelessly inadequate, but no other more apposite came to mind). It was a considerable shock. It made her head swim to think that through all these years of taking their closeness for granted, of assuming it to be closeness of the very first order, some unknown girl in a foreign land had been storing up a more favourable position. And was now sailing across the Atlantic ocean to stake her claim and enjoy her privileges.

'Answer your uncle,' Sabine Haddingham prompted; then recoiled with distaste as her daughter squinted at her across the table with the pupils of her eyes wildly diverging.

'Er?' Claire strove in vain to recall what had been said that required an answer. In the end she gave voice to her own concerns. 'How long's she going to stay, then?'

There was a squawk from her scandalized mother. But Peter Stone put out a calming hand. 'My dear Claire,' he protested. 'I don't believe you fully grasp . . . Foscote is to become Jeanette's *home.* And if, that is, *when* her mother recovers, she too will come here to live with us. That is why we want Jeanette to feel thoroughly welcome. Now do you understand?'

'Certainly, Peter, we shall do whatever we can to help the little poor one. *Shall we not, Claire?*'

Claire, stunned, managed a nod. This girl, she was telling herself, this hateful, pushing-in girl, is coming here to live for ever and ever. Unless . . . Here she conjured a perilous sea, and recalled the fate of the Titanic.

'I presume, Peter, little Jeanette is musical?'

'Naturally. I understand she is a useful pianist and has ambitions to be a singer. You will be able to assist her there, my dear.'

'But of course; I shall be delighted.'

'Sabine, do you think you could give me a hand this morning?' asked Margaret Stone, bustling by with a laundry list. 'I've got to sort out a room for Jeanette.'

'Ah, but I regret that is impossible. I must go somewhere very quiet and work, work, work on my neglected voice. Guy is coming tomorrow. I have promised we will rehearse "Chansons pour Sabine".'

'Yes, most important,' confirmed Peter Stone. 'Claire, I daresay you'll give Aunt Margaret a hand?'

Dumbly, she agreed; and Margaret Stone, who had bitten her lip with vexation, managed a smile. 'Come along then. I thought we'd put her in the little box-room.'

'But Laurie and I keep loads of our things in there,' Claire protested, scrambling up after her. 'And it's where I listen to the radio so I don't disturb Daddy.'

'Well, where else do you suggest?'

Somewhere as far away as possible. 'How about that room on the half-landing?'

'Much too cut off.'

She racked her brain. 'I know – the one across the corridor from your room. In case she gets scared in the night or something.' It was amazing – and somehow comforting – that she could speak so calmly and think so quickly.

'Mm, yes. But that's a particularly nice room. We often put Julian in there.'

'All the more reason. After all those sad happenings, she deserves a nice room.'

'What a kind thought. Very well; let's go and look at it.'

How galling to discover that 'poor little Jeanette', eight months younger than herself, was taller by several inches.

'But Claire is *petite*,' Sabine commented by way of explanation, for once mentioning her daughter with satisfaction.

'All that good American food has built Jeanette up,' Peter Stone countered jovially – an explanation which was not dwelt upon in view of Jeanette's plumpness and pasty complexion. Patently in need of fresh air and exercise, thought Margaret Stone as the child, in answer to inquiries as to her musical taste, offered Chopin's piano works and Schubert's Lieder.

Squinting at her, Claire listened avidly. Jeanette spoke with what the girls at school called a 'Yankee' accent – the mode of film stars and crooners (on both sides of the Atlantic): definitely a point in her favour. But would a glamorous accent offset the several and obvious negative characteristics – that she was fat, that she was plain, that she wore her sand-coloured hair in babyish bunches, and, worst of all, that her front teeth were bound in deforming wire ('A brace,' lisped Jeanette, putting a name to the horror). And if opinion went heavily against Jeanette, how would it affect her own standing? It had been difficult enough persuading the standard setters at the grammar school to overlook her unorthodox and (so local rumour had it) immoral home background. Now, in her second year, she was at last enjoying popularity. The liveliest girls had been to tea at Foscote and reported everything most respectable – Claire the clear possessor of two parents and in no apparent doubt as to which of Foscote's many residents these were; indeed, two parents sharing the same bedroom and Claire having one all to herself; also, they raved about Foscote's facilities, the enormous house, the outbuildings, the woods, the fields (but not, of course, those places private to Claire and Laurie of which they were never permitted a glimpse).

In the event, at school at least, Claire's anxieties proved misplaced. That Jeanette was 'a Yank' predisposed her classmates favourably, and frank accounts of her personal misfortunes prepared them to overlook, in this one case, unattractive physical attributes. Jeanette proved very adept at winning sympathy and had no shame in constantly re-winning it with graphic descriptions of her mother's illness, of her father's stone-hearted abandonment of herself and her mother and of there being no course left other than an appeal to their relations at Foscote – where to all intents and purposes she was now an orphan. She had also half a dozen ailments to confide, and when fascination with these failed could rattle off endless homey tales of teenage stars – for instance who Elizabeth Taylor and Debbie Reynolds were currently dating, what shade of lipstick they used, even their bra size. Talk of dating and lipstick and other people's bras sounded amazingly sophisticated to young English ears, and conferred on the speaker valuable credibility.

Though not particularly clever, she was dutiful, neat, and decorous beyond her years (and came, therefore, as a pleasant surprise to her teachers). Good reports of her soon filtered back to Foscote, and these, combined with her flair for music, established her as a firm favourite of Peter Stone's. Jeanette knew she had failed to win round Claire, but her cousin Laurie would be coming home soon for the Easter vacation. From many of Claire's remarks she deduced that Claire and Laurie were close: if Laurie proved a less stubborn nut to crack, might not Claire follow his example and at last succumb?

And so, on tenterhooks, both girls waited for Laurie's return.

'How do you do?' Laurie said smoothly, extending a large and very bony hand. He was fifteen; tall, with jutting bones and jutting curls and darkly dramatic features.

Jeanette, who couldn't for the moment speak, simpered instead. Looking on, Claire felt her mouth go dry.

Uncle Peter, of course, was supervising the introductions. He launched into an account of Jeanette's accomplishments, touched upon how well she'd settled in, how they all admired her for pluckily getting on with it, and recalled her charming rendition of 'Röslein of the Hedgerow' at a little soirée got up last week for Julian.

'Indeed,' murmured Laurie, his face affably polite.

'You must accompany her in a spot of Schubert, Laurie. Or rather, the two of you must make a duet: the Lieder, I always think, should be regarded as works for two co-principals – voice *and* piano. In fact, we must think of something for this Easter weekend. Eric and Konrad are coming, and possibly the Westermans. Margaret my dear, what do you think – a pleasing idea, eh? – the two young Stone cousins performing works of the incomparable Franz?'

'I shall be delighted of course,' Laurie said, studying then putting carefully aside his fingernails, 'so long as it doesn't take up *too* much time. I've an extended essay and a lot of swotting to get through this hol. They're putting me in for Maths and Science O levels a year early.'

This news, received blankly by his parents, proved a conversation stopper. Jeanette's preening expression drooped to sulky. Only Claire responded – 'That's terrific, Laurie.'

Laurie turned in her direction and made for the door, twisting his plastic features into a swift 'Come on, let's beat it,' message.

With relief singing in her ears, she followed him.

'My God, is she *drear*,' marvelled Laurie.

They were in the boxroom where, on a table beneath the window, Claire had arranged a display of annotated plant specimens. He went at once to inspect it. 'Mm. You've graded them nicely. I suppose you know what caused the tiny pimples on the underside of this leaf?'

'A fungus?'

'A parasite. I've got a book I can lend you.'

'Oh, thanks.'

'Now come and sit down. No, better still, lie down.' He gave her a push. He seemed excited. He always had something new and interesting to show her when he returned from school. She lay on the dilapidated couch under the sloping ceiling and waited expectantly. To her surprise and dismay, when he had finished rummaging in his case, he brought out a record. 'I know what you're thinking,' he declared, lifting the lid of the gramophone; 'but you're to forget all you've ever learned to loath about music: push it right out of your mind, simply close your eyes – go on, close them – and *listen*.'

She adored it when he was bossy; it seemed affectionately intimate. And of course, in another situation, she could as easily command *him*. She lay with her eyes obediently fastened, with no particular expectation, revelling in the loveliness of having Laurie restored to her.

But when the record began playing, her eyes opened in surprise; it sounded like – well, 'cheap music' would be Uncle Peter's description. (Laurie was watching her. 'Keep them closed, and don't say a word.') No, not 'cheap music' exactly, but somehow it wasn't serious either (as in 'serious music', an avuncular term of approval). The rhythm was relaxing, she found she could rely on it; the tunes jolly, haunting. Without knowing she did so, she smiled.

'I knew you'd like it. Want to hear the next number?'

He was standing over her. Heavens, had he been watching her all this time? 'Oh, yes please.'

'Budge up.' He lay beside her, felt for her hand and beat it to the rhythm against his thigh – and Claire felt a soaring sensation, as if she and Laurie and the couch were levitating. 'Wonderful, isn't it?'

'Wonderful,' she choked.

The next number was particularly jaunty. Her knees began bouncing. 'Jazz,' he said, by way of explanation; 'like *life* – like living and breathing. I mean, can you imagine sitting in rows, po-faced and earnest with this going on? What I think is, you can't be ugly enjoying this sort of sound. Remember all those ghastly festival faces?'

She giggled and wriggled – 'Hey, can you imagine Uncle Peter trying to conduct it? Or Maman *declaiming*?'

They laughed and jigged to the beat. 'So happy sounding,' said Claire.

'Hang on; I think the next one might be a blues number.'

Thankfully, the sadness of 'Basin Street Blues' was not the despairing kind, but a swaying, sharing, knowing kind of mournfulness. Their limbs flicked gently in sympathy. Claire felt as if her bones had dissolved.

When the music stopped, they continued to lie there for a moment, hearing the needle whirring in the record's centre, staring at the ceiling,

'I knew you'd like it,' he murmured. 'Personally, I'm besotted, specially with the Duke.' He heaved up, put his feet to the floor. 'But that's for later. I'm starting you off on the basic stuff.'

So there was to be a progression. Deliciously, she foresaw hours ahead of jazz and hand-holding.

And then without warning the door opened. 'Oh, here you are,' cried Jeanette. 'I've been looking all over for you guys. Then I heard some . . . music?' She put her head on one side and came mincing towards the gramophone. Laurie, in the act of removing a record, froze; his voice was stern – 'I'm sorry, I didn't hear you knock. Did you, Claire?'

'No, I didn't,' said Claire, sitting up.

'Oh, I'm, er, sorry?' (She seemed to make everything a question.)

'Can we help you?' Laurie asked. 'I'm afraid we're rather busy at the moment. Perhaps we'll invite you to join us later on.'

'Uhuh, I get it.' She retreated, looking arch, but paused at the door. 'See you later?'

'We'll look forward to it.'

They listened as her footsteps died away. Laurie looked thoughtful. 'We must establish some ground rules.'

'Oh God, Laurie,' cried Claire, relieved to let out her fears and annoyance at last. 'She's nosey, sly, always butting in and trying to land me in trouble. "Oh, what's that, Claire, what are you doing? Can I have a go? Oh look, you've got all messy." She's a devil to shake off. Never takes a hint. And if you tell her to clear off she goes running to tell. If we're not careful she'll ruin everything.'

'Then we shall just have to put our heads together.'

*   *   *

55

Laurie was suavely successful where, before his arrival, Claire had been like a terrier snapping possessively over a bone. His manner to Jeanette was rallying; the teasing style of an elder brother (particularly he was like this in front of his parents). He spared her spaced and measured amounts of his time, he at the piano, she trilling (shyly at first, then with more confidence), and promised that they would indeed give a brief performance together during the Easter weekend. But when her allotted time was up, his manner was like a door closing; and if she did not at once perceive this, he had no hesitation in making it plain. 'Not now, Jeanette. Run along please – things to do.' And though she did sometimes trail after them, or show up when they thought they had covered their tracks, those dollops of attention and cherished memories of mealtime teasing made his rejection tolerable. 'Hey, but Claire's here,' she once objected. 'You don't make her go.'

'Does Claire interfere when you and I are working on the Schubert?' he demanded – so fiercely, even Claire was taken aback.

Jeanette's jaw dropped. 'I guess not.'

'Well then.' He waited, looking stern, until meek and contrite she had slunk away.

Almost a year later, Jeanette's mother died without ever having been well enough to leave the nursing home where her brother had installed her. Claire – and later on his return home, Laurie – set out to be specially friendly. This, on Claire's part, was despite her fear that Jeanette would milk the situation for sympathy and the chance to get closer. But it was a subdued Jeanette who returned from the funeral (which had taken place many miles away in the village where Peter Stone and his sister grew up); subdued and somehow timid, as if losing a mother, even a sickly absent one, left her a prey to capriciousness. She gave hangdog smiles, spoke little and gently; and to Claire's amazement adopted physical expressions of affection – linked arms, slid a hand round Claire's waist, seeming to imply a wordless understanding that Claire, too, was moved by her loss. The fact that Claire was not, made her feel crass and stunted. She atoned for her deficiency by submitting to Jeanette's encircling arm, even going so far as to respond with her own.

And very embarrassed she was, too, to be caught linked in this way by a returned Laurie.

She and Jeanette had been set down by the school bus at the top of the drive and were dawdling up to the house. Jeanette was confiding how during choir practice she had been unable to continue singing the solo part (all those frolicsome 'hey nonnies' had got stuck in her throat, but Miss Bartlett was *so* kind, *so* understanding), when Laurie suddenly appeared on the path. Both girls dropped their arms, Claire in mortification, Jeanette in pleased surprise.

'Hello, Laurie,' Jeanette said shyly.

Laurie came forward quickly and wrapped his arms round her. It was a very brief embrace; almost at once he was stripping their satchels from their shoulders, insisting on carrying them. But he did not evade the awkward subject (as Claire had and still continued to do as far as possible). 'I'm very sorry about your mother, Jeanette,' he said walking between them, their satchels bundled under his arms.

'Oh,' – Jeanette gave the rueful smile Claire was now accustomed to – 'it's not so bad; at least I've got Aunt Margaret and Uncle Peter. And you and Claire are like my brother and sister.'

'I'm glad,' he murmured. Claire, who could look nowhere but at the ground, was relieved when he changed the subject. 'Full house again, I see. Lots of cars. Anyone new?'

'Oh, there's a dreamy violinist come over with Guy. Dreamy to look at, I mean. His name's Alex – don't you love it? At supper last night he sat between us.

We were almost swooning, weren't we, Claire?'

'Speak for yourself,' Claire snapped, 'I think he's soppy.'

'Oh what a fibber! Honestly, Laurie, she was drooling.'

Standing back to allow the girls to precede him through the doorway, Laurie squeezed Claire's arm. It almost reconciled her to tolerating Jeanette; it was a bonus to be sharing an experience, even a bad one, with Laurie.

That night Claire lay in bed and without compunction killed off her mother. Hearing of her loss, Laurie came immediately home from school (which he would be obliged to do anyway, to attend the funeral). He was waiting on the path as she came trudging up to the house from . . . (no, it couldn't be from school, she was too newly bereaved; and in any case it would be a shame to have Jeanette mucking up the scene) . . . from a solitary walk in the grounds. She approached, wan, hollow-eyed; he stepped forward and gathered her into his arms. Lying on her back in the dark, she imagined his large hands pressing her to him, her head coming to rest on his chest . . . Whereupon she blanked out sight and relied solely on other senses – concentrated on his heart beating, his solidity, the feel of his arms about her . . . And slept.

It was becoming a habit. During the twenty or so minutes before falling asleep, she would set her mind to invent a scenario permitting no outcome other than herself in Laurie's arms. What happened when she got there remained vague: usually at this point she lost consciousness, exhausted by the complicated plotting to render herself injured, pitiable, or even irresistibly appealing – though this last never rang true and was soon abandoned in favour of being trapped by fire or fallen from a tree, and Laurie happening on the scene or coming purposely to her rescue.

Tonight's plot flowed effortlessly from the scene she had observed earlier. She did not begrudge Jeanette having in reality enjoyed the starring role, for she knew Laurie had acted solely out of decency and his emotions, were she the one in need of comfort, would be entirely different. Of course, he often did touch her – slung an arm round her shoulder, hugged or squeezed her, grabbed her hand to chase off with her. But lately she had begun to yearn for something more than a comrade's salute (though she was neither ready nor able to be specific). Her hopes were pinned on Laurie nursing similar longings, only requiring, in fact, a precipitating circumstance.

'What a big bouncy girl,' said Laurie thoughtfully (and not, it was clear, admiringly) as Jeanette went bounding past them towards the practice rooms.

Two months had passed since the death of Jeanette's mother. They were beginning to feel at liberty to be less scrupulous towards her. At this very moment she was off on a wild-goose chase of their devising. 'I heard Mother say in the kitchen just now that Alex hadn't been in for his coffee,' Laurie had improvised in a bid to be rid of her. 'Why don't you do him a favour, Jeanette? – go and ask him if he'd like you to bring him a cup.'

'Oh yes, go on, Jeanette. I bet he's dying for an excuse for a tête-à-tête,' Claire urged. (The ruse relied on Jeanette's preoccupation with physical attraction – her own and that of various male visitors. 'Oh what a hunk,' and 'I think we clicked,' were two of her favourite expressions.)

'OK,' she said, grinning and smoothing down her skirt. 'I'll see you guys later.' She swung past them, waggling fingers in saucy farewell, her bosoms like jostling jellies under her straining blouse.

Laurie and Claire, their hands deep in their shorts' pockets, watched her bare legs flash under her circular skirt as she mounted the steps to the practice rooms. When they next met her, whatever had been the outcome of her visit, however mundane Alex's response, they knew what a very great deal she would make of it.

'Right, coast's clear,' Laurie said, and they set off at a brisk pace for the woods.

Half way to the stile, recalling his disparagement of bounciness, Claire surreptitiously peered down at her own bosom (which did not begin to approach Jeanette's, indeed, consisted of two small bumps). She was relieved to detect no movement at all. The pangs of inferiority she suffered in the school cloakroom while changing for games were suddenly forgotten. She was only thankful that no attribute of hers threatened to draw Laurie's offended eye.

(How mean we were to her, Claire would remember uncomfortably in years to come, and particularly when Jeanette came to visit them in middle age, beaming, hugging, bringing out presents, harking back – and this was the most shaming, wondrous part – with sentimental pleasure to their Foscote days. 'Laurie was so handsome, so remote, he was like a god; and you, Claire, were like a schoolbook heroine – so athletic and clever, such a daredevil. What a godsend you both were, distracting me from the gloom and doom of poor Momma dying.'

'We were selfish brutes,' Claire once tried to correct her.

'Nonsense, darling. I daresay I could be a pest and quite rightly you sent me packing; but if so, it was like water off a duck's back. You were both *wonderful*. No girl could have had a better brother and sister.'

Claire hardly liked to protest by stating the truth – which was that she and Laurie never gave Jeanette a moment's thought beyond how to evade, thwart or discourage her; that their single idea of her was as a threat to their way of being together and their sole concern to protect this from her prying eyes and forestall any tale-telling and subsequent interference.

And of course there was one embarrassing episode

they never referred to. Otherwise, Jeanette might have
been obliged to concede that for some months at least
they had virtually terrorized her.)

Laurie never did say much about school. Just snippets
remembered from lessons, the names of a few masters
and boys; none of the sort of detail *she* gave *him* – the
hilarious and odd things girls said and did – which he
was only too delighted to receive and ever avid for.
Perhaps boys were too dull to inspire gossip. Or was
it that he wished to hide from her his school persona?
(She did not doubt that he possessed a school persona,
for at Foscote she often saw how he would assume
new aspects of himself to serve particular circumstances.) Or possibly he sought to be patronizing,
and kept her chatting to save being pressed on matters
he considered beyond her level of sophistication.
Since becoming a sixth-former (he was now seventeen, she fifteen) he was more reticent than ever,
brushing away her inquiries, repeatedly firing
questions of his own with every expectation of being
entertained.

Well, she was beginning to resent it. It made her
indignant to have after all this time no clear picture of
Prestbury School, to know the names and nothing
more of Marshall, Gilmour and Walters – no striking
features, interesting traits, memorable doings, witty
sayings. What a cagey blighter. She smarted with
shame recalling all the stuff *she'd* confided.

It was the start of the summer vacation. They were
walking over downland – trespassing actually – on the
look out for specimens to add to her herbarium.

'What's the matter?' he asked gently when she failed
for the third time to reply with more than a mono-
syllable.

She stooped to inspect a small mound of grass.

'You haven't had a bad term? You're not getting cold

61

feet about going into the fifth? You'll find O levels a doddle, you know.'

'Of course not.' She straightened up, moved on.

He walked behind her. 'Is it something I said?'

She turned on him. 'What do *you* ever say? It's me who does all the saying – at any rate, the confiding.'

Digesting this, he went to peer into the side of a ditch. 'Here's something. Have you got this?'

With ill temper, she stalked over. ' Pennyroyal,' she scoffed. '*Mentha pulegium*. Of course I've got it.'

They walked on slowly, neither properly registering things they pretended to scrutinize. Eventually he asked, 'Is that how I seem, then – withholding? I thought . . . I mean, I'm always showing you things . . .'

She grew nervous, wondered whether by complaining she was putting something precious in jeopardy. But then the memory of him urging her to share every detail made her reckless. 'You never breathe a word about what it's actually like at Prestbury – what you do with your friends, things they say, what you think of them. I don't even know whether you like it there.'

He fell quiet, thinking of several aspects of school he would never talk about; not to anyone, not even to Claire; perhaps especially not to Claire. Yet he had to make amends. He would like, if he could, to convey to her what he had so far only explored in his head. He must at least make some swift attempt to mollify her. 'Sit down,' he invited as he got down himself and stretched out on his side with his head propped on an elbow. Dubiously she sat close by, hugging her knees, staring ahead over the rolling country. 'I suppose,' he began slowly, 'it's because you know what I don't. You *know* how you feel about school, you know how you feel about most things; you're sure in your own mind about what takes place and your part in it and how you stand in relation to it. You see, I'm not. When I'm at school I'm never really sure whether it's me saying what I'm saying, doing what I do. There's always a bit of me looking on and passing comment. In fact it's like that for me here, too; though not when I'm with you. Maybe I don't talk about school when we're together because I'm glad of the respite from that sort of confusion. To be perfectly honest, I don't know whether I hate school or love it. It's both at once, I think. I mean, as a set-up, the place stinks;' – he shuddered – 'it's a piggery. I couldn't bring myself to describe . . .' He broke off, sat up and grinned at her. 'Yet somehow I adore loathing it.'

She had begun to watch him closely, but as he turned to look at her, quickly resumed her observation of the skyline. Her ears were burning. She was fighting an urge to cry. She felt clumsy; she regretted mentioning the subject; she was frightened that by making him say these things she'd somehow hurt him. 'Sorry,' she mumbled into her knees.

'Oh, don't be.' He put out his hand, but she was too far away. Without being aware of it, she tugged up some grasses and now found herself intently examining them. Eventually, driven to know what seemed to her the worst possibility, yet unable quite to express it, she got out, 'You're not . . . sad at school, are you Laurie? Not, you know, dreadfully *sad*?'

'No,' he said, and flopped on to his back, shielding his eyes with an arm. 'Not just sad,' he amended, squinting at the tips of beech leaves shimmering against the sky. 'Never sad entirely.' (The qualification sent a lump to her throat.) 'Likewise, I find I am never purely happy without seeing something or other to be sad about. Fortunately, I know it doesn't matter a toss one way or the other, not in the long run. I mean, looking at all this . . .' He proffered his hand to the wind and sun. Then sprang to his feet and cleared his throat, and in a fair imitation of his father, rocked on his heels and continued: 'In summation, I think we can conclude that the prevailing mood is one of cheerful gloom, or, if you prefer, of morbid happiness.'

63

She smiled, but couldn't laugh. She had become very still, locked in her sense of something weighty having occurred. They had passed to a new level. Perhaps they'd suddenly grown up; although Laurie at seventeen might be considered grown up already. No, it was she who'd abruptly aged, she decided, recalling with shame her childish paddy of only a few minutes ago – despite which he had trusted her with his soul-bearing. She cast desperately in her mind for an appropriate response – not heavy, but not flippant – to indicate mature understanding. Inspiration came in the form of a list of titles on a record sleeve (last evening, unpacking his school trunk, he had passed her his latest acquisition, a concert recording by his beloved Ellington). 'Not so much "Mood Indigo",' she suggested timidly, 'as "Magenta Haze".'

She could tell she had scored from the way his eyes lighted.

'Exactly.' He put out his hands. She took them, let him haul her to her feet. Their mood had lightened; even so, before they moved on, he raised each of her hands thoughtfully in turn to his lips.

Foscote was filling up. One of the new arrivals, a music student who had come to earn vacation money, drew Jeanette's eager eye. 'Oh my Gard,' she groaned, nudging Claire in the ribs, rolling her eyes. His name, she discovered, was Nigel, and soon that Nigel was not only dishy but a pianist to boot. In no time at all (for Jeanette was adept at getting round her uncle) Nigel was relieved of his jobs putting up tents, digging trenches, hauling furniture, and promoted to accompanist – at least for a part of each day. When he was doing neither the work he was paid to do nor assisting Jeanette's artful cooing and eyelid batting through 'Who is Sylvia?' and 'You who have Knowledge', he was to be seen walking through the grounds hand in hand with his patroness. Landing a boyfriend at last was to Jeanette very heaven, and her only regret was that school had broken up and she had no-one truly receptive to share it with. She tried to enlist Claire's interest, but found her response incorrect for a good girly natter.

'Go on, did he really?' Claire yawned in response to an account of Nigel's latest amorous courtesy – and almost as a continuation, though muted, to Laurie, 'Then what a drip he must be.'

'Nigel,' remarked Laurie, as Jeanette departed to work on the Mozart, 'is a very good chap. He is doing us a large favour. God, but it's hot. Let's go and splash in the pool.'

'The pool' was a widening and deepening of the stream as it emerged from the wood and meandered through a meadow, and where on one side the bank had eroded. Bared tree roots laced its edge, providing excellent hand-holes for getting in and out of the water.

She went to her room to exchange bra and pants for a swimsuit, pulled on shorts and a shirt, collected a towel. Before leaving, she examined herself in the dressing-table mirror, looked into her close-set eyes – which stared back at her: dark wells of secret yearning. Perhaps it will be today, she thought, her stomach contracting as her mind ran ahead to the swimming expedition – no Jeanette to bother them, just the water with the sun on it and afterwards the soft grass . . . Then she cursed herself for having thought of it: anticipating a thing you want very badly was bound to make it not happen. But if this were so, it would be a very poor outlook, for there could be scarcely an activity left that her busy mind had not turned into lovemaking. She set off hopelessly down the corridor, having in all probability ruined her chances with a surfeit of longing and imagining.

The quickest route to the pool was not the wandering path through the wood, but round the wood's edge through the meadows. They took this shorter route automatically, but as their progress over the shimmering grass grew increasingly sluggish, Laurie wondered whether the circuitous but shaded path might not have made a better choice. He was too hot to say so aloud. Beside him Claire plodded wordlessly. The heat was sticking her eyelids open and roughening her throat, but compared to her thoughts these were minor nuisances.

Some minutes ago, stepping out into the courtyard, the light snatching away depth and colour with a blanket whitening, all her hopes, doubts and dreams seemed pathetic dross; she knew with clear-cut certainty that none of it would ever happen. He would never love her romantically. They were locked in their girl-boy, brother-sister relationship. She could never be sufficiently arresting to jolt him out of it. He, on the other hand, so dramatically good-looking, would have the pick of the girls at university and be all tied up – some raving beauty's own sealed parcel – by the time she got there. Ah well; so long as they remained close friends . . . She foresaw herself over the years bearing it well – Laurie's confidante, bravely making a chum of his wife. But how unlucky in these circumstances that she and Laurie were *not* brother and sister, nor even first cousins like he and Jeanette; for an indispensable friendship, even with someone you had grown up with, might well seem suspicious to a spouse. A married Laurie might prove more accessible to Jeanette than herself, she thought, thoroughly torturing herself. Her tongue passing over her lips tasted brine.

As their way veered round a bend, they came within the wood's shade. Feeling cooler, Laurie was able to speak. 'I wonder what I'll do?' he mused, his voice leaping on Claire's ears like a claxon, scattering her conjectures.

'When?' she asked; for her mind had already supplied him with a degree and a wife and an unspecified but satisfactory career.

'At Cambridge – always supposing I get there.

66

Possibly at Durham. Botany, Biology, Chemistry . . .
It's difficult to know. I must look into it thoroughly
this hol. How about you? What are you tending
towards?'

At fifteen it seemed too far off to contemplate.
'Shouldn't think I'll get to Cambridge. People from our
place don't. We're only humble grammar school girls.'

'Course you will,' he snapped. 'If I go, you *must.*
You're brainy enough, for heaven's sake. Set your
mind to it. If I'm already there, I shall warn the tutors
to look out for you and not miss the chance to snap
up a brilliant undergrad. And when you come up, I
shall show you off, I can tell you.'

The stream seemed to burst into sight. She broke
into a run.

'Hey,' he called, far too warm to chase after her.

She didn't want him too. She needed to be alone for
a moment, to open her mouth and silently whoop, to
burn off her sudden joy.

When he arrived, she was already lowering herself
into the water, gasping at the cold. He went behind
the stout tree trunk they used for a changing partition
– more demarcation line than effective screen – to
change into his trunks, while she, relinquishing her
grip of a tree root, slowly sank, suffering the heart-
stopping moment of freezing silk rising up and over
her. Some vigorous swimming soon restored her
circulation. After a while, she turned on to her back
and wafted in and out of the sun, her hands maintaining her position with lazy fluttering. She had only
half-registered the splash of Laurie's arrival. Their
submersion was not only into water but into their
childhood pattern of speechless communication, for
they barely spoke during the next half hour, though
they were often together at the same point, hanging
from a tree root, swimming to and fro between the
banks, drifting in the stream's centre. And at last
climbing out of the water.

She, as usual, went to one side of the tree, he to the

other. When she was sitting in her shorts and shirt, towelling her hair, he came round and sat beside her. Neither spoke, both disinclined to break out of the dreaminess cast by their long silence.

She leaned forward to press the towel between her toes. Her feet, he saw, were beautifully arched. As she laid the towel aside, he saw – as if he never had before – that she was very pleasingly shaped altogether: delicately boned, slightly angular like a boy, and in some respects quite unlike a boy: *gamine* he supposed was the suitable word. Her hair had been cut in a new way; it sprang wispily from her crown and layered towards her face like a cap of damp feathers. 'I like your hair done like that,' he said – not disruptively, more like thinking aloud. She smiled and tugged at the pointed wisps. A bead of water oozed out, crept over her face, ran out of sight under her chin and reappeared, gathering speed down her neck to trickle slowly, slowly over her breastbone and suddenly vanish in the V of her shirt. Through the damp thin fabric he saw the points of her breasts. An irresistible urge came over him; he reached out and with quick, deft fingers unfastened the top two shirt buttons. Her shirt gaped – and the droplet whose course he had wished to observe flew from his mind. In a dream, his hand reached inside until, like a bird he'd once held, a small warm breast beat in the curve of his palm.

Claire's smile had withered under his scrutiny. As he touched her, shock froze on her face and prevented her from moving a muscle. Only her eyes moved – slowly, to stare beyond him in disbelief. Trees, grass, sky seemed to roll away from her. She made no connection between what was now occurring and the habitual course of her dreams (a gathering into his arms, her name repeated between passionate kisses, her breast encountering only his). Unreality drove away all clues; she was taken by sudden shivering.

At once, he removed his hand. 'God, I'm so sorry.' He sounded dazed. 'Claire, I'm so sorry!' And as if to make amends, set both his hands to the task of refastening her shirt buttons.

But now his fingers were clumsy. Their frantic fumbling brought her to her senses. She saw that she had arrived at a familiar place by an unforeseen route. 'No, no,' she gasped, catching and stilling his hands. 'I mean,' – and she looked into his eyes and said deliberately – 'I don't mind. I mean, I want you to.'

Now it was he who was checked by surprise. He felt her hands relinquish his and slide upwards, over his arms to his neck; he felt their pressure draw him down as she lay back.

He kissed her. It seemed polite in the circumstances. After a moment he kissed her again, and this time she responded. He wondered whether he might now disengage, but found his hands were trapped between their bodies, in fact lay over her breasts. The discovery was electrifying; his embarrassed reluctance fled and the contents of his hands became all-engrossing. Eventually, he slid his face downwards to lay it near her breasts and as he did so glimpsed, risen over her waistband, the taut indentation of her navel. He found his face drawn here, as well, and was suddenly violently aroused. 'Claire,' he said, sliding up quickly to look at her. She gazed back steadily, and he knew that whatever he did she would welcome. The knowledge moved him, but at the same time raised his apprehension. 'Claire,' he repeated in a calmer voice, and fell to one side, holding her slackly.

For some minutes he fingered her hair and smiled into her eyes. At last he said, 'We should make a move, don't you think, darling?'

She watched his smile and her own – her own minutely reflected in his eyes. 'Yes,' she sighed contentedly, knowing she had gathered sufficient nourishment for a feast of dreams. Furthermore he had called her darling.

'Darling,' she would later repeat over and over to the dressing-table mirror; 'Darling,' she would whisper, clouding the dusty glass – substantiating a miracle.

The afternoon had pitched them into a new element, one in which Claire dwelt easily, Laurie less so. On the surface and before other people, nothing had changed. And alone together they were often as they had always been, engrossed in their interests, companionable, often silent. Nevertheless, Laurie noticed that whereas once they would only reluctantly raise their eyes when suddenly interrupted, now they were less innocent. At a knock on the door (Jeanette having been well-schooled) or his mother walking straight in (as was her right and habit) they took instant stock of where they were placed in relation to one another and how they might appear. This was nothing to Claire; merely the unconscious response of a woman surprised with her lover, albeit unremarkably. The massive leap forward in her relationship with Laurie, and the boost this had given to her self-confidence, had made her an adult, at least to herself. Her love was so central to her life that quite naturally she would defend it, and deception was an obvious and legitimate weapon.

He sensed her equanimity while squirming under his own doubts. It was inevitable that they would react differently – she sure, certain; he torn as ever, half wanting, half repelled. And the idiot thing was, their petting sessions always began at his instigation. Her response was immediate, but always she left it to him to choose the place and the moment. But he was full of self-deception. He recalled how late last evening he had purposely led her into the pottery, wanting *not* to, at the same time itching to experience again how she felt, moved, tasted. He was hurt on her behalf. Natural and trusting, she could have no inkling of his reservations, could never guess that while a part of him would – oh, would indeed – another was like a fastidious snail, closing up, retracting.

He was also afraid. Sex in his experience consisted of short, explosive, sometimes sordid episodes always leading to the same outcome: a sickening of his ability to tolerate the proximity of his partner. At the prospect of such an outcome with Claire, a void sprang in his chest. He dared not let matters go too far (and dreaded that he might) until he had conquered his ambivalence.

'Daddy?' A sound from inside her parents' sitting room – a low driven growling – prompted her to investigate. 'Is anything the matter?' Cautiously, she went in.

In the square window bay, newspapers heaped near his feet where he had evidently tossed them, Andrew Haddingham sat suspensefully, as if on the edge of a cliff rather than in his favourite leather armchair. He jerked an arm at her. 'Get my pills, will you? Bedside table.'

She sped into the adjoining room, found bottles ranged all over the table, gathered them, ran back. 'Which?'

'Tiny white ones.'

She proffered them tentatively; a wrong move might unleash his despair.

'Water.'

Dumping the remaining bottles on a stool, she hurried into the bathroom.

When the pills were swallowed, he tipped back his head and closed his eyes. 'Thank you, Sabine.'

'Claire.' It was an automatic correction which she immediately wished unsaid, for his blank gaze when he raised his head and looked at her was a wall of indifference – wife, daughter, nurse, cleaning woman: plainly, it was all one to him. 'Claire,' he repeated dully. 'Of course.'

'Would you like me to fetch Maman?' she asked, not really supposing this was the cause of his mistake, but just in case.

He waved a hand. She tried again. 'Anything else I can do for you, Daddy?'

The seconds crept by with no intervening answer, and eventually, she stole away.

Continuing to her room, light-heartedness returned with a buoyant lift as if it had been held briefly under water. A mechanically murmured 'Poor Daddy,' failed to rouse proper sorrow. Her father seemed not altogether to belong to her – though this was not a new feeling; Laurie had always possessed the power to distance her from other people. Nowadays that power was even stronger. She had customarily viewed her parents and everyone else at Foscote as though through the wrong end of a telescope; now the telescope was extended by several notches and they were shrunk to the size of pinpricks. It served them right. It was hard to feel close to people you constantly dismayed, who spoke in wearied tones as if you were a problem they'd been saddled with. Daddy, she had to admit, used to make efforts to reach her, but during the last few years when his health had deteriorated he'd evidently given up. She recalled a day last spring when she'd hurried home from school to tell him about a proposed trip to Stonehenge and Avebury. Once he'd been keen on pre-history; on this occasion he managed only a mumbled, 'I suppose you'll need some money,' and had simply ignored the explanatory booklets she'd placed on his knee. She had taken his money, despite having sufficient left from her allowance to pay for the trip, in lieu of enthusiasm.

'Poor Daddy', she repeated again sententiously, and sat down on her bed to change her shoes. At least she could absolve herself from the need ever to pity her mother. Not to be pestered had always been Maman's unspoken request, evident in the trapped wariness that came into her eyes whenever Claire, through carelessness or naughtiness, warranted attention. And Claire had learned to oblige. By not provoking attention, she made certain of being left pretty much to her own devices.

None of it had mattered, in any case, because she'd always had Laurie.

And the blissful knowledge radiated that she always would have Laurie. It brought her to her feet. On her bedroom carpet, she stood utterly still, thrilling at the memory of recent kisses, enraptured strokings. At last, feeling shaky, she tottered to her dressing-table.

Today they planned an expedition to Frean Hill, but first, Laurie said, he must put in a couple of hours' study. It was still not yet time to call for him – she was not impatient – they had all day. And days and days after this one, and years and years stretching ahead. No, there was nothing to be in a hurry about. His lovemaking could send her legs weak, make her nerves sing, but it did not arouse any sense of urgency. Rather, she relished the tantalizing delay; the prolonged exploration was a delight in itself; they had the rest of their lives to enjoy its culmination.

In the dust on the dressing-table mirror (it was her job to clean her room, so the mirror was usually dusty), she wrote with her finger, *Laurie and Claire.* When she had admired this for long enough, she rubbed the glass clean with her forearm. Her reflection showed with new starkness, and at great length, she examined it. Considering the drawbacks – narrow eyes which still, if she turned her head round far enough, were not entirely synchronized; a rather odd pallor for one so often out of doors; a pitifully meagre bust; still the look of a waifish girl – it was frankly amazing that Laurie found anything to be smitten by. But happiness allowed her to view these drawbacks lightly, almost with affection.

This had not always been the case. A few months ago, the comparative progress of some of her class-mates – from gawkiness to amazingly mature beauty – had brought her to the brink of despair. She'd be lucky, she considered in the light of the competition, to attract any man at all, never mind a prize like Laurie. It had terrified her to learn that he was a prize not only in her own estimation but in the more tested and valuable opinion of her friends who met him when they came to tea, including the stunningly attractive Gloria Doughty. Confidence in her continued importance to Laurie had sunk lower then than in those uncertain times when he first went away to boarding school.

All behind her now. She put her head on one side, grinned at her reflection, and thought she detected — not beauty, exactly — but a kind of racy appeal. In any case, Laurie, she suddenly saw, could not be expected to have conventional tastes; he would demand something out of the ordinary.

Certainly, she was that.

In the chalky grass on Frean Hill, she found what she'd been searching for all summer. 'Lizard orchids,' she screamed into the wind, in her pleasure hurling herself on Laurie's chest. Whereupon he caught her up and swung her to the ground, lay over her in a vain attempt to be sheltering, and sank his mouth over hers.

When she could breathe, she pushed him aside and lay panting for a moment, half wind-battered, half suffocated. 'Idiot,' she protested. She clambered to her feet and grinned down at him with a wondering expression. For not only were their eyes and noses running, the wind infuriating, the ground damp, there was important work to be done: the site to be investigated, neighbouring plants identified, a record made of all the particular conditions evidently favoured by *Himantoglossum hircinum*.

Just they two, she and he; and the unearthly trio — Duke Ellington, 'Sweets' Edison, Johnny Hodges — lulling, piercing, flirting with silence. (Oh, the suspense of those delayed beats.) Her eyes, he saw, were closed; sometimes she jigged her shoulders or rolled her head back; at the end, she opened them wide and grinned.

He got up, removed the needle, took the record from the deck, switched off. She was waiting, he sensed, to see what he would decide. And yes, there she sat in a perfectly relaxed fashion with her hands linked loosely on the table and her novel to one side – this was obliquely observed as he returned to his own seat and with an easy gesture reached for a book. At which, she promptly took up her own. After a second or two he covertly raised his eyes and saw that, as he had supposed, she was thoroughly absorbed, evidently content.

This was how they should be, how they always had been. His urge for something other (which, like a hobgoblin stirring from sleep, rubbing fists in its eyes, reassuming its wide-awake leer, he could feel already nudging the pit of his stomach) was perverse and possibly destructive. He despised himself (but was unable to prevent it) when he put down his book and looked across at her. 'Shall we go somewhere?'

She smiled, carefully marked the place in her book and put it down.

All at once, the part of him that was crying out against this was saved by a rapping on the door and Jeanette bursting in. She looked pink, heavy-eyed; and to judge from her portentous expression, bursting with news.

'Thank goodness you're here. I, er . . . Wait, I hafta sit down.' She grabbed a chair and sat heavily upon it with her legs splayed. 'I gotta tell someone, and you two, well I guess no-one else has more right . . .' She looked from one to the other. A feeling grew that what she was about to impart would not gladden them.

'Take a deep breath,' Laurie advised.

Jeanette heaved restively. 'Oh, I dunno; maybe I shouldn't. But it's goin' to be just *offul* for me carrying it around alone, no-one to confide in . . .'

'Something to do with Nigel?' Claire suggested.

'No. Well – it began with Nige. But I sure as heck wouldn't like Nige to know about it. I mean, what sort of impression would he get of this place?'

Claire flung herself impatiently to one side. Laurie tried prompting. 'You said it began with Nigel?'

'Yeah. You see, we fixed on a new place to meet this evening. I thought no-one went in there much, unless the weather was foul . . .'

'Where?'

'The old barn – where they keep all the old furniture and stuff. We thought one of those sofas'd be—' she giggled, 'snug? I got there first like we arranged, so no-one'd see us sneaking in together. So there I was waiting on the one we'd picked out – the long red one with the high back at the end of the barn where it's all dim and spooky – when the door opens. Naturally, I thought it was Nige. But I didn't call out 'cos I was lying arranged with my hair fanned out – you know?'

'We get the picture,' Claire said.

'But it wasn't Nige. Oh Gard – it was Uncle Peter. I nearly died. "Wait there a minute," he said to some-one, then started coming down the barn. I just rolled off the sofa and shot underneath. I mean, what'd he think if he found me? Anyway, he walked right round the barn then back to the door. Then said "All clear," and bolted it – he and this other person *still inside*. Gee, I didn't know what to think. Anyway, they started rustling about and talking low. Then after a bit – oh help! – there's a sofa squeaking, then going bumf, bumf, bumf, and Uncle Peter making horrible grunts and the woman, like, *moaning*.'

'What woman?' Claire barked.

Jeanette adopted a pleading expression. 'Your mom?' she mewed.

'Mom' seemed to bounce round Claire's skull. 'Liar. It couldn't have been. You said you couldn't see. . .'

'But I *heard*. "Peetair," she goes, "Peetair." It was definitely Aunt Sabine. I mean, who else says "Peetair" like that? With a *French accent*?'

Claire rose menacingly. Laurie caught her arm. Both girls turned to him – his face was impassive, he might have been considering whether or not to accompany Jeanette in some song. 'So,' he said at last. 'You've said nothing of this to Nigel.'

'I haven't *seen* Nigel. I heard him try the door soon after they came in. The rattle made 'em go quiet. Then she started whispering and Uncle Peter said, "Won't do them any good if they do, it's bolted;" and then all that stuff I told you about began. It was ages before they went. Then I made myself wait at least ten minutes before I dared sneak out myself. Luckily, it was getting dusk. Then I came to find you. Nige must be wondering what on earth's happened to me . . .'

'I think,' Laurie said slowly, 'we must go and put his mind at rest. However . . .'

'So you do believe me?'

'Of course we don't,' snapped Claire. 'You've always exaggerated, but this beats everything. Tell her, Laurie. Tell her she's a liar.'

'I'm not. I'm telling the truth. You believe me, don't you, Laurie?'

They were both staring at him, waiting. But Laurie was transfixed by Claire. Usually pallid, never more coloured by the summer sun than to a faint olive, her face and neck had sprung red blotches like nettle rash. A dispiriting sadness washed over him. With hindsight, he felt he had foreseen as she spoke what Jeanette would reveal. Memories burned in his head; gained a new significance. Playing for time, he propped his feet up on the table and crossed his legs, tipped his chair back, rested his hands in his trouser pockets (a laconic pose which had enhanced his reputation in the junior common room for man-of-the-world insouciance). He was certain Jeanette had told the truth; the problem was, how to manage it. When he spoke, he employed the gravitas which masters at Prestbury encouraged in their pupils and considered well exemplified by Lawrence Stone (though they little dreamt of the self-mockery underlying it in his case). 'True or false,' he pronounced, 'I fear poor Jeanette has landed herself in a perilous position.'

'How's that? I wasn't doing anything? I couldn't help . . .'

'Consider the matter from both suppositions. First,' (he directed a look begging tolerance at Claire) 'that Jeanette has described what is in fact the case. How then, do you suppose, my father would react to the news that his clandestine affair has been observed by his niece? – that she is the only witness, that she has blabbed about it? Second,' (and now a similar look to Jeanette) 'that Jeanette was mistaken, or fell asleep and dreamt the episode. It comes to my father's ears that she has accused him unjustly of conducting an affair with the wife of his friend and partner. I think, don't you, that in both cases his reaction is going to be largely similar and with the same outcome?'

'Outcome?' Jeanette echoed fearfully.

'Well, of course. My father is not a man to have his reputation besmirched and do nothing about it. Obviously, Jeanette would be sent away. Boarding school, I should imagine – perhaps some distant relative would be persuaded to put her up during the holidays. Failing that, perhaps a convent . . .' He smiled pityingly. 'Certainly, there would no longer be a home for you here at Foscote.'

Jeanette gulped. Laurie allowed sinking-in time.

'The point is,' he then continued silkily, 'in your own interest the story must never come out. You can rest assured neither Claire nor I will ever mention it. We shouldn't care for Claire's father or my mother . . .'

'My father's ill. He's very sick.'

'Precisely. And my mother is a very kind, a very decent person. I won't have her upset.'

'So . . .' Jeanette, pale and flushed by turn, blinked in confusion. 'So what you're saying is: I better not say anything.'

'Absolutely nothing. Not a word, not a whisper *to*

anyone. As I said, I couldn't allow my mother to be distressed, nor Claire her father. So, if – *if* it ever came to our ears that you'd breathed a word of this, we'd be obliged to take action.'

'Yeah?'

'Mm.' He raked long fingers through his curly black hair. 'I should imagine we'd go to my father and report that to our horror and disgust *you* have been putting round an outrageous rumour. I think I've clearly painted the consequences.'

She swallowed. 'I shan't say a word.'

'Well, we certainly shan't. So if ever there *was* a whisper . . .'

'Honest, Laurie, there won't be.'

'We shall watch you like hawks,' he promised, then swung his legs from the table. 'And now we'll all go and find Nigel. Let's see . . . You simply tell him that you were not aware when you made the arrangement that the barn is out of bounds in the evening. Then, when you failed to find him, you met us instead and went for a walk. I shall chat to good old Nige very chummily and suggest we all go into the kitchen and make cocoa. I think that's best: your first meeting with him got over with safely so you won't need to refer to this evening again.'

'OK.'

'Come along, girls,' he chivvied, springing to his feet, gathering them.

Not entirely satisfied, Claire went to play her part.

Thank goodness they'd stopped using the hayloft, thought Laurie, slipping into the pottery. Their hideout had not been visited for years, not since he went away to Prestbury and returned home with a more critical eye to see it as a hazard rather than a sanctuary, for it was riddled with rot and might collapse any time, specially under sudden weight. 'Promise you won't go in there while I'm away,' he'd insisted to Claire, alarmed by a vision of the supporting beams crumbling and the whole thing hurtling down through the barn to smash – Claire with it – on the stone-flagged floor. Now he speculated whether his embargo might have saved Claire from a different sort of crashing to earth. For it seemed, if Jeanette's report of the conversation was to be trusted, that the barn was used as a trysting place. Locking up had never been thought necessary at Foscote, it was too distant from any town and too alive with trusty folk. Evidently, his father privately held a key to the barn (and possibly keys to other places, too) for the purpose of guaranteeing measures of privacy with Aunt Sabine.

In his plimsolls, Laurie silently mounted the steps to the first floor and began the tricky feat of climbing over the shelves and opening and squeezing through the trapdoorway – tricky, because he was out of practice and considerably larger than the last time he did this. Safely in the roof space, he lowered the door behind him, and was suddenly queasy with claustro-phobia. He swallowed, breathed deeply, and tried to disregard the smothering dustiness. The air in the hayloft would be fresher, he reasoned, braving himself to crawl forward and feel for the rope. When his hands secured it, he began to flinch at the prospect of landing on the loft floor. But he steeled himself by rehearsing his conviction that tonight would be *the* night.

The last three evenings, following Jeanette's bomb-shell, he had known would end in no lovers' meeting; his father and Aunt Sabine were too taken up with visitors, rehearsals, or going over accounts. This even-ing, however, he had sensed a change. Watching them closely, he observed their brief but earnest exchange which seemed to end in agreement as they broke away. *Got you: tonight!* he'd exulted, jubilant to be on their track at last, momentarily forgetting the reason behind his decision to spy on them – a hope against hope that Jeanette's report and his own intuition would prove wide of the mark.

His feet met the floor of the hayloft sooner than he

expected. Gingerly, he gave them his full weight and relinquished the rope. In the half-light from the grill, he examined the tiny room. It was exactly as they had left it – a rug laid out and scuffed up on one side; a book propped open with its binding uppermost; bits of paper, pencils and crayons lying about; open tins revealing knives, scissors, string, rubber bands; Claire's old toy dog; a pile of conkers . . . Grave goods, he thought with sudden misgiving, and trod reluctantly over the boards to the aperture in the wall. And settled down to wait.

Laurie never was able to obliterate that evening – the mustiness stuffing his nostrils, the darkness pressing, as he knelt caged-like at the barred aperture peering down into a lesser darkness, where greenish limbs writhed and the moon of his father's buttocks heaved and a panting Aunt Sabine rasped, 'Yes, Peetair, yes!' and his father's ejaculating growl echoed and re-echoed. Like a death rattle.

vii

And neither would Claire ever forget that once Laurie had made love to her and now never did.

Realization, however, was a slow burn. For now, for the remainder of summer, Laurie's sudden anxiety about books still unread, essays still unwritten, seemed perfectly natural, and while he was occupied in reading and writing it was no hardship to Claire to find similar work. For she, like he, was increasingly engrossed in their mutual enthusiasm: the study of plants and other living matter. In fact, usually, it was *he* who broke into *her* train of thought, with a complaint that he was stiff from sitting so long, stuffy from lack of air, and required exercise or wished to explore some likely terrain for specimens. 'Come on, lazybones,' he would urge, dragging her out of doors. 'Wait,' she would wail, trailing behind. And he would yank her up the slope of the paddock in a reversal of their childhood roles (where she would easily outstrip him and wait at the top calling insults). These days, Laurie was the swift one, the energetic one with tireless limbs, while Claire, lightly built and nimble, was unaccountably taken by lassitude. He would pretend exasperation, which made her giggle and go floppy; if they were out of sight she would hook an arm round his neck and lean her head against his shoulder; at which he would turn, hold her in a steely grip at several inches' remove and plant a kiss on her nose or cheek. 'Now, come on; pull yourself together, dear, *do*,' he would order, giving her a shake. Which made her laugh all the more (Laurie was so monstrously bossy) and inevitably, with laughter bubbling out of her, she found herself revived.

However Laurie was occupied – working, reading, walking with Claire, talking to his mother, exchanging pleasantries with guests at table – part of him was grappling with the problem of how to escape. Flash memories of the copulation he had witnessed set off a refrain in his head: *I've got to get away from here*. Even Claire (at this moment) seemed part of what he needed to escape; for he craved complete foreignness, the cessation of everything in life he had so far experienced, and a plunge, total immersion, into bright clean newness. As soon as he returned to school he was determined to acquire the necessary information and knowledge to discover a practical means to cast off from Foscote.

viii

'Dr . . . ink,' Andrew Haddingham groaned out.

Claire rose from her chair, reached for the beaker on the bedside table and held it in front of her father's face. He took the spout into his mouth and with his good arm (the arm which had retained some mobility after his recent stroke) indicated that she should tip the beaker higher: higher still, his hand tetchily signalled, up, up. She tipped; his pursed lips appeared to draw; then he scowled and flopped back on the pillows.

'Was that it? Did you get anything?'

He shook his head. She said nothing (his frustration was palpable) but maintained the beaker in place, waiting for him to try a second time.

But this too ended in failure. Sensing his fury, she continued holding the beaker, watching *it* rather than him, determined not to get upset. She thought how easily she might panic and cry; she recalled Jeanette's puffy tear-stained face yesterday after one of *her* stints in this room. She pitied him, but would not let his despair undermine her. After a moment, she returned the beaker to the table, sat down and glanced at her watch, which told her that in twenty minutes or so she would be relieved by Maman or Aunt Margaret or Uncle Peter. And at nine o'clock the night nurse would come. Let *them* worry over his parched lips, let *them* discover the problem with the beaker, let *them* fuss and stew and be ground down by his misery. She sat, the picture of calm, beside him, holding herself in check.

'Claire,' he said suddenly, with difficulty. 'How's . . . school?'

This was more like it. Craning forward, her face brightening, she told him. School was fine, specially now she had Miss Thwaite teaching her. Miss Thwaite was allowing her to do her own project – it was like doing research really, as she hoped to do one day at university. Miss Thwaite was brilliant, and enormously kind. She even let Claire stay in the lab after school and afterwards, because the school bus had gone, brought her home in her car.

He had actually smiled when she began all this. But now, nodding to convey that he was pleased for her, closed his eyes. When she judged him to be asleep, she settled back in her chair. Talking of school had reminded her of why she was resolved to stay detached. It was because she had her whole life ahead and important things to do and a commitment to keep. This future seemed to hover over her head, strong and gleaming, like a platinum star; it seemed a thing of its own, as if she were not to live it, but be its keeper. If any person or happening threatened to obstruct it, she knew she would be ruthless.

A groan of pain came from the bed. She peered across. If he dies, she thought, Laurie will come home.

It was Aunt Margaret who came to relieve her, armed with sketching materials.

'He's asleep.'

'Mm,' Margaret Stone said vaguely, settling herself with her paraphernalia in a chair near a lamp; and then, 'Oh, Claire, dear?' – as Claire turned to go – 'Jeanette's in the kitchen all on her own ploughing through the most enormous pile of washing-up. You might be a darling and give her a hand.'

'I haven't finished my homework yet,' she said haughtily, and went out, pulling the door closed.

A hippopotamus on two legs – rather short it was true – went plodding down the corridor, limbs bowed under grotesque weight, features swollen by disgruntlement: that laden feeling had rolled over her again. At the top of the back stairs, she underwent a change of heart and turned and ran back, shedding pounds on the way. 'All right, I'll go and help her,' she conceded putting her head round the door; and was rewarded with the sort of knowing grin Laurie might have turned on her (he and his mother were so very alike). This sparked Claire's own lopsided smile and melted away the last trace of hippopotamus.

In the kitchen, Jeanette turned to see who'd come in. 'You don't have to,' she said, as Claire picked up a tea cloth. 'I bet you've got piles of homework.'

'That's all right,' Claire said carelessly, selecting a couple of drained dinner plates.

Walking between kitchen and scullery, putting away crockery and saucepans, she puzzled over the mysterious weightiness which would capriciously fall over and off her. Covertly, she examined the ample Jeanette. Now here *was* a hippopotamus. No, that was mean. But Jeanette was certainly large, head and shoulders taller than her, presenting a broad rear side, and, via a reflection in the night-blackened window, a bosom lurching over the foamy washing-up water like a hanging cliff. By the side of this Amazon her own reflection darted like an emaciated midget. So why, for no discernible physical reason, should she suddenly feel gross and hardly able to drag herself around?

'Any idea of my mother's whereabouts?' she asked eventually.

'Out there with Uncle Peter,' replied Jeanette with a nod towards the back door – before suddenly, very visibly, collecting herself. 'I mean,' she went on in a rush, 'they've gone to one of the practice rooms to rehearse their songs for the Bath Festival. There's an awful lot of work to do on Guy's piece. It's really tricky – Guy admitted as much at tea; he may have to do some rewriting. I'm pretty sure, in fact, that he's over there with them.'

Claire understood perfectly. Jeanette was at pains to convey her earnest belief in the total innocence of Uncle Peter and Aunt Sabine being 'out there' together: they were honourably and diligently engaged, and she hadn't the slightest intention of imputing otherwise. Claire also understood the reason behind Jeanette's anxiety to make this clear: it was due to her own behaviour and to Laurie's; for with their pointed looks and murmured threats they had driven Jeanette to such a pitch she dreaded uttering a wrong word. She strove constantly to appease them; there was no task which she would not do in their stead – which was why she sat for an hour with Claire's father every day after school, allowing Claire to come home late. Guiltily, Claire turned away and knelt on the stone-flagged floor to stack some dishes in a low cupboard. 'I need her to give me some money for the Science trip, that's all,' she mumbled.

'Uhuh? Where's the trip to?'

'Natural History Museum.'

'Yeah? That'll be interesting.'

Claire hung up her tea cloth to dry. 'That's the lot, isn't it? I think I'll just slip across and ask her now. The money was supposed to be in by yesterday at the latest; but I forgot.'

'Why not wait? They'll be out in a minute. You know how they hate being interrupted – which is understandable, all musicians do – gee, I do myself, and I'm no great shakes!'

Ignoring her, Claire went to the door.

'Say, I think I'll make some cocoa,' cried Jeanette desperately. 'You want some?'

'Thanks – when I come back,' she said, and stepped out into the courtyard and closed the door.

The evening air was cold and damp. It shivered coatless Claire to a standstill. As she grasped her forearms, very faintly her mother's voice drifted over – the high swoops which were such a recognizable part of the Sabine Haddingham armoury – and, sure enough, widely spaced chords from the piano. Blameless industry was obviously occurring behind the lighted window of the upper practice room. And yet, Claire reflected, it had been all too plain in the kitchen just now that Jeanette feared otherwise.

The sharp air seemed to rise in her nostrils and cut into her brain, piercing the cloudy blather she had been feeding herself these past months. It was all suddenly clear as day. Jeanette must have a reason for being scared that Maman and Uncle Peter were not now innocently occupied, and the most likely was that she had indeed overheard them that night in the barn having sexual intercourse.

Slowly, Claire crossed the courtyard and came to rest at the steps leading to the practice room. The sounds became ever more distinct, the agile soprano voice soaring, stalked by the piano's measured tread. Yes, she thought, it happened. And still does. It's been happening for years.

She moved quickly away over the cobbles. As the sounds made by Maman and Uncle Peter grew fainter, other sounds increased – the noise of a violin, a flute, the voices of men arguing: Foscote sounds, in fact; distinct layers combining in busy din. She covered her ears with her hands and discovered a worse noise in her head: her veins were full of seething blood. Her mind began rushing with headlong speed (as sometimes happened in nightmares) towards some point of catastrophe, and now (as never did happen in dreams, for she always mercifully sprang awake) that point was reached. *Laurie knows*, she thought. Laurie had known from the beginning Jeanette was telling the truth; only her own violent protests to the contrary had prevented him from confessing as much. Perhaps, though, he never would have confessed, but preferred to keep it to himself, to gnaw on it in secret. Perhaps, because she was her mother's daughter, his usual eagerness to confide in her was soured. T*ogether with all his other feelings for her*. She stood stock still, scarcely breathing, hunting through every moment spent with Laurie since Jeanette's revelation. And discovered there had been a change. He had continued to seek her company, laughed and joked with her, even kissed her and squeezed her arms. But in a comradely sort of way. There had been no more lovemaking. And she, having assumed a pledge in that first kiss and in every embrace thereafter, had been too complacent to notice. It hit her for the first time in her life that nothing, however precious and momentous, is guaranteed for ever.

When she moved, she found the mysterious

heaviness on her again. Trudging to the scullery door, she was a two-ton weight. But now an explanation dawned. Maybe she got heavy and weary from constantly denying the truth (the truth as described by Jeanette); maybe it was the truth dragging doggedly after her like a leaden shadow.

'Did you find your mother?' Jeanette asked, pouring cocoa from a saucepan into two of Aunt Margaret's pottery mugs.

'No. You were right. They were hard at work; it would've been stupid to interrupt them. But for heaven's sake remind me to ask her when they come in. If I don't pay up tomorrow, I'll lose my place on the trip. Mm, this is lovely, Jeanette. It always goes lumpy when I make it. Thanks.'

'Oh, that's OK,' said Jeanette, flushing at the compliment.

Claire dreamed she had gone into the woods to hunt for Laurie. In the first part of the wood, where vistas showed constantly through tall trees, she ran quickly, hopefully, over the hard ground. But now, in the tangled part, bramble stems snatched at her, clumps of fern stood in her path, and humped up roots lurking in undergrowth tripped her feet. Once, she glimpsed him – his face flashing whitely against the dark rhododendron he was speeding past. When she arrived at the stream, he was not waiting there, as she had hoped. She began to follow its course, knowing suddenly where he *would* be – the place where the stream broke from the woods to cut through the meadow, the place where it widened to form a pool. Keeping tenaciously to the stream bank, she thrust through all obstacles. And at last, burst from the wood.

But the scene was frozen, dead. No breeze ruffled the water or shifted the light dapples. There was no birdsong, no plop of fish; no rustling of leaves or sighing of grass. And no Laurie.

November – and nearly pitch black by five o'clock. At a quarter to five, driving out of the school gate, Miss Thwaite was obliged to turn on the Morris Minor's headlights. 'I do hate these short days,' she remarked.

'Oh, so do I,' said Claire, sitting neatly in the passenger seat, ankles and knees together, hands clasping the satchel on her lap. She would unhesitatingly agree with any sentiment expressed by Miss Thwaite, though as a matter of fact, her agreement in this instance was false. She adored slipping into the lighted lab at ten to four – all other girls gone (save Daphne Oxenbury, the only sixth-former currently taking Science; but Daphne sat quietly in a corner writing up notes, or waited patiently beside a distillation flask filling monotonously drop by drop, and was so far above Claire in age and remoteness – Daphne eighteen, Claire barely sixteen – as not to be counted with the chattering, stool-scraping, unappreciative throng implied by 'other girls'). The lab assistant, a taciturn mousy young woman, was usually about somewhere; so too was Miss Casey, the Head of Science, who had sole charge of Physics and shared the teaching of Chemistry with her underling, the Biology and Botany teacher, Miss Thwaite. And, brilliantly, at around a quarter past four Miss Thwaite herself would return from the staff room (smelling strongly of cigarettes) to check up on bottles bubbling softly on shelves, on the welfare of worms in wormeries and grubs in jars, to lay out a demonstration on the teaching bench for the morning, to chalk questions on a blackboard, and generally tidy up before driving home. With Claire as her fortunate passenger, sated with the pleasure of an hour denied the common herd in the peaceful lab, the privilege dramatically highlighted by the gathering dark at the window, the illumination within. But the truth of Miss

Thwaite's sentiment, as it applied to herself, was neither here nor there; not for a second did she consider it, but agreed at once and with sincerity – the sincerity of her wish to identify with her teacher.

This was no less than her duty. Not only because Miss Thwaite took a helpful interest in her work and was kind enough to allow her to continue with it after school and give her a lift home, but also because Claire felt drawn to protect her. No teacher of Science stood a chance of general popularity at the Girls' Grammar, for very few girls were drawn to the subject. But towards Miss Thwaite there was frank hostility. Particularly, she was despised for her dissection lessons. If she were honest, Claire would admit to unease herself at the sight of Miss Thwaite's knife splitting and splaying a fluffy white rabbit while Miss Thwaite's voice blithely expounded on the best technique, called for the naming of parts and estimations as to the number of hours passed since the deceased's final grassy meal. The girls mostly watched in sullen silence – broken by the noisy collapse of a couple of swooners. But those who fainted were of the sillier type. The consensus among respected girls afterwards was that the exercise had been rather disgusting and Miss Thwaite had shown an objectionable keenness. 'Butcher' had been murmured suggestively by one of them. Which prompted Claire to remark that fluffy white rabbits were daily to be seen hanging from hooks in butchers' shops, cardboard containers for the collection of blood round their poor little noses – an observation that did not entirely convince. There was something, the fifth-formers knew in their hearts, very much to be deplored in Miss Thwaite and her dissecting tools. Therefore Claire, who understood that it was single-minded enthusiasm for discovery and learning which cast her teacher in this unfavourable light, and a certain gaucherie where sensibilities were involved, was at pains to demonstrate with every opportunity that in some quarters she was appreciated.

'It's very kind of you to run me home,' she said now, as she did on practically every journey back in Miss Thwaite's car.

'That's all right. I have to pass by your gates. How's your experiment coming?'

'Very well, thanks. But I'm a bit worried about my silk worms. I gave them fresh mulberry leaves last night but they're keeping right off them; they're still crawling on the old holey ones.'

'Mm. I expect they need a good clean out. I'll take a look tomorrow.'

'Oh thanks, Miss Thwaite.'

They arrived in the Foscote gateway. Claire opened the passenger door. She was hesitating, forming in her head some pleasant phrase of farewell, when, above the quietly chuntering engine, a high-pitched yelping bore in on their ears. They peered through the windscreen. In the beam of the car's headlights a small woman in a large flapping coat and high heels came tripping and waving her arms, her white hands going up, down, out and in like semaphore flags.

'Good lord, who's that?' asked Miss Thwaite.

'My mother,' said Claire, bundling swiftly out of the car with her satchel. 'She's French, a singer.'

This information, it seemed to the teacher, was thrown like a bone to appease a dog, or an excuse blurted by some miscreant schoolgirl. She considered whether to switch off the engine or wind down her window, but when Claire called 'Goodbye,' and shut the car door and set off quickly towards the agitated figure, she concluded that she was not about to be introduced after all, so backed on to the road and drove wonderingly home.

Claire's legs plunging towards her mother felt lumbering. Headlights swinging had revealed a distraught Sabine – one hand at her throat, the other outflung. 'Claire . . . ma petite . . .'

'Is it Daddy?' she called (sensing how the life sped

from her mother's pose as the car's beam deserted). 'Is it *Daddy*?' she repeated.

A great sigh. Then, almost bitterly: '*Yes!*' – for her daughter's terse impatience seemed insensitive, a rebuke, and Sabine was tired of it. She had not at all liked Margaret's attitude earlier. How, for the good God's sake, could she be expected to know this would be the day? Andrew had been at death's door for weeks; she was not clairvoyant. As if the shock of returning home to learn of her widowhood was not sufficient, *questions* had been barked at her. Her mind reeling, too distracted even to divest herself of her outer garments (and what a blessing this had proved!) she had found remaining indoors, breathing air poisoned by panicky hostility, insupportable. Huddled inside her coat as she paced the drive and waited for Claire's return, a little saving scene had built in her mind: mother and daughter closeted together sharing their grief. Who would dare disturb that? And if someone were sufficiently brazen – 'Please go. We need some time alone,' she would simply, sadly, reproach them. 'Yes, darling,' she now said to her daughter, 'you will have to be brave. Daddy is dead.'

'I thought that was it. What happened? When?' She presumed he had died quite recently, since no-one had telephoned the school requesting her return.

'Earlier this afternoon. I don't know precisely.'

'You don't *know*?'

'*What is this, DAR-LING?* I am distraught – there has been nothing but turmoil – you expect me to keep my eyes on a clock?'

'Sorry, Maman.' She trudged by her mother's side, up the steps, into the hall, up two flights of stairs and along the corridor to the Haddingham apartment.

'Come and sit with Maman.'

But passing the door to the principal bedroom, Claire hesitated. 'Should I, do you think,' – she reached, half in dread, to the doorknob – 'go in and see him?'

Sabine frowned. 'He is no longer here, of course. The undertakers have removed him. If you wish it, I will drive you tomorrow to the funeral parlour.'

'Then he must have died ages ago. Why didn't you send for me?'

Sabine ran into the sitting room, fell into a chair, and let out a howl. 'Ow-ooo – and I imagined my daughter would be a comfort! But all she requires are the petty details – why this? – why that?'

'Shush, Maman. I'm sorry, I really am.' She flung on to her knees, took her mother's hands. 'It's a shock to me, too. I know we sort of expected it, but now it's happened . . .'

'There! – you see? We are different, you and I, but we can understand one another. Of course it's a shock.'

After a few moments, as Sabine began to talk nostalgically, Claire loosed her mother's hands and shuffled back a little way. 'You know, darling, I was recalling only the other day how reluctant I was in the beginning to come to Foscote. It was Andrew who was keen – and Peter, of course. I went along with it out of duty, to support my husband. And then. . . Well, we French women are pragmatic. We shrug our shoulders, roll up our sleeves, make the best of it. . .' On and on she went. And Claire took the opportunity to creep even further afield, to clamber into a chair. Primarily, Sabine appeared to be talking for her own benefit. Claire stopped listening and began to grapple with her own thoughts and reactions.

It surprised her what a blow the news was. She had anticipated her father's death; with equanimity she had contemplated its immediate consequences (for instance, that Laurie would arrive for the funeral); yet having fatherlessness suddenly thrust upon her was somehow shocking. That her father was *no more* (sickly invalid though he had been for years) seemed a momentous, an outrageous idea. For this reason she longed to be supplied with the petty details despised by her mother, details of how and when and why, to furnish a picture of the event, to make it real.

Suddenly, ringingly, her stomach rumbled. She clenched an arm across it.

Sabine frowned at her, as if she had forgotten who she was and why she was present. 'I expect you are hungry,' she conceded. 'Myself, I have no appetite.' (She did not confess that this was largely due to having lunched magnificently, but a faint taste of *moules marinière* at the back of her throat encouraged her to be considerate.) 'Go down and get something on a tray. Everything's at sixes and sevens down there, but there's sure to be ham and cheese. You can bring it up here, eh?'

Claire awkwardly rose, finding she was indeed famished and at the same time shamed by her mother's abstinence. 'OK, I won't be long,' she mumbled, and fled the room.

Noise of food preparation, footsteps, voices, caused Claire, running almost recklessly towards kitchen and scullery, to pause just before the threshold. Inside were only Aunt Margaret and Jeanette. But suddenly she was embarrassed. How, she wondered, ought she to *seem*? How was fatherlessness properly worn in public? Aunt and niece were passing between table, stove and sink, chopping, stirring, putting things to soak; their eyes glittered, their skin glowed; they worked and talked quickly, like people who have been on the go for so many hours they've forgotten how to stop.

Some sense caused Jeanette to look towards the doorway. Her stillness then prompted Margaret Stone to turn. Immobility gripped all three, until Margaret Stone, abandoning her saucepan, hurried forward with opening arms. While she was being held, Claire peered over her aunt's shoulder to the place at the long refectory table where her father would sit, and the place where, when Foscote was full of visitors, she and

94

Laurie as children sat squashed together. Then Aunt Margaret propped her upright, looked into her face, said how sorry she was, how sorry they all were, that although it was for the best it was still a terrible loss. Jeanette approached timidly, her eyes brimming. 'I really, you know, *feel* for you, Claire,' she offered.

Claire ignored her. She wished Jeanette weren't here. She longed for her aunt's undivided attention, to question her, to gain a picture of the day's events. As if Jeanette weren't present, she shrugged past her to the table and explained quickly that she'd come to fetch something to eat on a tray and take it upstairs where she was bidden to keep her mother company. 'I wish you and I could have a talk, though,' she added meaningfully to her aunt.

'Jeanette,' said Margaret Stone. 'I find I'm rather chilly. Be a dear and run upstairs for my cardigan, would you? It's hanging over the chair by the bed.'

'Thanks for getting rid of her,' Claire said, barely allowing the girl time to run out of earshot. 'I want to ask you . . . You see, Maman won't answer anything, like why I wasn't sent for, why didn't somebody ring the school. And what happened, exactly. Was it . . . awful? I want to know.'

'Of course you do. And tomorrow we'll talk as much as you like. But right this minute there's something I want you to understand: I could not have coped with everything today without Jeanette. Thank God she was off school.' (Jeanette, as Claire had frequently observed, often stayed home for piffling reasons – a bit of a cold, period pain, a headache.) 'Otherwise I'd have had all this to face on my own. And you have no idea . . .' But here she stopped herself, went to the stove and started stirring. 'I'm sorry we didn't think to call you from school, but quite honestly, what with trying to track down your mother and Uncle Peter . . . Apparently, they'd gone off to lunch with someone from the BBC – not a word to me to say where they were going, of course, and it was perfectly obvious soon after breakfast how very ill your father was . . . And then, of course, when the doctor left I had to call an undertaker – no-one here to consult . . . I'm only telling you this because I want it understood that Jeanette's been an absolute brick.' She stopped stirring suddenly, and turned, looking stern. 'So I won't have you snubbing her, you little monkey. Don't think I haven't noticed how you and Laurie make comments behind her back, and tease her and bully. . . I understand *why* you do it, of course,' (at this Claire's heart lurched; but Aunt Margaret soon showed that she didn't understand); 'you and Laurie are thick as thieves and determined not to let her butt in. However, you are no longer infants. And in this instance, you owe Jeanette a debt of gratitude . . .' At the sound of footsteps she broke off. 'So what would you like on your tray? Does Sabine want anything?'

'No, she doesn't, thanks. Anything will do for me – whatever there is.'

Jeanette came in and handed over the cardigan. Margaret Stone pulled it on. 'That's better,' she declared. The girls looked at her doubtfully; she appeared hotter than ever.

'I say,' said Claire, turning to Jeanette and endeavouring to sound casual, 'Aunt Margaret's been explaining how she couldn't have managed without you today. Well, me neither – other days, I mean. You were really good to poor Daddy. He was terrifically fond of you. And so'm I,' she suddenly blurted.

Jeanette fell against her and sobbed. Supporting her not inconsiderable weight, Claire braced her legs and looked awkwardly across to Aunt Margaret, who, with a pleased expression, was carving a ham. 'It was nothing,' sobbed Jeanette. 'I mean, I *wanted* to help him, I was glad to.'

'It was a lot,' Claire said. 'I won't forget it.'

At this, Jeanette grabbed a handkerchief and mopped her eyes. They examined the other's face, and the air between them shimmered with allusion. Did

Claire mean . . . ? Jeanette's face asked. Yes, I believe you; I know you told the truth, Claire's conceded. Impossible to say a word of this in front of Aunt Margaret; but perhaps this way was less awkward.

In any case, Claire thought, returning with her tray to the Haddingham quarters, even if Aunt Margaret hadn't been present she doubted whether she could have brought herself to mention the subject. She could hardly stand to think of it. So, her mother and Uncle Peter had been out to lunch with someone from the BBC, eh? It was possible, but she'd bet it wasn't the whole story. Things must have been desperate here – Aunt Margaret trying to cope with her father, deal with the doctor, then an undertaker, and with no way of tracing her mother; Jeanette run off her feet and fervently praying that the missing pair *wouldn't* be found – unless, of course, in innocent circumstances . . .

Bracing the tray on a knee, she turned the doorknob and pushed open the sitting-room door: it was like opening the lid of a jack-in-the-box, only it wasn't a garish face that jumped out at her, but Uncle Peter's voice. If her hands had been free, she would have caught the door to and crept away. As it was, she merely stood in the doorway holding her tray, feeling foolish and inadequate as she always did under the full gaze of Uncle Peter.

He came smoothly forward, removed the tray and carried it considerately to the table. Then turned to observe her approach. As she drew near, he reached out and placed two hands on her shoulders.

She would not look up.

'Claire, my dear. I know you will be brave. Your mother will be glad of your support.'

She nodded. When he released her, she pulled out one of the dining chairs, clumsily sat down, and with trembling fingers took up her knife and fork. 'Sure you don't want anything to eat, Maman?' she managed. At least her voice was steady, she was thankful for that.

'Quite sure, darling. But thank you for asking.'

In her peripheral vision she witnessed the long look that went between them.

'Well,' said Peter Stone at last. 'A great deal to do. Papers to sort through. Arrangements . . .'

'Thank you, Peter. So kind.'

He touched her mother's arm as he passed, and murmuring, 'Goodnight, Claire,' continued noiselessly over the carpet to the door.

In the pottery, Margaret Stone was pricking out a pattern round the fat circumference of an unfired urn. From the yard, Claire studied her through a window. A lamp's whitish glare showed an older looking woman than the image Claire held in her head, more worn, fiercely lined, her face colour similar to that of the clay she was working. Her frizzy bush of hair jutted over her forehead and nose like silverweed on a rock ledge. How hard she works; on the go at all hours, Claire thought, with, for some reason, a sinking feeling. She unlatched the pottery door and went inside.

'Hello,' Margaret Stone offered. And when there was no reply, followed with, 'What's the matter?'

'There's . . . something on your cheek – a bit of clay, probably.' Her voice had faltered. For a second she had mistaken the protuberance for a growth.

'Where? Pick it off, there's a dear.'

'You look tired, Aunt Margaret. You're not ill or anything?' People, she had come to understand, were liable to get ill, to fade, to die. *But please not Aunt Margaret* went up her appalled prayer, as a vision reared of Maman and Uncle Peter as parents.

The prayer might have been uttered aloud, so knowing was Aunt Margaret's snorting laugh. 'Oh-ho – I know what you're thinking. Don't worry, amazing though it may seem, people can go on for years and years looking pretty much as I do – mildly cadaverous.'

98

'I, er, just came to ask . . . I suppose someone's told Laurie . . . ?'

'Of course. He'll be home tomorrow on the five-fifteen train.'

'Oh, right,' she said carelessly, as though this were not the single most important piece of information concerning the funeral arrangements.

'If your mother can spare you, why not come with me to meet him?'

'Oh, she can. I mean, she won't want me *then*,' Claire said quickly.

'There you are then. It's a deal.'

Claire lifted a lid and closely inspected the contents of a clay bin.

'Go on, you don't need me; *you* go and meet him,' urged Margaret Stone.

They were sitting in the car, one of a short line of vehicles by the side of the road, waiting for the arrival of the five-fifteen train. It was pitch black outside, save for a half-hearted light over the junction entrance and pale amber showing in the gaping doorway; it was black also inside the car, where Claire peered often and uncertainly at the luminous dial of her wrist-watch. They'd arrived early; Aunt Margaret said there was no point getting out till the signal went down, it was such a beastly cold evening.

As if coldness mattered! Anything might happen to delay them when the signal fell – a lorry or tractor taking minutes to crawl by, the car door suddenly jamming . . . When her aunt bade her go – and furthermore go alone – she was like a released spring. (Seconds later, Margaret Stone watched the small figure shoot through the lighted entrance, and smiled to herself.)

Not many waiting on the platform, though quite a crowd was gathered round the cokey fire in the waiting-room. She glanced through the window and passed by; walked to the end of the platform, turned and retraced her steps. Where best to position herself? Calamitous to be caught in a crowd pushing on to, jumping from, the five-fifteen. On the other hand, if she took up a pitch in a deserted place, Laurie's long legs might carry him off to squander his first greeting on his waiting mother. No, she would stand by the exit and trust her eyes to rapidly scan the train and spot him from among alighting passengers. Then she would run to claim him. At the thought, a whole flock of flapping birds seemed to rise inside her. Exhausted by anticipation, she opened her mouth and hugely yawned.

At last the train arrived. And there he was, sailing by at a corridor window. As if she could have missed him! – so tall, gaunt and dramatic looking. Since he had no choice but to come her way, she went forward sedately.

'Claire!' Surprise at seeing her (he had expected his mother, dreaded his father), made him forget to be sympathetic; his response was frank and immediate. 'Darling!' Dropping his case, he gathered her up; her feet swung outwards like carousel horses. She laughed delightedly.

Recollecting, he put her down. 'Oh love, I'm sorry – I mean about Uncle Andrew.' He squeezed her hand then tucked it under his arm and retrieved his case. Thus linked, they walked into and through the darkness in completely satisfactory silence.

In the car, Claire retook her seat beside Margaret Stone. Laurie got into the back and leaned forward, resting his knees on the central hump and one arm on each of their shoulders. 'Now, girls,' he bossed, 'tell me about the arrangements.' His 'girls' immediately conferred a party-going air, and it was suddenly difficult to describe 'the arrangements' with proper solemnity. 'I've brought my grey worsted. I trust that will serve.'

'This is not an excuse to extend your wardrobe,' his mother warned over Claire's giggles.

'Certainly not,' he confirmed, the gravity of his tone belied by his fingers palpating their forearms.

'You really are a shocker. And you grow too fast. Next year you'll be needing all new for college.'

'But all new what, Ma? There's the question.'

'Is it indeed? I hope you're not planning to become a Teddy Boy. It would annoy your father dreadfully.'

'I wasn't, but that's certainly a recommendation. How are you, pet?' he asked in a different tone, and nuzzled Claire's neck. 'I know it's for a terribly sad reason, but it is lovely to see you.'

The dear children! secretly smiled Margaret Stone, and was taken by a feeling of driving not merely to Foscote, but securely towards the future.

Beads of glass stood under Claire's eyelids; her throat was stuffed by a steadily inflating tube. Turning stiffly from the open grave and the mounds of earth, she lurched over the grass to the path.

Laurie caught her arm. During the shuffle to the lychgate with the rest of the party, he covertly studied her. In the road, he tightened his grip and quickened his step and frogmarched her past the waiting cars. 'Claire and I will walk,' he called over his shoulder. Protests floated down the lane – 'Getting dark . . .', 'Spoil your shoes . . .'

'Sorry, can't hear,' he yelled back; and under his breath, growled to her, 'Keep going, keep going.' Soon, he pushed her over a stile, then along a muddy footpath, slithering, sliding.

'Wait,' she cried at last. 'Just look at our shoes!' Mud had gathered, inches of it.

'Right, we'll go back by the road. Give 'em five minutes to be gone, eh?' She nodded. He wrapped his arms round her. She leaned into him, and at last began to weep.

Many more than five minutes passed, and still they stood on the muddy track in the dank field with the mist rising, she shedding her pent-up tears, he holding

101

her. When they retraced their steps, Claire's legs felt trembly; she staggered and stumbled, and wondered how she would ever make it home. Lolled against the stile, she raised and dropped each foot in turn while he scraped her shoes with a stone. When he had roughly cleaned his own shoes, he decided to take her into the church porch to give her time to recover. Huddled on a bench, their backs pressed into the wall, she sank her head against him, closed her eyes; listened to distant sounds – the chink and thud of spades lifting earth . . .

The grave diggers had finished their work. Spades went flying into the rear of a pick-up truck, doors slammed, an engine fired. To Claire, starting awake, it seemed like the nightmarish dead of night. She broke into a fit of shivering.

Laurie pulled her to her feet; she swung her arms, stamped her feet.

'Better?'

'Much.'

Soon they were walking briskly, hand in hand, along the lane to Foscote. For the first mile, neither spoke. Then, with the house only half a mile away, Claire felt impelled to explain herself. 'I want you to know – I wasn't crying for myself. It was for Daddy. And not because he's dead, but because his life was sad. Maman said he was terribly eager to come here, to join with Uncle Peter in starting the festival. Thing is, somehow for Daddy it all went wrong. I know he was ill, but it was more than that . . .'

Laurie squeezed her hand. 'All the more reason to make sure life doesn't go wrong for us. Else what's the point in being born?'

She felt as if a leaden cloak had dropped from her. Her whole life was before her, she marvelled. There were so many things to discover and do. She began to tell him about Miss Thwaite and her latest study project.

He listened with attention. 'Claire,' he said, when

the subject of stick insects seemed exhausted, 'you remember accusing me of holding back . . . ?'

'It was stupid of me,' she said hurriedly.

'No it wasn't. And in any case, there's something I want to tell you. A decision I've made. I shan't tell them at Foscote till it's all fixed up, so you'll keep mum?'

'Of course.'

'I'm going into the army.'

'You mean, not the RAF?' she asked after a pause, the army her only cause for surprise. (All young men were required to do two years' National Service, three if they took a commission. Uncle Peter – with meal-time support from her father in the days when he was still well enough to come to table – had frequently outlined Laurie's best course: graduate first to become eligible for a commission and sign on for three years. In the RAF was taken for granted: his father's record would stand him in excellent stead. Of course, if Laurie had had enough gumption to join the cadet corps at school, the ex-flying officers had pointed out, he would have avoided the need to graduate first in order to become an officer.) 'Phew,' she said, 'Uncle Peter will go mad.'

'Won't he just? But no, what I mean is, I shall join up straight after A levels, as soon as I leave school.'

'And not go to university?'

'Go there afterwards.'

'Oh. I suppose because you only want to serve two years.'

'That's not the reason. I want a clean break. I'm sick of people's assumptions, of having my life mapped out. I couldn't care less what I do, so long as it's novel – in Foscote terms, I mean, and my own choice.'

They had reached the drive, and now began to drag their feet. There still seemed lots to discuss. Claire stopped to shove stones around with the toe of her shoe. She was calculating that in this case, she and Laurie would be starting university at the same time.

Also, it occurred to her, the army, unlike Cambridge, would not be full of witty, attractive, predatory females. 'Mm. I think it could be a good idea.'

'You do? I'm relieved.' This was an understatement. Back at school after the summer holiday, he had viewed the scene at home in sharper perspective, had got it clear in his mind which aspects he was desperate to escape from, and which not. For instance, he exempted his mother and the woods and the surrounding countryside. Above all, he exempted Claire. (He had been mad to have ever included her; but maybe, during the aftermath of catching his father at it with Aunt Sabine, he *had* been a touch crazed – looking back, it certainly felt like it.) He could do nothing about his mother or the countryside, which were fixtures; but he was determined to get Claire out of the place just as soon as possible. Nothing could be done for the present, she was only sixteen; a temporary parting was inevitable. However, her positive attitude to his own proposal was very heartening.

'I don't suppose Aunt Margaret will care one way or the other, so long as you're happy,' she went on. 'But, gosh you're going to have the dickens of a time telling your father. He'll have apoplexy.'

'I know,' he said, seizing her hand and merrily swinging their arms as he led her towards the house. 'But there it is. Into every life a little rain must fall.'

'Afraid I'm out of practice,' Laurie demurred; 'scarcely so much as touch an instrument.' Nevertheless he touched this one – the baby grand in the upstairs practice room where once, under his father's direction, he had laboured to accompany Aunt Sabine. However, on this occasion his hand brushing the keys produced no sound.

It was the evening following the quiet funeral – just a small party assembled – the family (which in Foscote parlance meant Stones plus Haddinghams), and a few close friends and associates – Julian Storey, Guy Lethersage, Marie Bowley, and the Emmersons. After the cold repast, they had been glad to repair to this, the most homely of all the music rooms, to discuss a more elaborate and public homage to the departed musician. An informal concert, a musical evening, a recital? – contemplative or celebratory? Peter Stone poured from decanters, and directed the discussion towards its goal (the memorial concert he had already devised in his head and outlined in private to the widow.) 'Of course, Sabine must have the final say,' he put in softly; and in response to further suggestions, 'Possibly, possibly . . . But whatever is proposed, I think we would all bow to Sabine.'

Not wishing to be patronized, Laurie and Claire had both sensibly declined his offer of drinks. But Jeanette elected to sample the brandy. Peter Stone wetted the bottom of a glass and with huge ceremony handed it to her. 'You do swivel a goblet *beautifully*,' Laurie said in mock admiration, as Jeanette followed more practised examples. 'Now, Laurie,' warned his mother. On the thin Indian rug, Claire sat with her legs tucked under her and chewed the two wisps of hair which normally lay flat against her cheeks in front of her bare ears. Laurie, grown bored (and therefore dangerous, his mother feared) took possession of the piano stool. It was his father's remark – to the effect that Andrew's memorial had better be postponed until the Christmas vacation since Laurie would hardly be allowed further time off school – which had led him to beg to be left out of their arrangements and to call in evidence his lack of practice.

All eyes were now upon him, as he very well knew. Knew too, and pleasurably, how his disclaimer in front of friends had bred paternal annoyance. 'Though now and then,' he added thoughtfully, 'I do play a little jazz piano.'

'Reah-lly?' drawled Marie Bowley.

As though to gratify her curiosity, he at once swung

to face the keyboard, scraped the stool back, hunched his back, flexed his fingers. Let rip with a rag.

The veins rose on Peter Stone's forehead. He slammed down his glass, strode to the piano. 'Stop! Do you hear, sir? Stop that FILTHY ROW AT ONCE.' He abruptly lowered the lid – Laurie retrieving his hands in the nick of time.

Claire scrambled to her feet. 'Why don't *you* stop?' she snarled. 'Pompous, overbearing pig . . .'

'Claire!' cried Margaret Stone. Sabine Haddingham shrieked and slopped her drink.

'Do not reprove her,' decreed Peter Stone, instantly metamorphosed from Wrath to Forbearance. 'We understand, it is only a few hours since her father . . .' his voice wobbled – 'our . . . dear . . . friend . . . Andrew . . .' – and altogether forsook him. He pressed Sabine's shoulder. 'I can only apologize, my dear, for my son's poor judgement of what is appropriate.'

'You think you're the only one who knows what's appropriate,' Claire shouted. 'Well, I don't think you know what's right for MY FATHER. In fact you're the last person who should be organizing a memorial, the very last person . . .'

Laurie, with eyes on his mother's face (which mercifully was all uncomprehending amazement) jumped to Claire's side. 'Come on, love,' he said gently, while grasping her forcefully, and led her away. He shoved her out of harm's way into the corridor, then turned back to the room. 'I believe a little blood-letting is traditional on these occasions,' he murmured before softly closing the door.

'Whad'yer do that for?' she demanded, jerking free of him.

'Let's go somewhere cosy . . .'

'It was time someone told him.'

'The wrong time,' he said evenly, and propelled her through corridors, round corners, down steps to the boxroom.

'I detest your father, he gives me the creeps.'

'I myself am not over fond.' He opened the door, ushered her inside. Had she discovered something – perhaps overheard her mother and his father planning an assignation – or stumbled on some revolting scene? he wondered, inwardly shuddering as he recalled what *he* had witnessed. Squinting at a record sleeve, he was turning over in his mind whether to question her: he would like to secure her promise not to unsettle his mother. But finally he couldn't bear to, and throwing down the sleeve, placed the disc on the turntable. 'A nice filthy row,' he joked, misquoting his father.

When he turned, she was lying full length on the sofa. Her arms reached towards him. 'Laurie,' she said, and he read in her eyes – dark pools of frightening depths – her desperate invitation.

For some years he had relied on a certain manner to extricate him from tricky situations. After the merest pause, he was all brisk bossiness – 'Budge up, dear, do' – bustling to the place where her head was positioned, making to sit down: 'Let me rest my aching back.' As his rear descended, she was obliged to sit up. 'Simply shattered. What a day!' he sighed, settling beside her. 'Bet you've had it, too.' He wrapped a sympathetic arm round her.

After a while, she leaned forward and detached from him; drew up her feet, clasped her shins, sank her chin on her knees. I'm utterly alone, she thought.

'There's Johnny,' he remarked brightly at the bouncing and insinuating entry of the alto saxophone (Johnny Hodges was her favourite musician). Playfully he ruffled the top of her head.

'Yeah,' she agreed absently.

He brought his hands together, clamped them between his thighs.

There are other things, she was endeavouring to convince herself. (Meaning other than Laurie, who, she now sensed, planned to leave Foscote and all its works – and all its inhabitants including herself – at the earliest opportunity: joining the army was simply his chosen method.) There were her studies, for instance. She entered, in her imagination, the bright laboratory. Her nostrils met its gassy acidic aroma, her fingers slid the slender length of a cool pipette. The deeper she lapsed into her reverie, the better she was comforted. Next year, she would be a sixth-former and able to spend hours exploring proper science . . .

The record had come to an end. Laurie rose and removed it, placed it in its sleeve and turned off the player. All the time his eyes indirectly observed her. Was she smarting? Did she know he had only pretended to misread her message? What was she thinking, sitting there like a worried elf – frowning, hugging her shins with her chin resting in the V of her knees, her hair stuck on end where he'd ruffled it: what so completely absorbed her? Little darling Claire, he thought, and a pang hit him. He yearned to protect her. But from what? From the situation at Foscote, obviously. But maybe from something else as well . . .

The idea began as a tease, a notion to toss and turn in his mind, to shiver over and sensibly dismiss. Only, it was not so easily obliterated. In fact, once considered, it proved impossibly stubborn. He turned sharply, braced himself on splayed fingers on the table, stared down. Stupid, but he couldn't get it out of his mind: that the threat to Claire, which he so much dreaded, was he himself.

X

Of course, Laurie's letters were largely composed of lies, Claire mused, conscious of his latest communication – as yet unopened – stored within her straining satchel, together with exercise and text books, geometry set, pens, pencils, penknife, an apple, a chocolate wafer bar, and a pottery vase (one of Margaret Stone's misshaped rejects and therefore possessing uncommon appeal) wrapped against breakage in a dingy aertex sports shirt. The satchel sat heavily in her lap, companionably bumping as her thighs bumped and the seat bumped and the ancient bus bumped, swayed and racketed through country lanes linking the several pick-up points. She rested one mittened hand on the satchel and with the other described a steam-free arc on the bus window. There was no sky to behold, just fields, trees, hedgerows, gates, a gaunt Dutch barn, an isolated straggle of stone habitation, and pitiless limitless grey.

When it arrived this morning she had noted how satisfyingly full the envelope felt. As always, the contents would require many readings, the first at mid-morning break – a swift skimming of the pages to isolate and underline the particularly important phrases and sentences. The remainder of the letter – that is, the bulk – could usually be divided into two parts: the purely fictional (reports of *his* doings and sayings); and the factual (commentary on matters *she*'d reported). During the more leisurely lunch break, she would take in this factual matter – the only part ever requiring her response – wherein Laurie keenly plotted and obsessively kept tabs on her scientific education. Where, he would require to know, had she got to in the study of X, Y or Z? Had Miss Thwaite mentioned the relevance of this to So and So? His letters were full of tips and opinions; they strained to contain his anxiety as to Miss Thwaite's worthiness as an accurate mentor. Indeed, over a study of the ecological preferences of allied species of violets he had questioned her method and conclusion. Tactfully, Claire had aired the matter with her teacher, and a stimulating little debate followed – Claire in the middle, both mouthpiece and conduit. Miss Thwaite had not minded in the least; she was not afraid of intellectual challenge; it was in other areas of life that she betrayed an embarrassing immaturity.

The remainder of the letter, the fiction, she would save for bedtime. Fiction, but fun: accounts of intimate conversations with a Colonel Honeypot, of bedtime japes and jolly mealtimes with a Corporal Catchpole, of a squad outing to a neighbouring town complete with tea and scones in the Spider's Web Café ('You be mother, Sergeant Major.'), of a visit to an art gallery, the finer points of a Francis Bacon discussed with colleagues, Ken and Terry. Beneath the ridiculousness she sensed purpose (a scarce opportunity to be his extravagant self) and reason (army life was too horribly mundane to waste time recording it). Now and then, his remarks confirmed her assumption: 'Alas, I have run out of paper; I must return to earth with a bump.' 'Looking over this letter, I find I may have exaggerated. However, I would simply collapse in despair if the tedium were made any more real by setting it down.' 'If you can't altogether swallow this, just imagine me in limbo. And don't worry – limbo can be an incredibly restful state; as well as boring, squalid, and administered by boneheads.'

She no longer, with resentment, set his insatiable desire for news of *her* life against his inability to confide the truth of *his*. Plainly though, he had not forgotten she once had complained: 'Don't be cross if I fuss about your progress like an old nanny. You can't conceive what it means to be able to take an interest, nor the pleasure your letters bring.' She pictured him (with acute perception, as it happens) huddled on the side of a bed with a blanket round his shoulders, his breath coming in puffs in the chilly air of a spartan hut, writing his flamboyant nonsense; for a while blessedly transported . . . Her own bedtime comfort was secured by selecting and concentrating on one of the sayings she had underscored; like a *religieuse* with a sacred text, she would fix attention on such mundane stuff as, 'With all my love, sweet darling Claire,' until bliss was achieved.

They had arrived in a village; the bus slowed towards its final stopping place before school. In the seat beside her, Jeanette threw off her daydream and leant over to give the window a further wipe. By the war memorial waited half a dozen small mortals – first or second years of both sexes – and one tall, nonchalantly handsome god: Barry Carswell, upper sixthformer, deputy Head Boy and Captain of Cricket at the Boys' Grammar. Claire stared at the foot of the war memorial where a wreath of poppies had lain since Armistice Day, its red and green virtually indistinguishable in uniform dullness, and observed out of the corner of her eye (and what she could not observe, easily imagined, for it was a weekday ritual) how the small mortals, at a curt nod from the god, clambered ahead on to the bus, how they fell swiftly into vacant seats to facilitate godly progress up the aisle to the double seat which was by common consent kept free in readiness; how the god chucked his satchel on to the window portion of this seat then lowered himself on the remainder, splaying his long legs so that the right foot disappeared beneath the seat in front and the left thrust up the gangway.

'Hi there, Barry,' drawled Jeanette.

'G'morning,' came the stiff reply.

At which Jeanette fell into animated conversation with any girls nearby willing to play her game. Most were happy to: Jeanette had not lost her American accent, indeed, had taken pains to make it more pronounced; thus the very sound of her voice signalled attractiveness, sophistication, sexiness, the world of films, entertainment, pop. (No-one in show business during the fifties spoke or sang in anything less American than a mid-Atlantic accent.) Claire turned benignly towards the chattering girls and drifted her eyes over Barry Carswell; confirmed that her supposition as to his seated attitude was correct (she was not sufficiently interested in him even to affect stony indifference), and turned back to the window.

They were moving ponderously through the village, past the church and the graveyard where tombstones lurched like ill-arranged teeth; past the thatched Three Pigeons where three straw birds were

111

sculpted untypically astride the roof's apex; past the village green with the still skeletal chestnut trees; past white blossomed almond trees in the Manor House garden, looking, in the freezing greyness, silly as women dressed for Bond Street caught shopping in Woolworths. At the end of the village street they turned onto the main road, gathered speed, headed for the town and the two grammar schools.

Perhaps, Claire thought with inspired perception, Jeanette was too sexy for any chance with Barry Carswell. It was possible that her come-hither figure (she had lost weight, but her reduced inches merely emphasized the forward-thrusting bosom and curvaceous behind), her pendulous lips and sleepy eyes, her long, turned-under hair, served only to intimidate; for by and large boys were nervous creatures, their noise and swagger mere attempts to prove the opposite. It was *girls* who were excited by Jeanette's charms, imagining how she must thrill grown men. However, according to educated sixth-form opinion, Jeanette had better make haste and cash in. The sex goddess was on the wane; a different type of woman was in the ascendant – lanky, angular, gamine. This, they deduced from diligent research in women's magazines and gossip sheets, taking particular note of the success of Audrey Hepburn. Eyes moved thoughtfully to Claire, who, though small in stature, possessed the right proportions and the perfect hairstyle to be a hit (if only she would follow advice in the magazines regarding make-up to widen the eyes and mouth). Claire laughed or scowled at this, according to mood. In her heart she could not care less. Her one ambition so far as looks went, was to approximate as far as possible to Laurie's notion of desirability.

Sometimes, her confidence that she ever could utterly fled. She looked back over a year ago to the night following her father's funeral when she had cast away pride and almost beseeched him to take her. A gift he had spurned, she recalled, wincing, screwing up her eyes in self-disgust. It served her right; what a daft moment to choose – he worn out after hanging about for hours in churchyard, field and church porch, she unattractive after her outburst against Uncle Peter. A better time, and she might have obtained the right result. Unfortunately, she had had no chance to test this theory. Laurie had spent the rest of the year studying like mad for A levels and afterwards had gone instantly into the army. Since when, neither she nor anyone else at Foscote had set eyes on him.

'What does he *do* when he's off duty – on leave or whatever? He must go somewhere. Do you know what he gets up to?' Aunt Margaret had asked the other day at breakfast, evidently finding his slim letter to her unsatisfactory.

The direct question had taken Claire aback. Chin propped on hand, she slid her elbow further into the centre of the table and with her free hand drew lines in the breakfast crumbs. 'I dunno,' she'd shrugged.

'Well, he writes to you.'

'He writes to you, too.'

Margaret Stone whipped off her reading specs. 'I tell you what – why don't we surprise him? I'll phone his commanding officer to discover when he's next on leave. You and I could drive up and pay him a visit.'

Claire's head toppled from her hand, she lurched upright. 'But that'd be an awful thing to do. He wouldn't like it. Why'd you want to?' she demanded.

'Hmm. Why, indeed? What time have I to go gallivanting? I suppose I'd better get on, before this place grinds to a halt.'

It had been a near squeak. She had better write and warn Laurie to mend fences or face the consequences.

Inadequate though his letters might seem to his mother, to Claire they came as life-savers, boosts to her flagging confidence, correctives to troubling memories. With his letter to hand, her doubts as to his feelings for her were easily repelled. It was sentiments such as 'All my love', and 'sweet darling Claire' that

113

she held to, that she resolved to believe in. For they were *written*, damn it, in black on white, as the Bible was written, as was Tansley's monumental tome on British vegetation.

Now, on the bus, nearing school, lending half an ear to the animated chatter of Jeanette and her friends, she pressed her hand on her satchel, and thought, with a little leap of her heart, of what lay within.

After school, she presented the vase to Miss Thwaite. 'A pot by my aunt,' she said grandly, thereby making the gift considerable. 'With thanks for all the lifts home you've given me. I hope you like it,' she added, with a faint note of reproof; for although Miss Thwaite deserved her gratitude, she also had earned her censure. Claire hoped to convey this.

Miss Thwaite was too thrown to notice. *A pot by my aunt*. Heavens, it was ART! – created by one of those culture vultures from Foscote. Art in all its manifestations habitually sent her into a panic, and she fell back now on her traditional response when confronted by it. 'What is it meant to be?'

'A vase,' said Claire, puzzled. 'To put flowers in and so forth. Personally, I think the way it *leans* suggests a Japanesey sort of arrangement. You know – with twigs. There'll be pussy willow out soon. Some pieces of that jutting at the right angles would look tremendous – don't you think?'

'I wouldn't have thought of it in a million years,' Miss Thwaite confessed. 'Amazing how *artistic* you are, considering you're so able at science. Your up-bringing, I suppose; you must have drunk it in. Somehow, one doesn't expect the two to mix – Art and Science. At Girton there were several arty types but we never had much to do with them. One tended to keep to one's own.' She gave a nervous giggle, then composed herself. 'But I shall follow your instructions meticulously, and I'm sure it will look very nice on my sideboard.'

114

Miss Thwaite often referred to her university days at Girton. Once, it had been Claire's fervent ambition to follow her there, but lately she'd found the reference off-putting. Miss Thwaite was so awfully gauche. Sometimes her behaviour made Claire feel old as the hills and infinitely wiser. Take, for instance, her hysteria over Daisy Monk.

Daisy had fallen violently in love with Phillip McNab, a second year sixth-former at the Boys' Grammar – and he with her – and because of this had suffered acute anguish (fifteen days' and six hours' worth, to be exact). Daisy was one of a large group of her friends. Within this group, Claire had always been rather excluded from a certain consuming interest: how to entice and ensnare boys. By tacit agreement, they did not include her in their speculative plans, nor in their self-improvement campaigns (enthusiasms for peculiar diets and mortifying certain body parts, specially waist, hips and thighs, and experiments with hair colour and clothes): an exemption granted on the grounds that she had already succeeded where they still strove, she had landed her man. Claire was aware that they knew about Laurie. Some had actually met him during visits to Foscote. But it was Jeanette whom she must thank (Claire strongly suspected) for implying a serious and possibly consummated love affair between them. Was this the reason Daisy singled her out as a confidante? The first Claire knew of something afoot was when Daisy was suddenly awarded the same tactful exclusion as herself. Other girls (the town dwellers) had spotted the lovers helplessly entwined in a bus shelter or staring into one another's eyes – oblivious of shyly called greetings – at the gate to Daisy's house; one girl had actually witnessed the fateful 'excuse me' foxtrot at the Regal Ballroom – the vehicle for their coming together. They could tell at once the matter was 'serious' and not just a delicious thing to giggle over. So when, at Monday break, Daisy Monk sat in a corner of the sixth-form room hugging a radiator with Claire Haddingham, the pair were left knowingly to their confidences.

'Oh, *God*,' groaned Daisy. 'Thank goodness I've got someone to tell. Someone who knows what it's like. Isn't it . . . ? *Is*n't it . . . ?'

Claire was noncommittal. 'Mm,' she said.

'I mean, don't you just . . . want to, you know, *burst* or something?'

Claire could empathize with the feelings, all right; it was where these feelings were cataclysmically leading (if she understood Daisy's clutching and groaning correctly) which left her rather at sea. (Churlish, of course to say so – it might seem unfriendly.)

The cataclysm duly occurred. Arriving at school one morning, Claire was flung upon by Daisy who implored her to skip Prayers and dragged her off into the deserted library. For some minutes Daisy failed to enlighten but sobbed incoherently and very soggily on Claire's shoulder. 'I want to die,' she choked at last. 'If nothing happens then I *will* die. I'll kill myself.'

'When, er, *should* something happen?' Claire asked cautiously, comprehension arriving only piecemeal.

'In about a week.'

'Not long to wait.'

'Not *long*?' Daisy gasped. 'I can't bear it, I can't believe I let him. I can't believe I did this to myself – just went ahead and probably ruined my life.'

'Er, when . . . ?'

'Last night. We nearly did it once before. This time he got to such a pitch, kept saying, "Oh Daisy, please" – like he was going to go crazy . . .'

'Just once?'

'But once is enough! They're always saying that in the bloody magazines. How could I be such a fool? God, I hate him. I hate him and I hate myself. I'm so . . . *scared*.'

'I bet the chances are you're OK.'

Daisy raised her head. 'You reckon?'

And Claire, who really had no idea but saw that a whole week must be endured one way or another, declared in the affirmative with all the authority she could muster.

And a terrible week it proved. But the following week, with Daisy still not let off the hook, was torture. Claire and Daisy, who both took Art at A level (they also both took French; plus Claire took Biology and Chemistry, and Daisy German), sat at adjoining easels, whispering contingency plans. Claire thrust Daisy into German lessons, and sat with her in French. She did not stay late in the lab, but went straight home on the school bus in order to spend an evening on the telephone. At the weekend she stayed at Daisy's house – two embarrassing days devoted to allaying Daisy's mother's suspicions, three sleepless nights bearing with suicide threats and ignorant speculation on the subject of abortion. She pleaded for patience: it was well known that emotional upset could play havoc with hormones; if Daisy would only calm down, all might yet be well.

And so it proved. One morning, descending from the school bus, Claire was met by an ecstatic Daisy. 'It's happened! It's the gut rot to end all gut rots, but who cares!' Poor Daisy: the pudgy, pasty-faced time-of-the-month look complete with spots, knocking back Anadins to deaden her pain, yet dizzy with relief and happiness.

'Shall you make it up with Phil?' Claire asked timidly at break.

'I might. Oh, probably. Yeah. *Yeah!*'

'Then I should tell him to get some, you know, precautionary thingies.'

'Don't worry,' said Daisy. 'I sure as hell will.'

A few days later Claire was in the laboratory cleaning equipment ready to be stacked in the apparatus cupboard, when a flash like a great bird winging past made her look up through the window. No bird, but Daisy flying down the path, her scarf trailing her like a slipstream. And waiting at the gate with his arms open, a tall fair curly-headed youth – Phillip McNab, thought Claire, recognizing him from a snapshot. He swung Daisy up and round. They earthed against the gatepost with their arms round one another and started a lengthier kiss than seemed sustainable. On and on it went. Unconsciously, Claire breathed *for* them, extra long, extra deep; while her hands slowly deserted the bowls in the sink and rose to her mouth . . .

A whinnying noise at her side made her start dreadfully. It was Miss Thwaite, drawn curiously to discover what had captured her attention. The whinnying worked into an explosion. 'Out . . . ra . . . geous! In her school uniform! Who is that girl?'

'Daisy,' blurted Claire, caught off guard.

'Yes, I see; it's Daisy Monk. Just look at her!' shrieked Miss Thwaite superfluously. Her pale face had sprung an ugly red flush which was spreading down her neck, and very likely, thought Claire, staring at the place where prominent breastbone met Viyella shirt collar, suffusing her entire body. (It was a repugnant image – naked, florid Miss Thwaite.) 'In front of those passers-by! And, oh my giddy aunt, aren't those first-formers? What an example! I must go and report this to the Head . . .'

Claire's wits were still not gathered by the time Miss Thwaite reached the doorway, where, fortunately, her passage was impeded. 'Whatever's up, Thwaite?' It was the carrying voice of the senior science mistress, dour grey-haired bespectacled Miss Casey – who would have addressed her colleague as *Miss* Thwaite if she had suspected a pupil's presence, Claire understood, hastening behind the door of the apparatus cupboard to save embarrassment all round. Miss Thwaite the while was describing what agitated her.

'Where?' asked Miss Casey, striding to the window.

'There, by the gatepost. Oh, they've gone.' (Miss Thwaite sounded vexed.) 'But it was disgusting.

Canoodling in full view of the road *in her school uniform*.'

'Your terminology is out of date. It's 'necking', Thwaite, *necking*,' cried Miss Casey with relish. 'That gatepost's a favourite place. I've lost count of how many couples I've seen making full and grateful use of it over the years.'

'I think the Head should be informed.'

'Rubbish. Grow up. Get a sense of proportion. Now, where did I leave my . . . Ah, *there* it is.'

It was some time before Claire thought it wise to emerge. Thankfully, Miss Thwaite had evidently reconsidered steaming off to the Head's office. A hush had followed Miss Casey's departure, then heavy sighs, then paper rustling disconsolately, and finally the sound of vigorous chalking on a blackboard. At which Claire crept back to the sink.

For some months Miss Thwaite's unravelling imperfections had been undermining Claire's wish to emulate her. This latest episode, which demonstrated that were it not for Miss Casey she would have made trouble for Daisy (who had only recently emerged from a worse trouble – and one beyond Miss Thwaite's experience, Claire guessed), simply finalized the process.

It was this episode Claire had in mind when she endeavoured to convey some reproof in her tone while making her gift of Aunt Margaret's vase. Of which gift Miss Thwaite was still making heavy weather on the journey home. 'I shall certainly be on the look out for pussy willow,' she promised.

'Oh, it doesn't have to be pussy willow. Forsythia would do – there's plenty of that about. A few sticks of forsythia of varying lengths.'

'Forsythia,' Miss Thwaite repeated earnestly.

'Anything you like, really,' said Claire, wishing she had given chocolates instead.

'By the way,' Miss Thwaite said, some minutes later, 'I'm going to Cambridge to stay with my friend for Easter. No doubt we'll pay a few calls. Professor Ellis

119

is usually around. Would you like me to mention your name?'

Claire hesitated. Not only was she disenchanted by this product of Girton, but Daphne Oxenbury on a recent visit to her old school had given a glowing report of Science at Sutton. Furthermore, Sutton University had evidently performed a miracle on Daphne, transforming her from a dull and dowdy swot into a confident and dynamic beauty. It had made Claire think she should consider all her options. 'No, thank you,' she said now. 'I haven't quite made my mind up yet where to apply.'

An astounded silence fell – taken full advantage of by the car's engine, which, incorrectly stuck in third gear, developed a hysterical whine. Miss Thwaite was still considering her response to this cavalier attitude to her *alma mater* when they arrived at Foscote.

xi

Someone was calling her name. Looking round, she saw a girl chasing through the open-sided verandah, fists clenched at her waist, the cold November air clouding her breath which came in spurts. Her pursuer drew close: 'There's a . . . soldier at the gate,' she panted importantly. 'He was asking people if they knew you. He said he thought. . . you'd be in the lab.'

Claire, who was just on her way to the lab, knew instantly who had asked for her. 'Thanks,' she told the girl – an anonymous fourth-former to whom she, as a sixth-former, was naturally well known.

'That's all right, Claire. Shall I go and tell him you're coming?'

'No, no. It'll be my, er, cousin. He'll wait.'

She sped off to the cloakroom for her coat and satchel.

It was Laurie, of course; though a Laurie she had never seen before or visualized – shorn, plucked-looking, with formerly hidden areas of neck and face cruelly exposed. His altered appearance was painful to her. With his exuberant black curls he had seemed heroic, and now was humbled, serf-like, a prisoner. She pressed her eyes into the harsh stuff of his greatcoat until all to be seen were zooming stars. When he relaxed his hold, she watched his face swim into focus: he was smiling down steadily enough, but – there was no denying it – sadly. This time when he caught her close, she stared over his shoulder at the traffic, at the bus drawing up, at people clambering on and off, at grammar schoolboys whizzing by on bikes. 'I'm sorry to turn up like this,' he said against her ear. 'I hope it's not a nuisance. I was just rather desperate to see you.'

Something was the matter; something infinitely more serious than close-cropped hair – which in any case he had had for sixteen months and must now be used to. She pulled away.

'Don't look so worried. It's nothing bad exactly, I'm not in disgrace, the military cops aren't after me – yet. No, really. It's very mundane. It just hurts like hell. It was a matter of coming to you or . . . Well, tell you the truth, I don't know when I've been in such a state before. Total panic.'

'Oh, Laurie,' she said, speaking for the first time. 'I'm so glad you came.'

He laughed and swung her round. 'I was on tenter-hooks watching them piling on to the school bus. I saw Jeanette, poor dear, hauling aboard – made sure she didn't see me: I don't want Foscote folks knowing about this – OK?'

'I won't say anything, of course I won't.'

'When you failed to show up, I guessed you were staying late in the lab.'

She was now facing the school, and at his words looked across to the laboratory window, from where, possibly, a reddening Miss Thwaite was even now observing her.

121

He felt her stiffen. 'Where can we go?'

'If we crossed over and turned the corner we'd come to Meadow Bank Gardens.'

'Then let's.' He seized her satchel, took her hand. Waiting at the kerb, practical matters rose in her mind (how would she get home since she had no money, and where would Laurie go?) for she was a very practical person, but she held these in abeyance, deciding the most important thing was simply to attend to his troubles. They ran across, then settled into an easy stride with their arms round one another, her hip jostling his thigh.

Meadow Bank Gardens, a wide strip of park running for half a mile along the river bank, separated the Victorian from the modern. A post-war development containing semi-detached houses and the two grammar schools was left behind as they passed through the high wide gateway into pleasure grounds laid out by Victorians at what had once been the edge of town. In the gathering dusk flower-beds mounded, empty for winter or covered in mouldering plants. At widely spaced intervals along the main thoroughfare lamps were already lit and casting a yellowish beam. The trees were bare, their leaves tidily swept away, save for those dropped lately which lay sparsely over the grass or lined the edges of asphalt paths. Here and there high clumps of dense shrubbery provided shelter. By one of these, on a bench seat, they arranged themselves – dumped the satchel, snuggled close.

'Now tell me,' she said.

He held her for a moment, his chin resting on the top of her head, his eyes closed; then released her and sank back. 'Thing is, I've got into a dreadful tizz over someone.'

She stared across the thickly shadowed park. Behind her, sensed the curving line of shrubs like arching arms. There was a dead inevitability about his mention of 'someone' (she had dreaded it for so long), and an inevitability about hearing it *here*, as if this place had always been waiting and now calmly became the grave of her hopes. She foresaw that walking out of here she would be a hollow creature, void.

Laurie was in difficulty – needing to reveal his wounds, dreading to affront or frighten her. 'I suppose,' he began hesitantly, 'it was loneliness that made us so leap at one another – I mean, coming unexpectedly, after months of not being able to relate to anyone other than superficially. What sparked it off? If I remember correctly it was just a grin – quickly smothered, of course; he caught me, and I caught him, grinning at something neither of us expected another soul to appreciate. It was like recognizing a kindred spirit. I must say, though, I was surprised to find *he*'d felt out of things. After all, you'd expect the odd flash of wit and flair in an officer's mess, the chance of intelligent conversation . . .'

Her hopes were reviving. She fell into a panic to be sure that she hadn't misheard or misunderstood. 'This someone you got into a state over,' she interrupted.

'Yes,' he sighed. 'He's an officer. That's the dodgy part – fraternization between officers and other ranks is virtually a hanging offence.'

He, she thought giddily with selfish relief; not *she*, not the effortlessly gorgeous and witty seductress of her worst imaginings.

'However, in spite of the danger we became close friends. It was an unbelievable happiness, like sunlight bursting when you'd got used to nothing but gloom. Not that life was all that awful before: I'd been doing all right, jogging along, marking time, taking my customary perverse pleasure in a fairly repulsive set of circumstances. But once *he*'d come along. . . Oh I'm sorry, it's really hard to explain . . .'

'You don't need to, I can imagine,' she put in eagerly; 'you were surrounded by oiks and suddenly met someone on your own wave-length . . .'

'Well, it was a bit more than that. I mean, I admired him. You could say I was obsessed – you know,

123

couldn't think about anything or anyone else, just lived for our meetings.'

'I suppose,' she said, rather embarrassed and casting round for an explanation, 'after all the monotony and drudgery, it must have been brilliant.'

'It was,' he said. 'While it lasted.'

'Oh, I see. Oh, Laurie.'

'Yeah,' he sighed. 'Maybe he got cold feet. Maybe someone noticed and tipped him off. Though never a hint was dropped in my direction. Mind you, they're inclined to treat me with a degree of caution – my caustic tongue, you know . . . What happened was, I went to meet him as arranged, hung around as long as I dared – no show. No show the next day or the next. I passed him once in the corridor. He looked straight through me.'

She slid her hands under his arms, held him tightly.

'The daft thing is, I felt ashamed . . . small. As if, because he'd withdrawn his notice, I'd turned into a contemptible object. My heart would pound like the clappers. Even when I lay down it went on pounding; I'd have to get up and pace about. One night it was so bad I had to run right outside – various scenes charging through my mind – like I'd go and find him, challenge him, or maybe beg . . . And if it was no good, then I'd just keep running till I dropped dead of a heart attack, or got knocked down on a road, or fell off a cliff or into a quarry. Then it came to me that I could run to *you*. It calmed me down. I thought if I could just hang on for a forty-eight hour pass . . .' His head jerked; she saw that his eyes glittered.

'Laurie, darling, you did the right thing.'

'I told you it was pathetic.'

'No, no.' She put her hand to his mouth, fingered his smile.

'I'm lucky to have you to turn to.'

'But of course you've got me. Silly, you'll always have me.'

'And you . . . me,' he said diffidently.

124

'That's *right*. Whatever happens, we've always got each other.'

They sat in silence for a time. Eventually, he suggested going for a bite to eat. Rather shakily they stood up, collected the satchel, and set off like convalescents along the lamplit path. And lapsed into silence again – he contemplating his life ahead and suspecting he would be often hurt, but that with Claire to hang on to, he'd maybe keep a grip on life and survive; she watching the lamplight cutting the darkness and reflecting that the sight matched her inner state – of sorrow for Laurie, joy at her importance to him.

The menu in the fish café window, set out in plastic orange letters on a blackboard, offered cod, rock or haddock, with chips, peas, buttered bread and tea included in the price.

'What's rock?' Claire wondered.

'The cheapest on offer. And therefore we should feel strongly drawn to it. We must be careful to allow enough money for your taxi fare home.'

It was time for those practical considerations. 'Where are you going to spend the night?' She had already gathered that he did not intend visiting Foscote.

'Oh don't worry about me. I'll catch the late train.'

'Well, I shan't need any money for a taxi, 'cos I can stay at Daisy's. I'll phone her first, and then phone home.'

'Are you sure? I'd hate you to get into bother.'

'Quite sure, I often stay there. Her mother's sweet. Anyway, it's got so late it'll probably be simpler.'

He reached into his pocket, sorted through coins, handed some over. She darted ahead of him to a kiosk outside a Post Office. He more leisurely followed, leant his back against the side of the box, hands deep in pockets; heard the coins drop, and indistinctly, between lulls in the grinding traffic noise, caught her voice. He studied the scurrying laden home-bound workers; and the occasional shopper pushing on the door of the newsagent, making it ping, soon emerging with an evening paper or ripping cellophane from a fresh packet of cigarettes. It was a drab end of town – the final straggle of shops plus a fried fish bar, a bank, a yellow-tiled pub, a darkly forbidding Congregational Church. The side streets, he guessed, would be terraces of meanly proportioned bay-windowed dwellings. For he knew it all off by heart – the same sounds, sights, smells, the same despondent listlessness as in countless other places where, in the past sixteen months, he had waited outside telephone boxes with a local paper folded to reveal the Bed and Breakfast ads. (There had had to be somewhere to go during short tedious leaves.)

'I was in luck,' she cried, flinging the door wide. 'I got *your* mother.'

Her vigour, her smile, seemed to erupt from another world. He shrugged upright, mentally shook himself. 'How is Ma?'

'Fine. Same as usual. Said, what was I up to? and all that – but, you know, jokey. I told her Maman could phone me after ten at the Monks' house, which seemed to reassure her.' She frowned. 'Will I be there by then, do you think, from seeing you off?'

'Indeed you will. But from having been deposited by me on your friend's doorstep.' It appeared she would object, so he continued briskly, 'Don't fuss. I can't bear goodbyes in stations.'

'Oh. Right. Anyway, I doubt Maman will bother. Aunt Margaret said she hasn't set eyes on her, or on Uncle Peter, since breakfast.' Immediately, she wished this unsaid and added quickly, 'Mrs Monk, Daisy's mother, was very nice about it.'

'Good. Let's go and eat. Now we haven't got taxi fares to find I think we might go as far as the haddock.'

A stout man tied into a stained white overall waddled towards them bearing two large plates – his face as grey as the ashy end of the cigarette stuck in the corner of his mouth (which, delicately, he kept averted to prevent spillage over the haddock). 'Rene?' he bellowed, dropping the plates on the table in front of them and snatching the cigarette between finger and thumb in one flowing sequence. 'Where's them teas?'

'Coming,' cried Rene, thrusting through clacking strips of plastic curtain. 'I given 'em their bread and butter, I've only got one pair of hands.'

'Thank you,' they repeated as items were set before them (quite superfluously, they were wholly ignored).

The fish, glowing bright orange, was studded over with crunchy batter barnacles; savoury greasy steam rose. 'Yum,' said Claire, sniffing deeply from her plate. She took up her fork, hooked up a waxy chip, dropped it into her mouth. 'Scrumptious. Food of the gods.'

He grinned at her, said nothing; to him the meal did not come as a novelty. But he was as hungry as she, and for the next few minutes ate ravenously.

The food steadied him. He began to feel hopeful. At last, laid down knife and fork, took up his cup and cradled it between his palms. 'I shouldn't like you to go away with the wrong impression,' he said. 'I think I painted a woefully inadequate picture.'

She glanced up briefly, reached for the plastic tomato, jerked out a dollop of sauce.

'I mean, really he's a splendid guy. Terrifically clever, sensitive, insightful. And capable of sticking to his guns, staying true to himself – I admire that. For instance, he speaks with a broad Lancashire accent – after three years at Oxford! – where, incidentally, he took an upper second in English. Honestly, Claire, he made me realize how ill-read I am. Take poetry for instance: I hated it at school, thought it was one big yawn. Yet he writes as well as reads it. Ever read any Auden?'

She paused in her chewing, and with her jaw slewed, stared – eventually recollecting that he had asked a question. 'Er, no,' she said, denying familiarity

127

with anyone or thing called 'Auden' – unclear as to whether it was the name of his officer friend. (Huh, some friend! Some 'splendid guy'!) Irritatingly, Laurie's face had gone dreamy.

'No? Well, I'll post you a paperback. Oh, Claire. He really is a super person. Beside him I felt only half-educated, narrow, lacking . . .' (It is always annoying when loved ones belittle themselves in the heat of infatuation. She seized her cup, swallowed a large gulp of tepid tea.) 'I wish you could meet him. Perhaps' – he brightened – 'one day, when our army days are behind us . . .' (She choked, grabbed the thin paper napkin, pressed it over her mouth.) 'Because I mustn't hold this episode against him. After all, we were taking an almighty risk. And he had the most to lose. Hell, when I get out I'll be a mere undergraduate; *he'll* be starting on a career!'

'What did you say his name was?' she asked, endeavouring to make it a kindly enquiry.

'I didn't. But it's Keith,' he said, after a tiny pause.

She pushed her fork through the debris on her plate, hunting for an overlooked morsel. Keith, eh? She'd keep a jolly sharp look out in future years for any poetry-spouting Lancastrian answering to Keith. Laurie could be as deferentially friendly as he liked, but let him introduce this Keith to her and there'd be no mistaking *her* opinion. Not that she'd say anything, she wouldn't dream of embarrassing Laurie, the soft idiot. She'd just deal him one of her looks. *Coward*, her eyes would shout. If he was so darned clever, he'd get the message.

'Still hungry, pet?'

'Not really. Just picking.'

'More tea?'

'All right.'

After much twisting in his seat and arm waving, he managed to catch Rene's eye. 'Two more cups of tea, please.'

'It'll be extra,' she warned.

'That's perfectly all right.'

Claire ducked her head and craned over the table. 'Cor – *extra*,' she leered.

'I know, dear. But let's be reckless.'

The trouble with Laurie was, he took so much longer than she to weigh people up (this decided as she hurried at his side through ill-lit streets). We can all be bowled over . . . Here she remembered her initial enthusiasm for Miss Thwaite and how all those dismaying little imperfections crept to her notice. Crept to her notice because she, Claire, had rapidly recovered her critical faculties and had not then flinched from adjusting her original perception. If only Laurie were as tough. But he was too impressionable. He required protection. At this, a worrying thought surfaced. Had she done wrong in deciding against going to Cambridge in favour of Sutton? Was she failing him? She bit her lip as she recalled her secret satisfaction in writing to him about her decision and demonstrating her independence. (He was so darn bossy about her work – meant well, of course, but as far as her studies were concerned, she knew what she was about.) Now though, her heart misgave her. His sudden sigh further alarmed her.

The cold tramp through the dingy streets had made him wistful. 'It was so good of you to turn out for me, love. I'm so grateful.'

'But Laurie, I feel I've hardly done enough . . .'

'Claire!' He turned her towards him under a street lamp. His eyes were earnest. 'You've done exactly as I needed. That wretched "small" feeling has gone – vanished, just like that! You know, sometimes, when I'm down, I get an urge to somehow waste myself – splurge, chuck it all away, as though my life weren't really worth the trouble. But you – you bring me down to earth, put me back in touch, remind me what's good . . .'

'Listen,' she broke in swiftly, fearing she might cry;

'it's not too late to change my mind about going to Sutton. I could apply to Cambridge . . .'

'Don't dare think of it! That course at Sutton is perfect for you. Think how I'd feel if you mucked up doing what you really want because of worries about me. Needless worries – OK? I'm looking forward to swopping notes – and to us visiting one another. I may get a little car.'

'Oh that'd be great!'

'Come on. It's freezing.'

A few minutes later, she led into the street where Daisy lived. 'Will you find your way back?'

'Easily.'

'Well, here it is, number eleven.'

He opened the gate, pushed her through, then relatched it. Over it, he pulled her close, kissed her on the forehead, the nose, the lips.

Did he linger on her lips? She struggled to recall, staring, as he hugged her one last time, over his shoulder at the houses opposite. Perhaps he did.

xii

'There is no need to go into details, I'm not asking you to break any confidences,' Margaret Stone promised, glancing round the boxroom (which had become Claire's study) at the high-piled table (piled with papers, files, textbooks), its cluttered window-ledge (she distinguished from amongst the debris a glass-sided specimen box, a magnifying glass, twigs, plants, and several peculiar looking metal instruments standing in a jam jar – like a futuristic sculpture entitled *Flowers*, she thought), at the sideboard where some effects of her son's were heaped – records, record player, a book entitled *The Duke* with a handsome black face large upon the cover, a framed photograph of meadow grasses obstructed by sandalled feet (Claire's, to judge from the style), and worming through this debris a Prestbury School tie. Towards this last her hand automatically reached. But no, it was a trophy of Claire's she reminded herself, and in any case she wished to lay hands on her blessed son, not his mangy old tie. 'I would simply like to know whether you've *seen* Laurie of late. Had any opportunity to cast eyes over the blighter. After so many months one does begin to wonder how he fares, whether he is healthy and reasonably happy. Or not.'

Claire, who had been staring fixedly at her book, looked up.

'My dear, there's no need for such a scowl. I'm not trying to pry. Just that, by my calculations, the army has very nearly had its money's worth. I do hope he's not going to keep this up – you know, never coming home, studiously ignoring all reference to his father . . .'

'I did see him once,' Claire conceded.

'Well! Good! And?'

'He was . . . all right. He looked sort of bare with his hair cut short. It doesn't suit him. I expect he doesn't want people to see.'

'Oh, you mean it's *vanity* that has kept him away for going on two years?' But while Claire mumbled excuses and worthless promises on her son's behalf, it struck Margaret Stone that her irony contained a grain of truth: Laurie would not risk letting his father treat him like a squaddie if he could help it, and in all fairness, she could well visualize the former Wing Commander condescending. 'Yes, I see,' she said aloud. And sighed – 'Well, he will soon be at liberty to grow hair long and thick enough to roost chickens in. Though I hope he won't go quite as far – Peter has such a bee in his bonnet about hairy beatniks. I blame that chap who came last year, the Californian . . .'

'He was from Oregon.'

'Yes, dear,' she agreed pacifyingly. 'Well, I won't keep you. Don't overdo it, or you'll drop fast asleep during the exam. Shall I bring you a mug of cocoa later on?'

'Yes, please. Thanks, Aunt Margaret.'

Your mother wants to see you (Claire scrawled on a pad of lined file paper). Please write and reassure her so she stops pestering me about it – that is, if you ever intend returning to Foscote. You profess to care about her, so I think you should – at any rate, as soon as your hair's grown.

She sent all her love and signed her name, ripped the sheet from the pad, then went to the sideboard to collect an envelope. While she was licking and sealing this she rather regretted the word *pestering*. But there was no time for second thoughts; and, honestly, she could do without these interruptions in the middle of A levels.

Of course I have every intention of coming to see Ma (Laurie wrote back). But what is this about my hair? You sound very tense at the moment. I suppose it's all the swotting affecting you. I've written to her to say I'll come to Foscote somewhere around the middle of August. . .

She wondered why August, since his two years would be up by mid-July. But of course – who was he trying to kid? – he needed time for his hair to grow. However, since he was postponing coming home, she might as well fall in with her friends' idea of a hitchhiking and camping holiday in France. Daisy and Phillip, plus two other girls and one of Phillip's friends planned to go straight after exams. Months ago, when the holiday was first mooted, she had written to Laurie asking him to join them. He had managed to decline without acknowledging that he had been invited.

Darling, your friends are mad (he had written). If I were you I shouldn't touch camping with a barge-pole. The very word *latrine* strikes terror. Take it

132

from one who has spent many a ghastly night — courtesy of the army — on a mouldy groundsheet. I should warn you that there is no time of day more achingly depressing than when the birds start up — specially when you're out there among the little beasts, the world reeking of bruised grass and damp canvas, and, dear God, *feet*. Oh, and the light of dawn thrusting at you like cold steel through the door-flap. Don't do it, dear, that's my advice.

Blow him, she said to herself now. Anything would be preferable to moping around Foscote waiting for Laurie to deign to return. And there were very positive inducements, such as acquiring a suntan and improving her French (a language she had come to enjoy, despite as a child resenting having to speak it with her mother at set times of the week and before certain guests — though perhaps the artificiality of those occasions had too closely mirrored their strained relations in any language); also the chance of adventure, of encountering a spicy mix of fun and adversity. It was just a shame, when Laurie would be free, that he declined to be there to share the experience. But since he did (and his oblique method of refusal allowed no scope for argument) it would be satisfying to demonstrate her insouciance. And refreshing for three whole weeks to put him right out of her mind.

Not that he inhabited her mind totally the rest of the time. When she was studying he stood no chance. Often, putting away her books or tidying the laboratory bench, she would notice this fact and offer herself congratulations. She devised a little test. If Laurie were in serious trouble, would she set her work aside? And concluded that of course she would, if the trouble were serious — though perhaps not immediately if it entailed some great cost such as missing an examination. How shocked her friends would be by this: in their opinion, LOVE was the number one commitment and absolutely everything should be dropped the instant it beckoned.

133

But then she was unusual in taking such positive pleasure in study – it had grown out of the thrill she experienced in childhood from examining and comparing plants and looking them up in books and hunting down specimens. Then, it had been her means of escaping other people's disapproval (she could still recall the bleak feeling she would get from their puzzled, worried or scathing looks). With no near-at-hand conventional outlets such as girls' clubs or school friends' houses to run to, she had turned to the outdoors and found plenty there to transport her. And so had Laurie. She and he had grown sharing the same enthusiasm. It was a waste of time to sit puzzling over which ranked first – her love for Laurie or her love for her studies. In fact, there was no dilemma; with simple happiness she saw that her twin obsessions were like two sides of the sun, complementary halves of a rounded whole.

However, it *was* possible to conjure a scenario in which Laurie took priority. If, by her presence, she could prevent some other person usurping her position in his life (here, her imaginary enemy loomed – devastatingly gorgeous, tall, witty), she would abandon everything, she wouldn't hesitate. Though what she would actually do to save the situation remained unclear.

'You look like a street urchin,' Laurie exclaimed, welcoming her back to Foscote with ecstatic appreciation. 'Is it all tan, or is there a dirt component?'

'We didn't use too much soap,' she admitted, 'but we were always in the water – a lake or a river and once in somebody's pond. This is Daisy's father, by the way,' she added in an aside, and more loudly to the man who was hauling bags out of the car boot, 'Thanks a lot, Mr Monk.'

She stood among her crumpled belongings, watching Laurie discover a point of interest to engage Mr Monk – a man of pessimistic countenance and very few words. The journey here from Daisy's house (where she had spent the night after arriving with her holiday companions very late in town) had taken place in awkward silence. But now Laurie hit on the subject of cars. 'I'm thinking of getting a motor,' he confided, resting his arm against the car's roof. 'How do you find the Anglia?' Mr Monk became so animated describing miles per gallon and reliability statistics she began to wonder if he would ever go. But Laurie managed this too. 'Well, I shall certainly know where to come for advice. And thank you for bringing Claire home,' he said, taking two steps back as one who awaits moving traffic. Calling through the window that it had been no trouble at all, Mr Monk obediently departed.

'Now, come and tell me all about it. We'll find somewhere nice and quiet, because, as you can imagine, this place is hell, in full and terrible spate. Quick, quick,' he muttered, as, from round the corner of the house, a party of eager festival participants advanced.

In the boxroom ('Shocking mess you'd got this room into, if you don't mind my saying,') they relaxed; she flopped down on the sofa, he turned one of the chairs towards her and sat on it. She had imagined she would be fit only for further sleep after the endless-seeming journey, but was soon regaling him with her adventures: describing the fun times and the bad, the times when they couldn't get lifts and half the party lost the other half for several days, of cleaning their teeth at village pumps to the mystification of on-lookers, of drinking too much wine in the sun and losing count of time, of the night it thundered and lightninged and gullies had to be dug round tents by torchlight to ward off storm water and save their belongings.

'What a wonderful adventure,' said Laurie when her voice faltered from exhaustion. 'I'm so glad you went. I told you you should.'

It took her breath away. But he carried seamlessly

on, and she, tongue-tied with fatigue, found no gap to make her protest – there was just a useless shout in her brain: *you did nothing of the kind. You said I shouldn't touch it with a bargepole, you devious, tricky so-and-so.* Her utter silence (surely he must notice it?) congealed in her ears.

'We've got a live-in help, did you know?' (She did, but gave no indication.) 'A Mrs Basket or Biscuit . . .' (It was Bascombe, actually, though she wouldn't say.) 'A marvellous lady, my hopes are sky high. For the first time in years I didn't have to clean the bathroom before daring to use it – customarily my number one priority on arriving home. Poor Ma, she could never grasp that a talented potter might not necessarily have what it takes to wage war on domestic dirt – however hard I might press the notion – more, I admit, out of self-preservation than concern for her. But I'm truly unselfishly thankful that she's letting up at last: simply ridiculous the amount of work she allowed people to foist on her. Shall we go and say "hello"?'

Why couldn't she challenge him? This sort of thing had happened before – he had said one thing, then, when it suited, blithely insisted he'd said the opposite. Always, she pretended not to notice. Out of embarrassment? Or fear of what might be discovered or provoked? In any case, to argue now would be a waste of breath. She could imagine how he would react if she gathered her courage and produced the letter in which he'd disparaged the holiday plan: 'Nonsense, dear, just my bit of fun, you weren't meant to take it seriously – as you very well knew, or why did you go?' His blather could tie her in knots.

Going with him through the white-walled corridors, passing sunny windows, she decided that life was too short anyway to start nit-picking and being miserable, and the chance to spend some of it now with Laurie too beautifully seductive.

'And then we'll go and visit all our old haunts,' he was saying.

*   *   *

Laurie, crossing the courtyard, maintained an amiable yet impersonal expression. 'Good morning. Might I . . . ? Thank you so much. Yes lovely, isn't it.'

It was always a problem getting from building to building during mid-morning coffee break (or lunch break or mid-afternoon tea break, come to that), and normally during the festival he wouldn't try. Wandering into the kitchen just now he had clean forgotten that it *was* coffee time (so many aspects of Foscote had slipped his mind during his two-year absence). The scene in the scullery – student helpers loading trays, spooning out coffee powder, staggering to the table with over-sized steaming kettles – jogged his memory; though it was presided over not by Margaret Stone but the new live-in help (Mrs Bascombe – of course!). He was certain his mother was not upstairs in the Stone apartment; nor, after her dramatic announcement at supper last night, in any of the rehearsal rooms. (Would everybody please take note, she had declared, that from henceforth she had abandoned the cello. Arthritis had begun to distort her fingers. She had held these in the air as evidence: 'See the joints? – see? – and the underside of the forefingers?' Having in the nick of time relieved herself of certain housekeeping chores, she now intended to go one step further. After all, potting was her first love, she had never been more than a jobbing cellist: from now on what nimbleness was left to her would be reserved for her craft. She then sat gazing about her in triumph – large and raffish-looking, her grey-frizzed hair jutting perilously close to her glinting eyes. Laurie's cry of 'Bravo!' had to some extent atoned for the more general silence. He drew her eyes with the brilliance of his approval, willed her to go on looking until the silent exchange he sensed between his father and Sabine was safely passed.)

He would find her in the pottery, no doubt.

137

Dusty, cool, faintly damp, a bluish deflected light – the feel and look of the place rushed over his senses as he stepped inside and closed the door. And heard a familiar sound – rhythmic bumps punctuating a constant whirring. Yes, there she was at the wheel, totally absorbed. He did not disturb her, but lolled against the wall, watching.

Something has happened to her, he thought. Age had happened to her. As she leant to her task, her face sagged; in the glancing light her criss-crossed skin seemed almost translucent. Once she looked up, smiling, and for a fleeting moment before she returned her attention to the wheel, cast off the years. He watched her fingers on the turning clay glistening with grey slick – arthritic fingers, he remembered. But had awareness, as well as age, happened to her? She could not have been *una*ware of the growing bond over the years between Sabine and her husband – even given that she was always so busily caught up in the job of keeping Foscote ticking over. Had her awareness received an extra boost lately – sufficient to cause her to reconsider her life, to re-order her priorities? And sufficient to bring on a faint air of battiness? He repressed this painful line of enquiry. His parents' lives belonged to his parents; they had built them; he was not responsible.

'Did you want me for anything, darling?'

'No, no. Just popped in to watch. It's compulsive viewing; almost hypnotic.'

After a little while longer he left.

Outside, the festival participants were thronging back to rehearsals. A great wave of A notes welled out. Friends called parting shots: 'See you at lunch – if I live so long; we're starting on the Schönberg!' So at home they all were, so in possession. It was he who didn't belong. Feeling less than a visitor, he strolled round to the front of the house, went up the steps and in under the portico.

Climbing the stairs, he pleasurably noted the novelty

of dust-free carved uprights in the balustrade, then raised his eyes to the paintings on the staircase wall. Perhaps the improved cleanliness everywhere encouraged him to view with new eyes, for he caught his breath and gazed upwards and around – amazed. Of course, he'd always been actively conscious of the Graham Sutherland; as a boy had craned his neck to peer at it, attracted by the fizzing conjunction of purples and greens, the dark verdant smell it seemed to give off, the jolt of a mechanical-looking object portrayed – so it appeared – as a living plant. But all these others on the walls . . . Slowly he climbed to the wide landing and passed along. For years these paintings were as dully familiar as wallpaper. Now each in turn leapt at him – a Bawden, a Gillies, a Pitchforth, a Piper . . . And how could he not have been hit in the eyes by this violently brash still-life, by . . . (he peered to read the signature) R. Macbryde? Good God, yes. He'd spent hours examining works by such painters in civic galleries during cold, wet, slow-to-pass leave from barracks. A thought struck him, and he moved quickly to lean over the banisters. Sure enough, down below stood a familiar but never before *observed* hall-stand, and near to it a carved chest. Discussions of long ago returned (at the time only half-heard): his parents and some Foscote *habituées* at the tea table arguing the merits of the Arts and Crafts Movement. He hurried along the corridor to the family sitting-room (knowing exactly what he would find): a finely crafted cabinet, a bureau, a stocky table. It was as though he saw these things for the first time. Looking back, he imagined he had moved about the place with his sense of sight only sufficiently engaged to prevent him crashing into things; he had been all ears, tongue, nose; had only properly scrutinized items he discovered for himself – trees, plants, bits of bark, the colour and texture of earth, small creatures. He was still grappling with his discovery when Claire tapped on the door.

'Come in,' he called, 'come here. Doesn't that strike you as beautiful?'

She gaped, nonplussed, at Uncle Peter's bureau; dislike colouring her view *because* it was Uncle Peter's bureau.

He seized her arm, led her off. 'And have you ever really *looked* at these paintings on the landing and over the stairs? You know,' he said as she frowned at a tremulous landscape signed G. W. Gillies, 'Father may be one hell of an overbearing bastard, but he certainly has taste, we must grant him that. I suppose even the worst of us has some redeeming feature.'

'Are you coming for a walk,' she demanded, 'or what?'

xiii

Claire, too, began to feel distanced from Foscote, though for her it was a more gradual process. And of a different, melancholy nature. She was struck, not by hitherto unappreciated satisfactions, but by faded glories. Favourite places seemed every year diminished. The bosky patch of stream where they would dangle their feet and cup fish in their hands now appeared gloomy, their magical den in the woods as a tangle of dilapidated rubbish; even the gleaming widening of the stream as it broke from the woods into the meadow, once so enticing, was perceived after river bathing in France to be shabby and uninviting. Digging into her memory she tried to rekindle lost charms. Some days she succeeded and blamed her morbid impressions on a passing mood. Other times, often in Laurie's company, larking, splashing and sitting about dreamily, she made a pretence of nothing being changed but all being still delightful. But the fading persisted. As if a series of veils fell over her eyes, every summer brought further clouding of her childhood vision. At first, this was accompanied by a sense of loss. Soon, she was too taken up with new scenes – a university campus, a city landscape, her digs, Laurie's new haunts – to care, or finally to notice. Foscote became simply a convenience. They inhabited the place as visitors taking advantage of kind hosts in order to indulge in the other's company.

Only in her dreams could the woods and stream shimmer with their former freshness. It was always the same dream – she in the woods searching for Laurie; but it was not now so pervaded with sadness. True, she never did stumble on him. However, her pounding progress through the trees, her weaving thrust along the stream bank, were conducted with new, mounting excitement. And the disappointing conclusion was no longer arriving at the place and Laurie not in it, but that she always, maddeningly, woke up. Damnation, she would curse, coming stickily awake. Another second and she would have had him. At last.

xiv

Every half-term they alternately visited one another in Sutton or Cambridge. The pattern was not decided upon in advance, but evolved.

Laurie's mother, as good as his hopes, had helped towards the purchase of a small third-hand car. When the time drew near to leave Foscote for their different destinations, and Claire bewailed the fact that these were so far apart, Laurie promised to drive to Sutton at half-term. Claire, in despondent mood, replied that this was only partial consolation; she could not foresee ever being able to afford a return visit. 'Have you seen the price of a train ticket from London to Sutton? Imagine London to Cambridge on top!' They were lingering over coffee in the kitchen at the time, and because Aunt Margaret was present, neither mentioned a further inhibition: that where Laurie's mother was generous, Claire's was mean.

Recently, the entire Foscote ménage had observed a

141

telling example of Sabine's parsimony. On being advised by the local education authority that it proposed to offer no grant towards Claire's living expenses (on the grounds of her mother's considerable earnings) — a communication Sabine had opened at the breakfast table and ringingly denounced — she proffered sharp words of advice to her daughter. Claire should please bear in mind that she was not made of money; success did not come cheaply; Sabine had standards to maintain, a public to please, important visits to make, hospitality to return; there were no grants for *her* either, despite that without her tireless work a modern repertoire for the soprano voice would barely exist in this ungrateful country. (This was not strictly true; grants from bodies promoting the arts regularly came Foscote's way — a fact the Stones silently considered as they bent their heads over their breakfast plates.) As Sabine harangued, Claire hit back. 'All right, all right! I s'pose you don't expect me to go to Sutton in my school uniform? I s'pose you can spare a few quid so I don't actually freeze? Or were you thinking of chucking me some of your cast-offs? Yeah, I bet that's it — you thought I could go round looking a freak in stupid *couture*,' (huge sneer) 'which'd give you the perfect excuse to go lashing out on new rubbish.' For once, Peter Stone had come to the rescue. 'Surely my dear, it will not bankrupt Foscote to clothe poor Claire,' he said, awarding the subject of his remark an understanding smile (she thought it supercilious); 'to clothe her becomingly, as she deserves.' (Not for the first time, Claire and Laurie noted an implication in this: that the finances of both families were inextricably entwined.)

When it was almost time to leave for Sutton, Margaret Stone drew Claire aside. Seizing her hand, she pressed into it a wad of notes. 'Of course you must visit Cambridge. Put this in the Post Office, and when you need to buy train tickets you'll have something to draw on. After all, one of us has to keep an eye on him,' she added, meaning to overcome any hesitation on Claire's part by pretending she would be doing her a service. Which was quite unnecessary: in the cause of maintaining her bond with Laurie, Claire was without scruple.

Claire could never decide which was the greater treat, her visits to Cambridge or Laurie's to Sutton; though it seemed clear from the way he was always begging her to return for some special occasion – 'Promise you'll be here for May Ball,', 'Don't forget Julius's party at the end of term,' – which Laurie preferred. Not that he would admit it (and, typically, always slithered from any quizzing on the subject), but she suspected he religiously undertook the trip to Sutton to make certain of her return visit. The scene at each place was totally different: they were a vivacious crowd at Cambridge, and somehow homogeneous; her friends at Sutton were simply a collection of characters, harder to know, less predictable.

When Laurie first introduced her around, though calm on the surface, inwardly she was all nervy suspicion. Smiling carefully, her casual-seeming sideways glance was checking for any sign of her long-imagined rival – who might, for all she knew, be a part of this group and already well on her way to capturing Laurie. But no-one ever came near to approximating the apparition. In any case, Laurie's circle was comprised of more men than women, and of these women, most were attached to blokes; and though many were pretty and a couple beautiful, not one, she sensed, was capable of arousing Laurie's interest. Her confidence soared. She was inclined to look back on her paranoia with pity, to view its mythical subject as the adolescent equivalent of childhood's bogeyman.

Her own singular appearance, once silently apologized for or shrugged off rebelliously, she now pushed to the fore – trained her wispy dark hair to stand in

143

spikes on the top of her head and trail like feathers down the sides of her face and the back of her neck; emphasized her eyes like mad, with the result that their cast no longer drew dismayed looks but riveted appraisal (with her lopsided grin, her fractionally unsynchronized eyes seemed reflections of inner, faintly wicked glee); developed a taste for starkly uncluttered clothes (a taste which, though she would never admit it, owed much to Sabine) – simple close-fitting shifts, slim trousers and turtle-neck sweaters, always in black or a dark colour to dramatize her pallor and smallness. However charming these Cambridge women, she perceived they lacked any memorable style. Certainly, they lacked her unique oddness.

The effect upon her and Laurie of suddenly becoming a pair – or more precisely, *displaying* as a pair – was psychedelic. At the very moment of meeting they became super confident, super bright, tirelessly inspired. Heightened awareness sharply defined the scene around them and, most vividly of all, via the smiles and stares reflecting them, the intoxicating brilliance of their own image.

If she were asked, Claire would be at a loss to offer any coherent explanation for how this metamorphosis occurred. One moment she would be sitting anonymously on a train, looking with bored eyes at the passing landscape or trying to fasten her attention on a book or grimly defend her share of an armrest, the next flying into Laurie's arms, airy, weightless, instantly becoming half of that glamorous phenomenon *Laurie and Claire*. From then on the rush from this excitement would build and build. Very likely, he had brought a friend with him whom she would greet at the barrier, and then they would be immediately off to join others at a theatre or cinema, or at somebody's party, or, if it was jazz night, to a pub or coffee house where Laurie and the rest of the band (he on piano, others on alto sax, trombone, bass and drums) were booked to play. Wherever they were headed, it would feel like a giddy excursion – Laurie filling her in with the news, complimenting, teasing, arguing, opening her out like full sun on a flower. As far as possible he liked to maintain contact; to walk hand in hand in the street, to stand chatting with an arm round her waist, to encourage her with a squeeze, nudge her at a private joke. He seized any opportunity to dance. She knew (and suspected he did) that as dancers they made compulsive viewing – exaggeratedly expressive, flawlessly anticipating the other's move.

Their shared intuition, they discovered, could be shown off in other ways. They evolved a game. Begun as a joke, as a piece of self-parody for the amusement of a few intimates, it became a famous success; repeat performances were constantly demanded, especially late at night when the lights were dim and everyone fuddly. Basically, the game was a trick, a pretence of telepathy; but to an extent it did depend on their ability to anticipate the other's mind. Via a secret code of touch and gesture (one press of a shoulder to represent A, two presses B; an upward brush of the neck to indicate the counting should begin at E, a finger click that it should begin at I, and so on), they were able to spell out words. Claire would leave the room with a minder. Those remaining would be asked to supply the name of some famous or currently newsworthy person. Then Claire returned, sat cross-legged on the floor with Laurie kneeling behind her. With great theatricality, with strokes and pressings and finger-clickings and swayings, he apparently urged her into a trance. When the words were safely communicated (never the *name* of the person to be conveyed in case some bright spark latched on to their code, but some pertaining feature or allusion which, with their intimate knowledge of the other's mind, Laurie could be sure of Claire recognizing), Laurie would move to sit cross-legged a few feet in front of her. This was the climax of the display, when 'thought transference' supposedly occurred, when hands reached, fingertips met, eyes held. Then Laurie snapped his fingers, and Claire shuddered and stage-whispered the correct name. Laughter erupted as the spell broke, as everyone knew they'd been had; but they always clamoured for more, fascinated as much by the touching and swaying, the unblinking mutual gazing, as by the mystery of the unerring result.

'Do it with me, Laurie,' Jessica (one of the beauties) begged one night.

He lightly touched her shoulder, swept fingers over her neck, tipped up her chin, looked into her eyes. And smiling regretfully, shook his head.

'Rubbish,' cried Toby (Jessica's boyfriend). 'Tell you what, come outside with me, Claire, and give me a few tips. I'll soon pick it up.'

'Certainly not,' cried Laurie haughtily. 'Claire is exhausted.'

Laurie was right. She was exhausted. But not from partying. She could have gone on all night – having fun, showing off, joking and dancing and listening to music – so long as she was accompanied by Laurie. Now, she lay on a narrow bed in a barren little guest room in a remote corner of Laurie's college, too lethargic even to remove her clothes. She was exhausted, all right. But from disappointment.

Weekends in Cambridge always ended this way – like a fizzing firework finally failing to shoot skywards as it was programmed to do. She had been fizzing all night (and if appearances were anything to go by, so had Laurie): all that body and eye contact was incredibly arousing. She had fizzed fit to burst, absolutely to the point of take-off, desperate to zoom, soar, spatter the sky with her starburst.

But here she was again, deposited by Laurie in her celibate's cell – and he gone after one chaste peck of her cheek before she could try some delaying tactic. He would come by in the morning to take her to

146

breakfast, after which they would go to the station (no doubt with one of Laurie's friends in tow). And that would be that . . .

Whoops, she had dropped off then for a second or two. She had better clean her face at least, or God knows what sort of fright she'd look by morning.

She felt better after washing, more optimistic. There was always next time, she told herself as she climbed into bed. Or, she yawned, when he came to see her at Sutton.

A quarter of a century later, Laurie and Claire were lunch guests at Toby and Jessica's.

The meal over, they sat over the remains of their wine. Jessica rose and went to a shelved alcove and hunted through a pile of old magazines and theatre programmes until she found what she was searching for. She brought it to the table – a photograph album, which they greeted with eager cries. They pulled their chairs closer together. Claire put on her reading spectacles. Jessica took charge of turning the pages.

Half-forgotten memories revived; reminiscences flowed; they groped for people's identities, wondered what had become of them in later life. Jessica was rebuked for turning the pages too quickly.

'Ahah!' Toby cried, lighting on a particular photograph. 'Now that stirs a memory. I do believe . . .'

'It's Laurie and Claire doing one of their stunts.'

'Turn the page over, Jessica,' Claire commanded.

But Toby wouldn't have it. 'Hang on, we haven't had a proper look. Gosh, do you remember . . .'

'No, I simply can't stand it,' Claire groaned. 'We were such God-awful exhibitionists. Doesn't it make your toes curl, Laurie? Turn over, Jessica, for pity's sake.'

'But darling, people were enthralled. You and Laurie were magic.'

'You were a star turn,' Toby agreed.

'I like to think,' said Laurie, raising his brows,

looking down his long nose, finger-brushing his sleeve as though dusting down hurt dignity, 'that we still are.'

'Merciful heavens,' sighed Claire.

XV

Sutton. By evening the Union Building was another world. No thronging of the concourse or squatting on the stairway, no gowns billowing by late to lectures, no cat-calls, no fug of noise. And no queue outside the refectory; but instant access to a tired-looking counter display, and a sight beyond of the reduced catering team, lounging desultorily or dragging off to stack plates, slam oven doors, run taps – unless, as somebody's favourite, your special requirements known and tolerated, you were cheerily greeted: 'Evening, love. Working late again? I can do you a cheese salad.'

'Thanks, Mary. You're an angel. Yeah, and I'm knackered. Bit of a crisis in the lab, couldn't leave it. How's your husband? Those new pills suiting him?'

'Doctor says he's doing all right. Can't say as they've done much for his temper . . .'

And no massed voices or clacking din of crockery, when, having paid for the food, you passed into the hall – with, at this time of day, no view of walkways and playing fields; just the nightmarishly lit and sparsely peopled vault endlessly reflected in blackened windows. Nor was there a need to go tracking through rows hunting a space; you simply joined the group at a long central table. Most people had arrived singly, as Claire now did.

'Hi, folks.'

'Hiya. Hey – cheese salad! How'd you come by that?'

'I have my sources.'

'Jammy devil.'

This exchange, between Claire and Anita, was attended to by the women present, but ignored by the men who continued to eat in stolid and famished silence or to argue about football. Most faces along the

148

table were familiar; Claire had eaten with, conversed, argued, joked with most folk here; but it was amazing how little she knew of any of them. The form was quite unlike that in the women's hall of residence where she had spent her first university year and where personal details were avidly exchanged. Here men set the tone, and therefore debated musical tastes, books read, films seen, political and sporting allegiances, the difficulty with landlords, where to get cheap food and booze, and who was fanciable on campus and who wasn't. First names could be gathered if you kept your ears open, and sometimes the subjects people were reading and which part of the country – or other country – they originated from and where were their present digs. But it was information imparted impersonally, banteringly, and engendered in Claire a feeling that here in this echoing, harshly lit space were huddled the day's left-overs, the rootless flotsam, too non-conformist to live in hall, too indolent to cook in a bedsit kitchen. Many here were postgraduate students, worldly, old-seeming. A few, like Claire, were mere second-year undergraduates who had taken the option to move out of hall. (Claire had done so, not out of a desire for independence, but for Laurie's sake, to provide somewhere he could lay a sleeping bag when he came to visit rather than waste money in a B and B.) The remainder were undergraduates in their final year, too busy swotting to spend time shopping and cooking. Some evenings, Claire cooked for herself and possibly a friend in the terraced house she shared with two Indian men from Kenya (Sadru and Krishna), Pattie from Devon, Eileen from London and Lai Sim from Hong Kong; often, after a full day in the lab she couldn't be bothered, preferred to come into the refectory, eat, drink coffee, smoke other people's cigarettes, and maybe if someone suggested it and she felt in the mood, go on with a group to a pub or a cinema.

Zak had come in.

Directing her eyes anywhere but in his direction, she

dumped her plate on top of a communal pile, cadged a cigarette from a neighbour, planted her elbows on the tacky table surface and blew smoke at the ceiling. And all the time her secret third eye was reporting: he's reached the table (wearing that God-awful shirt again), yeah and he's weighing the scene, looking to see who's here (looking to see whether *I*'m here). A place had been vacated almost opposite her. When he claimed it (as she had anticipated) her skin flinched. Of course, he couldn't simply sit down, but leaned over to deposit his tray, then tilted back the chair and straddled it massively. He was a massive bloke – tall, muscular, arms like tree-trunks, huge hands, broad face; everything about him *big* – except his eyes, which were piggy-small like Krushchev's. With his long lank hair scraped back and held in a rubber band, he was in fact pig-ugly. It was one of the reasons – not the main one – for her detestation. Everyone knew him. With his uncut hair (men were starting to wear their hair longer, but not that long) and his implied Californian decadence (heavy mention of drugs and beat venues, of cult writers and musicians) he was one of the sights on campus, a curiosity, a subject of speculation. He was simply Zak (no-one asked whether this was short for something, since to do so would reveal not being already in the know); he had arrived here from California, though he also let drop that he had been raised in Vancouver (again, no-one was so uncool as to enquire further); he was here to do a Masters in Political Science (or maybe it was Social Science or Political Economy).

Pretty soon it dawned on Claire that she had aroused the interest of this long-haired giant. Flattered by the way he sought her out, encouraged by his rapt attention, she innocently burbled to him her enthusiasm for a proposed field trip (part of her plant demography project), showed off her knowledge of jazz, confided her recent conversion to vegetarianism and with quiet pride her membership of CND. There were several such delightful little one-sided chats. Then out of the blue he simply took her breath away – stopped listening and started questioning in a rude sly manner. He rubbished her taste, threw her trusting remarks back in her face, picked holes in her answers, wound her reasoning into knots: 'Man, no-one digs jazz anymore,' and 'So why're you studying that, *exactly*? You know, I get the feeling you haven't thought this through,' and 'Where's the socio-economic justification for spending loadsa dough on esoteric stuff like that?' As for being a vegetarian, according to Zak she was breaking with her cultural norms, which would be OK if her motives weren't suspect. Most insultingly of all he found flaws in her reasons for joining CND – most insultingly, because he liked to advertise his own part in the Peace Movement: apparently, commitment was nothing while her logic was bad. How different was this to darling Laurie's reaction, he made no secret of not being fully persuaded of the case for nuclear disarmament (as usual he was inhibited by finding both sides of the argument compelling), but nevertheless heard her and her fellow campaigners out sympathetically and respected their passion. (Though he was not quite able to disguise his alarm when she proposed to join the march to Aldermaston. In fact, she strongly suspected an invitation to go with him to Jessica's at Easter had been engineered on purpose to prevent her, he having rightly calculated that she would not be able to resist. If this were so, she gladly forgave him; it was just another example of his loving concern.) Never did Laurie imply contempt for her powers of logic. Zak, who did, betrayed characteristics accurately mirrored by his peasant-butcher looks.

Of course, it wasn't long before she deduced the reason for this. Zak was attracted to her. He needled her deliberately to obtain a response. Evidence soon emerged to support this view. For though she now virtually ignored him, he continued doggedly to choose a seat as near to hers as possible, to wait to discover whether *she* was going before agreeing to join an expedition to the pub. Oh yes, he fancied her all right. *Lusted after her*, she would think deliciously, bent over her books under the unshaded light-bulb in her bare little room. *Lusted*, she would repeat under her breath, deliberately stirring lasciviousness.

Now, laughing at a joke that had gone rippling down the table, she allowed her eyes for an unhurried second to meet his gaze. Laurie's visit last week had terrifically boosted her confidence. It had been great showing him off, being flirty and funny right in Zak's face. When Laurie started playing the piano in the bar (Count Basie stride-style), Zak's contemptuous remarks about her musical taste had been thoroughly answered. (Wherever would she be without Laurie? she sometimes wondered. His visit here during her very first term – long before Zak's time – had saved her from an initial verdict: that she was a swot whose interesting looks were belied by a dull disposition. Overnight, accompanied by handsome and engaging Laurie and enlivened by the magic he always wrought in her, that opinion was reversed. She was no swot after all, it was decided, but interesting and clever and very probably heading for a first.)

'How about a noggin?' called Andy (her neighbour at the table). 'Anyone fancy a trip to The Ship?'

People agreed or declined. Zak said nothing – holding back, she guessed, for her reply.

'Claire?' Andy asked, shaking out his packet of Players.

'Oh thanks. I shouldn't really have another, I must owe you dozens.' (In fact, she owed scores of people dozens. Because Laurie considered the habit distasteful, she was reluctant to think of herself as a smoker, and never actually buying cigarettes allowed her not to.)

'Oh, right,' said Andy. 'But what I meant was, are *you* coming?'

Unfazed, she waited for a light. Breathing out smoke,

she could sense the deflation on the other side of the table when she shook her head. 'Er, no, I don't think so.'

People started preparing to leave – drained their coffee cups, gathered belongings. She and Zak remained still. Then he leaned forward, looking mean and calculating. 'Say, Claire,' he drawled, 'I don't get it. I mean, you act pretty straight. How come you hang out with a fairy?'

There was sudden silence, as everyone stopped what they were doing and turned and looked at her. She pulled in smoke (blessedly wonderful props, cigarettes); took time to exhale, to tap off ash. 'Now there, I fear, you are misinformed,' she countered, thankful for the cool tone of her voice. 'I am more than happy to testify to the contrary.' And nodding and smiling to herself, she actually purred – 'Mm, yes.'

Relieved laughter spluttered out. A great roar came from James (ex-public schoolboy). 'You see, Zak old sport, on this side of the pond, camp is *in*. It's a frightfully popular affectation in certain circles – theatrical, upper class. Laurie's a grand chap, most entertaining.'

'Why, thank you James,' Claire said, staring hard at Zak who was looking discomfited.

'Uh-uh. Guess I wouldn't know 'bout that,' he huffed. 'Guess I'm not what you'd call *au fait* with your British upper class.' He looked at her. 'You're not sore, I hope?'

'Not at all.'

'Come with us for a drink, then.'

'Afraid I can't. For one thing I have to make a phone call.' She got to her feet, reached for her bag.

'Phoning Laurie?' Anita asked. 'Give him my best. When's he coming again?'

'Soon, I hope. Must go. 'Night, all.'

Sailing to the door, his piggy eyes were greedily tracking her. She just knew it.

All the way home she was ecstatically pleased with

herself. Smoulderingly sexy on the bus (the conductor joshing and admiring her), sensuously swinging down Burnett Street. Her key was making heavy weather of the latch to number 37 before reality reasserted. She pushed open the door and switched on the light. That stuff she had implied about herself and Laurie, she remembered, and which everyone had eagerly swallowed: well, strictly speaking it wasn't true. 'Shit,' she cried, stumbling over the door jamb. Lumbering upstairs, she felt washed-out, as though, thoroughly doused and cruelly exposed, life had leached away her exuberance. She thumped down on her bed. The waste! she silently raged; the stupid waste of her longings, her energy, and yes, dammit, her *desirability*. Look, she was not going to be coy about this: Zak's attentions, other men's eyes, made it patently clear she was desirable. So why for pity's sake didn't Laurie *get on with it*?

She pummelled the pillows, flopped back, glowered at the ceiling. Her breathing calmed, soon became barely perceptible, and she noticed a quieter emotion taking hold. Soon she recognized it. Misery.

Her mind wrestled to resist. There was something she had forgotten, she thought, or perhaps overlooked. Some core to her depression which, if she could only bring it to the surface and examine and dispute, might cheer her up. Her eyes explored the pattern made by the light-bulb – bright streaks and shadowy blobs fanning out in a lopsided circle – while her memory raked over the evening. Perhaps it was something somebody said? For instance, 'fairy' (she heard it in Zak's voice), or 'camp' (as spoken by James). After a second, decided there was no problem with 'camp' – a word regularly bandied in Laurie's circle: 'Oh God, how camp!' would be exclaimed in tones of thrilled appreciation; or someone might ask if she knew so-and-so, because, 'You should, darling, you really should; he's so camp; terrifically amusing.' Clearly it was a term of approbation. Which was how James had used it tonight, and how Zak had heard it. So how about 'fairy'? – a rather different word. You could say 'fairy' nastily – as indeed Zak had. The word was not new to her. She clearly remembered the time she first heard it.

It was during her first term at university. She and a few others in her group were gossiping over coffee, swapping notes about their halls of residence. John said that in Fawsley Hall you had to be constantly on the look out for the sub-warden, specially late in the evening when he would prowl the corridors looking to chat up some greenhorn freshman, hoping to lure him up to his flat with a promise of a nightcap or a sight of his record collection. Later, this same sub-warden, who was also a lecturer in the French Department, had been spotted crossing a quadrangle on campus and pointed out to her – 'Oh look, here comes that *fairy* John was telling us about,' – a plump individual with a carefully arranged quiff of hair who was waddling towards them. So that's what one looks like, she had thought, having only recently become aware of the type's existence.

The word was so obviously and ludicrously mis-applied to Laurie (vigorous and forceful – nothing effeminate about him) that now she bounded impatiently from the bed and buried her unprofitable thoughts in a fit of desk tidying and mug washing. Then filled the kettle, plugged it in and squatted beside it on the thin carpet. When steam rose it seemed to clear her head; waveringly, she began to perceive what Zak had really meant to imply: *that Laurie was not turned on by her* – at least, not as he, Zak was. Zak was made sullen by desire, and therefore assumed Laurie's easy manner with her signalled it was lacking. As James had said, Zak had been misled by an extravagantly ironic and flippant manner. What it came down to: Zak was jealous. And also, where Laurie's feelings for her were concerned, so very wrong.

Stirring and sipping her coffee, rehearsing the evidence for this, her mind slid gratefully through the bosky scenes of her fondest memories – Laurie's passion for her that summer when she was only fifteen, his urgent caresses, his insatiability. And inevitably ran into a wall of frustration. However, understanding had long since softened the hurt of his ceasing to make love to her. From the moment she acknowledged the truth of the situation between her mother and Uncle Peter, all had become clear. Making love to her, in Laurie's eyes, had become tainted. Their selfish and baleful action (her mother's and Uncle Peter's) had cast incestuous undertones. She knew for sure that Laurie's feelings were merely suppressed, because sometimes, usually at a party, when he and she had maybe been dancing and were standing about with their arms round one another, laughing and joking with some other couple, or just one person (yes, she could definitely remember one particular occasion when they were merely talking to Nicholas), Laurie would suddenly go ramrod stiff, and as if he couldn't bear any remaining space between them, press her into his side, clamp her there, bone to bone, his rigid arm and side clenching her like steel pincers. Her flesh would catch his tensile throb. To excite him so much! she would exult, feeling her legs weaken.

If only he would be taken with desire for her at more convenient times. Alone with her, he always affected no memory of his previous arousal. Not that she had ever summoned the nerve to remind him outright, but her little hints with sultry music and cosy lighting and languorous displays of her stretched out body had so far failed to do the trick. (She understood why he behaved more cautiously in private. It was because of his over-anxiety for her, he seemed in constant dread lest she come to harm or get behind in her work. Sometimes she thought he was more bothered about her future than his own, less ambitious for himself than for her. It was so annoying of him never to take into account what she actually wanted. *He* was what she actually wanted, blast him.)

Hey – how about trying him out with a little competition? Details of another man's lust might just spike his guns. Laurie had been fascinated to meet Zak and measure his own verdict against Claire's – that Zak was the most repellent man she'd ever spent time with. She hadn't mentioned about him fancying her, though, which perhaps was a mistake. Maybe, soon, she would put Laurie more completely in the picture. It was worth a try.

Finding possible solutions to problems always gave her a buzz. She prepared her files for the morning and herself for bed on a surge of optimism.

xvi

Seizing Laurie's hand, Claire tugged him from the shop window and led towards the Charing Cross Road. They were going to the Happening at the Better Books bookshop. However much he tried to delay and deflect her purpose, they were *going*.

'What is a "Happening"?' he'd asked dubiously from Cambridge, during their weekly chat via the telephone box in Burnett Street and the pay phone in the lobby of his lodging house. He'd asked the same question again this morning soon after she'd met his train. And her reply then had struck him as equally vague. 'Oh, you know, it can be virtually anything, from music playing, and people dancing about and splashing you with water – stuff like that – to just wandering through a kind of exhibition. The point is to have a reaction. To be provoked – p'raps in ways you'd never expect. The Happening I went to in Sutton was a bit of a damp squib, really; nothing like they're supposed to be in the States. But this one at Better Books is the real thing – anyway, that's what Bill and Roz said.'

A group of her friends had already been. In fact, they'd asked her to join them, but immediately she'd seen how much more thrilling it would be to go with Laurie. (Doing things without Laurie always rendered them second best.) When her friends returned, hearing them talk about it (well, not so much talk as shriek and grab one another – they'd been careful not to give too much away), hearing all this had whetted her appetite. 'It'll be an *experience*, Laurie. We can't afford to miss it.'

Coming down on the train this morning, she'd felt almost ill with excitement. (She'd had the dream again – and as usual had woken up cursing; it had left her so nervily weary, she might have spent the entire night tramping the woods of Foscote, calling *Laurie, Laurie*.) She could feel her breakfast toast, rock solid at the top of her stomach. Some creature fluttered in her chest – a hawkmoth probably with long strong wings. Then the heat-haze lifted, and sunlight pouring into the carriage seemed to illumine her purpose. Suddenly she knew *why* she was passionately determined to get Laurie to this Happening. Imagine: he and she in the throes of reaction, clinging to each other perhaps, awestruck or moved: what was more likely to be provoked than his long reined in desire for her? The thought sent her molten, aching. She recalled how every time she set off for Cambridge she hoped this time would be the time – the time it happened. Never such luck – every visit planned and managed down to the very last detail. Nor did there seem much chance of it being achieved in Sutton – he was never sufficiently relaxed. And her recent hints about Zak being mad for her had crushingly failed to titillate. Which was all one big drag. Because – maybe it was the summer heat, but whatever the reason – wanting him was reaching such a pitch that it sometimes distracted her from work and kept her wakeful into the small hours.

Now, almost dragging him towards the Happening, she discovered another reason for staying resolute. Simply, for once she was calling the tune. She always fell in with him meekly, and he was always so full of plans. Today for a change he would do as she decreed. Though obviously not without a struggle. As he'd stepped from the train it was, 'You won't mind if we just pop into the Natural History Museum?' (endless delay there); and then, of course, 'If we don't eat soon I shall flake right out.' The afternoon had flown by, with shop windows to distract, and tempting theatre posters, and beckoning stills from the latest films – 'Gosh Claire, look what's showing here!' 'Laurie,' she'd said, 'we are going to Better Books – *now*!' His innocent agreement came smooth and quick as an eel: 'But of course we are, love.'

Halfway along Charing Cross Road, she discovered yet another motive. She was dishing out punishment. All along, deep in her heart, she'd known this visit would be torture for Laurie, who had a burning need to keep a tight control of situations (though he disguised this by fooling people into feeling not *checked* by him, but *led*). Yes, he was a devious sod. But she had taken his measure, and here was a chance to try him at his own game. 'Come on,' she cried boosily. And brooking no further nonsense, shoved him ahead of her into the Better Books store.

There was no queue inside at the small kiosk marked HAPPENING – as had been the case when her friends came. According to a newspaper clip she'd read, because no more than ten people were allowed through at a time, the line of people waiting often extended into the street. Four o'clock on a Saturday was a dead time, she learned from the man who took her money and handed over forms to be signed; the shop closed at five-thirty, which meant they would have little time afterwards to enjoy their free cup of coffee and browse through books. But this, thought Claire, was all to the good; she and Laurie would have the Happening mostly to themselves.

'What's this for?' Laurie asked, taking one of the forms.

'It's the shop's indemnity. You have to sign to say you agree to start at the beginning and follow directions to the end, and you won't sue them afterwards.' This last requirement increased the glamour of the situation in Claire's eyes, and the likely folly of it in Laurie's. 'Hurry up,' she said, jigging with impatience.

Against his better judgement he scrawled his name. The man took their bags and promised to return these with their coffee. Following an arrow as instructed, they went down some steps to a long bare room full of open-sided metal shelving. A voice they had heard faintly above in the shop, now loomed up close – that of an American male, droning monotonously. 'It's a tape of William Burroughs reading from *Naked Lunch*,' reported Claire (who had been told this by her friends). Trusting that the lugubrious voice was not in any way a scene setter, Laurie passed gingerly along the shelves inspecting open books on display. Claire glanced over the texts without properly reading anything; she was eager for more visual stimuli. But then some illustrations caught her eye – gosh, she thought, darting a look at Laurie to see what he made of them.

But he was merely sniffing the air and looking offended. 'Whatever's that frightful smell?'

'How should I know?' she snapped, worried in case he wasn't prepared to give this experience a fair try. Though actually there *was* rather a niff, which unfortunately seemed to be coming from the direction indicated by the next arrow.

They clambered down some more steps and reached a further room – on the threshold of which they hesitated, for they appeared to have stumbled on an intimate scene. Faintly, eerily, under wavy blue lighting stood four or five naked women. All had their backs turned, but were obviously beautiful, with sleek curves and long hair. Claire found it hard to resist her senses' report that these women were human and living – sounds of water dripping and soft breathing,

160

and the lighting's suggestion of movement, combined to give a strongly vibrant impression. But the women were giants and therefore wax models her brain over-ruled, and laughing to herself she went round the side of the group and slipped between them.

From this side the light glowed red. At first she was puzzled, then uncertain, then horror-struck. Laurie, whose sensitive nose had unerringly led him to the source of the reeking odour (a bedpan placed on a bathroom stool, whose contents he was busily identify-ing − raw fish roe, he told himself, probably cod's; gone off days ago) heard her sharp intake of breath. He hurried to her side. 'Oh-my-God-come-away,' he gabbled.

But Claire went on staring. Every woman was face-less, every woman had had her stomach ripped out. And what had appeared from the doorway to be tasteful drapes were now seen to be entrails hanging from meat hooks. Anger made her shake. What sort of bastard would conjure a scene like this?

'Come on!' Laurie insisted, tugging her to where the next arrow pointed. Sickened, sagging against him, she went towards the corridor.

Into which they stepped − once, twice − then jumped back: for the corridor's floor had a shocking give in it. But having signed the form promising to proceed as directed, there was nothing for it but to venture forward. Not only was the floor squashy, but the walls moved and bulged like windy distended stomachs. And as if this were not enough, they were suddenly aware of being watched by a youngish male, all in black with unnaturally blond hair, who was squatting at the far end of the corridor and squinting at them through glinting spectacles. It was very intimidating. Laurie's murmured 'Oh, dear Lord,' reminded her this was all her fault.

The squatting figure was probably just another wax-work, she was telling herself, when he confounded her by turning his head and nodding towards what she

161

now discerned to be a half-open door. Was she ever so glad to spot a means of evasion? (It meant they wouldn't have to actually pass the creature.) Almost lunging, she fell through the doorway, pulling Laurie after.

Was it relief or terror making them judder and cling to one another? Relief, they decided, looking around.

They were standing in a small carpeted sitting-room, snug as the setting of a 'forties Ovaltine advertisement – chubby settee, utility-style sideboard, matt-glazed china, a Clarice Cliff-type vase and a dish shaped like a lettuce leaf full of real tomatoes. Over the fireplace on the beige tiled mantelpiece stood family photographs. A wood and chrome radio rested on a side-table. All cosy and safe. A place where you'd be happy to curl up and relax.

'Phew,' sighed Claire, grinning and plopping down on the settee. She hoped Laurie would sit beside her. They could expel the terrors, laugh and grow mellow in each other's arms . . . Then, 'Wah!' she yelled, leaping to her feet. The settee was welling with water, wetness had seeped up her back and between her thighs. 'Oh, yuk. *Urrgh!*'

But Laurie ignored her predicament; he was transfixed by the contents of a sideboard drawer. She craned over his arm to see what gripped him. Inside, on a sheet of white lining paper, lay a single pink human finger. Her hand shot out and slammed the drawer shut. 'Everything,' Laurie was saying, like someone in the throes of a bad dream, 'everything . . .'

She started to examine things more closely. Sure enough, her senses had been again misled. All these lulling domestic signals were false, there was nothing here without hideous blemish – slugs in the tomatoes, nastiness portrayed in the seemingly happy family photographs, curdled vomit under the table, wires with spikes jutting from the back of the radio, even, she noticed, the floor sloped at a mad angle. Laurie's breathing was sounding wheezy. He was clutching his chest – don't say he was going to be ill! She wrapped her arms round him, 'Shhh,' she soothed, as he gasped in her ear that he had to get out of here – 'Sh, we're just going,' and watched over his shoulder in horrified fascination as the door slowly, firmly, closed. That horrid little man's doing, she supposed. She cast her eyes about the room: there had to be another way out.

By the side of the fireplace a curtain covered what appeared to be an alcove. Aware that if she hesitated for a second all would be lost, she strode across and yanked it back. Yes, thank heaven: here was the next arrow pointing the way, down yet another corridor. Just let it be the last!

There was something funny about this corridor, though, something she couldn't quite make out. 'Feathers!' groaned Laurie, and she saw that the floor, the walls, the ceiling were smothered in them. 'Well that settles it. I simply, positively, couldn't,' he choked. She, however, was determined: they were not going to disobey the rules and run back demanding to be let out, to the derision of watching customers. (And in any case, she doubted whether she could stand another glimpse of those carcass women.) At her first two exploratory steps, feathers rose and fell, emitting dirty warmth. Behind her, Laurie was still jabbering that he couldn't, that she must come back at once and would she please pay attention. He reached out, grabbed her skirt, yanked her backwards. Her protest died as she was distracted by a stealthy movement at the far end of the corridor. A door was opening on lighted space – revealing heaped up car tyres. Hurray! she cheered silently, remembering that Roz had mentioned crawling through tyres to reach a loft ladder which gave into the shop. 'It's all right; that's the end up there,' she promised.

But Laurie was adamant – 'Not feathers. Couldn't.' He retreated further into the deceitful sitting-room.

That light at the end, she thought: it was glinting on

something – and the unwelcome realization hit her that it was the glass in the blond man's specs. So somehow he had moved up there. And this time they would have to pass him – a prospect far more inhibiting to Claire than stepping through feathers. A drumming started up in her ears. Laurie was now worse than useless; he was a liability.

She closed down her mind and reached for him – seized his hand and *ran*, hauled him through the feathers and dust, past the lurking blond fellow, into the tyre-strewn room at the end. A split second of terror, and she'd done it! Got them to safety! Giddy with triumph, taking stock of their new surroundings, she was nudged by *déjà vu*: had done this before, seized and made off with him, effected a rescue . . .

'Hey, where're you going?' she barked. For he was leaving her, he was scrambling through the tyres, already had his hands to the ladder and was on the brink of climbing into the safe square of light in the ceiling. (From where his acute hearing had detected the chink of cups, a murmur of voices, even the ping of a shop doorbell). 'Wait, you bastard!' He was leaving her behind with that sinister man – who, now she came to think of it, might not even be part of this Happening but some crazed spying pervert. She thrust furiously after him, stretching for his ankle. There was no holding him back, but somehow, clutching his working limb, she too gained the ladder, hauled through the opening, and flopped like a landed fish on the floor of Better Books' coffee shop.

Raising her head, Claire saw there were several people sitting at tables with long-emptied cups, pretending not to stare, but in fact drinking in their discomfort. This was the enjoyable part of the deal, she suddenly grasped; having yourself been through the ordeal, what could be nicer than to sit casually observing the sweaty white-faced terror of those newly emerging? With proud defiance, she scrambled to her feet and went to a table.

'Our bags, please,' Laurie demanded of an assistant – who went behind a counter, then brought them out. 'Thank you. Come on, Claire.'

Every eye in the house was watching. 'But we haven't had our coffee. It's free,' she reminded him.

Laurie held open the door. 'Would you really allow anything they served in here past your lips?' he asked witheringly, and started briskly down the street. 'Think of the filth. Think of the germs. Personally, my requirements will only be served by hot running water, soap, clean towels, and an irreproachable WC.'

She hurried to keep up with him. Was he cross? Cheek if he was; what he ought to be feeling was mortified – leaving her behind like that . . . 'Where're we going, Laurie?'

'I'm not exactly sure, but the moment it appears I'll recognize it.'

Crossing the busy road, taking sudden dives into side-streets, striding along pavements, dodging round loiterers, swerving to miss oncomers – where the dickens was he taking her? At last he paused and looked thoughtfully into a hotel's wide open foyer where a man in livery stood chatting to someone. 'This could be it,' he said, and ran up the steps.

'Laurie, we can't . . .' But he was already inside speaking to the attendant. By the time Claire arrived, Laurie was receiving directions. 'Over there, sir, on your right. And to the left for the, er, lady.'

Laurie went ahead; after a brief hesitation, she followed suit.

The Ladies' was quiet, perfumed, flower-filled. She decided to make good use. Her skirt was still damp from the sopping settee; she hoiked a handful of it up to her nose and sniffed to discover whether it smelled bad. Not, she concluded, unless you got up close. And lavish use of this jasmine-scented soap would doubtless act as a countering agent. While she was larding and rinsing herself in as many places as she decently could, two smartly dressed women came in; and a little later two unsmart American tourists. Content that she would never have to face any of them again – directly or in mirror image – she continued to conduct a thorough toilet.

There was no Laurie waiting in the foyer, despite her spending at least ten minutes in the Ladies'. Keeping her eyes pinned to the door of the Gents', she positioned herself behind a giant plant pot so as not to attract notice.

At last he came breezing out. 'Spotless,' he proclaimed happily. 'Now for a wholesome afternoon tea.' This last he delivered loudly enough to attract the attendant, who came over and led towards a vast dining-room. 'Hey,' she hissed, scrambling after him. 'I hope you've got plenty of dosh, 'cos I haven't.'

'Of course,' he said – in that smooth murmur which meant you never could tell if he was speaking the truth.

'It'll cost a fortune,' she warned.

'And sure to be worth every penny. Thank you,' – this to the waiter who had shown them to a table near the window. Without consulting her, he ordered a pot of Assam. 'A robust tea,' he explained; 'I think we could do with it.' Having taken their order, the waiter was now clicking his fingers at a waitress in charge of a gilded trolley. She smiled and came wheeling over the carpet with her high-piled goodies. 'Now this,' said Laurie, 'is what I call a Happening.'

Of course, he was showing off to try and recapture lost face, Claire thought darkly as he, with a flourish, poured out their tea. But as the meal progressed, she began to suspect that he did not recall any face loss, nor that it was *her* courage, *her* decisiveness that had finally saved them. Happenings were supposed to tell you things you didn't know about yourself – and presumably about others sharing the experience. Well, this one certainly had. She now perceived that for all his bossiness and controlling bustle, in some aspects she was the stronger. A weird feeling grew in her, a presentiment that it would fall to her to rescue him again. And again and again.

'Delicious sandwiches.'

'Yeah,' she said, 'great.'

She was savouring a particularly jammy slice of sponge cake, when the feeling of *déjà vu* returned, slipping her instantly back in time. She was eating cake in another setting. Where? Why, here of course, in their hide-away hayloft at Foscote: just a few minutes ago she'd rescued Laurie from a vengeful Uncle Peter. She took a sip of tea, and the present was immediately restored. Nevertheless, a strong sense of earlier times remained, of when she was the odd little awkward one who couldn't do music, and Laurie the talented one who was anxious to stand up for her. He, she now saw, was always more bothered about people's opinion of her than she was herself; was more vulnerable than she on her behalf. In fact, he was altogether more vulnerable, she thought, covertly watching him behind her cup – his strongly boned hands, the mass of curly black hair, the long nose almost quivering and the dark eyes shining as he studied the room with frank enjoyment. Suddenly, she was so moved her heart seemed to pause; and the lurch of it hurrying to regain its stroke made her dash down her cup.

At which his pleased smile was directed across the table.

Giddy with love, she grinned back.

xvii

The summer heat continued.

Sticky-bodied despite the flimsiness of an Indian cotton shift, she stepped out of the bright dead afternoon into the breathable cool of the Cypriot grocer's (the only place in town, according to student lore, certain to be open at 2 p.m. on a Sunday). Not yet visually adjusted, she merely registered someone turning from the counter and their mutual tread towards one another, then looming bulk. But her ears identified him at once.

'Claire! Hi!'

'Hello, Zak,' she said.

'I didn't know you lived in this neighbourhood.'

'I don't. I ran out of food.'

'Uhuh? Great little shop they got here. They even got yams. You ever had yams?'

'Not knowingly.'

'You should. Say, how'd you like to try the way I cook 'em? You dig spicy food?'

'I can't say I've had much of it.'

'Well, c'mon! I'm right in the mood to do some really great cooking. My place is only a couple blocks. Save your money. We can have a nice afternoon.'

She paused rather than hesitated. It was too hot to shove her brain into action, too hot to muster resistance, too hot even to decide whether she *would* muster resistance if it weren't so enervatingly hot. 'Might as well I suppose.'

Zak's place extended over the top floor of a three-storey Edwardian semi. Perhaps he was here on a generous scholarship or funded by some rich American institution; or maybe dollars went further than pounds. Though considerably more spacious than the average student abode, it contained nevertheless the same beat-up furnishings, worn carpets, shoddy fittings – and the same familiar grime.

From the fridge he took two bottles of beer, pulled the caps off, handed her one. She looked round for a glass, but when Zak put his bottle to his lips and tipped back his head, she followed suit and gulped the cold tart fizz gratefully.

Then Zak set to – emptied carrier bags, rinsed things under the tap, chopped, scraped, all the time talking to her pleasantly. She was pleased by his improved attitude: evidently the way she had put him down a couple of weeks ago over the way he spoke about

Laurie had earned his respect. However, she remained cautious. When he asked personal questions, gave short noncommittal replies and soon retaliated with her own queries. She kicked off her sandals and padded barefoot about the living-room examining his books and records, then drifted back to watch him cook, lolling against the door-frame between living-room and kitchenette. Windows open everywhere made little difference to the stifling heat and failed to deflect smoke rising astringently from a frying pan. 'It has to be *hot*', he said, scattering in spices, 'to bring out the flavours and seal in the juices.' A further blast came as vegetables hit the pan. It made her gasp, but soon, breathing the pungent fumes, her appetite stirred. He seemed to sense this. 'Hungry?' he asked, peering at her through the smother.

'Mm. I am quite.'

'Won't be long. Grab a couple of those plates out of there.'

She bent to the cupboard he indicated and withdrew two plates. They were smeary; the pads of her thumbs met gritty dried-on specks. He ladled out the food, picked up the piled and steaming plates, turned towards her, and paused fractionally – his eyes dropping from her face and flicking over her body. Thoughts of food and hunger were at once dashed. It was only the briefest appraisal, the next second he was passing her and making for the table; but her nerves had leapt, she followed him warily.

Of course, she had known from the first where this meal was leading – or where he *imagined* it was leading. After weeks of hopeless pursuit, he assumed he was about to score. Well, he had another thing coming. She put a forkful of food into her mouth – then quickly grabbed a swallow of beer to ward off a coughing fit.

'OK? Not too strong for you? I went easy on the chilli.'

'Er, no, 's fine.' But her appetite could not be

rekindled; it was not the food's taste putting her off, it was the thought of what he had in mind for dessert. And the heat, of course. How mad of Zak to serve up stuff like this on such a torrid day. Though come to think of it, these were precisely the weather conditions in which this sort of food was usually eaten – perhaps with the idea of making you so seethe inside that your exterior felt comparatively cool.

'If you don't like it, don't eat it.'

'No, no, I *like* it all right. It's just . . . this heat, you know, it sort of saps your appetite.'

'Uhuh?' Chewing slowly, he seemed to be contemplating whether the heat had sapped *all* her appetites. Good God! Her mind lurched from the thought. She made to shift on her chair – and found she couldn't; her thighs, the damp muslin dress, the chair's sticky plastic, were thoroughly bonded.

'Like another beer?'

'Yes, please.'

While he was away from the table she took the opportunity to unglue herself, and on reaching her feet decided to visit the bathroom.

She returned feeling more composed; even managed to eat more of the quite pleasant food; praised it, and checked her remembrance of how it was cooked. He found a great deal to say on this and about other dishes in his repertoire. In fact, he so warmed to this topic that her faith was shaken in her assumption of his amorous intentions. Doubt stole over with a surprising chill. Was she fated always at the last minute to turn men off? Was she like one of those disappointing apples, round and firm and shiny on the outside and only when actually bitten into, found to be brown and mushy near the core? Perhaps it was this, and not scruples over the affair between their parents, that put Laurie off. And now here was Zak apparently going the same way – because, clearly, the only thing now on his mind was food and its preparation.

Miffed, bored, she shoved away her plate.

He looked at it.

'It was delicious,' she said defensively, 'but I'm bloated.'

'Too much beer. The gas fills you up. Want coffee now or later?'

'Oh, later.'

'Well then,' he paused, 'how 'bout a smoke?'

'Er, no,' she said nervously.

He grinned. 'It'd make you relax.'

'Thanks, but I don't need stuff to make me relax.' She detached each thigh from the chair in turn and casually rose – aiming to do this as languidly as possible – and glanced around: the greasy looking sofa did not appeal – where else to park herself?

'Wanna come here?' he asked diffidently, turning sideways on his chair, spreading his knees, raising his hands.

She squinted across sharply, and detected no hint of him seriously wanting her to comply. The bastard was mocking her! Right. With a challenging expression, she strode right up to him and inserted her body between his thighs.

'Hey, well! I guess I didn't really expect you to take me up on it,' he admitted, looking reasonably pleased none the less and resting his hands on her hips.

'No?' she asked, and deliberately arched forward, pressing as close as she could get, thighs into his crotch, stomach into his waist. Seizing his head, she jammed his great peasant face hard against her breasts. His cry came out muffled – 'OK! I get the message.' Her hands fell to his arms and gripped tenaciously; pulling and hauling him, she stepped backwards, sank to the floor.

'Jeeze,' he said, sprawling over her as she splayed her legs.

So he *did* want her, she gloried, tuning in avidly to all those signals which now – noisily, hotly, bulgingly, wetly – vindicated her earlier assessment. But as his hand moved high between her legs, insidiously her focus shifted, until, like stepping over a threshold and discovering new and brilliant territory, his wants were nowhere, and she was all self. 'Huh!' she squawked querulously when his hand paused. So he continued diligently – she grimly clasping him, holding him to the task. Finally, after a great flooding inside her, she subsided; lay still, gently pulsing. At peace.

'Well, thank you ma'am,' he said with heavy irony. But the allusion was lost on her. In fact it was doubtful whether she heard him. 'OK,' he said briskly, 'my turn.' And heaved up, and went away.

My turn drifted to her brain about thirty seconds later; its meaning thirty seconds after that. Christ, his turn, she panicked, as he returned, plastic applied, and quickly straddled her.

She kept her eyes tight shut, her nose averted from his matted chest, while her innards, it seemed, were knocked repeatedly into her throat. It was ended mercifully quickly and with a volley of curses. 'Aw – shit – goddammit!' Then he rolled off her and continued to pant out disgruntlement – 'Phew – nah – shit.'

His annoyance was a mystery, but she spent no time worrying about it. Sweat was congealing on her stomach and breasts, her thighs were itching. Disengaging from his heavy arm, she stooped to collect pants and sandals, and ran into the bathroom; there, so thoroughly sluiced herself that a few minutes later when she opened the door and peered out – hair on end, dress clinging – she might have been emerging from total baptism.

He was still lying on the floor but had placed his underpants over his privates. He looked pretty silly, she thought, going softly to the door which gave on to the landing.

'Hey!' he called, just before she closed it. She had reached the turn in the stairs when he came stumbling out after her. 'Where you goin'? Wait!'

Turning, she peered upwards. He was hanging on to

the banister rail with one hand, holding the pants in place with the other.

'So it was a lousy fuck,' he hissed. 'Isn't it always first try? C'mon, we got all day, we can get it together.'

She shook her head. 'I must have been mad – maybe the heat addled my brain – because I knew all along you were an utter creep.'

'You what?'

She started down the next flight, but after a few steps turned and looked back. 'And don't come pestering me,' she warned, 'or you'll end up sorry.'

'Hell, I'm already sorry,' he yelled – but her sandals thumping to the ground floor scuppered his riposte.

Along drab main thoroughfares and banal side streets she scurried, taking note of the traffic and occasional pedestrians, advertisements pasted on walls, hunched cats lurking, a purposefully trotting dog with lolling tongue and wicked eye, tiny gardens kempt and unkempt, varying curtain styles, endeavouring by such means to keep ahead of the uncomfortable thoughts which were bent on pursuing her. And which now and then caught up: *How could you? Why did you? Tart! Slut!* Their vehemence seemed to ruffle the dusty privet she was passing. Replies such as, *Because I had to*, or, *I was probably drunk*, were strangled at birth. Blanking her mind, she adhered ever more firmly to her visual litany: lamppost, gate, dog dirt, lotterbox . . . But soon, as she paused to cross a road, *How could you?* caught up again – this time with a force that moved her lips. Two women crossing in the opposite direction, curiously turned their heads.

She shot round a corner. 'Hello, darling,' came cheerily from soiled overalls half obliterated by a raised car bonnet. Jumping nervily, she sped wordlessly by. The cheery chap's appreciation of her made her remember Zak. God he was ugly, and not just of countenance but also of tongue. Remember his words to her down the stairwell? – *lousy fuck* and *isn't it always*? They made her ears burn even in retrospect, and certainly spoke volumes about his habits and attitudes. Be that as it may, argued her mind's awkward squad: however bad Zak, she was far worse. Because – let's not equivocate – she had made use of him; she'd had what she'd wanted and then made off, snarling abusive parting shots into the bargain. *So what?* she silently screamed back. Zak could stand it. Might do him good. Anyway, men were constantly using women – she knew this from sitting with so many of them at coffee break (men far outnumbered women in the science faculties) and listening in on their callous boasting.

Wilting, she was glad to reach Burnett Street. Her wearied legs had slowed considerably, but then so had her mind. A dull leadenness settled over. Feeling terminally dispirited, she opened the door and stepped into the hallway.

The house was steeped in cooking smells. Gales of laughter rang out in the shared front sitting-room.

'It's Claire. Hi, Claire – come in here.'

'Shh. Quick. Close the door. Guess what?'

'Oh, she'll never guess . . .'

Pattie, sprawled on the settee, Lai Sim on the floor with her legs tucked under her, laughed and interrupted one another and confided their tale – how they had inveigled the Kenyan boys to cook them a meal and afterwards to come with them to the cinema.

Claire sat on a chair arm. 'How on earth did you manage that?' For Sadru and Krishna were shy in the extreme, treating their female co-residents with inscrutable caution and sometimes as the subjects of a private joke. Sadru, thin almost to the point of emaciation, bespectacled, nervy, played the violin with plangent sweetness. Krishna, taller and stronger looking, had hooded eyes and a sardonic expression and floppy hair like black silk. The most the girls had ever got out of them was that they heartily despised

The Law – the degree course stipulated for them by their rich merchant fathers.

Claire listened to her friends with only half attention. She was struck by their openly gleeful faces, their soft-limbed gestures, the innocent way they disported themselves. Beside them, she was a hardened crone. Her gamine appearance was fraudulent. If they were to observe more closely they would discern lewdness marking her. She half turned from them as if conscious of pressing business. 'I'm just amazed they've agreed to go with you to the pictures. What's on?'

'*Summer and Smoke* with Geraldine Page and Laurence Harvey.'

'Oh, yeah – Tennessee Williams.'

'I think', Lai Sim said, 'we should bring the table in here. Make it look pretty.'

'Hey, that's an idea. We could put a sheet over for a cloth.'

'I could lend you my scented candle for the centre.'

'Thanks, Claire. That'd be lovely.'

'She could eat with us too, couldn't she, Pattie?'

'Oh – no – really. I've already eaten as a matter of fact. I bumped into a friend . . .'

'Come with us to the flicks afterwards, then,' Pattie invited.

'I wouldn't dream of it, honestly. But I'm looking forward to hearing how the evening turns out. I'll go and fetch that candle.'

The front door slammed at eight o'clock. For Claire, looking up from her desk, it was a bad moment knowing she was alone in the house. (Eileen, the sixth tenant of number 37, was away with her boyfriend.) The noisy meal downstairs and later people charging about visiting bathrooms and bedrooms, had held her from the consequences of what by now was an explosive weight of emotion. The door slamming sent a brief shudder through the house, then silence rushed over. She sat perfectly still, holding back; willing herself to

175

hold back. Then her breath shot out and tears rolled, and she left her chair and groped for the bed, climbed on top, lay down. Gave herself up.

If only, she blurted incoherently between spasms. *If only* . . . But got no further. When her tears were spent, she was not only exhausted but crushed by a sense of let down. Crying, she had seemed to be shedding some hindrance, pushing on to the crux of her grief. Dry-eyed, stiffly silent on a clammy pillow and rucked-up bedspread, *if only* was an empty echo.

Suddenly she sat up, as the phrase nudged forward. If only . . . she could . . . talk to . . . be soothed . . . reassured. *Go home!* she thought eagerly; and was then bewildered. Not to Foscote, that was for sure. Nothing for her there – at least, only an increasingly scatty and self-absorbed Aunt Margaret. Then she got it. *If only she could have a little time with Laurie.* Five minutes would do it. Just the sound of his voice . . .

The King's Head was hot and stuffy. Nodding to the applause, Laurie stepped between the tables and over the legs of skimpily-clad drinkers, and peered towards the bar where Jessica had the half-time drinks lined up – pints of beer for his colleagues in the band and his own orange juice. (Laurie rarely drank alcohol, and never beer; he did not smoke or snort anything or pop unprescribed pills. 'Certainly not,' he would snap if urged to share a friendly joint – which his friends – who mostly did – thought typically quaint of him. Privately he would concede that fear of lowering his guard via drugs of any kind sat strangely with his calculated carelessness in other matters. Often in his life he had taken decisions recklessly, as though prompted by personal disregard – take, for instance, his manner of joining the Army. He justified the conundrum to himself on these lines: to be reckless was fine so long as it was of his own volition; what he utterly shrank from was falling prey through loss of control to someone else's recklessness. He also dreaded this fate for Claire. He'd noticed that she often accepted cigarettes from people. Sometimes, unable to help himself, he would drift over to her and like an anxious parent signal *I see what you're up to* with a reproving smile, trying to disguise a greater anxiety that perhaps she accepted other things as well. She would jerk away from him – reading his mind, he supposed, and quite justly irritated.)

'Good girl!' cried Toby, grabbing his pint. But for once, Jessica ignored him. She tugged Laurie's arm. 'Claire phoned. I told her you were in the middle of a number and to call back about half past. So any time now . . .' She looked towards the phone at the end of the bar, then to the barman – 'I told Barry there'd be a call.'

Disorientated, with half a dozen questions clamouring in his brain, Laurie could only reach for his glass. He took a long slurp, and answered some of them himself – Claire knew where to find him because the band had a regular booking at The King's Head on Sundays; Jessica, calculating that it would be unprofessional to interrupt the band, had sensibly suggested a more appropriate time to call. But the most urgent questions remained unanswered. 'Did she say what she wanted? She's never done this before – something must be the matter. Did you ask her? How did she sound?'

'She said nothing was wrong, she just wanted a word. Honestly, Laurie, she sounded fine.'

'Thanks, Jessica,' he smiled, with false calm.

Something had to be the matter. He manoeuvred to sit on a stool as near as possible to the telephone.

When it rang, the barman took his time answering. Then, 'Hello, me old sport!' he cried, turning his back on the watching Laurie. 'Long time no hear! How's the world using you?' Tucking the receiver under his chin so that his hands were free to continue their glass polishing, he settled down for a chat. 'You don't say – cor, I like it!' Laurie tried to concentrate on other matters, but his head boomed with every inane comment; fatalistically he sensed there was no limit to what Barry and his old sport would find to say to each other.

But at last the call was concluded. Minutes went by; it looked as if Claire would not ring back. He began to panic, wondering what prevented her. Jessica, the silly cow, ought to have dragged him from the piano stool; she should have known it would take an emergency to make Claire phone. His eyes moved down the bar to where Jessica stood. He began to dislike her, to notice in her a certain smugness. Come to think of it, she attended every one of the band's sessions without fail, yet was no fan of jazz, for she sat placidly reading a novel while the band played, keeping an eye on the time so as to be sure and have drinks in place for the interval and coats to hand for swift exits. She came, he suddenly understood, to keep an eye on Toby. She was like a superior nanny, indulgently permitting him fun with his friends while her weather eye ensured he was not led astray.

From along the bar, Jessica caught his eye and raised her brows in a message of sympathy. Immediately he was ashamed of his assessment. Jessica was a good pal, a well-intentioned friend. Simply, with worry knotting his innards, he now wished she had interrupted the performance.

Then the phone rang again. This time, Barry held out the receiver.

'Claire?'

'Laurie, I'm so *sorry*. Soon as I got home I realized what a stupid idiot I'd been. So I thought I wouldn't bother you again – till I suddenly thought that not ringing back might make you even more worried.'

'Love, whatever is it?'

'Nothing. Well – nothing much.'

'Something's happened. I can tell it has,' he said authoritatively, 'so you'd better say.'

A pause. Then, 'Do you remember Zak?'

178

'Large chap with long hair?' Laurie enquired – calmly enough, though he was thinking, *Don't say, oh no, not that bloody great hunk of a fellow.*

'Well, I bumped into him today. He asked me back for a meal. So I, er, went.'

'Yes?' he gently prodded, as his flesh turned clammy.

'Oh Laurie, oh Christ . . .'

'He didn't rape you?' he blurted in a harsh whisper, jerking his head to one side.

'No,' she yelled. Then repeated 'No,' quietly, firmly. 'If anything it was *me*; I wanted . . . But that's it; I mean, it happened. Afterwards I felt horrible – spiteful, angry, and so *lonely*. I got this longing to see you, or just talk . . .'

But he was only half listening. That bloody great brute, he kept telling himself. And Claire so little, no more than a sprite. 'Are you sure you're all right?' he cut in. 'He was, you know, careful?'

'Uh? Oh, yeah.'

'You're not still with him?'

'No, no. I walked out.'

'And he won't be able to find you? He doesn't know your address?'

'Believe me, he wouldn't *want* to. But it's not that, Laurie. It's just that I came over miserable. You know – really, really blue.'

'I'm coming over.'

'What?'

'They can manage the next half without me. And I've got nothing on tomorrow that can't be postponed. Promise me to go straight back home?'

'Yeah, but . . .'

'Put your key in a mug and hide it in the hedge bottom by the side of the house. Then make some cocoa and go to bed.'

'But Laurie, I didn't mean . . . Look, you *mustn't*.'

'I'm on my way.'

*   *   *

If Laurie was really coming, she had better clean up. He was terribly particular about clean china and no grot in the bathroom. It rather narked her the way he squinted into her mugs for tell-tale coffee rings, scrutinized the tines of her forks, demanded fresh tea towels. ('My dear girl! What have you been wiping with this? No, don't tell me; just hand me a clean one.')

She got out the hoover (spread more muck than she got up, probably, but why should she be the one to empty it?), waved a duster over things, rubbed at stains, hid her dirty clothes, scoured her china. She then bathed and washed her hair and collapsed exhausted on top of her bed. Her mind – or part of it – drifted back to the events of the afternoon; another more wary part tried to embargo these musings in case of further depression.

The split in her mind seemed to be part of a cleft reaching right down inside – she recalled her simultaneous wariness and longing, her reactions of elation and almost immediate disgust: maybe she was schizophrenic? – she'd wanted Zak to desire her, had revelled in what he dished out; and had then turned round and called him a creep. Was he really so bad? If she'd hung around, who knows? – maybe he'd have been proved right about it working out better next time . . . Hang on. She loathed the man. That was the reason she'd yelled abuse: she'd been scotching any possibility of a next time, making sure that even if *she* got the urge again, *he* wouldn't come near her. Heavens, what a scary idea – it must mean she was a bit of a tramp. Because here she was admitting that she couldn't trust herself not to go with someone she didn't even like. She was that desperate! Whatever would nice people think if they knew? – the girls she shared the house with, Roz in her study group, her old school chum Daisy, people who thought well of her like her tutor and Aunt Margaret. And the awful knowledge dropped with a thud into her brain that the most important person of all, Laurie, *did* know. In her misery she'd gone and blurted it. Well, serve him right, she told herself defiantly; it was his fault things were so muddled between them: why couldn't they be straightforward like they were for Jessica and Toby, for Eileen and her boyfriend, for Daisy and Phil? Because of something to do with Foscote, she answered herself – their growing up there together, that business with Maman and Uncle Peter. It weighed her down thinking about it (because history couldn't be undone). Numbed, paralysed, she lay on her bed; if the house were to burst into flames she would be unable to lift a finger.

But at that moment the front door shuddered open and soon afterwards slammed – Lai Sim, Pattie and the Kenyans had come home. Someone – Lai Sim, probably – came running upstairs to her door and softly called her name. Normally Claire would leap at the chance to go downstairs and toy with a mug of something as an excuse to hear the news. But not tonight. She lay on her back in the semi-darkness with her ears burning – not as a result of imagining they were talking about her, but because the distant burble of sound made her feel soiled and alien. The noise indicated, however, a successful evening, and this thought pleased and gradually soothed her. For as long as the sounds continued, it felt like she had company. She relaxed; once or twice dozed right off.

It was when the house lapsed into silence, that she came wide awake.

A picture of Laurie driving his car began to haunt her. After a time, though fully alert, her mind strayed into dreaming. Laurie's car ran into obstacles – a fallen tree, an oncoming drunken driver, a wall rushing up as, white-faced, he grappled with the steering wheel. At first she was able to resist the worst outcomes, but as time wore on, her mind grew less biddable. She lay in the grip of panic, staring with hot sore eyes, crying, it seemed, from dried-out tear ducts.

With sudden effort, she flung off the bed and went

181

to the bathroom; returned, put on her lamp and tried to read. Her eyes had difficulty focussing; when they managed to, her brain failed to derive sense. After a time, she gave up, put off the light and lay watching patches of half-light drift over the ceiling.

She had done it again, she thought: made more trouble for Laurie. Last week she'd dragged him through that Happening at Better Books. He hadn't wanted to go, and in the event had been distressed. Now, as a result of her self-indulgent and hysterical phone call, he was driving dog-tired through the night. She was utterly contemptible and beyond the pale. If he did crash – oh God, if he died! – she'd damn well kill herself. Because she wouldn't deserve to live. And in any case, wouldn't want to.

Laurie, on the A421 driving towards Oxford, had found his thoughts going round in circles. Many times he dismissed them – whistled a tune, ran an Ellington track through his head, rehearsed the main points of a piece of work he was engaged on – but his feelings – shock, anger, repugnance, guilt, sorrow, alarm – refused to die down, and like irrepressible sparking plugs charged the same circular thought-process over and over.

He couldn't get over it. Claire – with Zak! Not Claire with anybody, he virtuously persuaded himself, for hadn't he often fantasized about becoming a brother to Claire's eventual husband, a favourite uncle to her future children? Changing gear to take a bend, he suddenly recognized this for the self-serving tosh it undoubtedly was: give her lover a face and he was jumping with jealousy – like a kid seeing some other kid handle a favourite toy and terrified he'd make off with it. That the face in question was ugly was some small consolation (Claire was very looks-conscious): Zak could only be a fleeting partner. Fortunately, he comforted himself, it was he, Laurie, whom Claire had her sights on . . .

'Pheew!' he whistled, shocked to catch himself out in such duplicitous thinking. He touched the brake, slowed down, and reflected guiltily on how his manner must encourage her. Had he been fooling himself, did he do this deliberately in order to hang on to her? Or did he simply behave with her as he felt inclined and close his eyes to the consequences? Either way he was a bastard. The poor girl could hardly help being confused. And he'd been doing it to her for years. Once he'd actually . . . For the first time since the summer when it happened, he forced himself to recall making experimental love to her.

But soon found he couldn't go on with it. The memories ran into others (of his father and Aunt Sabine). Raking up that far-off time was like lifting the lid of a dusty trunk, confronting the broken contents and having emotions stirred which he couldn't fathom and couldn't endure – like reliving in dreams, he supposed, an intense foetal experience.

He pressed the accelerator. Only three miles to Oxford it said on a road sign. And here he was, negotiating roundabouts, traffic lights, checking for familiar landmarks; following, as usual, the signs to Newbury . . .

So how did he come to be here, on the A423 heading for Wallingford? Damn and blast, he cursed, swinging full circle at the next roundabout. He drove furiously back in the direction of Oxford. Left at the *next* intersection, blockhead, he berated himself. For Pete's sake *concentrate.*

Safely back on the A34, he relaxed – and evidently let down his guard, for without warning a spontaneous rage sprang alight, and he was back on the same old thought circuit. But now his anger was directed at Claire. What had she said over the phone? – 'If anything it was *me* . . .' Christ, she'd done it deliberately! A picture of her inviting desecration was momentarily more vivid than his view of the road – she lying stretched out (as on that night in the boxroom after her father's funeral), arms reaching, dark eyes imploring, moist mouth gaping . . . He almost hated her, the reckless little bitch, going out of her way to spoil and shatter his . . . Yes, dammit, *his*, he yelled silently in waning defiance, knowing he was being ridiculous.

Because Claire was her own person. Just very important to him, he conceded more calmly. She always had been. All those hours he'd spent at Foscote conforming to other people's expectations, labouring to please, had only been relieved by the thought of Claire waiting for him – fleet of foot, agile, courageous: everything he longed to be but was not. She was self-contained, unimpressed by Foscote's poor opinion of her. He'd revered and adored her, the funny obstinate little scrap. He still did. Was it then so terrible to fear an irrevocable change?

Of course it is; it's *sick*, you blithering idiot, a voice snapped in his head.

Now here came Newbury. He willed himself to be super alert and not to go wrong as he had round Oxford. When signs confirmed that he was indeed heading for Sutton, he put his foot down. No more going round in circles, he told himself; just keep pushing on due south. But then, as he whizzed by a telephone box in a village street, back she came – clear as a picture in the telephone box in Burnett Street, squinting furiously as she made her awkward apologies, winding hair round a finger as she confessed about Zak. Brave and honest. If only he could be similarly frank. Sometimes he'd imagined making a clean breast to her, but always shied from the idea, terrified of what he might read on her face. Perhaps this was the moment to summon his courage and follow her example. *But it isn't the same*, squawked a frightened voice in his head; and his throat tightened and his hand shoved nervously at the indicator lever instead of the dipper switch.

No, he couldn't take the risk. Because he might as well admit it: he wanted the best for her, would make endless sacrifices, go to any lengths on her behalf, but for selfish motives. He needed to know that he could always turn to her; that in some form or other she could always be reached and would always be there. But, he supposed, that was how it was with love: selflessness and selfishness inextricably combined.

They lay side by side on her bed on the Indian bedspread. Outside, it was becoming light. When a milk float rattled by, she tossed restlessly. 'God, I haven't been to sleep yet.'

'Me neither,' he said faintly.

'Oh? Why?' She was suspicious in case he'd been kept awake after their long talk by bad thoughts about her. Perhaps the bad thoughts she'd had about herself earlier had been so intense they'd seeped into the bedclothes and now rose like sour mist to invade his mind.

'Because I'm still driving the blasted car.' Maybe he'd drifted off once or twice, but awake or asleep he couldn't prevent a fast flowing road running before his eyes.

'You know, I can't get over that you'd do this for me – drive all that way, just because I was miserable.'

'Don't be silly. You'd do it for me.'

'Yeah. Of course.'

'Well then.' After a while he asked, 'Remember that night we spent in the hayloft? My father had given me a thrashing. You'd come charging into the study and pulled me out . . .'

'Of course.' She remembered how they'd lain side by side, much as they were now. 'Mm. It was pitch black. Warm.'

'We had a carpet. I kept pushing my fingers through the holes.'

'There were mice rustling.'

'And it smelled good – oaty.'

'Yeah.'

'Pretend we're there now. It'll make you drowsy, help you drop off.'

'Mm. All right.'

xviii

1963 was the year Claire and Laurie graduated. It was also the year when Jeanette was married from Foscote. The wedding would see the final gathering there of the entire family.

The bridegroom, Richard Merton, was a violinist several years Jeanette's senior. During her time at Trinity College in London she had sampled the attractions of several men, and of more than a few during successive festivals at home. Then to everyone's surprise she suddenly committed herself, became engaged and married within the space of a single summer.

'She has plumped for Richard,' Laurie said in Claire's ear (making her snigger) as they lined up in the vestry after the register signing, and Jeanette, all dewy pink flesh and frothy cream lace, seized her bridegroom's arm in readiness to face their guests – among whom in the pews were several candidates she had considered and *not* plumped for.

Claire, as bridesmaid elect, had dreaded this day – dreaded the frock (which in the end proved not too terrible, silvery blue lawn having prevailed over peach satin), dreaded so many appraising eyes, dreaded parading as a united and quite wonderful family. For of course, as soon as the couple announced their intention, Peter Stone had immediately begun to devise the ceremony. This probably accounted for Laurie finding himself in the role of best man – though Richard did appear to lack suitable relatives. Laurie had risen to the occasion with a better grace than Claire with her constant grumbling. 'Don't be such a pain, darling,' he complained to her. 'It's all going to be lovely, simply wonderful.'

She'd glowered at him. 'God, I do believe you're actually looking forward to it.'

'But I am, I am,' he cried, and to prove it, shivered with anticipation.

She gave up wondering whether he were serious. To know him so well, yet never *quite*, she mused.

Back at Foscote for the wedding feast, some irresistible force overcame her. After the simple ceremony in the village church, the courtyard at Foscote was a riot of sound and colour. Bunting flapped overhead, flowering plants blazed in pots and twined over specially erected wooden trellises. Sumptuous food was set out on snowy linen on long tables. On a platform under an awning, musicians played light-hearted works by Vivaldi, Albinoni, Geminiani. Claire was suddenly awash with love. She loved Laurie (so much!); loved rosy blooming Jeanette (who had caught hands with her a moment ago and swung her round and round in cross-armed country dance fashion, and was now flirting and flashing her perfect teeth at a cluster of erstwhile suitors); loved stodgy Richard (standing with his feet apart, grinning and blinking at his wife as if he could scarcely believe his luck); loved very much indeed Aunt Margaret (eccentric and arty looking today in a purple silk caftan and with her forehead bandaged in matching chiffon); loved dear old Foscote and all these good-hearted people . . . And Maman? Here honesty checked her. Maman was hard to love. But she could at least privately extend some forgiveness. For example, she could forgive her for turning out far too chicly for a country wedding in a severe silk suit of the same pale straw colour as her burnished hair (which in any case was preferable to the matron's wedding uniform some women had on – horrible floral tents, hard straw hats banded with ruched silk – as if they had gone out of their way, paid good money, to make themselves as ugly as possible). Also she could forgive her for keeping too close to Uncle Peter's side. And if she could not quite forgive, she could at least begin to grasp how these two became drawn together. With a prevision of the way she might view similar situations in her later years, she saw what an undertaking Foscote had been – four lives plunging with varying degrees of faith into the unknown, and then, as is the way in human affairs, forces beyond their control taking a hand in the process. Small wonder that the outcome suited some more than others, that in shifting circumstances and very close quarters new alliances formed while others broke down. So – was a share of her inspired magnanimity to be allowed Uncle Peter? Not altogether; for when it came down to it, she could not overlook his character. However, (Jeanette was sailing towards him, reaching out her arms) she was inclined to honour him for giving Jeanette this blissful day.

An adagio had begun. With a reproachful and beautiful swoop, the lead violin cut into her thoughts. It was as if her father's voice wailed out for remembrance. She turned, looking urgently for Laurie.

He was leaning against the shaded drinks table, talking animatedly to a good-looking man and waving his free hand a great deal. When he saw her coming, he set his glass down on the table and hauled her into his side. 'Hi, love. Do you know Karl? Karl, this is Claire.'

He was another musician, a friend of Richard's, with a cultured voice and easy to converse with. But she could not for the life of her discover what about the situation so excited Laurie, who, as they chatted, continued to press her rigidly against his side. She could feel him down the whole length of her body, as taut and faintly tingling as a plucked steel string. His laugh seemed to erupt from a stranglehold. No doubt it was the champagne taking effect – he drank so rarely.

The adagio concluded, a brilliant allegro poured forth. During it, some people came up to join them. Laurie was charming, but his attention wilted. He reached for a bottle, began refilling glasses.

At last, with brio, the musicians reached the final cadence. Instruments were swept to their temporary rests, scores were substituted on music stands. Above the polite applause, a voice rang out – loudly, tipsily, suggestively. 'Well my dear, it was a rather *sudden* decision. No sooner did they become engaged than we had to send out the wedding invitations.'

Laurie put down his glass, took Claire's elbow. 'I'm afraid Ma gets worse,' he murmured. 'We had better go and distract her.'

Patiently, they weaned her from the Emmersons. 'Come and say hello to Kitty,' she protested, as each took an arm and led her away. 'You remember Kitty Gunn, my best and oldest friend?'

'Later, Ma. How about a bracing cup of tea?'

'Why? Do you think I need one?'

'I think Laurie needs one,' Claire put in swiftly.

Silence dropped from her remark like a stone into water; she heard the *plop*, saw the ripples spread, bringing him, she imagined, up against his behaviour of a few minutes ago. But no. 'I think we could all do with one,' he said smoothly, and the dropped stone became retrospectively her own self-consciousness. So often, if she ventured the tiniest criticism, the mildest questioning, this was the result: herself covered in confusion and wishing she hadn't.

'I suppose we're allowed in the kitchen? Mrs Basket won't object?'

'Bascombe,' his mother corrected automatically. 'Oh no, I dare say the panic's over by now. They'll be putting their feet up, having a cup themselves.'

There was indeed tea to be had. They poured out three cups, put them on a tray and started upstairs. 'The boxroom,' Laurie suggested. 'We'll get some peace in there.'

Taking her cup to the sofa, Claire sat down. Laurie waited to see where his mother would place herself, but when she continued to wander about the room, sipping her tea, removing a dead fly from the window-sill, squinting at the titles of books on the table, he too sat on the sofa.

'I'm thinking of going away for a while,' Margaret Stone said at last, and put down her cup.

'Yes?' Laurie encouraged.

'Kitty Gunn has asked me to stay at her place in St Ives. You know she takes quite a few of my pots to sell in her shop? They go awfully well, she could sell many more. I have always sent her my special things – not the mugs and teapots that go well here. Her shop, you see, is more of a gallery – with paintings, weavings, carvings, jewellery. I think it's time I was more selective.' She raised and scrutinized her fingers, back and front. 'There will be an exhibition at the gallery in October. She wants me to go down for it and stay on for a couple of weeks. Get the feel of the place, you know; gather ideas. I rather think I might.'

'You should,' Claire said eagerly. 'Shouldn't she, Laurie? It's time she thought more of herself.'

'If the idea appeals, then certainly.'

Margaret Stone laid the flat of her hands on the table and leaned on them. 'I've got an illustrated leaflet somewhere. I must show it to you,' she said vaguely, as if her mind were weighing another matter.

'Yes?'

'Mm. Kitty had them printed to send to clients. She has clients from the four corners – America, Japan . . .'

'Well!'

'I'm so glad to see Jeanette settled. Richard is a good fellow – reliable: Jeanette needs that, with such a rotter of a father.' Her eyes came to rest on Claire. 'Oh Laurie, just look. Isn't she a picture – that sweet dress – the way her hands are tucked between her knees? So puckishly demure – someone should paint her.'

'Ma, you're being embarrassing.'

'Am I?' She threw up her hands. 'I should like not to care a damn what any of you think of me ever again. To be totally free of care and responsibility. And

I should, I should; I should feel free as a bird, if only . . .'

'If only?'

'Oh, it would just be so lovely,' she cried, 'if you two were safely settled.'

Claire's ears turned inwards. She heard her blood coursing, heard the crack of a joint as her hand shot upwards to tug a side-wisp of hair.

'Dearest Ma,' at last sighed Laurie; 'you can't dispose of people in order not to have to think about them.' But when he turned, it was to Claire, not his mother. He wrapped his arms around her and drew her close, planted his chin on the top of her head. From which position he looked across at Margaret Stone. 'However, you need have no worries. Claire and I are perfectly safe.'

Slowly, Claire let out her breath. Laurie still clasped her, but now with a rocking motion which seemed to gentle away her intense embarrassment (which had veered towards terror, as if some delicate and precious thing were being rudely poked). And seemed to cast a promise.

Part Two:
LYDIA

i

SINGER IN DEATH CRASH

Sabine Haddingham, the well-known soprano, and her long-time associate, the musical director, Peter Stone, were killed yesterday when their car skidded off the A48 near Gloucester in treacherous weather conditions. They were travelling to the Cheltenham Winter Arts Festival where Miss Haddingham was due to give a recital . . .

The Times, 9 February 1967

Laurie held the telephone receiver at some distance in front of him, thereby sharing the call with Claire (who was sitting on the arm of his chair) and avoiding the full force of his mother's voice.

'You saw the report – *MISS Haddingham* – *her long-time associate* – and all that stuff about Foscote and not even a mention of Andrew or me? Well, my dear, I wash my hands of them. Shan't even show up for the funeral. In fact if I ever set foot in Foscote again, it'll be too soon. No, here I shall stay – where people appreciate me, believe it or not – safe and snug in St Ives.'

Laurie inclined his head. 'Ma, *we* appreciate you, you know we do. But if that's how you feel – so be it. Claire and I will take care of things . . .'

Claire's hand shot out to cover the mouthpiece. 'Like hell we will. My field project's at a critical stage. Anyway, of course she must come to the funeral . . .'

'Why?' he hissed – 'if she doesn't want to?'

They eyed one another over the noisy instrument. 'OK, OK,' Claire relented.

195

'What was that, Ma?'

'I said, is Claire all right?'

'She's fine. Look, don't worry, we'll manage. But you'd better inform the solicitor . . .'

'Oh, I have. Reggie Buckell says he'll ring you first thing tomorrow.'

'Right then, it's settled. You stay where you are . . .'

'I intend to. Kitty flies to the States next week leaving me in charge. And I've heaps to finish for the Spring Exhibition. No, I simply won't allow those two to rattle me ever again – dead or alive. Honestly, Laurie, you don't know the half of it. One of these days . . . Er, is Claire actually . . . ?'

Claire had risen. But Laurie pulled her back. 'Yes, Claire is here,' he sang out in a tone calculated to encourage cautious good sense in anyone threatening the contrary.

'I see – what does it matter, anyway? – history now. Though I might as well put you both in the picture – about Foscote and so forth. Can Claire actually hear?'

'Loud and clear, Aunt Margaret. You don't half shout.'

'Do I? That's what Kitty says. Must come from trying to make myself heard over the din all those years. Anyway, saves me repeating myself. Thing is, you two, the place is yours – Foscote, I mean. Eventually it'd be yours, jointly, in any case; it's just mine for my lifetime. However, I've no use for it. Have it now and do as you like with it – though I should hardly weep if you sold up, lock, stock and barrel. Don't suppose you're aware, but a couple of years ago I made them hand over my initial investment – plus a return, of course – which is how I came to buy this cottage and a share in Kitty's business. I shall leave the cottage to Jeanette, by the way. Trust that seems fair?'

'Certainly, but . . .'

'Claire? Did you catch all that?'

'Yes, it's incredibly generous of you, but I really think you ought to think it over . . .'

'Nonsense. Made up my mind ages ago. I want absolutely nothing from Foscote – do you hear? – NOTHING WHATEVER.'

'We hear, we understand. Now, dear, are you sure you are able to just hand it over? There may be trustees, the procedure might be more complicated than you imagine . . .'

'Don't worry, I've already gone into it with Reggie Buckell and it's quite clear I can do as I propose. He's going to discuss everything with you tomorrow; I'm just telling you so you'll be prepared. You know, it's long been my dream to see you two settled . . .'

This time when Claire rose, Laurie did not detain her. 'OK, Ma,' he broke in, his eyes on Claire darting to the window, 'we'll hear what Mr Buckell has to say, then talk it over. We'll keep you posted . . .'

'Tell her we'll come down for the Spring Exhibition,' Claire hissed, in atonement for her earlier selfishness. He sent her a smile and repeated the message, then re-opened the subject of Foscote: might some of the old gang want to buy them out – the Emmersons, for example?

Claire raised the curtain and watched snowflakes falling – singly, lazily – into the lighted street. It was quiet down below. But then the avenues – Westmoreland, Devonshire, Marlborough, York – were considered the quietest, most desirable area of Thorpe by the university set. A high proportion of these tall Edwardian villas were owned by academics, or rented out – floor by floor – to young single lecturers (such as herself and Laurie) or to research students. Laurie had been living on the first floor of number 27, Westmoreland Avenue for nearly four years. He was now a fully-fledged lecturer here at Thorpe, though still working on his doctorate under the supervision of his tutor at Cambridge. Claire was a relatively new member of Thorpe's academic staff. Having stayed on at Sutton as a full-time researcher and then put in a year at a commercial seed growers, she had already gained her PhD; five months ago, after turning down decent offers elsewhere, she had secured the post she coveted in the same department as Laurie, the Botany Department. Her lodgings, too, were in Westmoreland Avenue, but at the other end, in number 108. Laurie said when they had saved enough money they could look for somewhere more spacious – though whether he meant in one spacious lot or two was unclear. She'd been too involved in her budding career to care much where she lived. Or about anything else not work related.

Her first reaction yesterday evening when a young policeman called at her flat, was that her field study and its complicated arrangements were still at a delicate stage and she'd be blowed if this news (Maman and Uncle Peter getting themselves killed) was going to jeopardize weeks of painstaking work. But yesterday evening the tragedy had seemed unreal, just another example of indiscreet and extravagant parental behaviour. It was fast becoming less unreal. It was like a gathering black cloud, beyond her power to disperse. The damage might be considerable – not only the impact of her mother's death, and the time she'd have to take off work to attend the funeral, but all these unforeseen consequences, like the future of Foscote. This didn't strike her as terribly important, but she could tell from the tone of Laurie's voice that it probably was. (The tone being one he used when something significant was in the air and he considered it prudent to pretend otherwise.) Staring out of the window, it was Laurie she now tuned into, putting nearly a quarter century's experience into the exercise.

'And love to Kitty,' Laurie was saying. 'Now, Ma, put all this out of your head. Go into the pottery and produce a masterpiece!' He abandoned the telephone with a flourish, came over to her, and in a quite different voice asked, 'How're you feeling, love? Still too shocked to know?'

'I suppose I am really.' What a hard case she was – at a time like this to be so obsessed with her own concerns. Probably, she had shocked Laurie just now, carping because of her field project. But what he failed to appreciate was how much it *hurt* to wrench her mind away. Though losing your mother was supposed to hurt too, she remembered. 'I'm very sad of course,' she said defensively. 'But if they had to go, maybe it was good they went together.' Then added, not really meaning to, 'Saves a lot of hassle.' Oh hell, she thought, grabbing her coat. 'I'm tired, Laurie. I must go.'

'I'll walk you back.'

'Don't be ridiculous.'

Ignoring her, he reached for his own coat. Fastening it, a remark made by their senior colleague Zena Turweston rang in his ears – 'She's a cool customer, your Claire.' He looked at her – buttoned up to the chin in her long black coat so that only her white face showed and her wispy dark hair. 'Wait there a minute. I've got something for you.'

'So how do *you* feel?' she called, not seeing why only her feelings should be accounted for.

'Angry, moved; hurt for them,' he said, as he went into the bedroom, carefully selecting words to accurately express his feelings. 'Liberated,' he added, as he reappeared, prepared to elaborate on this if she signalled encouragement.

She did not. She hated to speak with him of their lover parents. Doing so gave her self-image a knock, as if the front she presented to the world hid a grubby underside (marks of her mother's transgression). When she was really low, she would suspect that by bringing up the subject Laurie was betraying that this was his secret view of her (and possibly explained why he never made love to her). Of course she soon calmed down and understood he could not be so unreasonable as to associate her with what her mother had done, or, come to that, consider her mother more culpable than

199

his father. However, much energy was to be saved by simply avoiding the subject.

Her eyes fell on the package he was holding. 'For me?'

He was disappointed. He would have liked to confess the sense of elation mixing uneasily with his shock and grief, and his sudden memory of how as a boy he had fantasized his father's death. He would have liked to confide how, briefly yesterday, an awed thrill of guilt shot through him – as if his secret boyish desire had metamorphosed into black ice, spread itself over the A48 near Gloucester and accomplished patricide.

'Yes, for you. I did some browsing in Princes Street.' (He had recently attended a conference in Edinburgh.) 'Close your eyes.' From the paper he removed a length of mohair jade-green lace, shook it out and draped it over her hair: 'You refuse to be sensible and wear a hat, so how about this?' The fine, virtually weightless fabric was woven through at sparse intervals with purple and gold twisted thread. He crossed it loosely under her chin and laid the ends over her shoulder and down her back. 'Take a look and see what you think,' he said, steering her towards the long bedroom mirror. 'I think you look enchanting.'

'Oh . . .' She stared at herself, then twisted to observe her rear view. 'Yes, yes,' she cried, 'thank you, darling,' and threw her arms round him.

'I simply can't bear the way you expose your most precious asset to these arctic conditions.'

'I won't mind wearing this,' she declared, turning again to the mirror. 'It's so incredibly light.'

'Coming?' he called, returning to the sitting-room to collect his own piece of head protection – a capacious wide-brimmed hat in black velvety material – the only article he'd managed to track down in various gents' outfitters, one penetratingly cold morning, large enough to accommodate his thick thatch of wiry curls. It provoked Claire's and others' scoffing amusement – which he steadfastly ignored. 'Before I acquired this hat,' he liked to declare in its defence, 'I was a veritable martyr to sinusitis.' He pulled it down hard on his head, squashing out hair and ears in the process. She giggled. 'Put your gloves on,' he said sternly, pulling on his own.

'We're only going a few yards. I don't know why you're bothering to come; it's quite unnecessary . . .'

He pushed her out on to the landing and locked the door behind. They ran downstairs. In the avenue, as they walked along, he seized her arm and pulled her against him. 'I sometimes wonder how long I can put up with the sort of weather they get up here.'

'Stop grumbling. You know perfectly well you adore to suffer.'

They had crossed the road and passed a dozen or so houses, when suddenly without explanation, he steered her into the cutting which lead into Devonshire Avenue.

'Hey – where're you taking me? Look Laurie, it's late . . .'

'Not far. I just want you to see something.'

She sighed, but allowed him to lead her left into Devonshire and on past a terrace of houses, then over the road to where several large detached Victorian villas lay in spacious grounds backing on to the park. Outside one of these he stopped. 'The Laurels,' he announced.

She squinted at it. 'Well?'

'It's for sale, I happen to know. Nice place, don't you think?'

'What I can see of it. It's awfully large.'

'Beautifully proportioned. Proper drive, huge garden, several mature trees.'

'You know it, then?'

'I know the tenant on the top floor. Tim Ryan, research assistant – ginger hair, pointy beard?'

'Oh yes, Paul's researcher.'

'Mm. Well he has the attic rooms. Apparently, they're trying to get him out because a sitting tenant makes it difficult to sell. Paul advised him to sit tight.'

'Uhuh?' She wondered where this was leading.

He turned to her. Snowflakes on her coat and scarf gleamed in the street lighting; a few had caught in and glittered her lashes. He slipped his arms under hers, pulled her against his chest. 'Love, we could buy it – if Ma really means to give us Foscote. What do we care about a sitting tenant – specially someone we know from the university? We'd probably want to let some of the rooms anyway.'

She was speechless. Had he really worked all this out since his mother's phone call? And even so, why would they want such an enormous place? 'But it's huge.'

'Do you know, I think that's the prime attraction? – room to live and breathe in. Ever since Foscote I've felt confined.'

'I suppose it would be nice . . .' She stopped. He clearly intended to please his mother by accepting her gift; maybe he meant to go one step further and accede to *all her wishes*. Maybe he now felt the time was ripe . . .

'You said it would be nice?' he prompted.

Oh Laurie, she begged silently over her heart's thumping. Say it, say it . . .

He wondered, when she kept silent, whether he'd miscalculated. 'Don't for one minute imagine I'm pressurizing you, pet. You must do whatever you wish with your share. It was just when Ma said . . . You know, I suddenly remembered Tim talking about this place, and I got this daft romantic picture . . .'

'It's not daft,' she blurted in exasperation. 'It makes sense.' Of course it did. Here was the 'somewhere more spacious' he'd talked about. 'It's a lovely idea, and it is . . . romantic,' she hinted. Why didn't he come out with it? She remembered the two occasions in her hearing when he'd referred to her as his 'fiancée' the first at a dinner in Cambridge (quickly, bluffingly), the second to the Dean of Science when she'd arrived to be interviewed for her present job (fluently, as if after practice). The formality of both occasions had prevented any objection or challenge; and afterwards, because the word described what she wished very dearly to be the case, she had been too inhibited to mention it. So, in a way she *was* his fiancée; he'd claimed as much in front of witnesses. Squeezing her eyes up tight, she willed him to spit it out in plain English.

Suddenly the suspense was intolerable. Opening her eyes, glaring, she bellowed, 'DO YOU MEAN WE SHOULD GET MARRIED, YOU DUNCE?'

Only the merest hesitation. Then, 'Of course,' he said swiftly in a tone she knew only too well (his 'playing along' voice; she had often grinned to herself hearing him use it on some other person when she alone was aware of his true feelings or intentions), 'if that's what you wish,' he went on – so seamlessly it took her a few seconds to recognize it as a let-out.

Without a word she turned and started briskly back the way they had come. She heard his feet sloshing behind, hurrying to catch up. She quickened her pace, hoping to arrive home still with an empty hole inside her and be safely alone by the time some dark emotion rushed to fill it. Through the cutting, right into Westmoreland (skidding a little rounding the corner), past number 63, over the road, past 84, 106, at last arriving at 108. Turning, her hand on the gate, she had a smile ready. (The last thing she wanted was to give an impression of having taken umbrage.) 'Goodnight, Laurie. Heavy day tomorrow.'

'Claire.' He caught her arm. It was time to say something, he thought, more than time. 'Can I come in for ten minutes?'

'Heavens, no. It's late and I'm shattered. And I've things to do for the morning, check over my graduate student's thesis, for a start . . .'

'It won't take long. There's something I have to tell you. Something I ought to have explained years ago.'

In an instant, in less time than it takes a lightning bolt to fall, she knew that whatever was coming would turn her life upside down – knew she did not want to hear these words, knew she must prevent him saying them – and threw all that she had, words, gestures, wiles, cunning, into warding off disaster.

'No, Laurie, really, I love the idea. It's a fantastically nice house,' she cried, deliberately misunderstanding. 'It just takes a bit of getting used to, I mean the idea we could buy it. But you're quite right, of course we could, if we sell Foscote. And we'd want to sell it, you bet! This way we could have what we've always wanted. Do you remember when we were kids, how we used to say we'd live in a house in a wood? I know it's not in a wood, exactly, but all those lovely mature trees, and the huge, huge garden, and overlooking the park. We must definitely look into it. Soon as we've got this funeral out of the way – and by the way, I was selfish about that, about your mother; but you know how I am, can't bear to switch off when I'm in the throes of something at work . . . How could I be so insensitive to poor Aunt Margaret? No, I'm really pleased we're able to take this off her . . .'

At last he got his mouth open – but she shot up her hand and pressed gloved fingers over it. 'Laurie, darling, I can't imagine anything more lovely than living in that house with you,' she said softly. 'But now I do have to go in.' She backed away, groping for her key in her pocket, 'I know the solicitor's going to ring tomorrow, but first I must get hold of Ken, persuade him to come out with me to Utterby, put him in the picture about the fertilizer trials. Then I'll come round to you and you can tell me what's been said – OK?' She put the key in the lock, turned it, called, 'Goodnight,' and lurched with the opening door over the threshold.

In her upper storey flat, unwinding the scarf he had given her, shaking it out and laying it over the back of a chair, she was comforted to reflect that she was very disciplined. So she was not about to waste time worrying over what he might or might not have been going to say. Unbuttoning her coat, she reasoned that as they were both in shock, what he had been going to say would have been regretted very possibly by morning. You know what he's like, she reminded herself, sitting down to strip off her boots: nothing is ever clear-cut; he's told you a hundred times that he's never sure about the truth of anything, or how he truly feels; that he's perfectly capable of feeling and believing two diametrically opposed things simultaneously. She undressed completely and went into the tiny bathroom, turned on the shower and put her hand under, waiting for it to run warm. More than likely, by shutting him up, she'd done them both a favour.

She stepped in and pulled the curtain across; turned the shower on full blast and let it rain down hard over her. It was particularly good on her back, this benign chastisement; as she stood there, bowed and pleasantly beaten, the world slid into normal: it seemed more than likely that her own reactions had been out of true this evening, and what Laurie had been going to say would have proved innocuous. As for their getting married: Laurie hadn't said they wouldn't, had in fact said they could, it was up to her. Well then . . . The marvellous thing was his proposing they bought that house and lived in it together. Things would sort themselves out – as things tended to if you didn't go pushing and probing. She turned off the shower, towelled vigorously, cleaned her teeth, put on a nightdress and dressing-gown and thick woollen socks. Then went to her desk because, compelled to take the next few days off work, there were one or two things she'd better look at straight away. (This was her excuse to herself. In fact there was another, more immediate reason for switching on the anglepoise lamp and settling down on her hard-backed chair, for putting on her reading spectacles.)

The process of shoving her mind into work orbit was never without effort. Its duration and difficulty depended on her physical state and whether there were competing matters (as there were tonight in the form of suppressed reactions to her mother's death and to Laurie's house buying suggestion). It was like hauling her loaded body up a steep and rocky outcrop; but once accomplished, standing tall and relatively weightless, the going got better and better until she could virtually fly. More effective than any drug or booze, it was a sure-fire method of cutting off from pain, anguish, irritation, frustration, and the vague background annoyance she was often prey to – unspecific worry, faint uncentred suspicion. And so tonight she did not seek refuge in brandy or a sleeping tablet, but in the papers spread out on her desk covered in graphs with neatly drawn lines in different colours and tables of figures running down the side – setting her mind to tackle the rocky climb leading to full and exclusive engagement with the population dynamics of *Lolium perenne* and *Agrostis stonlonifera.*

For some time there was nothing else in the world – until a pencil dropped and she bent to retrieve it, and feeling giddy all of a sudden, she noticed that two hours had passed, it was half-past midnight. Half dazed, she tidied her desk, visited the bathroom, sipped some water, climbed into bed. Idiot, she pretended to curse, really revelling in the high level of concentration she could achieve these days – aware, too, that it was not without consequence: concentrated efficiency in one area led to vagueness in others. It worried her sometimes when she couldn't remember simple things, like the day of the week or a person's name or what she had come into a shop to buy or where the hell she had put her library tickets; she worried in case other people noticed these mild eccentricities and whether they groaned when they had to deal with her or made comments behind her back. As plausible cover, she had developed a cool, offhand, noncommittal manner. However, it was a small price to pay for a well-tuned mind. She rejoiced that her work was good, that she'd had a paper published in a prestigious journal, that her field project had won extra funds for the department from local businesses and so enhanced her prestige. (If Zak were around now to question the potential use of her studies, she would have a swift and succinct answer: but she had forgotten Zak; he had merged with half a dozen faceless others to be logged in her memory under *sexual experience, miscellaneous*). Of course, Laurie was thrilled with her growing success, and lauded her at every opportunity. If only he were as keen to get on with his own research. But this proceeded slowly; he still hadn't completed his doctorate. Fortunately, a talent for teaching (undergraduates adored him) and a flair for diplomacy (invaluable to the department in its dealings with other bodies and to the Senate in its dealings with uppity students) were carving him a secure niche. We're different, Laurie and I, she thought, drifting comfortably towards sleep — sympathetically complementary, but different.

Apart from the faint greenish glow of his radio dial, it was pitch black in Laurie's bedroom. The World Service provided him with a companionable blur of civilized discussion. He was not actually listening; simply, it was a reassuring sound to have in his ears while chewing over some uncomfortable notions.

When she'd refused to let him into her flat, prevented him from speaking, refused to allow him a word in edgeways, but had just stood there burbling, he'd jumped to the obvious conclusion: *she knows*. Because frankly, burbling was uncharacteristic of Claire. She was direct (painfully so, he sometimes thought during departmental meetings); she lacked guile, used words sparingly. Very plainly she'd wished not to hear what he'd resolved to say. Ergo, she must have guessed the subject. Walking home, he told himself he'd been an idiot ever to suppose she didn't know. Sharp, quick, clever – of course she knew.

Now though, he was less sure. No question she was formidably bright; an intellectual by temperament in a way that he wasn't (already her research far outstripped his); she knew more, had read more, had been published; was dynamite when it came to setting up complicated field work, and dedicated – almost obsessively so – to studies in progress. All this cleverness, however, was quite narrowly focussed. She had none of his perception where people were concerned; he often noticed how she took people at face value until persuaded to do otherwise. The more he thought about it, the surer he became that he'd been right all along: Claire didn't know, she hadn't an inkling. The reason she'd shut him up tonight was the simple one: she'd sensed something complicated coming and couldn't face it on top of everything else. (She'd just lost her mother, remember?)

But now this didn't sound entirely convincing, either. 'Hadn't an inkling' was surely too emphatic. After all, it was possible to sense things pretty accurately without knowing precise details. (He thrust on to his side and curled up in foetal position.) Yes, he and she 'knew' all sorts of things about one another that they never put into words . . . (Still uncomfortable, he sat up, thumped his pillows, slid prone again on his back.) Take, for instance, that time she had made a big deal about going to the Happening in the Charing Cross Road. He had known perfectly well she didn't believe any of that justifying crap about self-discovery – was just wanting to put pressure on him, to make him comply. She'd had her own agenda, which was . . . (his hands went under his head as he groped for words to describe what he had sensed at the time) which was . . . *to exact a measure of control over him*. And why had she needed to? Possibly out of resentment at the way *he* seemed to control *her*, and because she feared she fell in with him too easily. Or possibly (this was a new idea, and perhaps a very likely one) because getting him to the Happening was a symbol for getting him into her bed – like sympathetic magic. But whatever the reason, it had been a kind of test: would he give in to her? He could remember the pang inside him, the sadness with which he'd acceded – and no wonder, having sensed (he understood now) that what they were about to engage in was a poor substitute for her true wishes.

Were they at times too close – as twins are said to be in some cases – tyrannically close? No; because unlike twins they had chosen closeness. So it was not unnatural for Claire to presume they were heading for marriage, and it must have come as a shock when he responded tonight with less than enthusiasm. No wonder she had reacted fearfully. (He pictured her on the doorstep, throwing words at him.) He might as well admit it: in the past he had often been just as fearful over the prospect of losing her; indeed had sometimes toyed with the idea of marriage as a way of making them safe, even referring to her as his fiancée – and not just to protect himself or help her get appointed to the department, but wanting to state some proprietorial claim. But of course, he wouldn't really marry her; he wouldn't do anything so wicked. . . Poor darling Claire – it was so much worse for her than for him; at least he knew the extent of 'the impediment', knew it was no real threat to them.

So after all he ought to have insisted on making a clean breast of it tonight. Bang went another missed opportunity. His hand reached out and snapped off the radio. He listened to the silence – dense, muzzy, it filled his head. Then turned on to his side and pulled the covers up over his ears.

Just before waking, Claire's dream began – but not in the usual fashion. She was pounding up the bank of the paddock on her way to the woods to search for

Laurie, when, from the courtyard below, her mother's voice interrupted the normal flow of events. 'Claire, where are you?' came the petulant cry. 'Come back here at once, you bad girl. Claire, come here . . .'

Not likely, Claire thought, putting on a spurt. But curiously, as she entered the woods, the trees on the perimeter did not, as normally, blanket out extraneous sounds. Her mother's cry persisted – 'Claire-aire-aire!'

She opened her eyes, lay for a second with her mind reeling and her heart pounding, then reached out and smacked down the alarm button.

ii

Claire put the tray on the sheet-swathed chest. 'Er, coffee,' she called, hardly liking to interrupt the deftly working hands, the fierce concentration evident in crouching body and bulging brows, in a forgotten cigarette stub stuck to lips and smouldering waste-fully into the paint smelling bedroom. 'Ta, duck,' said Mr Hennage, not looking up. The cigarette stub, trembling, went up and down with the words.

She remained there for a few moments, her eyes and Mr Hennage's marking the paintbrush's progress to the end of the skirting, her soul and his drawing deep satisfaction from an immaculate performance. When he rose, she tactfully left him to his refreshment, and ran downstairs with an appetite sharpened for her own task.

They took it in turns, Laurie and she, to work at home whenever possible while workmen were about. Not that they feared to leave Mr Hennage here alone, but plumbers were still coming back and forth, a delivery of floorboarding was expected, and one of gravel to replenish the drive. The Laurels (or number 97 as they had promptly renamed the house) had been part building site since the day they moved in four and a half months ago. This morning she had risen early and gone to the lab to check her pea seedlings, had then come home in time to eat breakfast (prepared by Laurie, as usual), before *he* had hurried away to a meeting. In fact it was quite convenient to work at home today; with a report to write for a scientific journal, she needed a measure of peace and quiet. Back in the dining-room, she took her chair again at the large oak table, glanced over her notes, reached for her pen. '10mm sections were cut with a razor-blade from the third internode of the epicotyls of 8-day-old etiolated pea seedlings,' she wrote in her neat rounded hand. And continued without pause for the next hour and three-quarters.

The table had been Uncle Peter's. When it first arrived from Foscote with all the other pieces she and Laurie (though really Laurie) had selected as suitable for their new home, she had been very conscious of its provenance. She had been glad of their habit of eating in the kitchen (for which the Foscote refectory table had fortunately proved too large). But after weeks of seeing the dining-table spread with Laurie's papers and lately her own, Uncle Peter's spirit seemed totally expunged; it was now *their* table, a handsome piece of generous size and perfect height.

She was interrupted by the doorbell. Hauling her mind from depths where white shoots peeped and curled under dim green laboratory light, fighting her way to the surface, to daylight, to the house and its urgent requirements, she started abruptly out of her chair. Belatedly her ears reported a lorry's arrival. (At least the doorbell had instantly penetrated!) Opening the front door, she remembered to assume a normal demeanour (a nice housewifely expression) and banish the stare-eyed countenance of a creature from another planet (which, according to her frank friend Monica Cage, appeared whenever her thinking process was disrupted and ought not to be sprung on the unwary).

'Yorkshire Building Supplies,' announced the front end of a couple linked by an armful of planks. 'Up here, is it?' He lurched forward, his eyes on the staircase.

'No, no,' she said, recalling Laurie's strict instructions. 'Round the back, please.'

'Round the back, Tone,' he repeated, ostensibly for his colleague's benefit, but meaning, she understood: why the hell couldn't you have nipped out and told us soon as you heard the lorry backing up the drive, you dozy female? Chastened, she hurried through the house and opened the back door, then led them to the back staircase. 'Stack them here, please,' she said when they reached the landing.

'There's more, yet,' he warned.

'Right.' She waited as they brought up four further armfuls.

'You counted 'em?'

'Oh yes,' she lied.

'Sign here then, duck. Ta.'

When they had gone, she stooped to check whether the quantity of boards matched the figures on the docket. Thanking her stars that it did, she went along the landing to a window on the front of the house and watched the tail-end of the lorry disappear behind trees lining Devonshire Avenue. Slowly, hand on banister rail, she descended the main staircase.

Against his better judgement, but following orders, Mr Hennage had recently covered these walls (of stairway, landing and hall) with thick plain paper in a colour Claire thought of as 'plum' and Laurie called 'magenta'. 'OK, magenta,' Claire had agreed (for Laurie had chosen it and ought to know). 'But mightn't it be rather dark? Mr Hennage seemed dubious.

'Nonsense. It'll be wonderful. The perfect backdrop for our paintings.'

The paintings (formerly Peter Stone's) were not yet hung, but waited safely in crates for the day when workmen with ladders and other dangerous protrusions no longer haunted number 97. However, walking downstairs, she had to concede that plum –

212

rather, magenta – wallpaper together with pale cream woodwork (stair rail, skirting, window-frame, doors) and dark green Wilton carpet worked marvellously. Squares of stained glass in pale green and lavender pink set in the top section of the front door (an original feature) echoed the colour theme. Laurie certainly had an eye. Reaching the bottom of the stairs and turning right she came face to face with Uncle Peter's Arts and Crafts Movement hall-stand. Fashioned from light oak with faintly deco carved relief, it bore a shelf (on which, when the danger from workmen was over, Laurie foresaw a bowl of tulips or chrysanthemums), and above this an oval mirror banded with beaten bronze. On either side of the mirror were two stout pegs. On to one of these Laurie had tossed his hideous black velvet hat. She had retaliated with her green mohair scarf draped from the other. And thus for some reason hat and scarf remained, like an announcement: *here reside Laurie and Claire*, perhaps. It pleased her to think this.

She'd often thought it strange, given his negative feelings towards his father, that he could bear to surround himself with so much of his stuff. Once, she'd said as much aloud. 'Got nothing to do with it,' he snapped. 'Ownership's transient. Beautiful things stand in their own right – for ever.' And his brows shot so high they disappeared under his jutting curls, evidently in surprise that this had needed pointing out.

Laurie's hand was everywhere about the house. And not, if she were honest, just because he was a bossy so-and-so. When it came down to it, he'd had a clear picture of what might be achieved while she'd had none. Even her own quarters had been chosen and designed by Laurie. 'I think it's all right as it is, really,' she'd said, looking round the front bedroom help- lessly, still reeling from the way he'd allocated their private space. (His very first stipulation had been a bathroom for his sole use – 'No offence, dear, but the army finished me for shared ablutions.' – and had gone

213

on to envisage this adjoining a study bedroom where, as well as a desk, he would place his orthopaedic bed – 'an occasional lie down does help one *think*, I find.' Later, it transpired that nights also must be passed on this bed if he were not to awake crippled by morning. He had then run upstairs to bag likely rooms. These were not the best rooms: those he afterwards 'discovered' for her: 'Now where shall we put you, pet? Oh, yes!' – throwing open the door to what was undeniably the most imposing room on the first floor. 'And we'll have an archway cut into the little room next door, which can be your dressing cum bathroom.' She'd agreed in a daze, and had been unable to think of a single objection or improvement, never mind a colour scheme.)

'What do you mean "all right as it is"?' he'd shrieked incredulously. 'This horrible dun colour? No, no,' he thought for a moment: 'Eau-de-Nil! We'll have it done out in eau-de-Nil and gold.'

'Good heavens, Laurie,' she'd giggled. 'Well, you can be the one to tell Mr Hennage.'

Repairs, alterations and decorations to all the rooms on the front of the house – upstairs and down – were now complete. Work was still underway at the rear of the house, where they proposed to close off some of the rooms and let them to students. (Tim Ryan continued to occupy the two attic rooms, which would have to wait for their improvements until he moved on.)

Claire found she was too happy to mind about the sleeping arrangements – though these certainly puzzled and provoked other people. (Laurie loved showing people round.) 'Oh, separate bedrooms,' had cried Monica, bluntly expressing what others noted and turned aside from.

'Absolutely, dear. One has to recover one's strength.'

'You mean, otherwise you'd exhaust one another?'

'Such an athletic imagination the girl has!' Laurie

retorted, his arm round Claire's waist, his fingers pinching. They'd laughed secretively together, and Monica had cleared her throat and the others had grinned and looked away – perhaps sensing an intimacy that couldn't be pinned down or defined.

And that just about said it, Claire thought, fixing herself a sandwich to take into the dining room and eat while looking over her morning's work. Having given the matter hours of thought (hours and hours, usually when lying awake in bed), she'd come to the conclusion that Laurie wasn't keen on sex – sexual congress, that is. Obviously, he was not a virgin. He'd confessed enough for her to know this and gain a strong impression of brief, perfunctory episodes best forgotten. (His partners remained faceless. Prostitutes? she wondered.) It rather matched her own experience: since coming to Thorpe she'd been celibate, seeing Laurie every day and her all-engrossing work had been satisfaction enough; but prior to coming here, there had been several snatched almost hostile couplings. Her analogy broke down, however, when she recalled that it was Laurie she had been longing for during those years, and that she always excused her behaviour on the grounds that if only he would claim her, she would not be driven to demean herself this way. So Laurie had a problem with sex. Which he certainly wouldn't want to foist on her. Ergo, much better to stop worrying and enjoy what she had got – *real* intimacy. Life was fine; it was groody to want more: she had Laurie, she had her work.

She put down her plate, rubbed her fingers down the sides of her jeans to remove any trace of food, read carefully from notes for a few minutes, then picked up her pen. 'After 12 hours in darkness at 25°,' she wrote, 'the sections were washed in 0.5% NaOCl, weighed and measured for length . . .'

An hour or so went by. Then a heavy rushing, like the sound of an avalanche, bore in on her. And the telephone rang.

'Hello,' Laurie said. 'Now, has the gravel arrived? I've rounded up some splendid volunteers . . .'

'Oh my goodness, I think I hear it now.'

'Then get out there quickly. And make sure they put it where I said. I'll ring you back.'

Heavens, heavens . . . She was just in time to see, over the mountain blocking the driveway, a lorry departing.

'Oh, Laurie,' she wailed when he rang again, 'they didn't knock. I'm sure I'd have heard if they had.'

He sighed. 'Tell me the worst.'

'Well, it's not too bad. It's more or less . . . Trouble is, though, it's blocking the drive. I don't think Mr Hennage will be able to get his van past. I suppose they didn't see there was a van parked round the back.'

Laurie's laughter ripped out. (She guessed he had an audience.) 'So it's an emergency: dig out Mr Hennage. Don't panic, we'll be with you in an hour. If you hear signs of packing up, you'll have to delay him. Cups of tea, dear, that's the ticket.'

Come to think of it, it was time she made a pot of tea. Mr Hennage brought his own lunch and sat in his van to eat it, reading the Daily Mirror propped against the steering wheel; but he enjoyed the courtesy of a morning mug of coffee and an afternoon cuppa. She stirred in two spoonfuls of sugar and put the cup on a tray with an extra blandishment of two chocolate digestives.

'Tea, Mr Hennage.'

'That time already?'

'Oh – I'm probably a bit early.' She glanced out of the window, checking that it afforded no view of the mountain in the drive.

Downstairs again, she failed to settle to work, but repeatedly went outside to stare, to walk round, to wonder whether she ought to make a start. But what with? Supposing she put a spade to it and the whole thing collapsed in the wrong direction? No – it was best left to Laurie and his tame students, she decided, returning inside to pace round the kitchen with an eye on the clock and an ear pricked for any sound of packing up above. When the rescue party trooped in, she fell thankfully on the kettle. 'Tea, everyone?'

'Not a drop till the job's finished!' cried Laurie, handing round implements – shovels, spades, blocks of wood.

The students laughed, all five of them – a couple of big strapping useful looking chaps, two weedy ones with John Lennon specs, and one short fellow: all with shoulder length hair.

'Now come along, and attend while I demonstrate.'

Tea and sandwiches would be all they'd get for their pains, she knew – plus a jolly good time: plenty of laughs, banter, argument; Laurie could be relied on to manage this, to bring out the shy ones, tease the bold, drop one or two indiscreet remarks about members of staff to make them feel privileged . . . But not until the drive had been levelled to his pernickety satisfaction. She could hear him now: 'What *is* the man doing? No dear, wait for him to shovel, *then* you spread. Nice wide sweeps! Oh, he's got the idea, what a relief!'

It was funny how people just loved letting Laurie order them around.

At about half-past-five, Mr Hennage's van was beckoned to safety along a track cleared through the gravel-mountain. Soon afterwards, two girls turned up. They hung about the entrance in their long velvet dresses, peeping shyly through long curtains of hair. A couple of the lads stopped work to shake back their own locks and grin at them. At which Laurie came bustling. 'In the nick of time!' he cried. 'Steve and Gary were positively wilting. Here, take hold of these. The idea is to spread and level the stuff. That's it. Splendid! I can see we're going to be finished in half the time. I'll go and see about something to eat.'

In the kitchen, Claire had been hard at work. 'Cheese and pickle butties,' she announced.

'Oh, you've done it.'

'Don't worry, I washed my hands.'

'I'm glad to hear it. What else have we got? There's a cake, if I recall.'

'And plenty of beer.'

'No need to go mad. I'll put the kettle on.'

Nevertheless, and despite Laurie's sniff of disapproval, when the gang trooped into the kitchen Claire passed round the beer and poured one for herself. When a couple of the students brought out cigarettes, Laurie was on to them at once: 'If you're going to smoke, you can do it outside.' Everyone laughed, but the cigarettes were returned to trouser pockets. It was a mystery to Claire, why, when Laurie snapped in that outrageous way, people thought him hilarious. Certainly – since the method invariably established his own wishes – it was very convenient.

The party was in full swing when Monica bounced in. Monica always bounced; her shapely but copious flesh was apparently more rubbery than most people's, and her undergarments – always supposing she wore undergarments – endlessly giving. She had simply opened the front door and walked in, for this was the habit among avenue-dwelling university folk. (Most socializing was conducted informally, people just somehow gathered; the sight of a familiar car outside someone's place, or bicycles thrown against a wall, or a crowd in a lit and uncurtained room, was sufficient spur to drop in – maybe to pursue an argument, or persuade colleagues of the merits of some pet case or theory, or hear the latest in a current scandal, or just browse through old so-and-so's books and records; and if old so-and-so wasn't in the mood for company, well, he or she would clear off to bed and leave others to it – last one to leave requested to drop the latch; conversely, no-one was offended by a request to bugger off, though this might not necessarily be complied with.)

'Well, well – a cabal,' Monica declared, misconstruing the situation. 'So, Mr Stokes,' (addressing one of the students) 'what are you planning for us now – another sit-in, or a take-over of the Vice Chancellor's Office?'

'Don't put ideas into their heads,' begged Laurie.

At this late stage, Claire recognized one of the students – Gary Stokes – as a leader of the current student agitation; his photograph was regularly in the university newspaper, his voice heard addressing crowds in the quads. He would be well-known to Laurie. In fact, Laurie would have made a point of cultivating him. Laurie's reputation as a skilled negotiator lay in his ability to persuade under-graduates to employ argument rather than action, while at the same time encouraging Authority's sup-position that he was a spy in the enemy's camp. It was a hazardous game, Claire suspected. Monica's assump-tion that she had caught Laurie actively conniving with the opposition, now made her nervous. 'Heavens, don't attack him,' she cried. 'Gary's been marvellous. So has everyone. They've spent hours shovelling a whole mountain of gravel over the drive. The least we can do is feed them.'

But Laurie was not in the least fazed. 'Monica, do allow me to put you forward for the Student Welfare Committee. Half of us come up for re-election next month – and not before time – we're in dire need of fresh blood. And this time we get a second student representative. How about you standing, Helen?' he asked one of the female students. 'Back up poor lonely Mike Bailey. He could certainly do with some, poor love; you should've heard him trying to make out a case for contraceptive dispensers in the Union bogs.' (Here, his sidelong glance checking for Monica's atten-tion warned Claire of an imminent indiscretion. She did wish Laurie *wouldn't*.) 'He hit on the ruse of calling them *Family Planning Facilities* – no doubt out of deference to our less worldly members, such as Dr Rose Hammond – who is not as fragile as she looks.

219

"But Mr Bailey," she quavered, "to the best of my knowledge you have no family to *plan*." '

'No thanks,' scoffed Monica above the shout of laughter. 'I've better things to do with my time than worry about the comforts of undergraduates. For whom, in my opinion, life *ought* to be hard and cruel.'

'Such a toughie,' murmured Laurie, and sprang to his feet. 'My goodness, look at the time! Ten minutes to wash up, then you must all disappear. I've piles to do this evening. Life is not a bed of roses for those of us who are not students, you know, as Mrs Cage here will testify . . .'

But Monica Cage was already half way to the door, joining Claire in pursuit of peace, quiet and an absence of students. 'We'll be all right in here,' Claire said, leading into the dining-room.

'Listen,' said Monica, settling heavily into Laurie's favourite leather armchair, 'I wouldn't say it in front of him, he's conceited enough as it is . . .'

'Who?'

'Laurie.'

'Laurie is?'

'Of course. But he played a blinder with that lot yesterday. Neville Hewson told me – he was watching from a window in the Senior Common. Apparently, big trouble was brewing, they were stamping and shouting and waving placards – all that, plus bloody reporters taking note, egging them on. Then Laurie got up and spoke . . .'

'Yes?'

No answer. Monica shot forward to yank off her spike-heeled shoes (which were her trademark, essential to her theory that an extra two inches of height conveys a slimmer impression) and grabbed the ball of a foot – 'You don't mind, do you, darling?' The action set her red curls tumbling, revealed her freckled cleavage. She sat up, bringing the foot on to her lap to nurse, pulling a face of agony and wry self-amusement.

Wicked was how she looked – green eyes glinting, cheeks so mottled with freckles they appeared darkly exotic, red-lipsticked mouth making a wide silent ah-ahh. Right now Claire felt she could murder her.

'You were saying . . .'

'Oh yes. Well, a large dose of the Lawrence Stone charm – no – more than that – I mean, fair do's, he's a very skilled operator. Anyway, he spoke, and they listened, and promptly settled for a meeting in the Mixed Common forthwith – trooped off like lambs, good as gold. Quite a coup. Laurie's star is very much in the ascendant, according to Neville. The hope is that with Laurie keeping the lid on the pot we can avoid the devastating sort of publicity attracted by Sussex.'

'Well!' said Claire, profoundly relieved. 'Have a drink. A proper drink.'

'Right y'are, dearie, don't mind if I do.'

'This room stinks like a still,' cried Laurie, coming in half an hour later. He went briskly to kiss Claire's forehead. 'I have to go out, pet. Don't wait up.'

'Oh Laurie, do you?'

' 'Fraid so. I'm meeting a bloke from the *Evening Telegraph* – to provide some background information and set our little local difficulty in the wider context. Good evening, Monica. I trust you didn't arrive here by car.'

'Did, as a matter of fact.'

'Then I should walk home, dear, if I were you, and retrieve it in the morning.'

'Bloody cheek. Just because you're too precious to take a drop,' she spluttered, waving her glass at him.

'Night-night, girls,' he called.

Giving the lie to her looks and carefully cultivated manner, Monica was not really wicked at all. She was fiercely loyal to her adored husband Paul (and evidently blind to a disinclination on his part to

221

reciprocate); she was a respected member of the English Department, and, despite an affectation of harshness, a diligent teacher and unselfish with her time (which could not be said of every colleague). She was a few years older than Laurie. In spite of being somewhat in awe of Monica's worldly sophistication, Claire had grown close to her. Monica, she knew, was one of the kindest people on campus.

Claire had been in trouble over a lost pass for the Library when she first encountered Monica. On the defensive, squinting fearfully over the result of a useless search (contents of case and handbag spilled widely over floor and counter), the situation had been saved by the miraculous intervention of a stranger. 'Perhaps you are under a misapprehension,' (addressed to the librarian) 'this is not an undergraduate, this is Dr Claire Haddingham of the Botany Department. I can vouch for her – presumably you recognize *me*? Jolly good. Then kindly issue Dr Haddingham with a replacement.'

'But how . . . how d'you know who I am?' Claire had stammered afterwards.

'My husband works with your . . . With Laurie. I expect you've come across him – Paul Cage? It was Paul who pointed you out. *Dr Claire Haddingham* rather stuck in my mind – such a long handle for a tiny shrimp. You can't really blame her, you know,' (she tipped her head in the direction of the librarian's desk) 'obviously took you for an undergrad trying it on. They get up to all the tricks. I'm Monica Cage, by the way. English Department. Come and have coffee.'

Half an hour of Monica's company left Claire for the first time feeling more or less at home at Thorpe, the place furnished with those cosy snippets of gossip so essential to a sense of belonging. (Item: that girl students are advised never to visit Professor Reed's room other than in pairs – advice possibly pertinent to attractive young female lecturers? Item: that a

Divinity don, the Reverend Charles Blackstock, had once sued the economist Dr Jeff Perks for publishing a blasphemy, and when this failed, had waylaid him one foggy evening to break his nose – only the full weight of the Vice Chancellor's appeal preventing a second court case and wider publicity. What? Good heavens, no, the Reverend Blackstock wasn't *sacked*; his academic reputation made him far too valuable. Item: that the Le Guinns' baby is pickled in the lab. Yes, really! Well, *foetus*, to be precise, inadvertently expelled by Mrs Le Guinn – having been sired quite properly by Professor Le Guinn – and subsequently donated, preserved in a bottle and placed on a shelf in one of the Bio labs, past which gangs of pop-eyed freshers are escorted every October. Owing to squeamishness, Monica herself had forgone the sight, but husband Paul absolutely assured her . . .)

It had been a riveting half-hour, with Claire's coffee left to grow cold. On subsequent occasions, Monica proved equally adept at more serious and intimate discussion – and, fortunately, utterly trustworthy. They confided their loves – and obliquely their anxieties. 'Paul is just too attractive,' Monica sighed. 'Which is not his fault, poor lamb. In fact he finds it a total drag, being constantly pursued by hormone-charged ex-schoolgirls.'

'Mm, he must,' soothed Claire, recalling without pleasure Paul Cage's habit of deliberately running his eyes over her. 'Can't think why they bother – I mean, once they've seen you. Who'd try and compete with the sexiest woman on campus?'

'Huh. Where'd you get that from?'

'David Guthrie, actually.'

'Oh, David's a tease,' she said in a disclaiming manner, but visibly cheered.

And on another occasion, this time with Claire feeling low: 'What I feel is, love shouldn't have to be expressed conventionally to be regarded as legitimate. It's quite sickening, really, the way people expect you to be married and so forth.' It was a sudden and fierce outburst, and took Monica by surprise.

'Mm, I know. People are just so conventional – when it comes down to it. But you and Laurie are lucky. I mean, you can trust one another, you're close enough not to feel threatened,' she hazarded, testing the water.

'Yeah,' Claire said. Then, after a pause, 'How d'you mean, *threatened*?'

'Oh, like you just said. . . You're not threatened by being in an unconventional relationship. I mean some people *would* find that threatening. They'd need a wedding ring to feel secure.'

'Right . . . Exactly.'

'Darling, if one thing is patently obvious, it's that Laurie adores you.'

'I know,' Claire said, her misgivings not exactly eased – for these were too vague to be baldly stated – but relieved to be sharing them with someone at last, in however coded a form. Monica seemed to have a knack of tuning into one's thoughts and feelings.

This evening, they were in the middle of a cosy discussion about the latest Thorpe marriage to come adrift, when there was a noise in the hall, at which they fell silent. Claire supposed it was Tim Ryan returning to his attic flat via the front stairs instead of the back for some reason; Monica wasn't sure who it could be but preferred not to be caught scandal-mongering. The door opened and Paul Cage stuck his head round.

'Damnation!' cried his wife, sounding vexed, but looking thrilled. 'Can't shake the man off. He sniffs me out like a bloodhound.'

'Saw the car outside,' he admitted, his eyes, as he casually squeezed Monica's proffered fingers, raking over Claire – who grudgingly offered a drink. 'Thanks.' He sat down and rested an elbow on a pile of notes left out on the table. Claire immediately abandoned what she was doing to gather these and shove them out of sight in the bureau. 'Pardon me,' he said.

She returned to the sideboard drinks cupboard.

'Well, what have you got to say for yourself? You saw my car outside, huh?' Monica spoke brightly, but Claire caught a forced note. My fault, she thought. Monica has sensed that I can't stand him. Willing herself to make an effort for her friend's sake (for after all, how would she feel if Monica disliked Laurie, if their verbal jousting sprang from antagonism rather than affectionate regard?), she handed him his drink and managed a smile. 'Yeah, Paul, what've you been doing with yourself?'

'As a matter of fact I've had a rather unnerving encounter with our famous resident poet.'

'Oh?'

'I was turning into Devonshire as he was coming out.'

'Really? But he lives on the Park'

'Yes. Wonder who he was visiting. Anyway, Paul?'

'Well, you know how he sort of glides rather than walks – nothing other than feet noticeably in motion – as though desperate not to draw anyone's attention . . .'

'Or take up too much space?' Claire suggested.

'No, no. . .' Monica screwed up her eyes, trying to get under the poet's skin. 'What I think is, he half resents having to be present among us, having to walk down dreary Devonshire Avenue, having to cross the tedious university quad . . .'

'Christ, Monica, whose story *is* this?'

'Sorry, darling . . .'

'So anyway, I didn't see him immediately. He was like a looming shadow, dressed as ever in that grimy mac, touting that clerk's umbrella. "Sorry – ah, it's you," I said – or something like that; then cheerily added, "Good evening." Hell, he must have recognized me, I've spoken to him often enough in the Senior Common – "Mind if I sit here? – Have you finished with *The Times?* – Cracking speech by the VC," sort of thing. To which he has always

225

conventionally replied. But not on this occasion. Not a flicker. Do you know, that man's eyes are dead? Behind those specs are two stones in aspic . . .'

'Darling, that's brilliant . . .'

'He just stepped to one side and went on walking – keeping himself to himself, as they say.'

'Weird,' said Monica.

'Poor bloke,' said Claire.

Paul looked at her sharply. 'Sorry for him, eh?' His voice was neutral but his face faintly sneering.

'Not . . . energetically,' she replied.

'Well he is rather pathetic. You know he had a pash on Liz Fullbright? Oh yes, pursued her relentlessly in a furtive sought of way – hung about outside her lecture room, sent her flowers. . .'

'Funny,' said Paul, interrupting his wife. 'I'd've put him down as a fancier of choirboys, or maybe the sort who hangs around parks. I can just see him opening that seedy mac for the delectation of schoolgirls . . .'

'No, no, you're utterly wrong. He goes for the mature and intelligent woman, and not altogether without success, according to Liz, who wasn't keen herself, but actually met one of his cast-offs – another writer, I believe. Hey, there's a thought: I wonder if he ever sent Liz love-letters? Now he's become famous, they could be valuable . . .'

While Monica speculated and Paul sipped his drink, Claire slyly appraised Paul. He was certainly handsome – lean and dark with long lank hair, in a black leather jacket over lime-green shirt and hip-hugging black trousers. But she couldn't like him, not even out of friendship for his wife. *Because* of friendship for his wife, she thought suddenly, sticking her nose into her glass. That was it, of course. Somehow, even when he was being nice to Monica, listening to her, making some casual gesture of affection, he seemed to convey calculation. She had no proof of anything; there was no particular gossip about him other than that he was fatal to a certain type of female student and maybe wasn't altogether discouraging. No, it was the way his eyes measured her that raised her suspicion. Also, what she sensed about his attitude to Monica.

'Laurie not around?' he asked.

'He had to go out. The press wanted to interview him about the student business.'

'Ah yes, our tireless troubleshooter. Laurie's quite a polymath, isn't he? So many talents, his clever fingers in so many pies.'

Claire frowned. She had been an academic long enough to know this was no compliment; *depth* was revered, *breadth* viewed with suspicion.

Monica knew it too. She groped for her shoes. 'Darling, we must go. I've a hellish day tomorrow, starting with a nine-thirty.'

'Poor you,' said Claire, who by seven-thirty would be in the laboratory tending her seedlings.

'They don't know they're born, these Arts people,' Paul said to Claire.

They exchanged smiles – which was something, she thought, relieved to be natural with him for a moment. She saw them to the front door and dropped the latch behind them.

From the dining-room she removed the used drinks glasses and took them to the kitchen to swill under the tap. She was climbing the stairs when someone tried the front door. 'Who is it?'

'Phillip. Laurie about?'

Wearily, she went down and let in Laurie's chum. 'No he isn't. And he'll probably be very late back.'

Phillip stepped into the hall and examined the carpet – a tubby, ginger-haired man – an unlikely friend for Laurie, she had always thought – a quiet civil servant with little to say for himself. His eyes darted suddenly towards the stairs, then fell again. He doesn't believe me, she thought indignantly, he thinks Laurie's up there in his room. 'Look, he had to meet a reporter on the local rag. He told me not to wait up. I'm on my way to bed, but you're welcome to wait in there if you like.' She nodded towards the dining-room.

'No, it's OK. It's nothing urgent. Just tell him I called. Goodnight, Claire.'

'Goodnight, Phillip.'

When the door was latched for a second time, she went to examine herself in the hall-stand mirror. She looked wrecked – stark-white face, hair more on end than usual, eye sockets so dark they looked bruised. Bed, she told herself – at the double and before Laurie gets back – for what's the betting he'll bring someone home with him? This house was a magnet to restless souls – workmen knocking and scraping and carting stuff up and down stairs by day, rootless wanderers with an insatiable desire for gossip and company most of the night. Bath and bed. This minute.

iii

The gathering, in twos and threes, moved out of the kitchen, through the hall, into the large front sitting-room, and eventually, after some furniture shifting, some debate as to whether to close the curtains, settled down. Then Claire had sudden misgivings. 'The thing scares me. Clive, you do it.'

'It's perfectly simple, you know. A matter of checking the aerial's engaged – yes; turning it on – so; waiting a moment to judge whether some adjustment is required . . .' (All eyes were on the screen where an image zoomed and wobbled and a frame hesitated over where finally to hold firm.)

'Laurie said it shouldn't be,' Claire put in nervously. (What Laurie had actually said was: 'For heaven's sake don't let anyone fiddle with it. Remember you'll have a roomful of argumentative so-and-so's on your hands. Just stay firm. Turn *this* for more volume, *this* for more brightness, *this* for definition, but *don't* alter that or that. Got it?')

It was their first television set (until now they'd

never felt the need), bought in honour of Laurie becoming a television performer. Or a television personality, as Zena was fond of repeating. Claire could still not quite believe it. Laurie was a *scientist*; to her this was as irrevocable as if he'd been born with the designation etched on his forehead; that he'd gone poking around in the murky waters of student agitation and was now considered an authority on the dubious subject of student affairs, was simply a diversion. Her faith in this view was undisturbed by evidence of his suitability for this new line of work (that he was endlessly kind and perceptive, trusted by young people in trouble and therefore able to offer practical advice of the sort which to Claire's own knowledge had helped turn one suicidal girl into a competent student). But part of her, her more instinctive and responsive self, could and did rejoice when interviews on the radio and then on the telly led to Laurie becoming virtually indispensable to any broadcast concerning students' demands, difficulties, drug-taking and demos; when so great was the impact of his talking face in people's sitting-rooms, he was asked to participate in a weekly programme devoted entirely to talk – talk about anything under the sun. But then Laurie, people said, was 'a natural'; he had only to be himself. In Claire's opinion this made light of an amazing talent. For as Monica put it: how many of us can think on our feet, talk fluently and amusingly without fluffing for minutes on end, suffer idiots and keep our cool while staying perfectly relaxed and appearing to enjoy ourselves? Of course the fortunate thing was, Laurie *could* enjoy himself under such conditions; to be paid for doing so he considered a fluke. As for those other attributes: 'Second nature,' he confided to Claire. 'I've trained myself to think fast, as if my life somehow depended on it – always in dread of being found out.' Found out about what? she asked. He thought for a moment. 'Do you know? I've been doing it for so long I've clean forgotten.'

On the television, the news had ended. People hissed for quiet. 'And after the break,' promised an announcer: *'Talking Triangle.* Tonight's conversationalists are Anne Fawcett, MP; writer and broadcaster, Tom Elliott; and taking part for the first time, Dr Laurie Stone.' Then, like a smack in the face, an advertisement blared for soap powder.

At the mention of Laurie's name, Claire's heart missed a beat. Both 'Dr' and 'Laurie' worried her immensely. For one thing, he wasn't a 'Dr'; Laurie had never completed his PhD. He had been distracted from this (as Claire had feared) by his involvement with university politics and latterly by keeping tabs on the student protest movement. Once or twice she'd noticed a reference in a newspaper to *Dr Laurie Stone*, and had heard him described this way on the radio: people playing safe or making an assumption, she had supposed, and had not liked to quibble about it. But now, in the presence of colleagues, hearing the title and not saying anything felt like condoning a felony. She half expected protests, sensed rows of knotted brows. For there were people here who were sticklers for accuracy, valiant for precise definitions; indeed, some who were more likely to go wild spotting a misused term than a misused dog or child. As for *Laurie* – wasn't it a bit matey? If it got bandied about, mightn't it undermine his weight as an academic?

Dissent had certainly broken out, but not over describing Laurie.

'I should like to see them defend that. It ought to be challenged. I'm surprised, frankly, they can get away with a clearly unsubstantiated claim.'

'Challenged, eh? Legally or scientifically? Speaking as a lawyer, you know I rather doubt there are grounds for complaint . . .'

'Well, speaking as a chemist . . .'

'Oh hell, we'd rather you didn't.'

'Yeah, put a sock in it, Bri. And you, Frank.'

'Look, everyone pipe down, or we shan't hear Laurie.'

Silence fell, and for the next couple of minutes rapt attention was paid to a jingle about sweeties, a furniture sale announced like the Second Coming and a homily about gravy browning – while Claire persuaded herself that she was worrying needlessly, that maybe people had forgotten about Laurie failing to complete his doctorate. After all, he was now a senior lecturer and likely to be made Dean of Students, so it could hardly be said to have harmed his career. And where had it got her, being Dr Claire Haddingham? She was still a lowly lecturer – which was fair enough, she was a rotten teacher; she could manage a couple of postgrads adequately enough, supervise and discuss pieces of work, but anything further, dealing with large numbers of students all requiring to be brought to a point of understanding or even inspired, was simply beyond her. Successful research had been her salvation . . .

'And now: *Talking Triangle*.' On the screen, three smiling people sitting comfortably in capacious armchairs took turns to utter greetings.

And the last of these three was Laurie.

The silence in the room – tense as held breath – gradually became easy. There were chuckles, murmurs of agreement and disagreement, some whispered comments to neighbours and the odd 'Rubbish!' or 'Absolutely!' (though anything properly audible was swiftly discouraged). Without realizing they did so, most viewers constantly smiled – both from enjoyment and self-congratulation. For here was Laurie on top form, funny, clever, compassionate, sharp (phenomena they had hitherto taken for granted) being shown to the nation, evidently to be admired and wondered at. Heavens, they'd been *privileged*. Of course, they'd long suspected that Laurie was a cut above the rest, and lo, here was gratifying proof of their taste and discernment.

Claire was sitting transfixed. The camera showing Laurie, luxuriating over him, zooming up kiss-close, was her ally. It was revealing things she'd only half-consciously noticed before. The expressiveness of his hands, for instance, the way, when he was thinking, they came together in front of his chin with the two index fingers forming an inverted V – on which he gently, with a nudging movement, leant the tip of his long thin nose. The way, for instance, when he tipped back his head and laughed, his hands smacked down over the ends of the chair-arms and lay there spread and curving. The way, for instance, when struck by an idea and eager to express it, he hitched his shoulders in an excited shrug. Oh, and those eyes . . . Dwelling on these, she was overwhelmingly moved. To think that for more than two years she'd lived with this man, in this house, and imagined herself utterly content! Fulfilled, even! Now she knew differently. It was as if her love had been a quiet sea and was suddenly charged by an electric current: it rose and rolled in a giant wave; it was *passion*. She grew so hot she felt her clothes sticking; her palms slid together wetly; a sharp odour burned in her nostrils (which for a split second triggered a childhood memory of lying in bed with a fever), burned and was gone.

And suddenly the camera was shrinking away from *Talking Triangle*. The conversationalists, growing steadily distant, continued to converse, but inaudibly. Then the credits rolled and someone – Clive – went to the set and switched it off. Claire rose up and staggered against Monica. ('Whoops, duckie!') She felt shakey as a drunk, but nobody noticed; they were too busy hugging her and kissing, patting her on the back, calling congratulations. It was a relief to be clasped, to loll against friendly shoulders.

They disappeared pretty quickly. The programme had been on at an awkward time for most people – six-ten till half-past on a Friday evening. Now there were dinners to cook, children to attend to, pieces of work to complete. And later on they would all return in their party gear. My goodness, the party! She called several goodbyes and see-you-laters, and gathered up glasses and took them into the kitchen. She stood at the sink staring out into the garden while her hands semi-automatically washed cups, glasses, knives, plates . . . And someone beside her started drying them with a tea towel . . .

'Phillip! I didn't realize you were still here.'

'Yes,' he said seriously, confirming his presence. And after a pause, 'Will Laurie come straight back, do you think?'

'Heaven knows. All we can depend on is he'll be back by ten – that's the time he told folks to come. I bet he arrives with some telly people.'

'Yes,' Phillip agreed. For Laurie never seemed able to go anywhere without making a human collection.

They finished the washing-up in silence. At least he's not a chatterbox, Claire thought, though that was about all she could say in his favour. He irritated her, the way he hung about. More than once she'd gone into a room supposing she was alone in the house, and discovered Phillip crouched near the bookcase, or slumped in a chair reading a newspaper. Once, looking out of an upstairs window, she'd spotted him below in the garden apparently scrutinizing an overgrown hebe. 'Give it a clip if you like,' she'd very nearly yelled down – before deciding against encouragement.

'Well,' she tipped water out of the bowl, 'I'm going upstairs for a bath and a lie-down.'

'That's all right. I'll go and straighten the chairs in the sitting-room.'

'Really, there's no need. Well, if you must, just shove them against the wall.'

'Anything else I can do?'

Evidently he was determined to stay on. 'No, no.'

'I'll get a book, then. Have a read.'

'All right,' she shrugged. 'See you later.'

The trouble with this house, she thought as she went

upstairs – and it was entirely Laurie's fault – was that too many people seemed to regard it as their home-from-home. Always someone about. Often gangs of people about. When the hell would she get the place to herself? More pertinently, when the hell would she get Laurie to herself, front door and back firmly locked? Oh, Laurie, Laurie . . .

She towelled her hair and put on her bathrobe. Then, because she couldn't wait another second, removed her Courreges dress from its cover in the wardrobe and looped its hanger round a hook on the bedroom door. More shift than dress, sleeveless and very brief, its severe black cloth was relieved by two thin strips of cream-coloured braid – one running vertically from left shoulder to hem, the other horizontally across the breast. Laurie had raved over the dress; they'd bought it together during a mad few days in Paris – he, pushing her at every step, to actually enter the for-biddingly elegant premises, to try on, to buy. Now, stepping backwards, viewing it from a distance, a thrill squeezed her stomach, shot down her legs.

She was hungry. Taking care not to dislodge the precious garment, she opened the door and stepped on to the landing. All was quiet; even so, she clutched the bathrobe tight against her as she ran downstairs in case Phillip was lurking somewhere. She made a sandwich (she could never be bothered to make proper food, Laurie took charge of the cooking), poured a glass of milk, and padded stealthily with these up to her room. On a table in the bay window she set down plate and glass, turned over a book which was lying there face down, and flattened its pages with a handy aspirin bottle. Then proceeded to dine in her usual fashion when Laurie was not at home – reading, chewing, swallowing, nudging along the aspirin bottle, turning a page . . .

Until tyres squelched on the gravel, and car doors slammed, and she looked up – not expecting to hear the front door closing (for Laurie was fanatical about everyone closing it gently in order to safeguard its stained glass panels), but trying to detect voices and how many. Thirty seconds later in the sitting-room below, 'Little Rock Get Away' came cascading out of the piano (the baby grand Laurie had brought here from Foscote) – a sheer tumble of sound, pounding exuberance. She grinned and closed her book. He was happy, evidently. When the piano stopped there was a whoop of appreciation, and a faint but unmistakable buzz of competitive excitement. She got up and looked out of the window. A car she didn't recognize was parked behind Laurie's. As she had anticipated, he'd brought people back.

She stretched thoroughly and went over to her dressing table where she sat on a stool and began to make up her face – not in her usual slap-dash manner, but slowly, sensuously. For some reason hurrying was out of the question this evening; her limbs were overlaid with delicious languor, a sense of portent hinting that only when *she* chose to appear could anything truly significant happen. So she took her time lining her eyes with kohl, painting the lids whitish slate, dusting her cheeks and forehead with silvery powder, darkening and curling her lashes, lining her mouth in dark plum and filling in with whitish pink. And then taming her hair – pulling pointed wisps forward to lie flat on her face, smoothing straggling streaks down the back of her neck, teasing the hair high on the crown. When the effect had been checked and approved with the aid of a hand-mirror, she selected and put on a flimsy black bra and a pair of pale tights, and then lifted down the dress. She stepped into it carefully, hitched the shoulders into place, fastened the zip. Finally, slid her feet into almond-shaped shoes of soft cream leather – low-heeled, button-strapped. An inspection in the long wardrobe mirror only confirmed her expectations: of a compelling effect, personification of the height of the moment, that she could have walked straight off the cover of a French magazine.

The house by now was very definitely populated. The plumbing chuntered, feet hurried, doors opened and closed, a record was playing. She went out on to the landing, saw his bedroom door ajar. 'Laurie?'

'Come in, you've beaten me to it. I was about to . . .' His eyes fell on her. 'Ah! Oh, yes, yes, *yes*!'

She ran to him. He gathered her. 'And you were so brilliant on the telly. I was *proud*,' she cried in his ear. They hugged and clung. His hands sliding downwards paused on her hips. 'Bony rabbit,' was what he usually said at this point (as though rabbits were specially bony), but tonight did not. Looking over her shoulder into a mirror, he caught a view of her straining against him, arms stretched up to wind round his neck, her feet on tiptoe. 'Hey, your bum's showing,' he lied, catching her forearms and setting her away from him. 'Pull down that skirt at once.'

Giggling, she smoothed herself down. 'I'd better go and say hello to people. Sounds like you brought plenty back.'

'Later, later. I've set them all little tasks which they're happily getting on with – putting things in bowls, polishing glasses . . .'

'Oughtn't I to do something?'

'You? You'd be useless. Anyway, they're falling over themselves in the kitchen. The stalwarts came early – Paul and Monica, good old Zena – and Phillip's about – oh, and Tim came down to lend a hand . . . Come to think of it though,' he raised his nose, twitched his nostrils, 'I'll just go down and open some windows; I think someone's lit up.'

'So people smoke. You can't stop them at parties.'

'More's the pity. An hour from now the whole place'll be reeking. Off to your room, you. Come down later and make an entrance.'

She laughed and kissed his cheek. He caught her hand and swung her round and dropped his lips to her fingers – a manoeuvre which nimbly deposited her on the far side of his door. She continued over the landing with a swinging bounce as if the soles of her shoes had springs incorporated.

Back in her room with the door left ajar, she was taken, not quite by *déjà vu* (she was too firmly stuck in the present), but a strong sense of this evening running concurrently with other evenings – those times when they were students and she was banished from a room while Laurie softened up an audience for one of their set-piece games. Finding she had forgotten to put on her thin gold choker, she took it from its box and fastened it on; and the contrary idea entered her head that the little scene she would presently enjoy (Laurie's public acclamation of her, their closeness paraded) was compensation for all those private partings which took place outside this very door – the goodnight hugs and kisses – when both happened to go up to bed at the same time.

Then she heard him – not his words, his tone of voice (though knowing him so well, she had no difficulty fitting words to tone: 'What *is* the girl doing? The time it takes her to get ready!'), and her body leapt as deliciously as if he'd touched her breast or put his tongue in her mouth. He was summoning her, she exulted. She flicked off her bedroom light and went quickly towards the stairs, buoyed by the hopeful conviction that it had not been simple lust she'd experienced earlier watching him on the telly, but *intuitive* lust.

'Here she comes at last,' he cried – at which everyone in the hall looked upwards.

Descending, smiling at the blur of faces, it was Laurie's her eyes reported. Before she quite reached the bottom, his arms reached, snatched, swung her to his side.

*   *   *

237

The party was getting noisier, brighter. Delicious to be getting mildly pickled with chums, at every turn to see open mouths and busy eyes, to hear Laurie's voice super-animated above the hubbub – amazing how her ears constantly picked it out. She had never felt so desirable, so wanted, so sexy. 'OK to drink it now, or are we waiting for it to mature?' she giggled when Paul Cage (Monica's husband) brought her a drink and then hung on to it (his leer for once striking her as funny and natural rather than just plain irritating). Laurie's new friends from television, when they were introduced, also helped themselves to long pleased stares ('Lucky old Laurie,' she interpreted). She was a witch, a siren, she was Cleopatra, moving from group to group, pausing here to hang on an arm, there to insert a quip, twirling onwards to share herself fairly. David Guthrie – whom she liked enormously (so grave and serious until you noticed his delayed glance and drawled 'Mm, well!' following someone's over-emphatic exposition) – approached her in the sitting-room.

'It's never struck me before what an amazing collection of paintings you have. I've just visited the bathroom: paintings lining the stairs and right along the landing. That is a Sutherland half way up?'

'It is. Come over here and look at the Gillies.' She linked arms, drew him towards the seascape hanging over the fireplace. 'All collected by Laurie's father. Not that we ever thought of them as *a collection*. In fact I can't say I really noticed them when we were growing up.'

'Of course, you and Laurie were raised in the same rather eccentric ménage. You know, I remember being taken as a child by an aunt to visit some peculiar artists' colony – though yours was for musicians, wasn't it? But to live in such an environment, to be reared in it, must have been . . . interesting?'

She laughed into her glass and considered which of their many Foscote anecdotes she would treat him to.

'I remember,' she began. Then stopped. For the front door had come open with a whoosh that shook the house.

'Mm?' he prompted.

She stared blankly. It had been Laurie who had yanked open the door – he who was so very particular about the front door being treated gently; this she knew because it was his cry of welcome which had accompanied the opening – 'So you did make it! Hurrah!' And something in that cry – a note of huge release – had frozen her mind absolutely.

'You said you remembered . . .'

'Er? Oh – it was a long time ago,' she said lamely. 'Can I get you another drink?'

'Not quite yet,' he said, tilting his half-filled glass at her.

People near the door were glancing covertly into the hall. What was going on? Who had arrived? Who was Laurie making such a fuss of? She downed the remains of her drink. 'Well, personally I'm parched. Back in a sec.' And dodging round bodies, went to investigate.

'Darling!' he cried, spotting her coming and seizing her arm, 'come and meet . . . Lydia,' he called to an elegant towering rear, 'this is Claire. Claire, meet Lydia.'

Who slowly turned . . .

And Claire, with disbelief, with a leeching away of blood from brain, saw who it was. *Her.* The long-dreaded apparition, the vision conjured in her unconfident youth of a witty and ravishing golden-haired beauty who would one day arrive on the scene to ensnare Laurie's heart and bear him away.

Ravishing, but not witty, was the private verdict with which, after a few hair-raising minutes, Claire attempted consolation. Though to begin with she could do nothing but gawp. Lydia's beauty was not of the soft and gentle kind. It was forceful, arresting:

239

cheek-bones and brows, the deep blue eyes (sootily made-up), clean-cut nose, lips, chin, thrust themselves on the onlooker's perception. Strong and bold was Lydia's brand of loveliness, and it terrified Claire. Collecting herself, she was not surprised to be spoken to coldly (after all, she had been staring – though with looks like those, surely Lydia was accustomed to being stared at); but she was disconcerted by the timbre of Lydia's voice – which was peculiarly flat, as if her vowels had been run over by a steamroller. Then Laurie intervened, and Lydia leaned towards him as a birch in the wind might lean, and drew him away.

Claire found she was swallowing on the same sort of queasiness that had once beset her at the Happening in the Charing Cross Road – where, she remembered, close inspection had revealed beauty to be disfigured and cosiness a con. Wishful thinking, she scoffed at herself. Then Monica came bustling up, and she endeavoured to hide her perturbation behind a grin and a shrug – 'Where on earth does Laurie find them?'

'You tell me!' said Monica. 'Good Lord, it's Dusty Springfield! I said to myself when I first clapped eyes. Then I was introduced and had promptly to amend to *Dudley* Springfield. Which was sad really. Rather banal.'

Claire gaped and gaped.

'You mean you didn't notice? Darling, you really must try and *grow*; you miss such a lot stuck down there. Oh yes, I clocked it soon as I got within a foot or so – underneath that hideous choker. His *Adam's apple*, dear. You couldn't miss it. Doesn't it make you utterly sick, the way when a man is got up as a beautiful woman, the beauty is very much more so – the females around seem to pale in comparison. Ne'rie mind. Come and get a refill.'

Claire, a dumb creature, followed her into the kitchen.

'What's it to be – more wine or some of the hard stuff?'

'Um, brandy. Yeah, brandy.'

Monica found the bottle and poured her a measure. 'Here you are. Hey, don't look so stricken, it's just Laurie's prank. And you're not the only one who's put out. You should've seen Phillip Grainger just now, standing by the dresser pulling petals off those poor dahlias – I had to smack his hand for him. I think I'll go, he kept saying. Well, cheerio, I said. Still hanging around though, I see.'

'Phillip's good at hanging around. Probably had too much to drink.'

'He's not tipsy, dear, he's jealous. He was doing to the dahlias what he'd dearly like to do to Laurie's glamorous companion – make her, though of course I mean *him,* disappear. Anyway,' her voice lowered cosily, 'have you heard the latest? The Le Guinns have split up. Honest, it's gospel. Yolande Mackay said she saw Mrs Le Guinn moving out, trailing backwards and forwards with leaking suitcases and armfuls of books and huge boxes of pots and pans. And guess where she took 'em? Straight over the road and into the house opposite, where apparently she's now installed in the attic flat, leaving the poor professor in sad isolation. I wonder if they'll get a divorce. And if they do, who d'you reckon'll get custody of the pickled foetus? Of course, their rows were always spectacular. York Avenue's famous for 'em. Maybe they'll start having them over the street – lean out of windows and hurl abuse, train their sights on each other, take potshots. Yolande thinks the avenue's in for a dull time, but who knows? – things could get even hotter.' She paused. 'What's the matter, ducks?'

'My head's started. Christ, I hope I'm not getting a migraine. Monica, do you think it'd be OK . . . Look, I just need five minutes . . .'

'Then for heaven's sake stop drinking brandy, you idiot.' She snatched away the glass, marched to the sink. 'Here – have some water.'

But Claire had already started to the door. 'I'll get some in my room,' she called. And fled up the back stairs.

But not, observed Monica watching her go, as one who nurses a headache. She moved thoughtfully out of the kitchen. Phillip Grainger was slouched against the sitting-room door-jamb. 'Still here?' sprang to her mind to say, but she bit back the flippancy: his eyes meeting hers were full of pain.

In a corner of the sitting-room her husband had a good-looking young woman pinned to the wall via an arm passing close to the woman's neck. The woman probably deserved it, had no doubt been chasing Paul from the moment Monica's eyes were distracted. One did have to watch out with a husband as dishy as Paul if one intended to hang on to him. And on the whole one did, she reflected, pinching his bum in passing. He swung round, came straight after her. 'Hi,' he said, slipping an arm round her fleshy shoulders. 'How's Claire taking it?'

'Taking what, exactly?'

'The competition. Fabulous-looking bird. No wonder Laurie's smitten.'

'Are you serious?'

'I'm serious about you, babe.'

'Mm. Been introduced?'

'Who to? The new bird? Yeah, briefly. Though Laurie bore her off pretty smartly. Not that she's my type.'

'Darling, I really think she isn't.'

'Exactly. *You're* my type, luscious.'

She shoved him away. Obviously people saw what they wanted to see, she concluded. Or else she was off her trolley, or her eyes needed testing. What was indicated here was a modest measure of empirical research.

For the next twenty minutes she circulated, eaves-dropping on conversations, buttonholing, dropping ingenuous remarks – with interesting results. Some people had clearly twigged, but a remarkable number – which included at least one social scientist and a brace of psychologists – had not. Well, well, well! Was this due to lack of perception, deficient eyesight, unworldliness or lack of interest? Not the latter: Paul wasn't the only one here to wonder whether Claire was put out by the 'dishy new woman'. People could be incredibly naïve. One would have thought the nature of Claire's and Laurie's relationship was patently obvious.

Laurie and Lydia were at the centre of a group in the piano's arc. Leaning casually against the back of a sofa, Monica sipped her drink and proceeded to a lengthy and objective stare. Laurie was clearly enraptured, people were not mistaken as to that; so why were they less perceptive about the subject of his attentions? Well, maybe because it was very well done. Here was no camp queen, no over-the-top caricature of a female. The hair was not a wig but the wearer's own, bleached for sure, but not brassily, and arranged in the latest style – smoothed over back-combing ending in flick-ups. The movements were contained and graceful, the voice flat but evenly modulated. In fact, the longer she watched the stronger grew her hunch that this was someone well used to passing as a woman. So the puzzle was, why Laurie should go for it? Oh Lord, speaking of the devil . . .

'Where's Claire?' asked Laurie. 'I haven't seen her for ages.'

'Blotting her dress,' Monica said smoothly. 'Some idiot slopped wine on it.' She heaved upright. 'I'll go and see how she's getting on.'

'Good, good,' nodded Laurie slowly. 'Yes . . . good. Thanks, Monica.'

A soft rapping on her bedroom door. Claire held her breath, hoped whoever it was would go away.

'Claire, you all right?'

Hell, hell, she cursed. Then, 'Yes,' she called cautiously.

'Let me in then.'

A pause. 'I'll be down in a sec. I'm just trying to get rid of this headache.'

'Headache, my fanny. Open the door. Hurry up, someone's coming.'

Wishing instant death to her friend, Claire dropped to the floor and lurched over the carpet. She turned the door key then returned to her perch on the bed. 'Well?' she demanded.

'Claire, lovey . . .' Monica drew up a basket chair and sat in it. 'Your absence has been noted and commented on. Shouldn't you come down?'

'I said I would soon, didn't I?'

Leaning back in the gold-painted chair, Monica surveyed the gold and eau-de-Nil room. 'I've always thought this quite the swishest bedroom . . .'

'Laurie's doing, not mine.'

'Ah. Look Claire, I don't get it. I mean, Laurie being *bi* has never upset you before, so why now are you so put out? And don't say you're not because I can see you are.'

No answer came, nor was any hinted at. Claire was sitting still as stone with her head turned away. So as usual when encountering an awkward gap in the proceedings, Monica hurled right in. 'I know one doesn't talk about these things, but I'd got the impression – well I think most people had – that what you and Laurie have is just too powerful to be shaken by his little, well . . . extracurricular activities.' She gave a nervous laugh: 'I even wondered whether they spiced up your love-life.' More silence – *horrible* silence. 'Well, you do read of such things,' she excused herself in a rush. 'Claire?'

'Go on,' said Claire.

'So, well . . . Is it the *drag* you don't like? I suppose it could seem a bit tacky, though actually no-one downstairs is offended as far as I can tell, and most haven't a clue. After all,' she sniggered, 'he's not dolled up like he's about to launch into "The Party's Over". So for heaven's sake come down and look normal.'

Claire's head slowly turned.

The look that went between them went on and on, with Monica (for once oblivious of the silence) grappling with a dawning idea, until, 'Christ, you didn't know, did you?' she whispered, 'My God, you didn't know,' and the pupil of Claire's left eye wavered closer and closer towards the bridge of her nose . . .

The spell was broken by Claire clapping a hand over the wayward eye and leaping off the bed; she loped to the table in the window – from where she snatched up her spectacles – and on to the dressing table where she leant down and peered into the mirror. 'My eye's going haywire,' she remarked. 'Perhaps I ought to put some drops in.' But instead of going into the bathroom where the eyedrops were stored, she sat down – elbows on dressing table, spectacles forgotten and clutched to her forehead – because the only remedy she could imagine being of real use to her at this moment was her occasional recourse as a rather driven postgraduate student. (A nice little spliff, she yearned, get right out of here.) Sadly, to her certain knowledge, no such means of escape was available in 97 Devonshire Avenue. Against her will, pictures of Laurie were taking over her mind, scene after scene featuring laughing, exuberant, popular Laurie; and herself an onlooker, little dummy Claire. To be such a fool, such a complete dunce . . .

Monica's thoughts – which had been fully taken up by condemnation of Laurie (men were so sickening; they had absolutely no conscience about poking some tart – of either gender – then hopping straight back into the marital bed – or the regular partner's bed), now jumped intuitively to an approximation of Claire's. 'For heaven's sake don't start feeling foolish. It's well-known that wives and mothers are the last to know. And you two grew up together, you saw each other daily for years and years. It's probably like ageing – you just don't notice subtle changes in people when you're right on top of them. So much easier for an outsider like me – meeting someone, sizing them up . . .'

She was finding excuses for her, it dawned on Claire. Excuses for her pathetic stupidity. Suddenly, Monica's first assumption – that she was some sort of sexual sophisticate – seemed infinitely more preferable. It was totally humiliating to be thought a goose. And it occurred to her how much worse she would feel if Monica had divined the entire truth – that not only had she spent years with Laurie in wilful ignorance, but also in undying hope and unconsummated desire.

She rammed on her spectacles and looked in the mirror. Dr Claire Haddingham, she thought; yes, she still had that, still had her work.

'Relax, Monica,' she said coolly, 'you're barking up the wrong tree. Of course, I *knew*. It's what you said in the first place – I felt insulted by that creature coming here. And believe it or not as you choose, I do have a raging pain in what might loosely be referred to as the head region, but since you are pedantic, this wonky left eye. OK?'

'Oh,' said Monica, sounding deflated; then, 'Oh,' again, this time on a note of revived interest. 'Well in that case, don't you think a word in his ear when folk have gone home might be more the ticket? You've played it so cool up to now, be a pity to rock the boat. I'm sorry about the eye, I can see it's playing up, but just bear with it for another half-hour, eh? What I'm saying is, you ought to be careful, things can still be very dodgy for gays – I dare say Laurie rather depends on you there. Generally speaking, as long as people are discreet a blind eye is turned, but should there be talk . . . Well, Laurie could kiss goodbye to Dean of Students.'

In spite of herself, Claire was shaken. The thought

of Laurie in danger was still galvanizing. She whipped off her spectacles – 'Yep, you're right. Hang on a minute.' – and began replenishing her lipstick and plucking at her hair. 'Right,' she rose, 'come on. We'll go down the back way and just sort of merge.'

'By the way,' Monica called, clumping after her down the stairs, 'someone was careless enough to spill drink on your dress. For the past half-hour you've been sponging and drying it.'

'Oh? Who?'

'Let's see. Ricky Howard's well plastered. Yeah – him I'd believe.'

'Clumsy blighter,' said Claire, and shot through the kitchen doorway aiming to put plenty of space and bodies between them: if she was obliged to give a performance, she'd rather not give it under Monica's scrutiny.

And somehow it wasn't too hard. She began a two-handed flirtation with Harry Knowlen and Paul Cage, then took pity on the bore of the Chemistry Department, Roger Urquhart, who, true to his reputation, gave a blow by blow account – which she heard to the end without impatience – of how he had recently played host to a luminary of the scientific world. Congratulating him, she passed on to one of the chaps from television, Jonathan, who, it emerged desired only to rave about Laurie. 'Isn't he *the* most amazing guy? I mean, he was just so terrific on *Triangle* you'd have thought it was his hundredth, not his first appearance. And to think he's a boffin, a physicist or something. Uh? Ah, *botanist* – yeah, right. But he's bright on whatever the topic. And then, *do you know*?' (she could tell from the mannered emphasis that what was coming would cause her no surprise) 'when we got here this evening he went straight over to that piano there, put up the lid, sat down, and – no, I won't say played – gave *a per-for-mance*.' 'I know,' she said gently, 'I was upstairs, I heard.' Out of the corner of her eye she spotted Eleanor Goodchild, a lecturer in

Sociology who had just failed at her second attempt to become a senior lecturer. She excused herself and went over, linked arms commiseratingly and heard out Eleanor's complaint (a not unfamiliar one at Thorpe) that now two of her male colleagues, both younger and with fewer publications to their credit, had been promoted in her stead. Then Eleanor's husband interrupted with a reminder about how much the babysitter was costing, and soon afterward the Goodchilds left. Making her way towards Laurie and spotting Phillip Grainger *en route*, she indulged in a few harsh words – 'Why, Phillip! Monica said you were on the point of leaving ages ago; maybe you've forgotten the way. See that door? Simply open, pass through and keep on walking.' She felt better for that.

'Hi, love,' she greeted Laurie, nestling against him as his arm went round – at which his slightly worried expression vanished. 'Hi,' he said, madly squeezing her waist and dropping a kiss on her crown, 'how's the dress?' 'Fine, fine, you'd never know it'd been splashed.' Zena and her husband were with him and, after expressing polite relief over the dress, returned to the topic she had interrupted. She listened rather than joined in, and was only inhibited when Lydia came towering over – at which her own body seemed to shrink and she averted her face in case her eyes had gone squinty.

The unease she experienced at being close to Lydia was not entirely due to the nature of her recent shock and confusion. Partly it was caused by knowingly confronting disguise. Disguise in its proper place, the theatre, the ballet – or even in the street so long as she could keep her distance – was fine. Forced up close she became frightened. (As when she and Laurie were watching a street entertainer last Easter in Paris and suddenly from a crowd of thirty or more it was she he fixed on, she he beckoned, she who was shoved forward by eager onlookers to be fawned over by a chalk-faced creature with triangular eyes: as also when

Jeanette came to visit with her five-year-old son, and the little wretch sneaked behind the settee, put on a crude monkey mask and then jumped out at her, and her stupid body went on reacting to the mask rather than to the child it scarcely hid long after her initial shock had died down.) Facing Lydia was upsetting, not because of any obvious falseness or grotesquery, but simply as a result of knowing that what she faced was not as it seemed. Fortunately, Lydia did not prolong the exchange, but soon placed a hand on Laurie's forearm and murmured something in his ear. (Something bloody hilarious, Claire thought, if his shout of demented laughter was anything to go by.)

Yes, she kept it up until every last person who mattered had taken themselves off – that is, every person before whom it was important to maintain appearances. Then she kissed Monica and a few other close chums goodnight, called her excuses in the sitting-room where Laurie was still ensconced with a few stragglers (including Lydia) and went thankfully upstairs to her room to wrench the cap from her bottle of Seconal.

iv

'Good morning! Tea's fresh in the pot. And by the way, I've a confession to make: Lydia's tucked up in one of the back bedrooms – the one next to the airing cupboard. Hope you don't mind, love, but I had to take pity on her. Thing is, she's had a nasty set-to with her landlord. I was aware of this in point of fact, which is why I was more than mildly surprised to see her turn up on our doorstep yesterday evening; I'd understood she'd be fully engaged moving into a new flat. Alas, that possibility is temporarily on hold – some mis-understanding over a lease – and the poor thing was simply wretched to be facing another weekend at the mercy of the brute landlord – who actually lives on the premises and is very much at large over weekends, liable to come charging upstairs any moment hot to go another six rounds . . .'

In a daze, Claire leaned against the kitchen table. Laurie was doing many things at once – stirring stuff in a saucepan, adjusting knobs on the stove, putting plates to warm, catching and buttering toast. While all the time delivering his prepared statement in what Claire supposed was his famously successful lecturing style – smooth, firm and authoritative, one any student would be abashed to interrupt (for instance to question the terminology – 'She?', 'Her?'). Yet a style which skilfully included the student with small directional asides (though not, this morning, 'If you refer to the diagram on page forty-four,' but 'Do sit down. Scrambled eggs coming up.'). Also a style which cleverly anticipated any gaps in a student's knowledge which might be causing embarrassment ('Lydia won't be coming down to breakfast; I took up a tray.'), and had a curious insulating effect, so that however startling the information imparted it was possible to take it in and stay with the flow, and not be so arrested by an item as to stay behind grappling with it and thus miss the peroration's development. (That Lydia had stayed the night, furthermore was *still here,* was one hell of a startling piece of news, but one easily assimilated – Laurie's even tone implied – via active and close attention to the twists and turns of the argument.)

He put a plate down in front of her.

She stared at it. 'Uh – sorry – but now I see it I don't think I fancy it.'

'No? Just have toast, then,' he said, whisking it away.

She took a piece and lightly buttered it, and reached for the marmalade – then changed her mind and went to a cupboard and brought out Marmite.

'I suppose you drank rather a lot last night,' commented the abstemious one – to which she made no reply, but bit into her toast, chewed and chewed, and

250

took gulps of tea to assist swallowing. Nothing further was said; evidently the lecture was over.

But he was watching her. Most acutely she sensed this, and when she moved her head again to take up her cup, obtained a confirming side glimpse. Though silent, he was still exercising control. Having said his piece, set the tone, outlined the parameters of the situation within which she was expected to respond, he now sat back and fiercely willed her to comply. For he had frequently interrupted his exposition to ask the same question in various forms: *did she mind?* (Of course not, darling; poor Lydia – what happened exactly with the landlord? – oh how ghastly; no, it's no trouble at all . . .) Yes, she could hear in her head all the right noises; after all, she was used to making them, whenever, in fact, he provided a cue. But this was a different kettle of fish, wasn't it? This was blatant. This required her to make even more of a fool of herself than usual. (Not that she'd ever thought of it before as making a fool of herself, but this morning she was seeing things in a sharp new light.)

The idea that today she would *not* be obliging was not embraced head-on in a rush, but circuitously; she made feinting passes at it, gathered it to her by sleight of hand. And as she did, sounds in the room magnified – the clock's ticking, the refrigerator's hum, a sudden eddy from the tap of gathered droplets, the jarring ring of her cup on its saucer, and most resoundingly the noise of her jaws endlessly masticating. At last, keeping her eyes on the table, clutching her fragment of toast in front of her like a talisman, she brought it out: 'Well, OK – we can have whomever we like to stay I suppose, I mean you don't have to ask me and I don't have to ask you. But what *is* a bit of a puzzle, Laurie . . . this is a *man* we're talking about, so why all the 'she' and 'her' business?'

And how long will the charade be kept up, and will he come down in a frock or in trousers? were questions she might have continued with, were it not for Laurie's hands suddenly withdrawing from the table top. She could almost hear his mind ticking over.

'You're right, of course,' he said smoothly. 'Lydia is a man. However, she doesn't *feel* like a man; her view of herself is essentially female. Since she wishes to be treated as such, surely it's a matter of courtesy . . .'

(Oh yeah? – well, courtesy to *my* view of *my*self, just call me Your Royal Highness.) She didn't say this, of course; no point in being cheap when some really pertinent point was begging to be made – if only she could put her finger on it . . .

She felt deadly tired. Her head was a ton weight. She propped it up on one hand while the other fed toast into her mouth – not to gain sustenance, but time.

The process of hunting dubiously for the right words began to feel oddly familiar – as if she had embarked on it many times before, but had always aborted before it could succeed. Was this because in some amorphous way she had long understood about Laurie, but was so fearful of the consequences that she had got into the habit, whenever her mind wandered dangerously near the truth, of stopping up any leading words or thoughts? No, she couldn't be sure. After all, last night when Monica spelled it out, her reaction had been one of total shock. And yet . . . Well, she could certainly recall one instance of her deliberately foiling an opportunity to learn something or other: the night after their parents were killed, when Laurie first suggested buying this house and she'd asked if this meant they'd get married. 'I've got something to tell you,' he'd said, and she'd half killed herself shutting him up. He never tried it again. Too scared of the consequences. Maybe they were both scared of the consequences. After all, once this thing was named they would never be entirely the same. And the devil of it was not knowing *how* they wouldn't be the same . . .

Well, thanks to Monica she was now in possession of a few key words (and one, 'bi' – presumably short for bisexual – so way off-beam it merely betrayed

Monica's touching assumption of a roaring sex life between her and Laurie); she had only to relate some of these handy terms (*gay? drag?*) to what he had just said. But this was by no means easy.

'Actually,' she began, then stopped (embarking on speech was like stepping off a cliff and falling, falling . . .) 'Actually, I'm still very puzzled. I take what you say about Lydia, but in that case . . . what's in it for you?' (Getting these last words out was like ending up in the sea – with strong waves propelling her nearer and nearer to an unknown shore.) 'I mean, Laurie, a *woman* – or someone who purports to be one: how come you're so. . . enamoured?' (At this his body jumped as if a dart had entered it. Now they were both in it, she thought, both being swept to God knows where.) 'You see why I'm puzzled? Take Phillip Grainger – every inch a bloke and happy to be so, I dare say – eating his heart out: of the two I'd have thought he'd be more to your taste. Or take dashing and manly Jonathan from your TV show – I am right about him? – I bet he's available. As for *the lady herself,*' (she couldn't help investing contempt in the words) 'why isn't she looking for a man who – not to put too fine a point on it – finds women fanciable?' (Phew, that did it – she couldn't have hammered home her new knowledge more pointedly.)

A pause, during which, for the first time she ventured a proper look at him.

Slowly leaning forward to the table, he put his head between his hands. 'So you do know,' he muttered. 'I could never be sure.' (His voice came to her over the roar of blood in her ears – or was it the noise of breakers meeting the shore?) 'I used to dread that once you found out it'd be the end of *us*. Later, I decided you must have an idea. And that being so, I'd say to myself: she's intelligent enough to see that as I *am* gay, have been all this time, that's the package she knows and loves. Then I'd change my mind: If she really and truly knew she wouldn't want to waste her time. God, the arguments I've had with myself . . . So,' still looking at the table, 'how long have you known?'

If she kept very still the question might go away.

'I knew,' he went on, 'I ought to make it crystal clear before you decided about buying this place. And I did try – maybe not hard enough – but somehow you always cut me off. I suppose that was deliberate? There again, I could never work out why you'd do it. Is it because she knows but doesn't want to talk about it? I'd wonder; or because she doesn't, but suspects there's a fly somewhere in the ointment and prefers ignorance? Yet all the time . . .' He ventured a rueful smile, but she quickly ducked her head.

'Yes – Lydia,' he agreed, reading her gesture as one of impatience. 'So what's in it for me? you ask. Not a great deal, is the short answer – in the terms you imply. For, as you rightly point out, I can't be the sort of guy Lydia has her sights on; presumably, to confirm her view of herself, she needs to attract a man who gets turned on by women.' (Only days afterwards did she recall this remark and wonder if he'd presented himself to Lydia as such – with herself as the evidence, the live-in girlfriend. But at this moment she was merely hanging onto his words – and battling against unreality.)

'I'm not sure what I want,' he reflected, 'apart from being able to see her, admire her, be with her. She knocked me out the first time I saw her (well she is rather an eyeful) – though I admit what I thought I was seeing was a bloke flaunting his gayness, glorying in it – which was quite a turn on. I soon learned that if you want to get close to Lydia you damn well take her at her own estimation. And suddenly I was hooked, couldn't get her out of my mind – infatuation, I suppose, of a particularly virulent kind – which promptly turned sex between us into a no-go area. You see, when I'm overwhelmed emotionally I never can . . . perform. Afraid I need a certain detachment for sexual congress – though I don't have to explain that to you, do I? – I mean that's been your experience, more or less?' And when she threw up her head in frowning amazement: 'Those brief encounters you told me about,' he reminded her, 'taking those men in somewhat goal-orientated fashion. Worried me like hell, made me wonder whether we'd both been warped by our upbringing or something . . . Come on, you remember,' he persisted (for she was frowning harder than ever), 'Zak, and . . . Charles was it? and the German zoologist, and the bloke you picked up at the conference in Bergen?'

She dropped her eyes, bit her lip.

He decided he'd better stick to his own case. 'For my part, I suspect I never came to terms with sexual intercourse – a candidate for celibacy, perhaps? Anyway, for several reasons nothing of that sort is likely to work for me and Lydia. Sad but there it is: fall for someone and I can't damn well make it.'

By now her emotions had taken so many turnings she'd lost count of where they'd ended up, or indeed which was uppermost. Then her mouth opened, became hugely square-shaped: a square red funnel for huge red anger.

'Don't you dare say I'm like you!' she yelled. 'It's not true at all, it's the reverse. *I* fell for *you* years and years ago . . . and I've been dying to make it – years and years . . . *bloody dying*.' She was crying wildly now as well as shouting, her words coming between heaving gasps like bursts of gunfire. 'Yeah, I screwed those men . . . because. . . *you didn't want me, you bastard!* I only told you about 'em . . . to make you jealous, to show you. . . some blokes fancy me, though I couldn't. . . actually fancy them, to try and . . . make you think of me that way.'

She lurched over to the sideboard, grabbed a handful of tissues, blew, cried some more, blew and wiped. He came after her. '*Leave me alone!*' And putting up stiff arms to keep him off, she threw back her head and howled. When he seized her wrists and hung on to them, they shook in unison, as if caught on live wire.

It was the sight of his tears that caused hers to falter. Gulping, she watched them stand in his eyes and finally spill. When his grip slackened, she took the chance to grab more tissues, to blow her nose and mop her face. Then moved away to chuck the sodden handful into the waste bin; leaned against the sink, stared out into the garden.

Red leaves of Virginia creeper lay on the lawn like blotches of blood. Signalling an end, she thought. There were other signs of the closing season – yellowing leaves on the willow, orange rosehips, the spent black stems of gaunt shrubs . . . When behind her Laurie spoke, his words registered belatedly.

'I'm frankly terrified to think how I've harmed you.'

They impacted on her slowly, with shock.

She turned round. 'That's perfect nonsense. No, listen,' for he was shaking his head, 'I'm not a fool, and I'm twenty-seven years old. Of course in some sense I must have known you were . . . gay.' (The word was difficult, but practice, she remembered, made perfect). 'I suppose I wilfully blocked it out, determined you'd fit in with what I wanted. Sheer bloody obstinacy. I've been perfectly free to find someone else – and if I haven't bothered to, that's my look out. So please, Laurie, forget what I said – or at least the way I said it – making out I had reason to be bitter when it's perfectly clear I don't. Simply I was angry, jealous as hell, to discover you love someone else.'

'Yes, but it doesn't mean . . . Claire, you don't imagine it means I've stopped loving you? Claire?'

Damn and blast she was going to start crying again. Unable to speak she nodded, then lost the question and shook her head instead. He put his arms round her. 'I could never stop loving you. Surely you know that?' He held her away from him. 'Please say you do.'

She nodded. 'Yes, yes.'

'Lord, you had me worried for a minute.' This,

sounding more like the Laurie who liked always to be in control, made her laugh. Relieved, he tucked her head under his chin. 'How I feel about you is utterly different from how I feel about Lydia. Loving you is like breathing; I can't *not*. Loving Lydia – well, it's a form of madness. I know it can't last, though right now the thought that it mightn't makes me feel quite desperate. So bear with me, love. Don't go against me.'

'Of course I won't. I couldn't.'

For some moments he held and rocked her in silence. Then, recalling what started all this, declared, 'I shouldn't have asked her to stay. It wasn't fair on you. I'll find somewhere else. Maybe she can go to Phillip's – hell, no, there I go again, hurting people. (Yes, you were right about Phillip, he does terribly yearn for me; I'm afraid as far as I'm concerned he's simply a friend.) No, but I will think of somewhere Lydia can go.'

It was a chance, she suddenly saw, to make amends. 'Don't. Leave things as they are. I mean it, Laurie,' she cried, freeing herself. 'In any case, I'll be out most of today and tomorrow – I'll be at the field centre, we're lifting some of the trial potatoes. So I won't even be around.'

'Well, if you're absolutely sure . . .'

'I am, I am. Good heavens,' she laughed bravely, 'it's only for one weekend.'

v

Jumping from the bus at the end of the avenue early on Monday evening, striding along the pavement lined with garden hedges and gates on one side, lampposts and plane trees on the other, Claire was all happy anticipation. She swung her case to and fro and pictured her empty house. Or maybe it would be empty except for Laurie. Come to think of it, she would not be altogether dismayed if a couple of chums were discovered drinking tea in the kitchen, or a gang of students taking their ease after being inveigled by Laurie into raking up fallen leaves; her high spirits should even survive a visit from Phillip. (Poor Phillip, as she now charitably thought of him. Since learning the reason why he called so often and stayed so long, of the secret he covered with his look of a bulbous frog, her attitude to him had softened, she planned to be specially nice to atone for her spitefulness the other evening and also several crushing remarks made on previous occasions.) All that mattered was that the house be empty of Lydia.

It had been a terrible weekend. Arriving totally drained at the field centre on Saturday morning, she had mixed up the labels on trays of potato specimens – created just the sort of confusion, in fact, her presence was supposed to prevent (it was student helpers, not academic supervisors, who were supposed to make silly mistakes); luckily, in the lab on Sunday she managed to retrieve the situation, for under magnification the various batches were seen to have distinctive markings. On both evenings recuperation had been impossible. At supper on Saturday she was too hideously uncomfortable wondering how much of her outburst had been overheard by Lydia and what Laurie might have said to explain it away. By Sunday she was finding it an ordeal to so much as raise eyes to their guest, who in her tired mind had begun to loom like some mythical creature, larger than life, a bringer of doom. Also, a *frisson* of embarrassment sometimes leapt between herself and Laurie (of the sort that afflicts friends who have rowed and made up and now must rub along in the light of passionately exchanged home truths). Perhaps this was to be expected after their mutual soul-bearing. Their relationship had taken a jolt. It was in convalescence. They needed time and privacy to adjust to their altered perspectives. For all these reasons, she was avid to re-establish with Laurie the easy-going normality of life at home.

She unlocked the front door and stepped into the hall, gently closed the door behind, then looked as usual to her left, to the hatstand. That Laurie's hat was hanging there did not at this time of year (when it was still quite mild) guarantee his presence. She unwound her lacey green scarf (not being worn as head protection at the moment but as a loop of colour on her shoulders, and because Laurie had given it her) and draped it over the second peg. Then walked down the hall looking first into the dining-room and then the kitchen. Both were deserted. It began to seem that she had returned indeed to an empty house. She retraced her steps. The sitting-room door was closed, and in any case the room was seldom used at this time of day, so without bothering to look inside she turned and headed upstairs. Then she heard something. It took her a few seconds – hand on the banister rail – to work out the nature of the noise. Of course, she'd forgotten about the television: Laurie was amusing himself with their new toy. Grinning, she ran down and went to join him.

As she had supposed, in the sitting-room the television was on. But she was taken aback to discover the furniture re-arranged – the settee dragged from the wall to stand across the front of the set, so that all to be seen was its back and a pair of large white feet sticking over one end, and beyond this the animated screen. The sight was so unexpected – as was the absence of Laurie's usual greeting – that she hesitated and with some caution approached the feet, which disappointingly turned out to be Lydia's. Lydia was sprawled there full-length. Expressionless eyes flicked momentarily from the television to Claire and straight back again. There was no greeting.

Claire felt her blood rise. This was the first time she had found herself alone with their guest. So far, their exchanges, though distant, had been polite; but now with Laurie absent, Lydia evidently felt free to forgo even the minimum courtesies. In which case, she'd be

259

damned if she'd bother with them herself. 'I didn't expect to find you still here,' she observed baldly.

'Didn't you?' came the careless answer.

'No. I thought you were staying for the weekend – because that's when your landlord gets restless or something – and were returning today to crack on with finding somewhere else to live. That's what I thought Laurie said.' When no comment on this was made, she asked, 'Where is Laurie?'

'No idea.'

'Well, do you mind telling me your plans? I am the joint householder here.'

This aroused faint amusement. 'Actually,' a languid wrist was raised, a watch consulted, 'my immediate plans are to get ready for work.'

'What work? What do you do?'

'I'm a doctor's receptionist. Evening surgery starts in an hour. Time I got a move on.'

'You're kidding!'

'You know, I'm not sure I like your tone. You're not trying to be rude by any chance?'

'I'm just surprised. You're not my idea of a doctor's receptionist.'

'U-huh. Maybe on that score I'll give you the benefit of the doubt. You do get some hideous old dragons guarding doctors' appointments. That's because most doctors loathe their patients and wish to be saved from them as far as possible. My boss is not that sort.'

'And what sort is he?'

Before the arrival of any reply, long legs were swung to the floor and hands reached for a pair of mules. Then: 'A very clever and understanding and enlightened gentleman. Any further queries?'

'Yeah. How long're you staying?'

'My, you *were* at the back of the queue when they were handing out social graces.' Unravelling to full height (which Claire suddenly found intimidating and stepped back from), Lydia sighed. 'Really, I haven't a clue. Who can say what the future holds?' With which, slippers swinging from fingertips, she sashayed across the carpet and out of the room.

Claire switched off the TV. She was still staring at the blank screen, baffled by the unpleasantness of this exchange (all right, they were never going to like one another, and she had been pretty blunt about wanting Lydia to make haste and leave – but this hardly justified Lydia's contempt for her), when the front door came open and Laurie called, 'Back at last! Anyone home?'

She went into the hall.

'Hello, pet. Ghastly meeting – thought it would never end. And there's another in the Union tonight which I ought to look in on. Lydia about?'

'Upstairs. Getting ready for work. Um . . .'

'Ah, yes.' He strode to the stairs. 'I might as well give her a lift.'

She watched him bound upstairs and disappear along the landing; heard him call out his offer of a lift then retrace his steps to his own room; heard his bedroom door close. She went into the kitchen, filled the kettle.

Laurie came in as she was sipping her tea.

'Like a cup?'

'Yes, *please*,' he said emphatically on his way to the fridge and the food cupboard. 'I'll just make a sandwich for now, and have supper later. Don't forget there's heaps of salmon left from yesterday, and some salad in the box.'

'Yeah, I'll find something.' His bustling haste made her feel lumbering. Her tongue seemed to cleave to the roof of her mouth as, bringing his cup to the table, she forced herself to remark, 'Lydia's still here, then.'

'Yes.' He darted a look at her. 'It seems sensible for her to flat-hunt from here, rather than keep moving about. That's not a problem for you, love, is it?'

He made it sound so reasonable. 'Well,' she shrugged, 'I suppose not.' He darted over to the cutlery drawer, brought out a bread knife. There was no time now for a discussion, he seemed to be signalling. And perhaps in any case she wasn't up to it so soon after all the talking on Saturday. After a moment, she said, 'Right, I'll leave you to it.'

Sawing slices from a loaf, he dashed a smile at her.

On her return from work the following evening, Claire was greeted by Laurie's familiar call from the kitchen.

'Hiya,' she replied, stopping by the hatstand to divest herself of jacket and scarf. Behind the sitting-room door, the television was giving out. Of course, it was too much to hope that Lydia would have found a flat and moved into it all in one day. And perhaps it would be better not to ask, this evening, how the search was progressing. Don't pile on the pressure, be patient; give them a chance, she persuaded herself.

Laurie's car was not in the drive when she returned home on Wednesday. Going into the house, she encountered silence, and a brief look into the ground floor rooms encouraged her sense of the place being deserted. Her sprits rose. Maybe Laurie was helping Lydia move in somewhere. She went into the kitchen, filled the kettle, plugged it in, then turned to collect a cup from a cupboard – and nearly jumped out of her skin: Lydia had arrived in the doorway, was lolling against the door-frame, watching her.

Claire hesitated, took down her cup and saucer, then hesitated again as the pressures of normal politeness caught up. But hell, no, she would not offer tea to someone who by rights shouldn't even be here; to someone, furthermore, who couldn't even manage a civilized greeting. Waiting for the tea to brew, she wondered why her ears had missed Lydia's approach. It was not the first time this had happened. Hateful, the thought of somebody creeping about like a spy. It was a nuisance, but she'd have to drink her tea in her bedroom, the possibility of relaxing anywhere else in the house was now nil. She filled her cup and turned

– yes, still under silent and expressionless observation; really, if she wasn't purposefully exercising detachment it would be quite unnerving. Taking care not to slop her tea, saying 'Excuse me' in a neutral tone, she passed through the occupied doorway then bore her cup upstairs.

An hour later, Laurie knocked on her door. 'Can I come in?'

'Of course.'

He stood in the doorway, looked at her lying on the bed. 'Not well, pet?'

'Bit of a headache, that's all.'

'What a shame. Have you taken something?

She nodded. 'Um, Laurie . . .'

'I do hope it hasn't spoiled your appetite, because I'm making one of your favourite dishes – ricotta and spinach filled crêpes.'

'Oh,' she laughed, the wind rushing out of her sails. 'With tomato sauce and béchamel?'

'Naturally. Topped with parmesan.'

'Cor! I'm hungry already.'

'Just mind you're down by eight sharp to eat it,' he warned, turning away, then closing the door.

She laid down her book and sank back with relief. That had been their old selves talking again. His desire to please her and her own quick response of pleasure had banished, at least for the moment, the cautious embarrassment that had marred their exchanges these past few days.

Sadly, Laurie's labours on Claire's behalf resulted in no pleasure at all for Lydia. 'What in heaven's name is it, Laurie?' she complained, prodding her crêpes with her fork.

'It's very delicious and very good for you. Give it a try,' he ordered.

She obeyed, but with a reluctance that could only result in rejection, Claire foresaw.

'Oh yuk, no thanks. I hate that sort of sloppy stuff. I need *meat* when I've been on my feet all day.'

263

Laurie laid down his fork. 'Well then, let me think. How about grilled ham and tomatoes?'

'Much more like it. Would it be a terrible nuisance?'

Laurie left the table and went to the fridge. When Lydia made no move but merely commented that he was an absolute angel, Claire also got up – found some foil to cover his plate which she set in the oven to keep warm.

'Ah, thanks, love,' he said, looking harassed.

And Claire, who had hoped to find an opportunity during the meal to enquire after the progress of the flat hunt, decided after all not to mention it.

On Thursday she worked late, and afterwards ate dinner in the Senior Common Dining-Room – where penance turned to reward when David Guthrie joined her. She made amends for having cut him off when they were talking about Foscote at the party the other evening by recounting one or two amusing anecdotes. Afterwards they took their coffee to the large lounge and sat opposite one another in deep armchairs. She hinted that she'd quite like to see the Jean Luc Goddard film being shown later on. He didn't rise to the bait – so maybe, she thought, he had work to finish. But he had evidently enjoyed her company because when he got up to go he said they must do it again.

She went to film soc on her own. Only afterwards on the bus home did it occur to her that David might have assumed she'd arranged to go with Laurie. Even so, he could have joined them. But if he wasn't a film buff why would he want to? No, there was no cause to feel discouraged. And at least she'd managed to spend an entire day out of the house, away from enemy occupation.

Friday morning was misty and cold. In the kitchen, Laurie grilling kippers and buttering toast and pouring coffee was producing marvellously inviting smells. She'd intended to hurry off to the university and grab a bite when the coffee-shop opened, but his greeting, 'Hello – horrid morning – compensation coming up!' combined with the aromas was simply too much for her will-power.

'You're a treasure,' she said, sitting to table.

'You were late in last night.'

'Not very,' she objected. 'I stayed for a film. Oh, but first I had dinner with David Guthrie.'

'Did you?' he cried.

Finding his pleased excitement at this news suddenly riling, she kept to the subject of the film.

When the kippers were ready, they stopped talking and concentrated on the job in hand – picking and spitting out bones, mopping up butter, wiping mouths. Almost she felt underhand, enjoying his cooking while preparing to ask a straight question. However, it had to be done. 'So,' she began, 'here we are at the end of the week with our guest still in residence. What are her plans, do you know? Any luck with finding a flat?' (She was relieved to have put the question at last, but embarrassed about that 'her': all week she had avoided feminine pronouns like the plague, and blow if one hadn't slipped out! Actually, she had also shrunk from using masculine pronouns, for fear of appearing to be taking a hard-faced stand. As far as possible she had stuck to 'Lydia', 'your friend' and 'our guest' – though the results were sometimes disgustingly convoluted. Trouble was, she was beginning to think 'she' and 'her'.)

Reaching for her used plate, he asked, 'You remember it's my day for the TV studios? Well . . .' he took the plates to the waste-bin, 'as Lydia has a couple of days off and since a friend of hers – someone who works at the studios – is having a party tomorrow, we thought we'd make a weekend of it. Though I'm sure,' he added, his tone changing to formal, 'you're most welcome to join us.'

'You mean come with you and Lydia to Manchester? Do me a favour!'

He rinsed the plates under the tap, then ran water into a bowl adding a hefty squirt of detergent. Watching the bubbles rise (so intently he might be gauging the foam's density) he asked, 'Is it such a bother to you, my having a friend to stay?'

Put like that it was hard to say 'Yes'. Jeanette and family had been for a week (at Claire's invitation), Rosie her old school chum had spent time here last summer, and never a word from Laurie other than welcoming ones. Likewise, she had not objected when he asked Toby and Jessica to stay, or when his ex-colleagues from the jazz band came for a weekend jam-session. But this, as he knew full well, was different – though her objections were not the obvious ones. How could she put it to him? That she was not objecting out of jealousy (true, it was far from ideal to be sharing her home with her rival and perhaps she would rather not, but this could not be the cause of such shrinking dislike). Nor honestly and truly was she objecting because of the transvestism. (She had thought hard about this, and believed she would keep an open mind about any person – including a man who needed to live as woman or a woman who needed to live as a man; she would simply judge how they came across as a human being and respond accordingly.) The crux of the matter was that Lydia came across as a bitingly cold fish and faintly sinister to boot. So please, Laurie, she asked silently, don't get the wrong idea. 'The thing is,' she said aloud, 'I don't feel comfortable with Lydia.'

'Ah.'

'Look it's not . . . because I'm jealous or anything. And it's not because of the transvestism . . .'

'Don't use that word,' he put in hurriedly.

'Why ever not?'

'Because she's not . . .' he glanced nervously at the door (which was shut) and lowered his voice to a whisper, 'not just a cross-dresser; it's more fundamental than that. She's actually saving to have surgery,' he shivered at the word in spite of himself. 'We'll talk about it another time; just remember the correct word's *transsexual*.'

'Oh. Right.'

'My goodness,' he cried loudly, turning to look out of the window, 'the weather's certainly turned. Button-up securely today, dear. If you can hang on for an hour I'll run you in; I have to call at the office to pick up the mail. You know you really ought to get yourself a car.'

'With buses going by at both ends of the avenue?' she responded automatically (while thinking: so the discussion is over).

'But it'd save waiting for them in such miserable weather. And think of the inconvenience when you have to go to Utterby.' (Utterby was where the department had its experimental field sites.)

'It's perfectly convenient to borrow the van.'

'And how many times have I heard you grumble about Paul hogging it, or moaning about it being taken out and not signed for?'

He was talking for the sake of talking. They'd had this argument before. She got to her feet. 'No, I can't wait, I have to be off. Thanks for a delicious breakfast. Have a nice trip, and good luck with the programme – I'll try and watch it,' she promised, going over to give him a hurried kiss. 'See you.'

'See you,' he agreed absently. 'I say, why don't you have someone round?'

'Oh, I expect Monica'll call. And possibly Yolande . . .'

'You could ask David Guthrie.'

She stared. 'Why the hell would I want to do that?' And stomped away to dig out her winter coat.

She strode down the avenue with her green scarf pulled high against the fog, teeming with tension. She decided to give the bus a miss – it was only twenty-five minutes' walk to the university, and perhaps the exercise would help her feel better. It was not until she came within sight of the university gates that the kernel of her frustration became clear. The tricky bastard had never answered her question. She was still none the wiser about Lydia's intentions. For all she knew they were stuck with her.

Looking bleak, Laurie brought the tray back downstairs. It was relieved of its cup of coffee, but still bore buttered toast and a plump brown kipper – the plumpest and moistest kipper of the three he had purchased yesterday in the fish market – of this he was sure, having prodded and scrutinized each in turn this morning before deciding which to reserve for Lydia. Cooking it just now, he had imagined her fork hooking up the blackened backbone, lifting it with all its crispy skin attached, and the pink-cream succulence revealed beneath, and how tender it would feel in the mouth, and how deliciously would ooze its juices. But it was not to be. His beloved had spurned his offering. A cocotte of smoked fish pâté might be made from it of course, but he hadn't the heart. In the kitchen, dumping the tray on the table, he briefly considered next door's cat (for he hated waste): but – No, he admonished; just get it over. He dumped the toast on to the kipper, seized the plate and a knife, swept over the room to the waste-bin, applied foot to pedal and scraped. As he moved away the bin's lid clacked down nastily behind him.

Washing the dishes, he consoled himself that at least Claire had enjoyed her kipper, his efforts were not entirely wasted. Then his hands fell still, he raised a frowning face. Claire might have breakfasted well, but she certainly hadn't obtained the satisfaction she'd asked for. Quite the reverse, he'd deliberately thwarted her. She'd had every right to ask her question, but he'd manipulated her to feel badly about doing so. Because the stark fact was, he was desperate to keep Lydia under this roof. (Yes, he had better face up to it – he had deliberately misled Claire. For, if she only knew,

268

it was *he* who had prevailed on *Lydia* to stay. He had brushed aside the subject of flat-hunting – 'Plenty of time for that. Relax here for a while. You deserve a break after all you've been through.' And when it was necessary to collect items she needed from her rooms, he had driven her over himself to make certain of her returning to 97 Devonshire.) His obsession, his violent desire to hang on to her, to keep her with him, he supposed would pass in time; violent desires usually did – he wasn't so utterly changed that he couldn't acknowledge this and imagine how he might feel about this episode some time in the future. Angry, puzzled, ashamed? Probably all of these. Once passion goes cold, though one remembers why one behaved as one did, the reason is no longer sufficient; memories are not passion-tinted, they can provoke disgust. For instance, he knew absolutely for certain that years hence the look on Claire's face at breakfast this morning would return to him – and how he would then castigate himself.

Good Lord, he must be besotted! All his life he'd looked out for Claire, sought to protect her, fretted if he suspected she was neglecting her studies, or accepting dubious smokes, or getting messed up by some insensitive guy. Now here he was himself doing the messing! He sighed lengthily, deeply . . .

Then his hands became busy again – there were things to do, he must get on. Anyway, it was pointless and contemptible to start agonizing when he knew damn well he would pursue his infatuation, come what may, at least for the immediate future.

Overhead, a door closed. He fell still, listening. Soon water ran in the cistern. She was up and about. Oh, just live for this moment, he thought, shutting his eyes. And a pre-run of their weekend excursion leapt through his mind like a brilliantly lit film, full of pace and vivacity; and joy pouring inside entered his ears like an ecstatic song.

*   *   *

Monica, handing her a glass, observed, 'Your visitor's still with you, then,' as if making an everyday comment for the sake of politeness, like, 'I see your pea project was mentioned in the *New Scientist*,' or 'Are you enjoying that novel I lent you?'

'Yeah,' Claire mumbled, and said no more in case Paul was about.

'Paul's seeing his research student this evening – in The Hesketh Arms – so he won't be home for hours and hours.'

It was very disconcerting the way Monica read your mind and made no bones about it – like an eavesdropper suddenly inserting into a private conversation her own comments. Still, at least they were not likely to be interrupted . . .

'Although,' Monica warned, 'I did ask Eleanor and Joyce to come round later, and Liz Fulbright if she's not too bushed after the Birmingham conference – oh, and Yolande might make it. I thought it was time we took a serious look at the way this dump fails to promote women.' She paused – her green eyes considering Claire (in, Claire felt, a peculiarly penetrating way). 'But they won't be here for ages yet. Have a nibble.'

'Oh – thanks,' said Claire, only now noticing the plate; and because Monica seemed to be willing the words, agreed once more that Lydia was still installed in number 97 Devonshire.

'So, how long's it been? Must be three weeks.'

'Four to the very night,' Claire corrected her, 'the night of the party.' (Not taking her eyes off her friend, Monica opened her red-lipsticked mouth and popped in a giant potato crisp.) 'In my opinion, she's using Laurie. Sorry, by the way, but I have to say 'she' and 'her'; I find it's the only way . . .'

'Of course.'

'Laurie is completely in thrall. Waits on her hand and foot. She has everything for free – free food, free booze, the very last comfort. Yeah, she's using him all right.'

'Mm.' (Reaching forward for her drink, Monica delivered a riveting view of her freckled cleavage.) 'Well,' she gulped some of her wine, 'mm, that's inevitable, I'm afraid. We all use people.'

'We do not.'

'Course we do – all the time. Say you feel bad about not being appreciated at work, or because an inattentive hairdresser cut off two inches of hair when you'd said half an inch, ten to one you relieve your feelings on your nearest and dearest. Or say you feel wildly happy – maybe your lover's come back from abroad; ergo, hubby gets a kiss and his favourite supper. Kids in a paddy take it out on their mothers, and mothers only have 'em in the first place to fulfil a biological urge. Men marry to be serviced and to enhance their careers, and when they go and make arses of themselves in public you can bet their wives'll stand by them in order to protect their meal-tickets. Friends give each other earache working out personal problems (and no, I'm not getting at *you*), while others wheedle out confidences because knowledge is power and gives a bit of a thrill   Admit it, I'm right: everyone uses everybody.'

'Yeah, well, see what you mean,' Claire mumbled, shifting in her chair and crossing her legs. Sometimes it was hard knowing quite how to take Monica. 'Obviously it depends what you mean by *use*. What *I* mean is: using someone deliberately, in a calculating fashion. Which sums up Lydia. It's creepy the way she'll sit staring at you, her face totally blank, no expression; you can almost hear her working things out. Of course, when Laurie's around he's half killing himself supplying her every need, so he never has time to notice.'

'Sounds like, if he's keen as all that, he likes having her there. Maybe its more *him* using *her*.'

'Look, I concede he wants her around (though take it from me, he's not getting the traditional quid pro quo). But there are consequences: he's missed more than one lecture I happen to know . . .'

'Has he really?'

'He has, and resigned from the NSCC . . .'

'Er?'

'Natural Sciences Co-ordinating Committee. And that's a body blow, we were depending on Laurie to fight our corner. You know Bot and Zoo come under Bio as from next year? – well, think of the resource implications, not to mention the scramble for chairs. Laurie's such an asset for us botanists. I mean, who else is there?'

'Paul?' mildly suggested Paul's wife.

'Er – yeah,' she agreed, trying to sound both enthused and amazed that she hadn't thought of this herself. 'I say though, you will keep it under your hat about Laurie missing lectures?'

'Of course.'

'Paul hasn't said anything?'

'No – well not about that.'

Relieved, Claire took up her glass. 'But you see what I'm getting at?' she cried, returning triumphantly to the point: 'If Lydia wasn't such a selfish bitch she wouldn't let him do those things.'

Monica nodded. She crunched another crisp – 'Mm, you said just now,' and paused to swallow, 'Laurie wasn't getting a quid pro quo. You mean..?'

'Oh, but I shouldn't have, it was a confidence.'

'Then not another word,' Monica declared, and to cover her disappointment peered down her front and hoicked out a crumb. 'But Laurie's still going strong on the telly, I see.'

'Of course. Lydia revels in that. She's in with that crowd, which is how they met, I take it.'

'What's his – pardon, her – real name?' Monica asked curiously.

Claire looked blank. 'Do you know, I've no idea – isn't that weird? – not even a surname. Gosh, I wonder if Laurie . . . Oh, he must. I suppose those people they meet in Manchester would know . . . That's another thing, taking her with him to the TV studios: it shows how completely dotty he's become, how he's changed. OK, he's probably sailed pretty close to the wind before now (I know for a fact he did when he was in the army), but generally, professionally speaking, he's circumspection itself. I mean he really does take appearances seriously.'

'I shouldn't worry. I expect everything's different in media circles. He's not so far gone that he escorts her about on campus. As long as he keeps the two worlds apart . . .'

'But plenty of people have seen her at our place.'

'Yes, but *friends*. And you're there, too, maintaining the proprieties. Sweetie, don't look so agitated. Drink up and have another.' She reached round to the table and grasped the bottle. 'You know, I'm sure this thing will pass.'

'But God, Monica, when?'

After dinner in the kitchen they went into the dining-room and sat on either side of the fireplace, as they had on countless evenings before Lydia's coming Claire sipping the last of her wine, Laurie with a cup of coffee cooling beside him. It did not happen by chance this cosy tête à tête. After nearly two months (thanks to her training – 'OBSERVATION!' her tutor at Sutton would cry, urging the acquisition of this most essential scientific skill), Claire was now quite adept at anticipating Lydia's work pattern – which shift she was likely to be working, when a free day was due. This enabled her to make her own plans, to decide whether to spend the whole day at work, eat in or out, spend an evening at a friend's house or, on golden evenings like this, stay at home with Laurie. She did not always guess correctly, but scored a hit often enough to feel she was regaining some control. Now that dinner was over she knew she would only have Laurie to herself for another half-hour. She rather hoped a friend would call and prevent Lydia dominating the rest of the evening. But this was unlikely; these days people seldom dropped in.

'We could go in the other room and watch television,' Laurie suggested.

'But it's nice sitting here, isn't it?'

'Of course. Absolutely. Well now, how are you getting on? I hear there's been a roar of approval for your work on pea cellulase. Owen showed me the piece in the *New Scientist*.'

'Yes. Funny, but they've been doing something pretty similar – though more high-powered – at McGill. I had a smashing letter from a professor there – he'd read my report for the B. A. symposium. Enclosed some stuff about theirs.'

'But that's marvellous,' he beamed (though he did not insist, as he surely would have two months ago, on a sight of the correspondence). After a moment he glanced at the clock.

Yes, only another ten minutes, she thought, following his eyes.

Laurie was praying that Lydia wouldn't be late. He couldn't bear it when she was, having to steel himself to appear calm while secretly agonizing over where she'd gone, who with, and whether she would come back at all. He must get a grip on this need to control. To an extent he'd been the same with Claire – wanting to keep tabs on her, to keep her near. But Claire, who loved him, did not resist; Lydia, if his anxieties proved irksome, would simply cast him off.

'So – you're fast becoming the star of the department,' he boomed, making an effort.

She didn't respond, merely gathered his abstractedness – not so much from his voice but the tight look of his face, his hunched posture and his knees clamping his hands.

When a noise came in the hall, he was like a released spring. 'There she is!' he yelled, bounding to his feet.

His suddenness made Claire flinch. She stared at his empty chair, listened to his blather in the hall. 'Oh my

274

dear, you look frozen. Give me your coat – I insist, it's wet. Go in and get warm while I hang it to dry.' Bracing herself with a slurp of wine, Claire sensed (but did not hear) footsteps behind her. (Lydia moved noiselessly as a cat.) The only approach she could swear to was Laurie's bustling return. 'Sit down, sit down; pull up the chair. We'll soon' – he flung on to his knees in front of the gas fire and struck a match – 'have it cosy and warm,' he promised, as if the radiators were not already blaring heat. 'Now what can I get you? Something on a tray? Hot drink? Something stronger?'

Sinking gracefully into the chair Laurie had urged upon her, Lydia stretched out her long hairless nylon-encased legs; and bringing her arms through the air like a swimmer, allowed her head to fall back. (Light from the wall bracket pinpointed her larynx's give-away protrusion.) 'Nothing,' she said, flinging her head forward with a flying swirl of pale gold, 'nothing at all for the moment. Just to sit by the fire in perfect . . . *peace.*' The final word was so affectingly dwelt over that Laurie, pausing with his head on one side, seemed to be tracing its susurrating flight. And Claire, in spite of herself, was unable not to admire the grace of movement, or to acknowledge that the feminine fluidity expressed by those long angular limbs was disconcertingly stirring. Laurie was first to collect himself. 'But you must want something.'

'For heaven's sake, Laurie, she said *not for the moment,*' snapped Claire, banging down her glass.

And Lydia smiled – at least, the corners of her mouth moved. 'Though when I'm properly thawed I might welcome a bite. I'll have it in front of the telly if you don't mind. Lovely Sean Connery is on at nine-thirty.'

Laurie returned meekly to his chair.

The dream ran as usual; the same pattern, the same detail: she pushed through the woods and followed the stream with the same fanatical persistence. But somewhere along the line, a sense grew of it all being futile.

Laurie was certainly here somewhere. It was just not in her to find him. Maybe this was because of some fault, like her squint preventing her picking him out, or she was too clumsy to be sufficiently quick, or too small to reach him, or too insignificant to be worth his waiting. Then she woke up, the dream heavy in her mind. A bitter grin came on her face, and her conscious self addressed her dreaming self: none of those things necessarily, duckie. Just the wrong bloody sex.

Claire was leaving the Dining-Room with her case and a cup of coffee when David Guthrie came in. His face fell. 'Ah, what a shame. We could've eaten together.' They had eaten at least six dinners together recently, by happy chance.

'Well I'm in no hurry,' Claire said smoothly. 'See you afterwards for coffee?'

'Great.'

'Or,' she called after him two seconds later, 'we could go completely wild and have a drink in The Hesketh Arms.'

He hesitated. 'Why not? See you in about half an hour.'

The drinking area of The Hesketh Arms was one vast room broken by high-backed upholstered benches forming open-ended cubicles. Forty-five minutes later, Claire and David were seated in one of these cubicles, deep in red plush, their elbows and drinks resting on a polished wooden table. David was an historian, not a scientist; even so, news had reached him of plaudits she had received in scientific journals. He congratulated her. She talked about her work for a while, then returned the courtesy by asking after the book he was writing (on British foreign policy between the wars). Then David mentioned Laurie's continued success as a television performer. 'The mystery to me is, how he fits it all in – Dean of Students, and still teaching full-time I take it?'

'Oh yes.'

'How does he manage?'

'With difficulty I imagine,' she said. 'And I say *imagine* advisedly because we rarely have a chance to talk these days.'

'I'm not surprised – all those commitments.'

'And not only professional ones,' she said cryptically, picking up her glass (not to drink from it, but to occupy her hands while she waited for his signal to enlarge).

But he changed the subject. 'Talking about television . . .'

Feeling slightly cheated, she listened patiently nevertheless to an account of the latest documentary on the Vietnam War. And was soon engaged in animated discussion.

'Another one?' he asked eventually.

She jumped up. 'My turn.'

'No, no.'

'Yes, yes. Same again?' While she was getting the refills, he went to the Gents. They arrived back at their table more or less simultaneously.

'Thanks,' he said. 'Cheers.'

'Cheers. No, I hardly set eyes on Laurie these days, never mind talk,' she said, as if twenty minutes' despairing analysis of the war had merely punctuated a superior topic. 'As well as all these work commitments, he and Lydia evidently possess an insatiable circle of friends.'

'Uhuh,' said David, grasping his glass rather soon after his last slurp. As he drank, his eyes sought and found the bar clock. 'Mustn't be too long, I'm afraid. Got to lay my hands on some lecture notes when I get back. My filing system's a mess. I keep promising myself I'll sort it. You have that problem?'

'Er, not really. I'm pretty neat and tidy. Can't work otherwise.'

But he wasn't listening, he was gearing up to go – she could tell from the way he hung on to his glass when not actually drinking, and constantly eyed the clock. She should not have brought Lydia's name into the conversation. It had put him off, made him nervous.

Never one to flog a dead horse, she got to her feet. 'Time for me to go.'

His eyes went to her half-full glass, but he didn't protest. 'Walk you to the bus stop,' he said, and swilled down the last of his beer and retrieved his case. When a bus failed to materialize after three or four minutes, she urged him to leave her – there were plenty of people waiting, it was silly to waste time. He demurred half-heartedly, then went.

Sitting on top of the bus, swaying and swinging from stop to stop down Little Coates Road, she thought what a shame it was to have made him wary, for she truly liked David. Though she had to admit, he never aroused in her the tiniest flicker of desire. Perhaps though, if she were given the chance, in time this snag would be corrected. Or she could make herself keen by conjuring some sexy scenario. That is, if the occasion arose. Didn't look as if it was going to, though. Shame. Because David was nice . . . It was a bit worrying the way people (and not only David) shied away from any mention of Laurie's connection with Lydia. This could prove limiting for her, too, if she were associated with it in people's minds.

'Devonshire,' called the weary conductor. At which she abruptly got out of her seat and pushed down the aisle against the bus's erratic forward thrust to grasp the stair rail at the back.

vi

The only TV programmes Claire ever seemed able to catch were those featuring Laurie or Vietnam. There were films she might have enjoyed and science-based programmes, but Lydia hogged the television, and Lydia's taste was not her taste. *Talking Triangle*, of

278

course, was switched on whether or not Lydia was at home, and it was generally possible to catch one of the showings of the evening news. The war had gone stale on her, she had followed it in the newspapers, it seemed, for ever, attended protest meetings, signed things, written letters to MPs; but now television bulletins revitalized her anger; the least she could do was watch and suffer vicariously. Also, as she often reproved herself, such wickedness and misery did put some perspective on one's personal problems.

One Sunday evening in February, she was following a televised debate on the subject when Lydia came in. Claire was sitting on the floor with her back resting against the settee (which was now left permanently in the position Lydia preferred – right across the TV set).

'That morbid stuff again,' Lydia tetchily observed. 'There's a good programme on in a minute.'

Clasping her knees, squinting at the screen, Claire endeavoured to ignore her – until the settee quaked behind as Lydia upped the pressure by settling down on it full length.

'How long's this go on for?'

'Where's Laurie?' Claire asked, in the faint hope of support.

'Out.'

'Where? When will he back?'

'How should I know? I'm not his keeper. He's probably gone down the docks to pick up some hairy-arsed trawlerman. I thought he was a bit restless earlier on.'

It took Claire a moment – staring sightlessly at the screen – to digest this. Then she scrambled to her feet and switched the set off. 'You don't even like Laurie. *Do you?*'

A muffled snort. 'If you're not watching any more, put on channel three. There's a dear,' she added, her eyes bright with some private joke.

'You don't even like him,' Claire repeated, as if trying to understand this herself.

Losing patience, Lydia heaved up, bounded past, pressed two buttons in quick succession, and flopped back down. 'Shift your carcass, you're blocking my view.'

But Claire stayed put.

'God, you're a peevish little twit. Anyway, what would you know about it? I wasn't slandering Laurie. Fact is, he likes a bit of rough, it's the way he gets off. So what? – each to his own. Though if there's one thing I do dislike, it's the way he hates himself afterwards. That's just pathetic in my book, hypocritical.' She had watched Claire closely throughout this, and now gave a pleased laugh. 'See? I was right, you haven't a clue. You really are as green as you look – I've often wondered. Let's see: how many years is it you've been Laurie's cover girl?'

'What?'

She laughed delightedly, nodding and raising her brows. 'A cover girl, *dear*, is how gay blokes refer to poor dumb chicks who act as their convenient girl-friends. Provide them with *cover*. Get it? Now will you please MOVE?'

This time Claire obliged. Moved right out of the room.

A bit of rough. Cover girl. The words haunted her for the rest of the evening. Later, lying in bed waiting for sleep, it was *a bit of rough* that distressed her most, with its hint of hurt and cruelty, of journeys Laurie took where she could never follow, of his deliberately courting danger which she would never understand. When his car sounded in the drive, she bounded up to the window and watched him come across the gravel and disappear under the porch. At least he was safe for tonight.

But the relief was insufficient to permit her to sleep. Eventually, her dreaming self grew impatient and imposed waves of her familiar search through the woods. Her conscious self resisted, feared that if the dream took hold she might actually come upon Laurie on this occasion, and in circumstances more upsetting than when he remained out of reach. The dream sucked at her. She pushed it back. Finally, summoning strength, she flung out of bed and put on the light. It was twenty past two; in a few hours she had important work to attend to. She took half a sleeping tablet and forced herself to read for a while; then lay back in bed in the dark and concentrated on the procedure she would use in the lab tomorrow. Until proper sleep drew her down.

Half an hour before the alarm was set to ring, she woke with a start. She lay staring at light beginning to show against the curtains and recalled the night before. *A bit of rough* had a stale ring to it. She had over-reacted, she decided, had proved easy prey to what had surely been spite on Lydia's part. She decided to get up and dress. Gradually, as sensible Monday morning asserted itself and fearful Sunday night dwindled to a sickly hung-over dream, the clearer she became in her mind that *a bit of rough* was merely a blast of sour air, a venting of Lydia's malice.

Cover girl, however, proved more tenacious. Over the following days, whatever she was doing, however firmly she squashed the phrase to the pit of her mind (way, way beneath all that she had recently learned about regulating pea growth, about the preference of certain types of potato for fishmeal fertilizer, about the effect on human beings of getting sprayed by defoliant, about Monica's strategies for winning pro-motion, about the Le Guinns' reconciliation, about Zena Turweston's hysterectomy), back they bounced: COVER GIRL. 'Cover girl, cover girl, cover girl,' taunted various persons inappropriately (from the Vice Chancellor to Mrs Smethurst, their cleaner) during the uneasy course of her dreams.

In one of these, Aunt Margaret used the expression – not in a hostile manner but as though it were an accepted fact, as though being 'cover girl' to Laurie were Claire's principle function in life. The dream stayed with her for days. It had never struck her before, but wasn't it odd of Aunt Margaret to have promoted a marriage (or at least 'settling down') between her son and the daughter of the woman who had stolen her husband? She had supposed that in her offhand manner Aunt Margaret was too fond of her to allow what her mother had done to come between them. But now a more likely explanation occurred to her; that guessing the truth about Laurie and fearful for him in this prejudiced world (and with Claire at hand, fiercely loyal, madly adoring, and patently and conveniently innocent), Aunt Margaret saw their union as a means of safeguarding her son.

Stupid to let two small words unsettle her. (It was like having a notice stuck on her back; she longed for someone to rip it off and authoritatively declare that it didn't apply.) Sometimes she rehearsed trying the words out on Laurie, dropping them casually as a silly saying of Lydia's. But she wouldn't let herself. Because however humiliating the revelation that it was possible for the world to view her this way (and at least the revelation that Lydia viewed her this way had cleared up the mystery of Lydia's contempt for her), she was convinced in her heart that they did not describe what she meant to Laurie. And since what she and he meant to each other formed probably the most precious part of her life, she was not going to insult or undermine this by so much as breathing the words in his hearing. She doubted whether Lydia would either. Every passing week brought evidence that the side Lydia presented to Laurie hid much that she allowed Claire to see.

But she did consider (in the hope of hearing it rubbished) testing the phrase out on Monica. Then thought better of it. For hadn't Monica recently remarked (meaning to reassure) that if people encountered Lydia when visiting 97 Devonshire Avenue, not to worry because she, Claire, was there 'maintaining the proprieties'? And then on another less recent occasion (possibly the night of the dreadful party), Monica had reminded her that life was still made difficult for gays, and then had added that in this respect Laurie must rather rely on her. How nearly, Claire wondered, did these notions of Monica's approximate to the convenience of a so-called cover girl?

The next day, as she was passing through the doorway to the Senior Common Room, Claire spotted Monica sitting inside. And swiftly changed her mind about coffee, turned and walked out.

'Hello,' said Paul Cage. Having ignored the 'KEEP OUT' sign on the side-lab door, he only cautiously put his head round.

'Close it,' said Claire, her voice muffled by a mask. 'Can't you read?' She squinted into the gloom. 'Who is it, anyway?'

'Paul,' he announced, stepping into the circle of light thrown by low green lamps. 'What've you got there?'

'If you mean to come another step nearer, put on a mask.'

Deciding to stay put, he watched from a distance one gloved hand holding a tiny seedling, the other wielding a blade. 'That's neat.'

'Shh.'

Eventually, peeling off the gloves, she looked up. 'What do you want?'

'To talk about the van. I say, that light does incredible things to your eyes – specially with a mask underneath. *Full of eastern promise!*'

She stepped away from the work area and removed the mask. When her eyes adjusted to the dimness she saw he was leaning back against one of the high benches in the centre of the lab, feet and arms crossed. As usual, he was entirely in black – leather jacket, crêpe shirt, narrow tie, cord trousers; a smooth black streak of a man. Endeavouring to convey an impression of scarcely even registering him, she demanded, 'What about the van?'

'I see you've booked it out next week, Tuesday to Thursday.'

'So?'

'Can't you be flexible?'

'Sorry, I've got people coming down. It's all fixed up.'

'Mm. Well do you think you could squeeze some of my stuff on board? I need to go down to Utterby on Tuesday. I can take my car and Jamie can take his, but . . .'

'Oh, that'd be OK.'

'Thanks. Load up Monday night, then. By the way, Monica thinks you're avoiding her.'

'Nonsense. 'Course I'm not.'

'Well that's what she thinks. Said you dashed into the Library rather than cross her path in the quad.'

'No, never. That it then?' When he said nothing, but carried on staring, she growled, 'Something bothering you?'

'You are,' he grinned. 'It's just occurred to me that you've got nothing on underneath that overall.'

'I certainly have.'

'Not a lot.'

'In case you haven't noticed, it's pretty warm working in here. This job needs a constant temperature . . .' Her voice faded as his grin broadened. He was loathsome, she thought, utterly disgusting. Monica wasn't so darn bright as she made out – always pressing her advice on people, yet look what she'd married! She'd like to wipe the smile off his cocksure face, show him two can play at this stupid game . . . She stepped forward aggressively and raised a suggestive hand to the top button of her laboratory overall. 'Like to see more?' she jeered.

Well, it was meant to be a jeer, but she heard with dismay that it didn't quite come off; it was left unclear whether she was calling his bluff, issuing a challenge

284

. . . Or *offering*, she thought, half-appalled, but all at once feeling in truth half-naked, her nerve ends jangled by the coarse cloth of the overall. Seemingly without any conscious go-ahead, her fingers slipped the button free.

'Any time!' he wowed. His eyes on the gape at her breast were large as a kid's spying a treat.

He glanced round, spotted a bolt on the door and went quickly to secure it. Returning, he slipped off his jacket, dropped it on a bench. His expression, which she plainly read (knew she'd come over for me sooner or later) gave her pause: it seemed a shame to confirm him in this sanguine view. But already his hands were making swift work of further unbuttoning, and as they slipped beneath the overall to clasp her waist and pull her against him, a dull distant soreness inside (which had plagued her for weeks, making her ratty and constantly on the verge of snapping at people) suddenly intensified in a hopeful direction. What had been negative promised to become positive, and that positive to achieve relief. She broke away from him, whipping her overall off in the process, and quickly removed plimsolls, bra and knickers. 'Now you,' she directed hoarsely as he stood surveying her. He fell to at once – off came the knitted tie, the Chelsea boots, socks, trousers plus underpants. When he was down to the shirt with the top few buttons undone, his jutting erection made her lose all patience: she came for him; he backed her against the nearest laboratory bench and she, hoisting herself up via arms behind his neck, wrapped him round with her legs.

'Yeah, yeah,' he exulted, 'knew you'd make a sweet little armful. Phew, yeah!' when she dug her hands into his back and thrust on to him. Soon, under her direction, he was working strenuously – but not for long: 'Let's get down on the floor,' he gasped when his legs buckled. She pushed him down before her, determined to stay on top in unhindered pursuit of her own salvation. Which was coming nearer and nearer . . .

At last, calm and empty as an expanse of sand from which water has receded, she lay utterly still.

For a moment he too lay quiet, until, constrained by what he felt to be the etiquette of the situation, he drawled in her ear, 'That was fan-tas—'

She cut him off, 'Shh.' For outside in the corridor a door came open; a cold gritty draught licked their flanks.

Claire had not really been unsettled by someone coming into the corridor, but by Paul himself, who by speaking had reminded her of his identity. In her fantasies her partner was always Laurie. It was Laurie for whom she contrived circumstances such as these culminating suddenly and at last in his overwhelming desire for her. (As once upon a time actual circumstances *had*, she frequently recalled with anguished insistence. During the past few weeks she'd even considered reminding him of this – for after all they were now being honest with each other; she'd thought of asking how it was possible at age seventeen to kiss and fondle her without apparently violating his nature. But she shrank from the possible explanations, shrank from hearing her cherished memories relegated to adolescent experimentation, or even – horror of horrors – that such episodes had been decisive in turning him off women.)

'It's all right. No-one's going to come in here,' Paul murmured, his breath irritating her eardrum. 'They wouldn't dare. Everyone knows this is your territory.'

The words made him wholly and entirely himself. Paul Cage in all his aspects. Not least, husband to Monica. By rights it should be Monica sprawled on top of him – a thought which projected her into Monica's body, lending her an additional thirty or forty pounds so that her flesh enveloped him, her breasts squashed up voluptuously, and her arm extended on to the floor in a dimpled curve. Then,

'Claire,' he murmured, 'I don't want to rush you . . .'
– and her body shrank back to puny, her arm to an angular stick. What a jerk he was to desire her when he could have Monica. And not only her, but the countless students, lab assistants and secretaries who had lain with him on other floors. He was a jerk all right. She hated the thought of his spermatozoa even now swimming around inside her (swimming around uselessly, thanks to the pill). Abruptly, she pushed on to her feet, collected her overall, went to a cupboard.

The disengagement brought him great relief. When she'd continued to lie on him, he'd begun to worry whether she had further ambitions. She was certainly a goer. And probably didn't get it all that often. However, in his considered opinion, enough was enough and as good as a feast. Free of her weight, he could minister at last to a familiar post-coital loss of spirits: another notch on the bow, he reflected (consciously rallying himself); yes, another submission, another great score. Restored, he reached for his trousers, felt into a pocket for a handkerchief and gave himself a cursory mop. Then stood up and rubbed at the grit embedded in his buttocks.

As he did so, it struck him that strange rifling sounds were coming from the cupboard, accompanied by grunts of exertion. 'Whatever are you doing?' he asked. (She was known to be a devil for work, but surely she hadn't resumed it already?) With no answer forthcoming, he began to dress – pulled on underpants and trousers, leaned down to haul on socks and boots. Straightening up, he glimpsed her backing out of the cupboard with an armful of equipment including a trailing length of tubing – but it was hard to make out what she was up to in this poor light. 'What the blazes?' he puzzled, as she carted the load to a sink and dumped it in.

'I'm *trying*,' she grunted, giving something a twist and a squeeze. 'Uh – got it! I've been trying, and I believe I've succeeded, to fix up' (a pause as she climbed on to a stool) 'an impromptu douche.'

His hands fell still. Not until water rushed from a tap did full enlightenment dawn. 'Sweet Jesus!' he gasped, and began frantically grappling with his tie ends, half strangling himself with the knot. 'You might give me a chance to get out of here,' he growled, appalled and deeply offended, 'before *seeing to yourself.*'

He made it sound like a perversion, she thought, climbing down to comply with his wish. (It would be better to be rid of him.) She held the door open. He seized his jacket and sped to safety. Upon which she closed it and shot the bolt.

She felt sick. I will never, ever do that again, she vowed. Then, in her tiny office, sat down to consider how this might be achieved. An hour later she had found a solution. She must leave here, leave Laurie and the situation he had landed her in at home, leave Monica and the need to smile falsely on a friend. The professional part of her life was perfectly fine; the rest was a mess. After further thought, she cleared a space on her desk and laid out a sheet of notepaper.

'Dear Professor Fergusson (she wrote)
It was kind of you to write to me recently. I was most interested in the material you sent. I've concluded my project here – that is, as far as it goes. I wonder: is there any possibility of my continuing this work in your department? . . .'

When the letter was sealed in an envelope, she set it aside and went off to the Senior Common Room to study the job ads in various journals. On the way, she called in at the Head of Department's office with a request for an interview.

*   *   *

It was her last night at home: she had been granted leave of absence from Thorpe in order to fulfil a two-year contract in Montreal. (Two years in the first instance, Professor Fergusson had written.) So who knows? she thought, stashing in her chest of drawers various items she had decided against taking.

'Shall I put the house on the market?' Laurie had asked when she first told him.

'Why? No! Of course not. I mean, you don't *want* to sell?'

'No – not unless you do. Very well, I'll send on a share of Tim's rent, and more if I can let that room . . .'

'Don't be stupid. I'll be all right. You'll need every penny to keep the house up. Don't forget there won't be my salary.'

'We'll see how it goes,' he said.

He had taken the news calmly, but gravely; had listened to her reasons and agreed they were sound ones for her career. 'But I'd be sorry if my having Lydia here has driven you away.'

'Not at all,' she lied. 'I just want to stretch myself.'

'Sure,' he nodded. 'Of course.'

Now, on her knees in her bedroom, she heard the piano start up. She couldn't place the tune at first; then it came to her: a Beatles number – 'She's leaving home'. She pushed a drawer shut and stood up. After a moment, slipped quietly downstairs.

Only Laurie at the piano, no Lydia in the room. (Good heavens – was Lydia capable of tact?) She went and stood behind him, placed a hand on each of his shoulders. He smiled and played on.

He was wondering what he should say to her. *I'll miss you?* So far he had refused to contemplate the extent of his missing her during the coming months, for fear of inadvertently loading her with his feelings. *Come back soon?* Oh yes, please do, he thought, then wondered how much harm he had done in the past by always encouraging her back to his side. This time he'd let her go lightly. On the other hand, she'd be hurt if he said nothing to mark the occasion.

Eventually he brought the music to an end on a single note near the top of the keyboard, then raised both hands to one of hers. 'I'll miss you,' he said, after all.

'Oh Laurie, I'll miss you too.'

'Of course you will. But you're going to have a marvellous time. And when you feel like coming back, everything here will be waiting for you. Right?'

'Right. Laurie, though, promise me one thing.'

'U-hm?' he said cautiously

'No, you must.' She swivelled the piano stool round in order to perch on his knees. 'If you ever need me – say something went wrong – I'm not thinking of anything in particular – but say it did, or you got really down, or ill, or in some kind of difficulty – promise you'd let me know?' Her hands were linked round his neck; she leaned her head back, earnestly looked into his eyes.

His hesitation lasted only a moment. 'All right, I promise. On one condition.'

'Yes?'

'That you'll get over there and give it your very best shot.'

'That's easy,' she answered, 'I intend to.' And solemnly kissed him.

vii

From the top of the steps at the entrance to the Arts Building, Monica surveyed the scene before her. There was no-one of interest in the immediate quadrangle or walking the broad path leading to the Library and the Senior Common Room. Turning to her left, to a partial view of a second quadrangle and another broad path – this leading to the Students' Union Building, her sharp eyes discerned Laurie. He was leaving the Union in the colourful company of a group of students. The sun intensified the psychedelic shimmer of their velvety clothes – greens, reds, purples, yellows, flashed and glowed with their weaving progress; and at the centre of the throng strode Laurie – she would recognize that salmon-pink corduroy suit at double the distance. As he came nearer, she noticed he had knotted a dove-grey scarf at his neck. Not taking any chances, she thought to herself wryly; after all, it was only April, still a nip in the air. Then she remembered that it was also Wednesday afternoon. So Laurie would have attended the Union debate and then taken tea afterwards in the Union refectory. (One or two other academics supported the event from time to time, but none as religiously as the Dean of Students.) Evidently, the dear young things were reluctant to part with him – or perhaps he was escorting them somewhere, or they him.

When he was near enough to hear, Monica hailed him from her vantage point. 'Good afternoon!'

'Ah – one moment,' he told his companions, and came bounding up the steps. 'Well met, Mrs Cage. I've had my eye out for you.'

'Indeed? And I for you, as a matter of fact.'

'In that case, you first.'

'No, no, go ahead.'

'A letter from Claire arrived this morning – unfortunately I don't have it on me. The main thing is, she sounds happy and enthused.'

'Good. I had a postcard a week ago – view of the St Lawrence River – just a couple of lines on the back. Very busy of course.'

'Quite. This is the first letter of length she's managed for me. Perhaps you'd like to read it?'

'Tell you what, come and dine with me soon. Then you can show me Claire's letter, and I can give you *my* news.'

'How intriguing,' Laurie said cautiously.

'So when can you come?'

'Let me see.' He cast his mind through Lydia's

schedule. 'Tomorrow would be possible.'

'Tomorrow would be perfect.'

'Though do bear in mind, Monica, eating too late is tantamount to suicide with my digestion.' (Also, Lydia would be home by ten at the latest.) 'So earlier rather than later, if it's all the same.'

'Come at six, darling, for a teeny weeny gin, then we can start dinner at seven. It'll be just the two of us.'

He raised an eyebrow, but made no comment. 'Six on the dot.' He promised no more.

Five past six on Thursday evening found Laurie Stone sitting with Monica Cage in a very large room (formerly two rooms now knocked into one) on the first floor of number 118 Marlborough Avenue. By his side on a table stood a glass of orange juice, by Monica's one of gin. He reached into his pocket, then leaned towards his host. 'Claire's letter.'

'Ah yes.' Settling back in her chair, Monica removed several flimsy sheets of paper from an airmail envelope. Meanwhile, Laurie got up and went over to the bookshelves lining half of one wall.

'Darling Laurie,' (Monica read.)
Thank you for your lovely letters. Sorry mine have been scrappy so far, but here goes with a proper one. As you will see from the above address, I have at last moved into a flat. (The hall of res. accommodation was unspeakably spartan – despite its grandiose title of assistant director's suite!) The flat I have rented is smack bang in the middle of the Latin Quarter – which people seem to think very odd of me. (There are undercurrents here, great Anglo-French suspicions.) However, it's cosy enough and will do for the moment; and it is nice to use my French.

You anxiously enquire after the all important subject. Let me reassure you at once: work is just fine. In fact, it's terrific. You can't imagine how exciting it is working in this department. Botanical science has always been financially well supported in Canada – for reasons which I'll come to later . . .' (Dearie me, thought Monica, scratching her thigh.) 'I think I told you that the Biological Sciences Building was only built four years ago. So as you can imagine, everything is virtually new. And talk about state of the art! For instance, I've got a project on the go in the Phytotron . . .'

'What in heaven's name,' Monica cried, 'is a phytotron?'

Maintaining a hand in a gap on one of the bookshelves, Laurie turned. 'Basically, it's a large greenhouse in which various climatic conditions can be created – useful for testing how plants will react in different environments. I say, a number of Paul's books seem to be missing.'

'Ah,' said Monica. 'Tell you about that over dinner.'

Intrigued though he was by this, Laurie was also apprehensive. Paul Cage was not the sort of dear old friend he would miss if no longer around, but his 1860 edition of *Manual of British Botany* certainly was. To cover his disappointment, and for something to do, he pulled out, with scant hope, Virginia Woolfe's *Mrs Dalloway*.

By now Monica, having stumbled over further unalluringly technical terms, had decided to skip to the second sheet.

'This is a stunningly beautiful campus.' (Monica sighed.) 'New buildings such as ours on the periphery are interposed with very grand houses – almost mini palaces – formerly the homes of the rich, now owned by the university. At the heart of the campus is a sort of park – vast lawns, spreading trees, an imposing avenue – stuffed with Scottish baronial-type mansions – grey stone, mullioned windows, towers and turrets. There's such a feeling of space and grandeur . . .' (Well, it made a change from Thorpe, Monica supposed. She skimmed quickly to the end of the paragraph, and began the next.) 'The students here are incredibly bolshy. Honestly, Laurie, even you would have your work cut out with some of these . . .' (How terribly grim, thought Monica, zipping on to the next page in search of some gossip. Her eyes lighted hopefully on a named person.)

'Prof Fergusson is very high-powered. I hadn't quite appreciated what an honour it is to be on his team. Which includes, by the way, Li Wan and David Sculley. Have you come across their report on massive synthesis of ribo . . .' (*Ribo what?* puzzled Monica, squinting at the word. But why bother? Heavens, how earnest the child was. She skipped on.) '. . . underground malls linking the two big stores.' (Saints preserve us, she was now on about shopping.) 'I adore the old quarter. It's full of ware- houses and cafés and artists' studios, and craft shops and way-out clothes shops . . .' (Yeah, yeah, sighed Monica. Oh, but this might be promising:) 'Last Sunday I had a trip to Parc des Îles . . .' (But who *with*? she groaned, finding nothing but sparkling water and dazzling grass, a biosphere and some pavilions still in place from *Expo 67*. A few lines further on, an intimate jazz club on the rue St Denis featuring a piano player who had reminded Claire of Laurie afforded a brief flash of hope, but sadly the pianist was admired from a distance and no other person awarded a mention. She gave up – leapt to the final paragraph which was a series of questions: had Laurie managed to let the back room yet, was the boiler now functioning properly, was Laurie well, and was *everything* – underscored twice – still OK? Then lots of love and write soon etc.)

Monica folded the letter and put it back in the envelope. 'Tell you what,' she called over her shoulder, 'Claire is quite obviously engaged in a passionate love affair. . .' (she paused, as *Mrs Dalloway* fell to the floor and Laurie stooped to retrieve it) '. . . with the city – and every blessed stick and stone therein – of *Montre-al.*' (She pronounced the name in cod Canadian.)

'Ah, yes,' said Laurie, sliding the book back in its place. 'Marvellous isn't it? She's quite bowled over. I'm relieved the job's lived up to her expectations. Sounds as if she could make quite a name for herself out there.'

Smells of garlicky cooking were seeping into the room. 'I think dinner's ready. Take a seat at the table. Pour yourself a drink. I hope you're not going to abstain absolutely. My news could not be properly appreciated stone-cold sober.'

'Certainly not,' Laurie said defensively. 'I'll have a small glass of wine.'

On her way to the kitchen, Monica stopped off at the dining end of the room to light the table candles and extinguish the overhead light. This made Laurie nervous, and more acutely aware, when Monica returned, of how very much she *rustled*. Because of all those silken folds chafing one another, he supposed, only now taking in her shiny scarlet dress and – when she leaned to him across the table – her shiny scarlet undergarments. There was an awful lot of Monica, he reflected. Then pulled himself together: if she was good enough to cook him a three-course dinner, the least he could do was preserve an uninhibited appetite.

'This is de-*licious*,' he said stoutly, when he had swallowed a few mouthfuls of Monica's fish soup. He spoke as if there were others present who might disagree.

'I'm glad you like it.'

'Yes, indeed,' he said, so there should be not a smidgen of doubt. Privately he was worrying about the ingredients: a quarter pint of cream, he guessed, and very likely the same of wine. He reached for some extra roughage in the shape of a second brown roll. 'Well now, dear, don't keep me in suspense. What is all this mystery over Paul?'

'Oh, very well, if you like. Though I had planned to kick off with the really big item.'

'I leave the order of play entirely to you.'

Monica rested her spoon, and swept a hand through her lustrous hair; a smile hovering on her lips got bigger and bigger. Something huge was coming, Laurie sensed, and laid down his own implement.

'My book's going to be published!'

'Oh,' said Laurie flatly. Most academics had at least one title to their credit – if only as co-author with half a dozen others; one's job, or at least one's chances of promotion, rather depended on it. He was surprised by Monica's gushing like a novice when in fact she was a senior lecturer and a pretty ripe one at that. 'Remind me, what is your subject?'

'No, no, no. I mean a *proper* book. A novel.'

'You've written a novel?'

She beamed and nodded.

'My dear, forgive me, I had no idea. But how absolutely thrilling!' Sincerely impressed, Laurie took up his glass and recklessly emptied it. Glad to see him enter into the spirit of things, Monica promptly seized the bottle and gave him a refill. 'You are a dark horse,' he continued. 'What sort of novel? Will you be spilling all sorts of beans?'

'Oh, a novel sort of novel. As to the beans, you'll have to wait and see.'

'When will it come out?'

'Early next year.'

'You clever old thing, I'm truly delighted. And Paul,' he hinted after a pause, 'must be immensely proud.'

'Now there,' said Monica, flashing him a deep dark look, 'I fear you are mistaken.'

'Surely not,' he countered, looking suitably shocked. 'Tell me.'

She hesitated. 'Let's wait till I've brought in the meat.'

Obediently, Laurie finished his soup in silence. When she had removed the bowls, he allowed a few well calculated minutes then followed her into the kitchen – now permeated with delicious roasting odours – to collect the vegetable tureens. 'Leg of lamb studded with garlic and rosemary,' Monica announced, bringing a glistening joint to table. And Laurie, with the scented fumes in his nostrils, felt an inner melting of the restraints he constantly imposed to hold his desires and their satisfactions in check (fearing the self-disgust he might land up in otherwise). He could always forgo pudding, he reflected, allowing her to carve him several chunky slices.

Monica savoured a few mouthfuls, then re-opened the subject. 'Well, as you can imagine, the person I immediately hurried to with my good news was Paul. And his reaction, I should say, was correct. The right words did come out, but with little warmth. Ne'rie mind, I thought, give the lad time. After all, it must come as a shock when, having for years indulgently regarded your wife as a bit of a scribbler (*keeps her out of mischief* sort of thing), you suddenly discover she scribbles to some purpose. He'll recover, I thought, and be pleased as punch. In the meantime, my own joy felt large enough for both of us.' And the beam she sent across the table was so full of delight, Laurie didn't doubt it. He smiled back. For a couple of minutes they attended to their plates.

'Then last Friday,' she continued, 'I had to go up to London – lunch with an editor and so forth. So picture this: half-past eight in the morning, and there am I pacing platform four at Paragon Station – when who should I discover doing exactly the same, but David Guthrie!'

'Really?' said Laurie, surprised by this turn in the story.

'Yes. And going up to London for the precise same purpose.'

'You mean David's written . . . ?'

'Not a novel; a tome on his subject. Though actually I believe it's quite an important book. Anyway, you know David – a perfect sweetie under that dry, droll manner. He was thrilled by my news. We spent a very pleasant journey together, ate a British Rail breakfast (about which I will not hear a word of criticism, it was scrumptious!), got talking about the plays and films and art exhibitions on at the moment; and soon began wondering where was the *sense* in scurrying back to Thorpe that very evening. So we didn't. We met up in the afternoon, booked two single rooms in a faded little hotel and went on the razzle. Had such a marvellous time we decided to do it all over again on the Saturday.'

'I see,' said Laurie, helping himself to more roast potatoes. 'And I suppose you kept Paul in touch with your changing plans?'

'Naturally. I rang him on the Friday afternoon, then again on Saturday morning after we'd decided to stay on, then again on Sunday when it was clear we wouldn't make the earlier train. I told him precisely whom I was with and what we were doing. There was nothing to be secretive about. Just two people who are friends and colleagues happening to be in the same place at the same time with nothing particular to hurry home for. More wine?'

'No, thank you. This meat, by the way, is done to a turn.'

'Mm. Thanks.'

To allow her time to enjoy her own portion, he spoke inconsequentially for a while about how he hadn't been to London for ages, not since he and Claire spent a day at the Natural History Museum *en route* to visit his mother in Cornwall.

'Imagine my feelings,' burst out Monica (giving Laurie the impression that she had not merely been stoking her appetite but also her anger), 'when scarcely had we set foot on the platform at Paragon, than this . . . this malign streak of a vengeful husband comes hurtling towards us yelling abuse. Abuse primarily directed at David, I may say. Talk about humiliated!'

'Dear, dear,' murmured Laurie. 'And how did David take it?'

'With considerable gallantry. Stood his ground and in quiet and measured tone said that if he *were* guilty of luring me into adultery he would gladly accept the rebuke and consider it an honour, since he only wished it were true. All wasted on Paul, I'm afraid, who was quite determined to believe the worst. You know, Laurie, I must be naïve: married to Paul for eleven years and never once thought of him as a jealous person.'

Laurie doubted whether anyone was less naïve than Monica. Not so much jealous, he guessed, as guilty; there was no-one more keen to launch an intemperate and self-righteous outburst than someone with a chronically guilty conscience.

'Actually, things did then get very nasty. I said he must be lacking in self-esteem.' She hesitated. 'All right, I put the knife in. Accused him of acting the way he did because he knew he couldn't measure up to me,' she admitted. 'So then he got his own back – and I must say it took the wind out of my sails. He claimed to have rogered most of the fanciable crumpet on campus, including some of my dearest friends. His point being, that it showed how little I was esteemed, how people giggled at the poor fat cow behind her back, et cetera, et cetera.'

Laurie's jaw was stilled. A list of Monica's friends loomed in his mind – headed by a name very close to home. 'It is not unknown,' he suggested, 'for people to tell lies in anger.'

Her mouth twisted downwards, 'Yeah.'

It was some time before he could resume mastication with any purpose. When it was apparent that Monica considered her story told, he shook his head, sighed.

'Have some more?'

She was holding the carvers, he considered, at an unnecessarily businesslike angle. 'I'm tempted, but simply can't. Er, where is Paul?' he enquired – and would not have been altogether amazed to hear her reply, 'Under the floorboards.'

Monica put down the carvers and folded her hands in her lap. 'I have thrown him out,' she said grandly. 'I've dispensed with the smarmy sod.'

'Ah. And, er, did Paul agree to be dispensed with?'

'You bet. The sort of grief he was getting he was glad to get out. Jamie Cryer took him in, I understand. But I've no doubt he'll soon charm some daft dolly into taking him in – and into washing his socks and generally stroking his ego.'

'Well, I'm very sorry your marvellous triumph was spoiled so disagreeably.'

'Darling, it wasn't spoiled. Let me tell you, nothing can take away from my novel being published. Now, let's have some pudding.'

'Monica, I'm quite defeated.'

'Oh well, it was only a shop cake. Coffee, then?'

'Lovely. But first we'll wash up,' he said masterfully. She didn't demur. Towards the completion of the chore, testing the ground, he casually inserted Claire's name into the conversation. 'That was an interesting point in Claire's letter, didn't you think, about the historical reasons for botanical research being so well financed in Canada?'

'Er? Think I missed that.'

'Well, their large influx of Irish immigration was a result of the potato famine, so there was a tremendous dread of crop failure in people's minds, which acted as a stimulus to the study of plant diseases and how to control them.'

'Oh, I do vaguely remember . . . Mm, interesting.'

'I shall write to her at the weekend. Shall I give her your news, or would you prefer to send it yourself?

She'll be so delighted. Did she know you were writing a novel?'

'I may have mentioned it. I'll be writing later on, but do go ahead and tell her yourself. Although . . .' she paused to unplug the coffee pot and set in on a tray, 'no need to go into details about Paul. Just say we've split up by mutual agreement. Hateful to think of all that nastiness winging across the Atlantic.'

'Of course,' Laurie soothed. 'Now let me take in the coffee.'

viii

In the kitchen, Laurie was setting out the utensils he required to bake a cake. It was to be a peace offering (Lydia could never resist chocolate cake). For this morning he had offended her by asking what the pills she seemed these days to swallow by the handful were actually for. Was she sick? Who had prescribed them?

'Mind your own flaming business,' she had shouted, very angry indeed. It was the first time he had ever heard her voice raised.

He was in such a hurry to get the cake into the oven and have it cooled before she returned from her shopping trip, that he did not first wash up all the stuff lying about from this morning's breakfast and last night's supper – still lying about because he had given a nine-thirty a.m. lecture and then gone on to an argumentative meeting.

'Tablespoon, tablespoon,' he muttered, turning over the cutlery in a kitchen drawer in a vain search for a clean one. He gave up and went into the dining-room where a seldom used canteen of silver cutlery from Foscote was housed in a drawer of the sideboard. He opened this confidently. Then paused – as his eyes met unaccountable disarray, some implements not in their proper place but lying sideways over others. Frowning, he took time to remedy this disorder. And an uneasy feeling grew. When every tool was back in place, there could be no doubt: two of four silver tablespoons were definitely missing. With some difficulty, he manoeuvred the canteen out of the drawer and reached to the back. Found no spoons, only rolls of dust and some wooden cocktail sticks. He then brought out all the table linen from the other sideboard drawer in case the spoons had been put in there by mistake. They had not. Standing at a loss with his fingernails hooked over his teeth, he persuaded himself that they would turn up somewhere, sooner or later. Meanwhile, he had an oven wastefully heating. He took one of the two remaining tablespoons from the canteen and returned to his baking project.

The club was on the city's main shopping street, which at this time of night was almost deserted – just cars and taxis going by, and now and then people in pairs or small groups hurrying across the pavement from vehicles to the narrow doorways (passed unnoticed by shoppers in daylight) between broad shop-fronts. These doorways inevitably gave on to stairs – some flights leading upwards, perhaps to a top storey gaming room, some leading down, as in this case, to a club in the basement.

Except for the bar at one end and the platform at the other, the club was only faintly lit. Peoples' faces shone (for it was warm and smokey), drinks glasses and pieces of jewellery glinted. The audience was unusually attentive for this stage in the programme – the halfway fill-in spot between the two main bookings, being provided tonight by Laurie Stone on piano accompanied by bass player and drummer. He was a great pianist, people thought, playing a great tune ('Misty'). He was fascinating to watch – those long flying fingers, those dramatically dark and handsome features, the silver threads in his hair catching the spotlight and highlighting the thick black curls. But most significantly of all, he had been seen on the telly, and thus emanated that aura of extra and more vivid existence not possessed by ordinary untelevised mortals.

The applause at the end of the set was warm. Lydia's was ecstatic, and made the risk Laurie was taking seem worthwhile. There were already rumbles of discontent at Thorpe over his television appearances which nowadays had no connection with his academic role; he had been asked to account for the number of hours he devoted to this activity and the rate of remuneration. If it were known that he also gave the odd performance in a Manchester nightclub to which detectives from the Drug Squad made occasional visits (and to which similar club did they not?), he could find himself in unpleasantly hot water. Lydia stood to applaud him back to his seat, making certain, he understood with amusement, that everyone present saw who he was with. Briefly, he was Lydia's possession, and more than happy to be so. Someone had kindly put an orange juice on the table for him. He settled back and observed how his companion now became the focus of everyone's attention. It was natural that she should, she was a fabulous eyeful, affectingly lovely as she turned her head and reached her arms to people. Her only competition right now were the men hauling electric cables and instruments on to the stage. It seemed wonderful to Laurie that such a glamorous creature would be coming home with him afterwards to Thorpe.

At last, to whoops and cheers, the main band of the evening came on. This particular band featured a *sitar*, a very popular instrument at the moment. Normally Laurie did not care for its plangent swooping tones, but tonight the sound was inspiring; it seemed to elevate him to a point where he became far-seeing. What an artist was Lydia, he suddenly saw. By sex male, by gender female: as lived by Lydia it was a gloriously defiant and successful dichotomy. And therefore (the conclusion he arrived at swept his breath away) what a profanity to surgically remove one side of the equation, or slow-poison it chemically; what a pathetic lessening of her. *She must not do it*, he thought. It would be his mission to persuade her not to.

In the car driving home he was still possessed by this mystic vision. Fog seeped up to the headlights, swirled sulphurously at the windows.

'Hell's teeth,' said Lydia. 'We should've put up somewhere.'

'Nothing to worry about. Sit back and relax.' He had never felt more sure and steady. 'I thought, by the way, you looked utterly beautiful tonight.'

'Thank you, darling.'

'You are beautiful – period. You are quite perfect,' he hesitated, 'in every way, just as you are. You should be proud of that.'

Beside him, Lydia started winding down the back of her seat. Then she lay with her chin tipped up and her eyes closed. 'Just concentrate on the driving, Laurie. OK?'

He smiled to himself, he had plenty of time. 'OK.'

Two hours later they were home, and because they had spent nearly forty-eight hours away, found a pile of correspondence on the door mat. Lydia swooped to gather it up as Laurie turned to close and bolt the door. 'Oh, one for me for a change!' she cried, 'and another, a card. Who can be on holiday in Corfu, I wonder?' She proffered the remaining letters, and when he had taken them, took two steps towards the staircase.

'Um, isn't that Claire's handwriting?' he asked. In fact he had seen no handwriting, just the edge of an airmail envelope which might have come from anywhere. He was embarrassed to know that she knew this.

'Oh silly me, I've picked up *three*. Sorry! I'm past it, half asleep.'

He pocketed the letter and smiled. 'Hot drink?'

'No thanks. Beddy-byes for me. Goodnight, darling. Lovely, lovely weekend.' She inclined the side of her astounding face – which was just beginning to roughen up, he noticed.

'Night-night, sleep well,' he murmured into her hair. And watched her mount the stairs before going into the kitchen.

He fancied a mug of cocoa to accompany a reading of Claire's latest letter. Standing by the stove waiting for the milk to rise in the saucepan, he wondered whether Lydia had really intended to deprive him of it. But why on earth should she? He felt the idea sink him in his own estimation, from the high-minded resolution he had entertained earlier towards her, to this – this mire of unworthiness.

Disappointed, feeling he had crassly spoiled a special evening, he whisked cocoa powder and sugar into the heated milk, then poured it out.

Darling Laurie—
I'm simply bursting to tell you: I've met someone. Actually we met back in the summer, bumped into one another – literally – jogging in opposite directions round the base of the mountain. (Do you know about jogging? Has the craze hit Thorpe yet? Here there's an official campaign; they put notices up in the buses – 'Jog to the back of the bus, it may be the only exercise you get today!' Mind you, I can see why the authorities bother – the number of fatties in this city is truly staggering. And I mean *gross*. Whole families – mum, dad, and the kids, each as broad as they're high, waddling down the street clutching bags of fries and bottles of Coke. The people who take the exhortations to heart, of course, are the trim and healthy, belting round the parks in jogging suits and sweatbands.) So that's how I came to crash pretty vigorously into Rob McAlister. Rob is from Ottawa, a partner in his father's law firm. He's here to do a post-grad business course to widen the firm's expertise. He is *sweet*. A great big guy, blond, open-faced, funny, clever and guileless, a

year younger than me, and very physical – I mean sporty. (I'd forgotten how much I always loved sports.) Besides jogging, Rob has got me into swimming, sailing, mountain walking, tennis, and has promised to take me skiing when we get some snow – though he is also very physical in another department, but tender with it, which is something of a novel experience for yours truly. Anyway, Laurie, I do believe I'm keen. If Rob and I last – fingers crossed – I hope you'll come out and meet him. I don't mean during the winter (quite simply, dear, you wouldn't survive – twenty or more degrees below freezing is not uncommon), but will you promise to try and fit in a visit next spring? Lydia can surely spare you for a week or two.

By the way, something mildly upsetting happened last week. I was having a meal in Nick's Diner (a haunt of the arty crowd), when a girl I know introduced me to this gink of an Englishman, who (a real heart-sinker this) turned out to be an academic musician. He latched on to 'Haddingham' like a leech on a vein – 'You're not related by any chance to *Sabine*?' he cried, and when I stupidly admitted she was my mother, went into orbit – wailed on about the tragedy and the loss to music and how her interpretation of something or other was considered definitive. Well, the most awful feeling of stale misery descended; I went all inadequate – spilled food on the table, fell over the chair when I tried to get up. Brought on, I suppose, by not knowing the half of what he was on about. Also because he gave me this overwhelming sense of the Foscote world, that serious important world, still pursuing *proper* business, while here I am with my bits of peas and coloured charts, still playing, still messing about (like the hopeless little tyke with the box of crayons who drove Maman to distraction). Then it hit me how wonderfully lucky I was in those days to have had you on my side sticking up for me. Made my eyes water to think of it. Love you, Laurie Stone.

Write soon – your Claire.

PS. And before you start worrying because I haven't mentioned the magic word, work is top-hole; going swimmingly.

Monica turned the door handle and pushed. The front door opened – she had not been certain that it would, there being a new regime at number 97 Devonshire. Voices in the kitchen hesitated as she closed the door, ceased altogether as she walked through the hall.

'Ah, Monica,' said Laurie, sounding relieved.

'Laurie, my pet,' acknowledged Monica – though looking at Lydia to whom she offered, 'Hello.'

'Hello,' came the reply, without enthusiasm.

'You find us over post-prandial coffee rather than afternoon tea,' Laurie explained. 'Lydia is on duty this evening, so we ate early. Like a cup?'

'I'd rather have a gin,' she declared, and with every confidence settled herself down at the table. Lydia's forthcoming absence was a piece of luck. She had come prepared to outface *that shitbag* (Claire's expression – as in her written request that Monica 'pop into 97 from time to time and keep an eye on that shitbag, who, I'm convinced, cares not a jot for Laurie and is only out for what she can get.'); if necessary, to hang around all evening in order to get Laurie to herself for five minutes. 'You're on duty,' she repeated, 'that's in a doctor's surgery, I understand. Interesting work?'

'Not particularly.'

'Oh, d'you know I'd have thought it would be?' rattled on Monica, staring at Lydia, shocked to notice the beautiful face was marred this evening. Frankly, it was dirty.

'Here we are,' Laurie cried loudly, coming up with the gin. 'How are you, dear? To what do we owe the pleasure?'

'Oh, fine,' said Monica, only choosing to answer the

first question. She embarked on some fulsome chatter – described ideas for illustrating the jacket of her novel, quoted a thrilling endorsement of David Guthrie's forthcoming book by A. J. P. Taylor, who was generally thought to regard the interwar years as exclusively his own to comment upon. But with only half her mind. For she had just tumbled to the fact that Lydia's face was not dirty at all but in need of a shave. The realization gave her a jolt. It tipped her perspective of this little social occasion. She had come on the scene as a woman joining another woman and a man – all unconsciously, of course, but now, as she consciously adjusted to her new situation – that of a woman joining two men – she glimpsed the significance of hundreds of tiny assumptions constantly and thoughtlessly made and adapted to. So Lydia's choice of gender was not just a matter for herself and those close to her, but to everyone whose path she crossed. She grew tremendously excited and tried to file away her feelings accurately so that later she could consider them in depth. One never knew, in the novel-writing business, when such things might come in handy.

Monica also noticed that the initiator of these insights was not unaware of her facial condition. During the exchange between herself and Laurie, Lydia's hand rose surreptitiously to explore her chin. Then, 'I must go,' said Lydia, uncrossing her long and shapely legs. She rose gracefully, rested fingertips on the table to say a bored 'Goodbye,' to Monica and an equally bored 'See you later,' to Laurie, then swung away and left the room.

Monica decided to delay the main purpose of her visit – a little hint to Laurie about jealous common room gossip concerning the time he was spending on non-academic business – until Lydia had gone absolutely. (Laurie was special to her, it had long been her habit to cover his back.) 'Paul has been pestering to come home,' she said, opening a new topic.

'Has he?' said Laurie, his voice carefully neutral in

case he might soon be called on to rejoice over a reconciliation.

'He has come up with the idea that all his philandering was my fault. Because, he now discovers, for the past four or five years I have been secretly devoting any energy surplus to job requirements on novel-writing. Which more properly ought to have gone into wifely attentions. Isn't it perfect?'

Laurie nudged his cup and saucer a couple of inches.

'Naturally, I told him where he could stuff his pathetic excuse. Honestly, Laurie, I must have been blind. Tell me truthfully: I bet you knew Paul was fooling around?' And when Laurie inclined his head merely to convey the faint possibility: 'Of course you did. Didn't everyone? Maybe I did myself. Phew, aren't I just glad to be rid of the bastard. You're keeping pretty schtum, I notice.'

'Well Paul, of course, is a valued colleague – though I have never been as close to him as I am to you. I'm sure you've acted for the best. Now, let's go into the other room where we'll be more comfortable.'

'First I'll help you wash up.'

'Certainly you will not.'

But she ignored him. Ten minutes later as they left the kitchen to go into the dining-room, she heard the front door close.

'I expect you'd like another?'

'Thank you, I should. Laurie dear,' she began, sitting down and accepting the drink, 'you look rather wan. Could you be overdoing things? You're always so busy, you have such a lot on . . .'

'Monica, I have the feeling you're leading up to something. If so, do come to the point.'

'Oh – the usual spiteful murmurings from types who are worried by others' success. Just, darling, be a little discreet.'

'I can hardly do television discreetly.'

'No. OK. Then try not to send your apologies quite so often.'

'Ah – the Financial Forecasts Committee. I've been trying my damnedest to get off that. I do my share, you know – all these student committees . . .'

'I'm sure you do more than your share. But you're quite right. Better to come off altogether than regularly draw attention to conflicting commitments.'

'Yes, I'll be absolutely firm about it. Thanks for the tip.'

'You'd do the same for me, I know. It's good to have chums watching out for one. Talking of chums, I had a nice long letter from Claire. She does seem to be enjoying herself. And this gorgeous-sounding young man. . .'

'Oh, I'm glad she's told you,' Laurie burst out happily (for if they were corresponding normally it was unlikely Claire had been one of Monica's 'dearest friends' cited by Paul as his adulterous lovers). 'I mean,' he tactfully explained, 'if she's mentioned Rob to you as well as to me, she must be keen on him. Which is rather nice.'

And Monica, reading his mind with perfect ease, smiled enigmatically into her gin.

Laurie had been relieved when it was Monica who had walked uninvited into the kitchen and not a particular friend of Lydia's who had lately taken to calling – a tall and hefty crinkle-haired man, of about forty-five years (Laurie guessed). A man who sported a camel coat and other rich trappings such as a jewelled signet ring, a Jaguar car, and a seemingly endless supply of fat cigars. And who answered simply to 'Jack' – or, when addressed by Lydia, to 'Jackie darling'. Laurie had been hard put to discover anything much about Jack other than what his eyes reported. Lydia vouch-safed that Jack was some kind of dealer, but dealt Laurie such filthy looks whenever he directed questions at the horse's mouth that he quickly desisted. Jack, Lydia explained, couldn't stand being interro-gated. And when Laurie wondered aloud whether this was as a result of having been interrogated under due process, she left the room and slammed the door. Where had she met Jack? he asked on one occasion. But Lydia was suspicious as to his motives for wanting to know; it seemed to her that Laurie had taken against Jack for some incredible reason. He was just puzzled, Laurie explained, because Jack was so different from her other friends – the artistic and show-biz crowd in Manchester and Leeds. At which Lydia had disbelievingly snorted.

In December the car insurance became due. When he had detached and signed the appropriate form and put it ready for posting, Laurie refolded the documents and put them, for future reference, in one of the compartments inside the desktop of the bureau. Then brought up the bureau lid and turned the key. His fingers, however, did not quite relinquish their hold, for what was the point, it occurred to him to wonder, of a key left in its lock for all to see? He and Claire used the key as a kind of handle – turned it one way to open the bureau lid, the other to fasten it. Silly really, he thought, pulling the key clean out – with, unfortunately, no clear idea of what to do with it. It lay annoyingly in his palm – a dull stick of metal just an inch and a half long with a double tooth at one end and a ring handle at the other. He folded his fingers over; thrust his hand in his pocket. Another futile gesture, he soon realized. Becoming irritated, he pulled open the shallow drawer directly under the bureau desktop and laid the key inside. But might it not slide about and be lost if he left it at that? After a moment's consideration, he broke off a piece of Sellotape and with this stuck the key to the drawer's bottom. Then strode out of the room and away from the embarrassment (taking care as he went to keep his eyes averted from the mantelpiece and the vacant place which had doubtless precipitated his sudden concern for security).

311

Last Thursday Mrs Smethurst (the two-mornings-a-week cleaner) had arrived quarter of an hour before her usual time, specifically to ask a question (Laurie was usually gone before she arrived). 'What's happened to the ballee dancer on the mantelpiece, then?' she demanded, jerking her head in the vague direction of the dining-room. Laurie was nonplussed. Mrs Smethurst stared belligerently up at him. 'You know, what stands on tiptoe on a big ball.'

'Oh, you mean the silver statuette,' he said, realizing she meant the art deco ornament that had once belonged to Sabine – and which Claire despised but he thought amusing.

'Yeah, well it's gone. I thought mebbe someone had knocked it off accidental and it'd gone to the menders.'

'No, no,' said Laurie, hurrying into the dining-room – Mrs Smethurst hurrying after. 'It's not here,' he discovered.

'That's what I said. It weren't here Tuesday, neither. I hope you don't think . . .' She left what she hoped he didn't think rather aggressively to his imagination.

'Certainly not,' he said, tumbling to her meaning. 'I'm just . . . puzzled. But I'm very glad you pointed it out, otherwise I mightn't have noticed for goodness knows how long. Doubtless, there's a perfectly simple explanation.'

'Well I hope there is,' declared Mrs Smethurst, drawing in her chin to convey scant faith. Then stomped off to the cupboard under the stairs to yank out the vacuum cleaner.

Staring at the baleful space, a weary sense of inevitability brought Lydia to mind. The idea of her as a thief was shocking; it brought a sharp physical pain. But not because he was thinking *How could she do such a thing to me?* but *How could I be thinking such a thing of her?* It was not the first time treacherous thoughts had crossed his mind. He was sickened by himself, he was the lowest of the low. As for the blasted silver ornament – he wished he had listened to Claire in the first place, for she was quite right about it, he saw in retrospect; it was indeed a coy and odious bauble, and he hoped never to set eyes on it, never have it drawn to his attention again.

And now a duller piece of metal, the bureau key which hitherto had innocently projected from its lock in the bureau lid, lay inefficiently hidden in a bureau drawer, to serve – whenever he had need to use it – as a depressing reminder.

When, in early January, Monica next pushed on the door of number 97 Devonshire, it did not yield. Someone was home, for a light glimmered on the stained-glass panels. She pressed the doorbell. No-one came. She pressed it again, twice in quick succession, heard it shrill in the hall, heard – as she stood with her head lowered and her feet apart and her merry greeting, Happy New Year, dead on her lips – the faint sound of a television. Then the television noise zoomed and a figure loomed. The door, at last, was opened to her. 'Oh, it's you,' said Lydia.

'Laurie about?' Monica asked, stepping purposefully over the threshold.

'I don't know. I think he went up for a kip.' Lydia looked at the visitor with annoyance, clearly not caring to invite her to share the TV programme, clearly not wishing to turn it off. 'I'll go up and see,' she conceded, settling for the least evil.

Monica watched her go, then took herself off to the dining-room. There was something different about Lydia, she thought. Then it came to her. During the couple of months since she had last set eyes on her, Lydia had gained weight. Not a massive amount, but suffi- cient to blur the line of her jaw and produce a hint of plodding as she mounted the stairs. The result, no doubt, of living too royally (she remembered Claire describing how Laurie obsessively prepared her delicacies and waited on her hand and foot). Well, it was a titbit to pass on in her next letter to Montreal.

Laurie, in his socks, stood in the doorway.

'Don't *do* that!' squeaked Monica, clapping a hand to her throat.

'Sorry to startle you. I was having forty winks.'

'Then I'm sorry, too, for getting you up. But there was no need. I would have been happy to sit here and read for a while. However, since you are here,' she went forward and kissed him, 'Happy New Year! I was sorry you didn't come to my rave-up. You missed a jolly good time.'

'Lydia and I flew to Majorca for a few days.'

This surprised Monica, for Laurie looked far from refreshed. In fact, he looked haggard. She decided not to mention this when she wrote to Claire.

Laurie was at the sideboard bringing out the gin. 'Your usual, or something other?' (She nodded confirmingly at the gin bottle.) 'Anyway, it's lovely to see you. Make yourself comfy. Bottoms up.' He had poured himself a tiny glass of Cointreau.

'I've had a lovely letter from Claire. She was so pleased about me and David . . . You do know,' Monica asked in response to his frown, 'that David and I are an item? Good Lord, Laurie, where have you been? It's the wonder of the Common Room, on account of my being the elder by one or two years. All right, five,' she confessed with a grin. 'Anyway, I gave Claire the news at Christmas, and she wrote back immediately saying the nicest thing: that she herself had made a play for David and now understood why he'd remained impervious. She recalled that he'd always said I was the sexiest woman on campus. Rubbish of course, but sweet of her to say so.'

'Gosh, Monica, I am behind with the gossip. But I'm terribly glad. You and David strike me as the perfect combination.'

'Thanks.'

'We must do something to celebrate.'

'We will . . .' Funny, thought Monica, how *when Claire comes home* seemed to hang in the air. But

Claire's contract with McGill still had a year to go, and with a boyfriend in the offing, she was unlikely to come home for a visit in the meantime. Possibly, if the romance prospered, she wouldn't come home at all.

'She wants me to visit her out there soon,' Laurie said (thereby confirming to Monica that their thoughts coincided). 'She wants me to meet Rob.'

'Of course she does. She's probably contemplating a very big step. You will go?'

Lydia – and various matters concerning her – visited his mind briefly. Then, 'Yes, of course,' he said. 'When the temperature out there is sufficiently high to support sensitive life. I thought I'd go in the Easter vac.'

'I'm relieved to hear it.' The look she dealt him over her glass was severe.

There'll be hell to pay if you don't, he interpreted.

ix

As the plane completed its laden upward thrust and lightly coasted, Laurie was suffused by a warm, clean, airy sensation. In a word, *escape* – escape from all manner of earth-bound nuisance. From Monica, for instance, skitting about on her high heels, ever anxious to detain him: 'Are you quite sure you're all right, Laurie dear?' From troublesome students who would not be content, he had begun to think, until they won total dominance of the university; and from one student in particular, a pale sharp-featured young man who sat on many of the committees Laurie chaired and seized any opportunity to air his belief in the duty of homosexuals to declare themselves – airings which Laurie could not but suspect were aimed at him. From jealous Senior Common Room mutterings regarding his TV appearances; indeed, from those very appearances which – with Lydia's encouragement – were beginning to incorporate blatant show-biz elements. From the sad remains of his thesis that he would sometimes come across staring accusingly up at him

315

like some neglected elderly relative (though quite unlike, thank heaven, his seventy-year-old mother who was still vigorously pursuing her craft and as pleased to see him after a year's absence as a month's). Escape most overwhelmingly from Lydia, from the lure of her beauty and its weakening effect on him; from the anger and hurt she caused by refusing to grasp that her ambiguity was the essence of her mystique – indeed, by seeking to destroy this very ambiguity with quantities of vile pills prescribed by her 'understanding' doctor, and unscrupulously scraping together every penny she could lay hands on in order to purchase her life's goal, a sex change operation. And escape from himself, of course, the self who would pathetically grieve whenever Lydia was caught out in a lie ('No-one's been round, Laurie, honestly,' – and the sitting-room reeking of Jack's eternal cigar); and the self so pathetically grateful whenever suspicions proved groundless. For instance, the time he came home unusually early one afternoon and from his bedroom heard sounds across the landing seeming to emanate from Claire's room. Praying, *Please, don't be in there* to an image of Lydia, he had gone to investigate, had opened the door to a furious batting on the outer side of the wall, soon followed by the affronted flight of a starling across the window, evidently from a nest under the eaves. Merely a falling out among birds. *Thank you, thank you*, he breathed (to the starlings? – to an innocent Lydia?), locking the door on the outside nevertheless, and removing the key to secrete under a pile of shirts . . . As the plane strained skywards, he seemed to shred these and all his life's conundrums – the whole complicated unedifying pawky mess.

Freedom, he exulted, as the jet broke from the clouds into limitless blue – where nothing on earth mattered a piss! – and was so intoxicated by the thought, that he accepted a small bottle of wine from a kindly stewardess and proceeded to make a proper job of it. Then the meal was served, a barely hot foil-covered dish of chicken and vegetables plus cold accompaniments. Thinking of all the microbes within swelling and multiplying (for the meal was prepared how long ago? and plainly the reheating was perfunctory), he set the tray aside and finished the wine, and when the stewardess next passed by, detained her with a request for a second bottle.

And then, for three and a half hours, undisturbed by announcements over the intercom concerning flight path and weather conditions or enquiries from the aisle as to duty free requirements, deeply, and sometimes stertorously, slept.

It took a tugging of his sleeve to bring him awake. 'Sir! Will you please fasten your safety belt. Our descent has commenced to Mirabel Airport.'

Descent resounded like the knell of doom as he fumbled with the belt's catch. His mouth was caked over. His head hurt. He felt hopeless and helpless, for down he must go and face a thing he was dreading – though quite what this thing was he couldn't tell. It couldn't be Claire, he reflected (as the plane bump-landed); not darling Claire who was invariably well-disposed towards him (as he wrestled a canvas bag and a mac from the overhead luggage box). Perhaps it was the foreignness of Montreal, the feeling that he lacked the energy to cope with newness. No, it was something less amorphous, he thought, approaching the end of the aisle and smiling farewell to the stewardess. What it was, he all at once realized, stepping into the plane's exit mouth and getting smacked in the face by cold air and bright sunlight, was Rob – a great big hunk of a man according to Claire's account, handsome and strong and bursting with health. While here was he – creeping unsteadily down an iron staircase, grasping the handrail for dear life – a total wreck. With a hangover, he added, cursing his foolishness. And went lurching over the tarmac.

*   *   *

317

He hung on to her, and hung on . . . How good she felt
– proportions and contours as reassuringly familiar as
a treasure from childhood; and how good it was to
enfold her – like coming to rest. She was the first to
break away (though not very far), her raised face
reflecting a mixture of delight and concern. He gravely
placed his lips on her forehead. Then, with their arms
round one another, they turned at last to Rob who was
standing tactfully at a few yards' distance. A hearty
handshake, a 'Good to meet you, Laurie,' and he
hauled the luggage from the trolley and led off to the
glass-panelled front of the terminal building. They
followed behind, blissfully free of bags and the responsibility of finding the way, Laurie pulling Claire hard
into his side in the perambulatory style he had always
relished.

Outside, waiting to cross the first of two roads, he
was suddenly disorientated. Claire freed herself and
seized his hand, gauged the traffic and pulled him
across. The car park lay ahead, spread over a rising
bank. She continued to pull him, up, up. Plodding to
keep pace with her, he was engulfed by *déjà vu*: they
were on the rising track of the paddock at Foscote,
heading for the woods; in a moment she would scold
him: 'Laurie, come *on.*'

But she didn't. Instead, 'Here we are,' broke the
spell, and there was Rob lifting the bags into the boot
of an enormous and ugly car, calling that the doors
were unlocked. Claire opened both doors on the right
of the car and hesitated, waiting to see if Laurie would
get into the front beside Rob, or into the back and pull
her after him. In the event he climbed into the back
and spread himself over the seat, 'You must excuse
me,' he said faintly, letting his head loll back, 'I fear
I'm severely jet lagged.'

Getting in, Rob grinned and leaned his mouth to her
ear. 'I've heard that airline's pretty generous with the
booze.' Laurie the worse for drink? – that was a laugh,
she thought – but not with true amusement, for she

was shocked at the change in him. Was he simply fatigued, or could he be ill? She turned to peer into the back.

From under his half-closed lids he met her gaze, smiled, then shut his eyes completely. For a few seconds her silhouette loomed in negative. Which seemed significant, for he was as impressed by the change in her, as – he guessed – she by the change in him. Claire, he thought, had sprung more fully alive during these Canadian months; there was still the lopsided grin, the faint squint, the impish haircut, but her skin glowed, her eyes gleamed, her vigour was palpable. It soothed his conscience to see she had rebounded from the bad time he had given her (he remembered her howls that morning in the kitchen, and her hemmed-in frustration afterwards). With typical courage she had taken hold of her life and changed it for the better. She always was a brave little toughie, and now her courage had paid off. It was a well-deserved triumph. Just as his fate was deserved – to feel always enervated and crumpled, barely in control; virtually past it.

Claire was staring ahead along the straight and boring freeway, blind to the passing industrial outlets, to the rivers they crossed and their bordering scrubby terrain. Rob drove fast in a relaxed fashion. Once or twice he turned and grinned at her – meaning, she knew, to be reassuring, because he guessed and was sorry for the fact that her reunion was not turning out as expected. She had rather built Laurie up, naturally foreseeing that Rob would be as bowled over as most people on their first meeting. Anticipating the scene at the airport, she had been inspired by all those times Laurie had zoomed into her life and instantly charmed it on to a higher and more exciting social plane, as when he had visited her at Sutton, and later when he presented her around Thorpe. And so she had assumed it would happen today: Laurie descending on them, witty sayings and droll manner at the ready, taking charge of their itinerary, adjusting the plans they had made, organizing tiny details such as where they would sit and how the conversation would run. In spite of them, he would take them over. He would take over Montreal, in the sense that nothing of it he experienced and pronounced upon would ever strike them quite the same way again.

She returned Rob's grin with extra brilliance, knowing she would never allow anyone, however close, to presume Laurie had disappointed her. But she was certainly worried. All those months with Lydia had taken their toll, sapped his vitality; she hoped they had not killed his spirit entirely. Damn and blast Monica for not spelling out clearly what was going on. Her letters had given an impression of Lydia's hold slackening, of Laurie less content with her. If they had contained the slightest hint of Laurie being actually undermined, she would have been on the next plane home, never mind her job, never mind even her lover. She darted another and now rather guilty smile at Rob, and as she did so, experienced a rising wave of familiar bad feelings – resentment, jealousy, insecurity. Laurie might as well have brought Lydia with him – as, when she first invited him to visit, she had briefly tormented herself that he might. To her relief he had never suggested the idea. Even so, Lydia, or the effect of Lydia, had succeeded in crossing the Atlantic and getting to her here in Montreal where she had felt safe and renewed.

Her reverie was interrupted by Laurie lurching against the back of her seat. He slipped an arm over it and his hand over her shoulder. 'I'm sorry, pet. The thing is, I'm exhausted. Up at five, the most ghastly journey down to London, and now, by my clock, bedtime feels urgently indicated. It's alarming to see everything here so very mid-afternoon. I shall be wonderful tomorrow, I promise, so long as I get twelve solid hours between nice clean sheets.'

Now she felt happier, and put her hand over his.

She could certainly promise the nice clean sheets. 'I was lucky enough to get you into the Faculty Club,' she reported proudly. 'I had to praise you up to the skies; they don't take just anyone. I know you'll adore it – it's the last word in civilized comfort.'

'Sounds marvellous,' he said, squeezing her hand.

'But you can't go straight to bed. I mean, you'll want to eat first.'

'I've been eating all day,' he lied. 'There was little else to do.'

'Tell you what, when we get to the club I'll ask them to fix you a sandwich and a flask of something hot. Then you'll have something for when you wake up. I remember my first day here, waking up ravenously hungry with hours and hours to go before any chance of breakfast.'

'You think of everything.'

They were in the city now. Laurie fell back in his seat to admire the various sights pointed out to him – the Champlain Bridge, Dominion Square, Mary Queen of the World Cathedral, the Sun Life Building. Rob added the statistical information so beloved by North Americans – the tallest this, the longest that, the precise billion dollars' worth handled per annum – and Claire, not daring to turn her head, was taken by disloyal silent giggles, all the more delicious because she knew Laurie shared them.

'Mm, imagine,' came a drawl from the back.

'Yes, sir!' cried Rob. 'At one time that was the largest building in the British Empire.'

Claire laid her head against the window. It was the best feeling in the world, this knowledge of invisible threads between her and Laurie – which now trembled with their secret laughter.

The next day found him recovered as promised. When early in the morning she came panting up McTavish Street to the Faculty Club, he was already waiting under the canopy at the top of the grand stairway entrance (which he had found so impressive on his arrival the day before). He bounded down to greet her, full of praise for his comfortable room, the discreet service and congenial atmosphere. She felt glad to have taken the trouble and gone to the expense; a made-up bed on her tiny sitting-room floor, her stained WC and cracked wash-basin would have made him miserable.

It was a beautiful day. They began with a tour of the extensive and hilly campus. By mid-morning they were taking a breather on the steps of the Arts Building, he sitting on a step one above hers with his legs stretched on either side of her and his arms around her. Before them lay the tree-lined avenue; on either side were wide lawns backed by handsome limestone buildings. It was the vacation, but there were plenty of people about, strolling along the pathways, jogging under the trees, or standing around gossiping. 'I like Rob tremendously,' Laurie said, though he had only been in his company during the ride from the airport. 'Be seeing you the day after tomorrow,' Rob had declared after depositing Laurie's bags on the pavement; 'that'll give you and Claire a chance to catch up with each other.' What a splendid attitude, Laurie had thought.

'I'm glad you like him,' Claire said, rubbing her face against his arm. For some time neither said another word, but by common consent fell into one of their traditional silences. When at last Laurie stirred, Claire suggested coffee and afterwards a visit to the Biology Building.

'Wonderful,' he murmured, pulling her back against him and nudging his chin into her hair.

Another ten minutes went by before they finally got to their feet.

After all, Lydia was not so very tenacious, Claire decided, watching Laurie watching the accordion player.

It was Laurie's third day here. She and he had spent the day exploring the Old Port of Montreal, and were now drinking lemon tea in a sheltered café garden off the rue Saint-Paul. Yesterday had been spent with Rob walking the trails and wooded paths of the Morgan Arboretum – where childhood memories had been stirred and their fantasies of living together one day in a wood. 'Of course, we should have come here!' Laurie had exclaimed. 'It's the obvious place.' 'Well, it's never too late,' Claire had suggested – though knowing it was. She had been charmed by Laurie eagerly recounting, for Rob's benefit, stories of their childish escapades in the Foscote woods. It had seemed like Rob being shown another dimension of herself. She felt enriched. And it was good to see Laurie and Rob take to one another easily. Rob had tactfully found other things to do today but would be joining them this evening for dinner.

The accordion player, attired *Québécois*-style in smock, floppy bow, draped trousers and soft boots, now started singing – an old French song, "bitter-sweet". Laurie hummed softly in harmony while his eyes wandered the garden – the central tree with its spreading branches, the iron tables dotted over the flagstones where customers sat gossiping or dreaming. His eyes rested finally on Claire. 'You have found your perfect setting,' he said, after a moment's consideration. 'It brings out your Frenchness. Delightful.'

Laurie always miraculously said the right thing. The one difference she had with Rob – and also with friends and colleagues – was their disparagement of French Montreal. The heat of her indignation, her sense of Gallic solidarity in the face of ignorant slurs, surprised even herself. She smiled warmly across the table as he joined openly in the singing of the plaintive chorus; she started to join in too – until she remembered the sort of dreadful noise she made and contented herself with mouthing the words and swaying her shoulders. How at peace Laurie looked. There was no doubt about it; Lydia had definitely failed to penetrate *Le Jardin de Bonsecours.*

When the musician's stint ended and he had passed round the tables collecting tips, they discovered they were hungry. Laurie beckoned the waitress. She came over with her notepad, neat in her white blouse with its cape-like collar, her black skirt and stockings, her buckled shoes, and took down their order for jam-filled *crêpes.*

'I thought yesterday what a good-looking couple you and Rob made,' he remarked. This thought had struck him as Claire and Rob posed for his camera beside the lake. But he did not go on to confide his subsequent reflections as he peered through the viewfinder: that Claire in time would *become* this snapshot; that he would frame it and stand it on the mantelpiece and look at it whenever one of her letters arrived from Canada; that by pressing the button he was recording the moment when having Claire as his partner in life had run into the buffers; that he was taking the one bit of Claire he could carry away with him and keep.

'He's asked me to marry him,' she confessed. 'Though don't let on that I've told you because I haven't actually said yes. Though I dare say I will in the end.'

'But you're hesitating?'

Their food arrived. She waited until it had been placed before them before answering. 'Well, it's a mighty big step. I suppose it'd mean committing myself to staying over here for good. Mm, these are OK!'

'They're delicious.'

'Next month I'm going to Ottawa to meet his folks. I think I'm supposed to have decided by then. From remarks made, I gather he plans to announce me as his intended.'

'Otta*wah*,' Laurie repeated in Rob's voice.

'Yeah,' she grinned. 'I adore the way he drags words out. I probably will get hitched. Everything's so great out here. And I'm really excited about the project – it's been broadly hinted that if I do stay on I'll get tenure.'

'I'm very happy for you,' he said. And did not lie. He had been aware for so long of his ability to host diametrically opposed emotions that the facility no longer fazed him.

'Well, don't let on, that's all. If he knew I'd told you he might assume I've reached a decision.'

'I believe you have. But I promise I won't breathe a word.'

However (and perhaps as she might have known), before the week was out Lydia had reasserted herself.

It was Laurie's last evening. As Claire walked up McTavish to the Faculty Club to collect him (they were meeting Rob downtown), she reflected that this time tomorrow she and Rob would be returning from seeing Laurie off at the airport. Never mind. After a dodgy start, the week had turned out perfectly – Laurie commending her lover, her work, and her favourite city. Furthermore they had some terrific wining and dining ahead of them in a Greek restaurant on the rue Saint-Denis.

But when she arrived at the Faculty Club there was no Laurie waiting. He would be down in a minute, she supposed, and made herself comfortable in the sitting room with the latest issue of *The Macdonald Journal*. She was beginning to get very apprehensive indeed when the door burst open. 'Sorry to keep you waiting,' cried Laurie. 'But I've been trying to ring home.'

'Why? Whatever is it?'

He frowned. 'I simply wanted to speak to her – to Lydia.' (It was the first mention of her name all week.) 'Since I'm going home tomorrow I thought . . . However, no reply. Shall we go? I'll try again later.' He spoke, she thought, as if their evening at the restaurant (Rob's generous treat) was to merely pass the time before he could accomplish what really mattered – making contact with Lydia.

'Perhaps you'd rather stay here and keep trying. Perhaps we should ring the restaurant and say we can't possibly come until someone in England has picked up the phone.'

Ignoring the sarcasm, he seized her arm. 'Come along. We can't keep Rob waiting.' Anyone would think, she thought as he bustled her down the steps, that she was the one who'd caused the delay. But later in the Metro, where the light dealt harshly with his bony face, her indignation melted, was supplanted by concern.

For a time he seemed to rally, to relish the aromatic cooking if not the tart white wine. Then out of the blue, and before Rob had properly concluded the tale he was telling, he grew fidgety, started looking about, and failed at its conclusion to grant Rob's story more than a distracted smile. 'What's the matter?' Claire snapped.

'I was just wondering . . . Is there a public phone in this place – or is it possible to use the proprietor's, do you suppose?'

'I dare say it's perfectly possible, though he'd hardly expect you to use it to call the UK.' She jabbed her fork into a *baklava*.

'No, I suppose not.'

'Like to go on to a club?' Rob suggested when they had ordered coffee.

'No, no,' said Laurie. 'In view of my journey tomorrow I think I should get an early night.'

'Christ Almighty, you can sleep on the plane!' Both men viewed her outburst with surprise. She sighed. 'OK. As you will, Laurie. And do cheer up: by the time you get back to your room, Lydia might be home to answer your call.'

Rob raised his eyebrows. This was the first he had heard of any Lydia.

Claire nodded to him. 'The bill?'

'Uhuh,' he said. 'Right.'

In the car, all the way along Sherbrooke, she was asking herself how could it happen. How could the pleasure and ease and fun and joy they had found in each other's company all week just dissipate? The answer was the same as it had ever been: Lydia.

When they had dropped Laurie off, Rob turned in his seat to look at her. 'Back to my place?' (As a place to make love in, his shared house was preferable to her tiny flat where the bed was too narrow and the facilities crude.)

'Not tonight, love. Tomorrow.'

'When Laurie will be out of the way,' he observed.

'What d'you mean by that?'

He stared ahead. 'Nothing, I guess.'

'I'm tired, that's all. It was a crummy evening.'

'Thanks.'

'Oh God, I'm sorry. It was sweet of you to take us out. Laurie was crummy, not the evening.'

'Yeah, he did seem kinda different. What was that about some woman – Lydia?'

'I'll tell you tomorrow. Promise.'

'Just as you like, babe,' he said, and started the engine.

For both of them the leave taking was terrible. It had hung over them all day, augmented by Lydia's shadow. Hurting, they had affected a degree of detachment, sticking mainly to the safe topic of botanical research while shopping in a desultory fashion for useful gadgets and attractive novelties not seen in the UK. At the airport, Rob and Claire waited with Laurie in the short queue to the check-in desk. Then, with still an hour to go before take-off, Laurie suggested getting their goodbyes over and done with. At which Rob clapped him on the back with relief, shook his hand thoroughly, and took himself to a bench twenty metres off to study the sports pages of an evening paper.

Claire and Laurie looked at one another. Laurie put

327

down his travel bag. She fell on him, wrapped her arms around. 'You will come again?' she asked, wishing last evening's ill-tempered remarks unsaid, terrified lest these should stick in his mind to the detriment of warmer memories.

'Of course I will.' He looked over her head to where, beyond passing travellers, he could see Rob with his newspaper. 'I shouldn't be surprised if I'm back soon for a wedding.'

'Don't say that,' she said quickly, pressing her face into his chest. Clasping Laurie, the weight of loving him was so immense that other loves seemed puny, any other liaison a mockery.

'Well,' he said softly, 'I shall come anyway. And I hope one day you'll come and see us at home.'

She stiffened, raised her face. 'Us?'

'Monica and David and Zena and Yolande. All the old gang. And me, of course. I certainly hope you'll come and see me.'

'Yeah,' she choked, 'you bet . . .'

'But listen.' He took her by the forearms, held her at a few inches' distance. 'I can't tell you how impressed I am by the life you're building here. If I thought for one moment that by visiting I'd distracted you . . .'

'You haven't, Laurie, honestly. The reverse: you've encouraged me.'

'That's all right then.' He kissed her, 'Bye-bye, pet,' and turned her to face away from him. 'Go on.'

'Goodbye, Laurie,' she said over her shoulder.

'Go on,' he repeated.

She went tottering over the concourse in the direction of Rob. And Laurie, satisfied that she had almost reached him, turned into the maw of International Departures.

'Phew, let's go,' she said, sinking back in the car seat and closing her eyes.

'Your place or mine?'

'Yours.' She badly needed someone – anyone – to hold her.

'You got it!' He checked the lane of the car park left and right with a pleased expression.

In a solid semi-detached villa in Westmount, the tenancy of which Rob shared with another well-heeled post-graduate student, Claire relaxed on a sofa while Rob prepared a meal. 'Something light, and not too much of it,' she had ordered.

He made a ham and mushroom omelette, a leaf salad, and buttered some slices of the wrapped bread disparaged by Claire (on the grounds that it was sweet and pappy), there being no other to be had in the house. 'Get that inside you,' he said, putting a plate in front of her, 'and you'll feel one helluva sight better.'

'Thanks.' She ate slowly and steadily; eventually cleaned her plate.

'Coffee?'

'OK.' She wandered back to the sofa, switching on the TV *en route*. Nixon's face loomed up, his voice bloating about Vietnam. She was interested: though no fan of Nixon, she had a feeling that here at last was someone truly prepared to bring the monstrous débâcle to a close. However, since on political matters her views and Rob's did not coincide, and having no stomach for an argument this evening, she lurched up from the sofa and switched the set off.

He brought in the coffee and settled beside her. 'So, when are you going to tell me?'

'Tell you?' she frowned.

'What was eating Laurie last night. And what was eating *you*. Something to do with this woman, eh? What was her name – *Lydia*? I never heard you mention her before. Who is she, anyway?'

'She's . . . She's Laurie's girlfriend. Sort of.'

'Sort of,' he repeated, taking a thoughtful slurp of coffee. 'That's a funny thing. You know, I'd've had old Laurie down as a fairy.'

329

'The word's *gay*,' she barked. Then added, 'Which he is.'

'Pardon me. But if he's gay, how come he's got a girlfriend?'

She let out her breath in a long hard sigh. 'Lydia's . . . a transsexual.'

'You mean Lydia's not a woman?'

'No, technically Lydia is a man,' Claire enunciated in the clipped tone of an instructor with a wilfully stupid child. 'But to all intents and purposes, if we are guided by gender identity, Lydia is female.'

He whistled, shook his head. 'Now I get it. Now I see why you were so darned scratchy last night. Can't say I blame you. Must be sickening having someone close mixed up with a . . . *transsexual*.' ('Trans-sex-yew-ahl' was how he drawled it.)

At which she flung round to face him. '*You get nothing, you jerk*,' she yelled. 'What d'you take me for? – one of your Presbyterian bigots? I'm not against anyone because of their label. I detest Lydia for one very good reason.'

His clean-cut chin collected her insults calmly. 'Which is?'

'Which is, that she shares Laurie's life, takes the poor smitten bastard for every damn thing he's got, and doesn't care a jot for him. Feels for him nothing whatever. Zilch. She even let me know this. And when I protested *she bloody well laughed*.'

'Hey,' he said leaning over to smooth her down.

She shook him off, and slumped back against the cushions. 'Now do you understand?' she asked in a softer and more reasonable voice. 'Do you see why I despise her? Why I'm fearful for Laurie?'

'Yes, I do. Come here.' He reached out, tugged her arm and brought her on to his lap; gathered her up, much moved. What a fierce, loyal little scrapper. And what great qualities to have in a wife – specially for a man making his way in the legal and business world. 'You know what? – you're really something.'

330

His arms round her felt wonderful. 'Let's go to bed,' she said.

'Yes, ma'am!' He took her hand and led her upstairs. Helped her undress, got stripped himself. Then joined her between the sheets and made love to her with such expressive sweetness it took her breath away.

Some time later as they lay back – her head on his chest, their legs entwined – she told him, 'You're a proper darling, Rob McAlister. And I've decided, after long and careful consideration, to take the position.'

'Eh?'

'To become *Mrs* McAlister, of course.'

She shot upright in the bed. It stunned her to realize that only two or three hours after making very satisfactory love with Rob, she had dreamed that pathetic old stuff about the Foscote woods and hopelessly searching for Laurie. Christ, what was the matter with her?

Rob was woken by a draught down his front. 'Hey! Wha's matter?' His hand reached to her back. 'Bad dream, huh? Not about me, I hope?'

'It wasn't about anyone, really,' she lied. 'Except me, lost in a wood. I've been having it for years.'

'Come here.' He took hold of her arm and tugged her down. 'I'll show you something to dream about. Happy ending guaranteed. Every time.'

x

Darling Laurie,

A doleful letter, I'm afraid. Because I *feel* doleful, dammit; also indignant, bewildered and heartsore. I'm also a martyr to panic attacks – around midnight usually, when I'm too tired to resist and phrases like 'old maid' and 'dried-up spinster' worm their way into my mind. However, as I keep telling myself: one lives and learns; it's all for the best; I made the right decision.

I can see you getting twitchy: 'What is the girl on

331

about?' Well dear, the girl is fumbling around for a way to say: please ignore the effusions of my last letter for I am not after all to become Mrs Robert McAlister. To do so would spell disaster for both of us – a conclusion arrived at and mutually agreed soon after my visit to Ottawa a couple of weeks back to 'meet the folks'.

Don't groan – I know you thought you had me safely settled. Let me try and explain. Has it ever occurred to you that proper houses (I mean as they are generally lived in) are quite foreign to us? As I recall, the doors at Foscote were usually unlocked, people came and went (often by the score), no-one was ever sure where any other person was unless they were marked down for one of the practice rooms. (Remember Maman and Aunt Margaret wailing 'Laurie and Claire,' and never a clue where to direct their cries?) And when you think about it, we began a similar sort of set-up – on a reduced scale – at number 97: people free to barge in and help themselves, and in the summer wander through to the garden. So imagine my claustrophobia chez McAlister, where doors and windows are not only locked and bolted, but wired up to an alarm system (on account of burglars and all the worldly goods on show – for which reason there are also handy wall safes in most bedrooms); where everyone has their known timetable; where you never go outdoors except for an organized purpose such as tea in the garden, golf, tennis, boating, or to watch the match; where you climb into your car from a garage built into the house and arrive like as not in some other garage or car park integral to a club, restaurant or shopping mall; where, on visiting some other family residence, you drive straight to the front entrance and nip indoors past the waiting servant – who palms your keys and parks your car at a discreet distance and brings it round later when it's time to go.

I'm not carping. Just trying to convey the culture shock. The McAlisters are a perfectly pleasant and welcoming bunch. Keen as mustard they were to take Rob's fiancée to the collective bosom and fit her into their scheme of things. Such as, into Maggie and Don's present house. Maggie and Don are Rob's sister and brother-in-law who plan to move into a larger house (a McAlister house, needless to say) before the arrival of their second child. It was thought that Rob and I might as well start off where Maggie and Don did. Though I was also shown two further possibilities on a tour of the residential district. 'See that one on the corner with the big bay and the ornamental pool? That's a McAlister house,' confided Mrs McAlister – a house occupied at present by an employee who could easily be persuaded to move elsewhere should I take a fancy to it. You see, Laurie, why I was so impressed by the central importance of houses?

Anyway, when I recovered sufficiently to recall who I was and what I did etc., I mentioned that I was a research botanist and planned to continue as such. They received this politely but were baffled as to its relevance. Mrs McAlister implied it was something I'd grow out of, and when I doubted this, her old man barked, 'What does it make?' From my embarrassment (simply couldn't bring myself to name the pittance) they concluded there was no contest. You will appreciate how slow I am when I confess that I did not at first associate Rob with any of this. My worries were along the lines: Crikey, we're certainly going to have trouble with Rob's folks.

To be honest, I still can't quite take it in. I mean, what's loving someone got to do with wanting to totally change them? Expectations – there's the nub of the matter. Mine were only that we'd continue beautifully as we were; I thought of marriage – when I thought of it at all – as setting the seal on the *status quo.* His were that by agreeing to marry him I was agreeing to abandon my mode of life and adopt his. That, at any rate, is how I see it when I'm cross. Lately I don't feel so much cross as ill-fated and regretful. From the outset we were flawed as a long-term couple; I was in my milieu when we met (a university campus, in the throes of my work), whereas he was right out of his. Now I've had a glimpse of his background I feel quite sorry for having wasted his time. Perhaps it was being out of his milieu that got him sufficiently confused to imagine I could be right for the rôle. To be fair, he's as blue as I am about us breaking up – and utterly bewildered. Why, if I love him, won't I share his life? What's wrong with it, goddammit? Nothing, I say, and I'll gladly share it, so long as my career can be accommodated. But sweetheart, he reasonably points out, when we have kids . . . Which brings me smack bang into the proverbial brick wall. (Remember when we confessed how daunted we feel faced with Jeanette's brood, and Toby and Jessica's? It's such a relief to know you and I share the same peculiarities – no great fondness for sprogs and certainly no yearning for parenthood.)

I miss Rob unbearably at times. I suspect in one way I always will. (He was such a tender lover.) But I know if he ever looks back on his time with me he'll think of it as an aberration and thank his stars for a lucky escape. Fortunately, he finishes here in three or four weeks and there will be an end to the risk of running joltingly into one another.

Now, love, you are not to think of me as badly troubled. My work hasn't suffered in the least, you will be relieved to learn; in fact I was richly complimented only the other day by Prof Fergusson. So no cause for concern. This is merely an update (as they say over here).

All my love – your Claire.

*   *   *

When her tutorial with a group of second year students was concluded, Monica was free for the day. She grabbed her baggage and stamped resoundingly down the main staircase to the front of the Arts Building, where she paused to open an umbrella before hurrying through the rain to the car park. Considering the obstacles – high-heeled sandals and a restricting skirt – she covered the ground speedily, and was soon at the wheel of her Triumph Vitesse attempting to spur it into action. Perhaps water had seeped under the bonnet: 'Come *on*,' she cried, kicking the accelerator as the engine wheezed and coughed and died. At last it fired. She let off the brake and drove – the car lurching like a camel – to the gateway and out on to the road.

As she approached the traffic lights they changed to red. She smote the steering wheel. Gossip overheard after lunch in the Senior Common Room rendered her impatient to be visiting Laurie. Who was ill, apparently, and on medical orders had taken sick-leave. This information, initially conveyed and received with due gravity and concern, soon drew its natural concomitants – jealous asides and catty speculation: Laurie's television work was touched upon, there were references to a hectic private life. At which Monica broke cover – rose majestically from her high-backed easy chair, shook out her cashmere shawl and with a contemptuous gesture flung it around her shoulders. (As she had had occasion to remark before, when it came to scurrilous gossip, these male habitués of the S.C.R. could knock spots off any woman.)

But now such observations were far from her mind. Driving through the rainy streets, her only concern was for Laurie being ill, or, worse, in some sort of trouble.

She was not in love with Laurie, exactly – for a decade she had been passionately in love with her husband, and was now more maturely and securely in love with David. But from the moment Laurie arrived at Thorpe he had fired her interest. He possessed a quality she had discerned in no other person, which set off echoes in herself; it was as if, when they met, she already knew him. He was terrifically handsome, of course, in an unconventional and romantic way (she was not a bit surprised he was such a hit on the telly), but to Monica there was more to his looks than magnetic eye-appeal. Something in her responded to what was expressed by fleeting sadness in the eyes, wry twists of the mouth, quick glances and shudders; she understood him, she felt, in an intuitive, wordless way. And had ever after striven to put this way into words – for her own private satisfaction – though lately it had occurred to her that Laurie might be just the sort of character to explore in a novel. Consequently, she delved and dived into him, grappled for explanations.

For instance, why his reluctance to commit whole-heartedly to a single direction in life? Because he had too contrary a nature, she decided, too keen a sense of irony – not to mention of the ludicrous; he was always conscious of the downside as well as the up, and could never totally embrace the positive with the negative pressing its case. No wonder he made such an excellent committee chairman. Having so many conflicting impulses of his own to arbitrate, it was child's play to manage people opposing one another in simple single-mindedness. But the restlessness of never being able to settle on a particular line must come at some cost, she guessed.

And in his personal life, too, Monica sensed the same reluctance to commit himself one way or the other. (Though from conversations with Claire following the advent of Lydia, she gathered she was mistaken in her original assumption that Laurie was bisexual.) No, it was more interesting than that. Claire did not spell it out, nevertheless, Monica divined that Laurie was unable to find both emotional and sexual satisfaction with the same person. And thus it followed, she reasoned, that no one person could ever hope to embrace Laurie in his entirety. Claire could be his darling and his life companion but never his lover; Lydia must remain his untouchable goddess for worshipping purposes only; and his sexual partners were anonymous shadows, divorced from his life proper. She wondered about his mother – how much of her son *she* had managed to know, and, indeed, whether she had been disposed to try.

His ambivalence touched her, his intuitiveness called to her; the jealous mutterings he provoked made her fiercely protective. The gossip-mongers aroused her scorn: he was too complex for them, she thought; he baffled their inadequate imaginations. Hers, on the other hand, fearless and wide-ranging, was fired by him.

Heh! – as she swung the car into Devonshire Avenue she was struck by an exciting idea: was it possible that she, Monica Cage, via her novelist's imagination, would of all his intimates most nearly encompass him? She braked quickly, finding she had over steered in her eagerness, and the tyres skidded a little on the greasy road. When she had regained control, she made herself calm; held the wheel straight, put her foot down, made a beeline for number 97.

She parked as near to the front door as possible, then scuttled through the rain to the porch. Jabbed the doorbell, registered its short sharp ring and turned as she waited to glower at the glowering sky. It was nearly the end of June. When, she would like to know, were they to have some proper summer? She pulled her cashmere shawl tightly round her arms – otherwise clad only in thin silky material – and stamped her feet to encourage her circulation. And then wondered why no-one had come to the door. Laurie's car was standing in the drive, so he was surely at home. Lydia, it was to be hoped, was out, though on that score Monica had decided to take a chance. She put her finger to the bell a second time and held it there, hearing the shrill summons resound in the house, picturing it searching

337

him out. Sure enough, as she raised her finger preparatory to a third attack, blackness loomed against the
stained glass and the door was opened.

'Laurie,' she said, stepping in without invitation,
'they tell me you've taken sick-leave. I've come to
check up on you.'

He very obviously continued to hold the door
open: 'Monica,' he began crossly – when a dull thud
in the dining-room made him start and turn quickly to
close it. Evidently the thud was significant, Monica
deduced, and hurried to investigate. 'You really are an
infuriating woman,' he complained, coming after her.
But she barely heard. She was staring aghast at the
littered room – drawers pulled out of bureau and
sideboard, their contents piled over table and floor (it
was one of these piles, she guessed, that, collapsing
and falling, had caused the thud just now), the bureau
lid hanging down. 'What a tip! Have you been burgled
or is this a belated spring-clean?'

Laurie rested against the back of a chair. He really
did look ill, she thought, and urged, 'Don't just lean
there, sit in it.' When he hesitated, she clasped his
hand (finding it cold and clammy), pulled him gently
round the chair and pushed him down. 'Shall I get us
a cup of something?'

He let his head fall back, looked resigned. 'A cup of
tea would be very welcome.'

'Don't move,' she commanded, and went into the
kitchen to put the kettle on.

Laurie obediently did not move. In spite of his
irritation with Monica and her ill-timed arrival, now
his frantic search was halted he found he had little
inclination to carry on with it. It dawned on him that
it was the middle of the afternoon and he had not yet
had lunch. When Monica brought in the tray of tea
things plus a packet of biscuits, he accepted the
sustenance gratefully. She let him enjoy it in peace,
merely complained about the weather and a review of
her book, and expressed the hope that Claire would

soon find someone else – mere chatter interspersed with silences to forestall him bothering to make any effort. She also made some rude remarks about a mutual acquaintance. He grinned tiredly. 'You do me good, Monica.'

She certainly hoped so; he looked in need of it – so thin that his wrist and knuckle bones made her wince; and the shadows under his cheek-bones almost had her out of her chair and clasping him to her bosom. 'There, there,' she longed to say, but was stayed by the knowledge that this would produce an opposite effect to the one intended. 'Darling,' she said instead, pouring him a second cup, 'tell Aunty Monica. You would be perfectly safe to do so, and they do say two heads are better than one.'

He sipped some more tea and considered the matter. Monica affected to be tough, they were old sparring partners, but she was intelligent and kind and utterly loyal. He knew he could trust her. 'Some things of mine have gone missing,' he confided. 'Some letters someone once wrote to me, plus an ill-considered photograph.'

'Mm. Incriminating things, I take it?'

'Not criminally so. Though professionally is a different matter. One could certainly say that, were they to turn up on the wrong desk, my career would not be enhanced.'

'So – Lydia is a thief. Is she also, do you suppose, a potential blackmailer?'

His hands shook violently. She restrained an urge to leap for his cup. 'I have no evidence whatever that Lydia took them,' he reproved. But when Monica said nothing and he had drunk the rest of his tea, he conceded, 'And if it turns out she did, I will consider myself partly to blame.'

'How's that?' she asked, taking his cup and putting the tray aside.

'It will mean I've totally failed her. Failed to dissuade her against this horrible ambition of hers. A sex

339

change operation,' he explained, when Monica looked startled. 'I've spent the last twelve months trying to convince her she's right as she is, that such gross interference would almost certainly be diminishing. Yes, well,' he bristled, as Monica snorted behind her hand, 'definitely diminishing in the crude sense, but I think you know what I mean.'

'Sorry, dear. Go on.'

'I do find the idea upsetting. And not necessarily because of the mutilation.' (But at his violent shudder Monica's mouth twisted in disbelief.) 'No really, it's more . . .' he beat his fingertips together as he strained to express the nub of his objection — 'more that it'll destroy my *dream* of her — of what I imagined she could be.'

'You know, sweetie, I think that's your trouble. You're an incorrigible dreamer and you've a strenuous imagination. Very strange in a scientist. Maybe you took a wrong turn somewhere, and should have been a poet, or a painter. Can you draw?'

'No I can't,' he snapped.

'No, no, of course — you were meant to be a musician, only you wanted to disoblige your over-powering pa. I remember Claire telling me . . .'

'Look, do you mind sticking to the point? I was explaining why Lydia might need to lay hands on some cash. If, as I fear, I've failed to dissuade her and she intends to go ahead, it could prove costly. Presumably it could be done on the NHS, but in that case she'd have to be patient — no doubt there's a waiting list as long as your arm. But look, Monica, I really can't believe she'd try her hand at extortion.'

'No, but you'd better be prepared for it. What you've told me does provide a motive.'

He sighed. 'It's not so much Lydia who worries me, as her latest pal — a rich, flashy bloke, and probably unscrupulous. Mind you, if he's as wealthy as all that, where's the need? No,' he cried, clapping his hands down on the arm of his chair, 'this is ridiculous. There must be a simpler explanation. I can't believe . . .'

But to Monica the case was already proven. 'Is she in at the moment?'

'Lydia? Oh, no, she went out to lunch.'

'Right then,' she stood up, 'let's go and turn over her room.'

'Are you serious? Sit down at once, or I'll be sorry I told you!'

No-one argued with Laurie using that tone of voice. 'Well, if we can't retrieve the bloody things,' Monica said, retaking her chair, 'let's at least take stock of the Lydia situation. Surely you've had your eyes opened by now? I know you're obsessed, but she just ain't worth spoiling your life for. Time to get rid, Laurie. More than time.'

There was a pause. He played his fingers along the chair arm as if it were a keyboard. 'You mean,' he said slyly, 'like you did?'

'Oh! Right. *Touché.*' Feeling herself redden, she was annoyed that any reminder of her wilful blindness to Paul's betrayals still had power to hurt. 'OK then, as one fool to another, let me advise you: there will still be life after Lydia. Just don't put off facing the facts for years and years, as I did. And take heart that you're not a laughing stock around campus. You won't be sneaking looks at people and wondering if they had a go with your erstwhile darling. At least you're not facing public humiliation.'

'I'm not sure,' he said slowly, 'that one of these days I shan't look back and consider myself humiliated in my own eyes.'

'Good Lord, we're all of us that – if we're honest. I'd like to know anyone who could face public exposure of their most private moments with perfect equanimity. I sure as hell couldn't. So forget about feeling bad in the future, and concentrate on doing something now. Here's a thought: imagine Claire in your shoes – or mine, come to that. Would she have any compunction? Not likely. Look how she faced up

341

to the Rob problem – obviously loved him, wanted the relationship to continue, but the moment she saw it threatened her chosen way of life, she had no hesitation. Finito – and bugger the heartache.'

They exchanged wistful smiles.

'Yes,' he sighed. 'I dare say. And I'll certainly think it over. You're quite right, I know that.'

'Good.' She rose. 'Now let's tidy this mess.'

'Not you, Monica. You've done enough.'

'I insist. Come on. Be awkward if Lydia came home and caught you in the middle of it.' She started fitting drawers into their spaces. 'I'll pick the stuff up, you say where it goes.'

'Really, you know I'm not an invalid.'

'Well, my dear, I understood that you were. And as you've taken sick-leave, perhaps it'd be better to maintain the pretence. Where do I put this?'

He gave in. 'Bottom drawer of the bureau,' he sighed.

When order was restored in the dining-room, Monica encouraged Laurie to think about an evening meal. During its preparation, Phillip Grainger arrived and Laurie asked him to stay and share it. (Lydia had evidently gone straight from her lunch date to work at the surgery.) Contented that she left her friend in better spirits, Monica took herself off. Laurie found he was glad of Phillip's company. They ate supper, then took their drinks into the dining room, where Phillip as usual became engrossed in the contents of the bookcase and Laurie sank into his chair and caught up with work-related journals. By half past nine, with evening surgery long over and plenty of time allowed for the journey home, Lydia was still absent. Phillip caught Laurie checking his watch against the clock. 'I must go,' he said, returning a book to its place on a shelf.

'No, don't rush off; stay and have coffee.' He could say this with confidence, Phillip was as tractable as any student and would leave the moment he gave the signal. For the time being his presence was helpful. It prevented him rehearsing in his mind how he would be and what he would say when Lydia did arrive. During the afternoon, crawling over the floor picking up bits and pieces with Monica, he had become conscious of a slowly forming resolve – albeit a rather vague one: to start retrieving his dignity. To this end, it dawned on him, he would have to speak to Lydia, though to say what precisely he had not begun to consider. Better, he sensed, to keep his mind blank and his nerves steady and rely on the inspiration of the moment, than compose a speech he would inevitably find fault with and possibly decide he hadn't the stomach for. With his fate seeming to hang in the balance, he wanted not to speculate but to remain as he was – cold, vacant, calm.

Phillip was as good as he had anticipated. The moment the glass panels in the front door rattled, he was on his way. 'Must you really go?' Laurie murmured, nevertheless leading the way into the hall where he called informatively to Lydia, 'Phillip's just going.'

Lydia, looking as if she could not care less, made for the stairs.

'Come again, and don't leave it so long another time,' Laurie said, ushering his guest past the front door and quickly closing it. 'Aren't you going to have something to eat or drink?' he called up the stairs.

She didn't pause. 'I'm still stuffed from lunch.'

'Then I'd like a word with you, if you don't mind,' his voice going from solicitous to determined.

Now she did halt. 'What about?'

'We can't have a conversation here. Come into the dining-room.'

'Sorry, but right now I'm exhausted.'

'In the morning, then.'

She turned and stared down. 'You're being very mysterious. Anyway, you'll be at work in the morning.'

'No I won't, I've taken sick-leave. The doctor thinks

I've been overdoing things. I told you I was going to see her about my neuralgia – don't you remember?' (Or is what I say so boring you just shut it out? he thought better of adding.) 'I'm not doing the next two telly programmes, either.' He then recalled that the doctor had also advised him to consult a dentist, which he had arranged to do in the morning.

Lydia was plaintively defending herself. 'If you did tell me, I'm afraid I've forgotten. I've had a lot on my mind lately, what with one thing and another.'

'Mm. Look, it'll have to be the afternoon. I'll be out in the morning; I've just remembered I've a dental appointment. You're working late again tomorrow, aren't you? – so shall we meet here for lunch?'

She was no longer looking down at him, but pensively at a painting hanging level with her eyes on the staircase wall. 'All right,' she said absently, 'see you lunchtime tomorrow.'

At which, calling a brisk 'Goodnight,' Laurie went towards the kitchen.

'Darling,' said Monica to David over a cosy nightcap, 'you know Laurie's on sickies? Well, I called round to see him today. He was in the most awful despairing mess. Do you think I should write and tell Claire?'

Head on one side, David raised an eyebrow. 'I thought you'd decided never to bother Claire about Laurie – it being unfair to distract her from her new life in Canada and so forth.'

'Mm, motives are such shadowy unknowable things,' mused Monica cryptically. 'However, I am truly concerned for the dear old chap. And Claire did make me promise . . .'

'Very well,' he said in his best tutorial manner, and laid down his glass. 'Answer me this: what – if your letter brings Claire winging home – do you suppose she can do about Laurie's despairing mess?'

'Mm. There you have me. I suppose it is up to Laurie.'

'It was up to Laurie before Claire went away. I can't see that her coming back now changes the fact.'

'You're right of course. What a sensible man.'

From his visit to the dentist and a city bookstore, Laurie let himself into the house and stepped into the hall. Straight away it felt unoccupied. He went slowly about, checking the rooms. Lydia was nowhere on the ground floor. He ran upstairs and knocked on her door; when there was no reply, looked inside. The bed was tousled, drawers hung open, the wardrobe gaped; but, of a thing belonging to its recent occupant, the room was bare. She had had her work cut out, he thought, and had probably been assisted. His hands trembled on the handle, closing the door. Light-headed, he returned downstairs. Then, as he turned towards the hall-stand, a sense of oddness struck him, of some lack, and he looked back up the stairway. Two blank and deeper coloured rectangles of magenta wallpaper showed between the hanging pictures – dark shades of their missing companions. The two smallest oils had gone, as though, Laurie thought wryly, they had been chosen for their fitting conveniently into a bag or suitcase rather than their appeal or merit. Beneath one of the rectangles he sank down. He could imagine where she was – or rather, where she was headed: a clinic somewhere abroad – in an exotic and teeming city perhaps, or some fresh mountain region. There very soon she would lie – begowned, scrubbed clean of artifice, drugged for surgery. They would wheel her through corridors gleaming with antiseptic, place her on a table beneath a large circular light. Laurie pictured the scene with vivid clarity – the ventilation bag going in and out, the surgeon taking up the knife; and found he felt absolutely nothing. Nothing at all.

In a bus shelter under a street lamp, Laurie sat watching the rain – rivulets and eddies over the road, waves swelling from the flooded gutter and shooting across moving headlights, a million streaks of spitting steel. His cold calm of the afternoon, which had allowed him to make a dispassionate inventory (two further spoons, a carriage clock and a transistor radio missing), had deserted him. He had left the house on an impulse, as if its boundaries intensified a rising panic which the open air might allow to dissipate. Walking briskly through the evening drizzle towards the town centre, he had passed the door of a bar sometimes frequented by Lydia's crowd; had suddenly turned back and gone inside. He'd sat alone, a campari soda at his elbow. The time passed. Once, thinking he heard her laugh, he jerked round. But there was no-one anywhere remotely resembling Lydia. For which as well as relief he felt a sharp sense of loss. Abandoning the drink, he hurried out onto the pavement. It was now raining heavily, even so he felt impelled to walk. He had walked for hours, and could not recall actively deciding to come into this shelter. Nevertheless, here he was – his trousers sopping from the knees down, also his socks and shoes. An umbrella had not saved damp from penetrating to his very bones. Gloomily, he foresaw worse aches and pains than neuralgia, even long-term debilitation – rheumatism, bronchitis. One way and another he had really gone and done for himself.

It had come to him during the afternoon's methodical search that he did not greatly care what she had taken. Only that one package. The thought that she had acquired a small lever of control – or rather, that due to sentimental carelessness, he had lost it, had upset him then, and it gnawed at him now. Undermined by one stupid slip! He could not let go of the error, but worked himself up into what was very possibly an overreaction compared to the degree of threat. But then, as Claire was fond of saying, he was a controlling bastard. It was a failing in him which people laughed over, and he denied; but secretly admitted to himself. And with no sense of shame. In the circumstances, it was a perfectly sensible thing to be. Anyone, he told himself, waking up to the fact that their very essence was deplored by the world at large and ringed round with unfair prohibitions, would, if they had anything about them, set out to develop survival tactics. His had been to take a grip of every situation in which he himself featured. (And he had learned, using self-mockery, to do it inoffensively.) He had no throbbing desire to dominate for domination's sake – people who did wearied him beyond measure, the colleagues who argued to the death and must always score the winning point; indeed, his usefulness in committee sprang from a readiness to rein in his own opinions and promote those of others, particularly those of more hesitant others. If he was a control freak – as Claire with amused exasperation insisted – it was of *situations*, not minds and wills, and was the fault of boneheaded prejudice which might otherwise do him down. So yes, it *mattered* that part of him was now in other hands. And there could be no comfort in false bromides – such as, that nothing would come of it, and anyway it was pretty mild stuff. The fact was, he had let himself down and had been doing so for months. Dammit, he *ought* to feel despairing, anguished, wrung out!

He sprang to his feet, finding it impossible to take this punishment sitting still. He pushed open the umbrella, edged out of the shelter, set off along the greasy pavement.

Everywhere sodden and bleak – the dead-looking church, tattered hoardings, yawning station entrance with a few scurrying stragglers, a desultory taxi rank. On he trudged, heedless of ankle-sloshing puddles, of hammering rain. He would cross at the lights. Not that there was any need to wait for the pedestrian signal in this downpour with so little traffic about . . .

When the car came skidding and screaming at him from nowhere he rather limply jutted his umbrella at it. He reeled on to the pavement and caught hold of a post for support, and could not believe the umbrella – wrenched out of his hand and now lying in the road – worth going back for. It was almost certainly broken and useless. A man came lurching – 'You all right, mate?' 'Perfectly, thank you,' – he steeled himself to let go of the post and continue in the opposite direction (all he needed tonight was a drunken companion!). Holding his smarting wrist – the one which had taken the car's force, it occurred to him that he had not tried to save himself just now with any alacrity. Almost, he had let fate take a shot at him, as if fate scoring a hit would at least put him out of his misery. He thought how little impact his no longer being around would have on anyone or anything. Science would scarcely notice; the university would be briefly incommoded; a few television viewers might be disappointed; a couple of students who currently depended on him would be upset and put at a disadvantage, and his mother and a handful of friends genuinely regretful. On the other hand, Claire . . .

He grabbed at a garden railing as he rounded a corner – and not only because of wetness underfoot. Claire's reaction, which he could clearly imagine, rocked him. She would be distraught, inconsolable; and then, as is the way when grievous things happen beyond our control, would turn on herself. Soon it would be all her fault – she should not have left him at the mercy of an obsession; she had always known Lydia was poison . . . All this she would suffer when she had hardly got over Rob.

It would take a selfish swine to cause her such misery, he thought, and began instantly to employ circumspection negotiating the puddles and crossing the Little Coates Road. In his mind, he lined up various saving measures against the flu and lumbago – a hot bath, a hot toddy, a light but nourishing meal, an hour's read or watching the telly, and to bed with the World Service and a hot-water bottle. And felt marginally less irresponsible.

On the corner with Devonshire Avenue was a tele-phone box. As Laurie drew level, the phone inside began ringing. There was no-one waiting to answer – which was hardly surprising in view of the weather. The ringing continued, hope against hope, as he moved further and further away. When his ears could only hear the memory of the sound – vain, desolate – waves of his black mood returned, not at full spate, but as lapping reminders. Reminders also of another time when he was this low – when as a National Serviceman he had fallen in love – doubly forbidden – with an officer. . . Ah, yes, Keith: Keith the poet and fan of W. H. Auden, who at first had reciprocated his affection but then thought better of it. What a black hole he had plunged into then. He'd been terrified as to what he might do. And had saved himself, of course, by seeking out the one person who could be depended on to value him, come what may. He could see the scene now: the park at dusk, her eyes glittering as she looked into his face. And he could hear her: *Laurie, darling, you did the right thing.*

It began to seem an almost sacred duty to deliver himself up to her in one piece, before destructive self-loathing sprang another attack.

xi

In the blinding sunlight, baking like a lizard on a concrete slab, Laurie sat waiting for Claire. The slab was a bench, precast, as was just about everything in the courtyard – square concrete flower tubs, slotted concrete cycle stand, concrete paving, and the three concrete and glass towers which comprised the Biology Building. Red geraniums provided the only splash of colour in all the gray-whiteness. The sun beat and beat on him. It penetrated his hair and tingled his scalp. It was heaven to be so hot and sticky. If only the summer were half as decent as this back home he could never have fallen so low in spirits. With the sun blasting your mind, dark thoughts, black emotions, were too much darned trouble.

Every now and then, students came by. Some rushed past silently on bicycles, directing front wheels skilfully into a slit of the cycle stand. Noisy groups would suddenly emerge from one of the towers and amble to another across the courtyard, their lab coats swinging undone, their arms full of books, files or rucksacks. They were taller, stronger, healthier looking specimens than those at Thorpe, was his impression. None gave him more than a cursory glance.

He wondered how long he had been sitting here. His watch, when he flexed his arm, gleamed at him piercingly. Shading it, he checked the time. Over an hour. Not that he cared. He was pretty certain she was inside one of the towers, either the one straight ahead straddled by the phytotron, or the one behind where she had her study. Of course, she might well walk from the phytotron and through the tower building on his right in order to reach her study, because, if he correctly remembered the layout, the tower on his right contained the Common Room. His eyes wandered from one building to the next, but not with any purpose; the gleam from the glass made an effective blind. He knew she wasn't in her flat because he'd gone there to check straight from the bus station. He had slipped a note under her door telling her of his arrival and promising to return there later if she proved elusive. There was no urgency. Just by getting here to Montreal he had virtually accomplished his mission.

Now, after one large exodus, fewer people came through the courtyard. When they did it was singly and usually from the building housing the studies and offices. Academics finishing for the day, Laurie surmised, turning to face that direction. A triangle of shadow had deepened across a corner and now extended across the open doorway. When Claire arrived in this, he at first took her for a child – a waif, she seemed, after the strapping creatures he had watched all afternoon. When he saw who it was, he stood up, and from his vantage point took in every detail. In flowing flimsy blue (which he recognized as an Indian smock dress, and the little glints of gold on the ends of ribbons hanging from her neck as tiny bells), she stood holding a case in one hand, a paper cup in the other. When she had drained the cup, she dropped it into a bin and stepped forward. 'Claire,' he called.

She, looking into the sun, could see nothing beyond a figure standing between two flower tubs. The voice was instantly recognizable, but she quietened the leap inside her with the stern observation that it couldn't possibly be.

'Claire!' he laughed. She shielded her eyes. It was a dream, a mirage, but she pelted towards it.

Her case dropped as he swung her round. She dug her hands into his back, her head into his chest. And briefly, before the questions and protests and self-recriminations ('What are you doing here? It was my letter about Rob, wasn't it? – I made it sound too miserable. Oh Laurie, you shouldn't have; I never meant you to be worried . . .') there was only pure sharp joy; a moment when she knew all that truly mattered to her – not Rob, nor even her work in Montreal – was here in her arms. As the questions gathered, she purposely held them at bay. If time must stop, she thought, let it be now.

In the tiny slant-ceilinged bedroom of her apartment – to which they had come for a rest and a shower before going out to eat, he stood watching as she changed the sheets. 'You have the bed,' she was saying. 'I'll sleep on the living-room couch.'

'No, I'll have the couch.'

'You will not. I know what you are. You'll be miserable as sin on that couch – it's a horrid greasy old thing. You'll be much better off here.'

'No, I mean to have the couch.'

'You're having the bed. Why the hell do you think I'm changing the sheets?'

'Then stop changing them. I'll take the couch.'

Dropping the bedcovers, she raised shaking fists to her screwed up eyes. 'For once in your life will you do as you're bloody well told?' she shrieked.

There was a pause. 'Certainly,' he sniffed, and went and sat on the bed.

'This is my place for chrissakes!'

'Indeed.'

She moved to the window. 'I'm sorry,' (she didn't sound it in the least), 'I'm just so darned mad about Lydia robbing us. Though it's not so much the stuff she took as her getting away with it. Hey – do we even know her surname?'

'Devlin,' he answered shortly.

'Any idea of her real first name – or his, I should say?'

'Yes, I did happen to see it . . . Liam.'

'Sounds Irish.'

He sighed. 'Is that relevant at all?'

'No,' she said defensively, 'but it's something to go on. I mean, we are going to do something about it, aren't we? Why the hell didn't you go the police?'

Her fury took him aback – and he hadn't yet got round to mentioning the incriminating package, only the paintings, the clock, the radio and the silver. 'I hardly like to draw attention to my living arrangements.'

'Ah, I hadn't thought . . . But *she* had, I bet. Of course! – that's what she banked on, that she could thieve with impunity. Which, when you come to think about it, is rather like blackmail. Shit! Give me five minutes alone with the cow. I'll show her where she gets off. I'll . . .'

She was interrupted by the bedsprings crying out, as Laurie, exhausted by the tirade, the travelling, and his body's insistence that it was really bedtime, flopped back. He closed his eyes and decided it might

352

be prudent to forget about the missing package – she was roused enough as it was.

Staring down at the bed, at the darkness of him – the black curls and shadowy clefts and violet wells under the eyes, her heart misgave her. 'Sorry to have gone on,' she mumbled, stooping to pull off his shoes. 'You know I don't really care twopence for that Foscote stuff, I just hate it that Lydia took you for a ride – after all you did for her . . . Yeah, well, have a good rest.'

From his utter stillness and even breathing he might already be asleep. Feeling foolish, and rather cross with herself, she tiptoed out the room.

When she woke in the morning he was nowhere in the apartment. He had eaten she noticed, from all the china, cutlery and packets lying about. She ran to the front window and looked out. And there he was below in the square (a square of grass and trees with seats, where later in the day the square's elderly residents would sit for a gossip and laden shoppers pause for a breather). On one of the seats, Laurie was sitting reading a newspaper. She pushed up the window. 'Best part of the day!' she called. He looked up, waved, half rose. 'Don't move. I'll get dressed and come down.'

Descending the curved iron staircase with her mug of coffee, she decided not to apologize again for her outburst last evening. This morning afforded a fresh start. Beaming, she crossed the road, then the grass, and settled beside him. 'You slept well?'

'Like a log. And I ate two breakfasts.'

'Bet you needed them.' (They had not, after all, gone out to eat last night: it had seemed sensible to let him sleep on.)

'I can't get over this glorious weather. It's been atrocious at home. Now dear, you must carry on as normal. Don't let my being here interfere with your arrangements.'

'Well, I am supposed to be . . . But no, look, I can ring in . . .'

'You'll do no such thing!'

This morning his bossiness seemed endearing, as usual. She grinned, guessing he'd welcome some time to relax alone. 'OK. So long as you don't disappear as suddenly as you arrived.'

'I'll come and meet you from work. Same time again?'

'Oh yes,' she said eagerly. 'Promise?' They could have a repeat of yesterday's rapture and this time she wouldn't blow it by laying into him.

'Promise,' he confirmed.

Towards the end of the meal that evening, he confided the true reasons for his flight to her: not the thefts (he didn't even mention the stolen letters), but the conflicting emotions stirred by Lydia's departure – pain at the disintegration of a dream, bewilderment at having built so insubstantial a dream in the first place, corrosive self-hatred for having refused to admit its worthlessness. He had been riven by similar feelings once before. Did she remember?

Oh yes, Claire remembered. And she understood him exactly. Across the table she reached for his hand, sought his eyes over the flickering candle. 'Thank God you had the sense to get on that plane. What the hell would I have done if . . . ?' She shook her head, words failing her. 'I'm just so thankful.'

One afternoon, as he walked alone down Maisonneuve Boulevard, Laurie thought he saw Lydia. The air shimmered with heat, the pavement ahead was apparently awash: into this mirage the phantom erupted, hurriedly, from Eaton's doorway. She strode for a full block ahead of him (that swinging walk, those stiffly-held shoulders, the haughty sideways turn of her head!), then paused to look at a window display. He, drawing level, stood alongside. It wasn't her, of

354

course, nothing approaching her: it was a svelte blonde beautiful female (female by sex as well as gender). Not for the first time he was struck by the size of people here; the women, many of them, were as tall and broad shouldered as British men. She gave him a sidelong glance. At which, smiling an apology, he backed away and turned confusedly into the blessed cool of the Hudson Bay store's air-conditioning.

It grew hotter, the atmosphere closer. That evening, while they dined in a restaurant on the rue Saint-Laurent, thunder rolled, lightning flashed, and the skies emptied. At their table in the window, they ate *moules* from shells and slurped up the liquor and watched the rain as if hypnotized. When she had devoured every mollusc and every last drop of juice, Claire, with an air of abstraction, reached into her bowl of fries and popped one into her mouth. ('*Moules marinières* with fries? It's an obscenity!' Laurie had scoffed when the food arrived, and she, because *he* had said so, had been disposed to agree.) However, though by now tepid, they were tasty and deliciously squelchy. It was a pity he should miss such a treat. 'Actually, these are nice,' she said.

He tried one, then another. The rainfall was enormously liberating. He felt relaxed and free, as if weighty baggage had recently slid from his shoulders. And ate a third potato chip.

'I thought I saw Lydia today,' he casually confided. 'This statuesque blonde blew out of Eaton's. I walked behind her as far as The Bay, then she stopped to look in a window, and I got a chance to look at her face. Of course it wasn't Lydia, nothing like. I felt a chump – she'd obviously noticed me staring. Had to escape into the store. Maybe the heat's getting to me . . .'

'How fortunate, then, that it's Saturday tomorrow and I can keep an eye on you. Prevent you disappointing some other poor woman.'

He raised an eyebrow. He had thought he was the

one who'd been disappointed. But of course, really he hadn't been. Good God, what would he have done if it *had* been Lydia? 'So, you think she was disappointed, this woman, when I sheered off?'

'Naturally. She thought she was in with a chance, and that on closer inspection you didn't reckon her. You do know you're devastating, that you're a loss and disappointment to womankind?'

'Hmm. No doubt you're right. You are, at any rate, about these slimy little potato worms. Scrumptious.'

He was beginning, she thought, to sound like his old self. She hoped the progress would continue, that his going home on Monday wouldn't cause a set-back. 'You know, darling, this thing I'm working on at the moment – it'll be finished in a couple of weeks. I'll have the paper to write, but I could come home soon afterwards. I don't have to stay here the whole two years.'

He pushed away his bowl of fries, wiped his fingers thoroughly on a napkin. 'I wouldn't hear of it. Don't dare offend Professor Fergusson. He could be useful to you.'

She lingeringly disposed of her very last chip. 'But I shan't stay on *longer* than my two years. I'm coming home at the end of February – I'm determined about that.'

A look went between them, as both had the same thought and were aware of the other one thinking it: if Lydia had not removed herself from 97 Devonshire Avenue, Claire would have reached an alternative decision.

'In that case,' said Laurie, fiddling with some leftover bread and patently endeavouring to restrain undue eagerness, 'we should play it carefully. You shouldn't come back for less than a Senior Lectureship. But I'd wait and see, if I were you; they might make you such an attractive offer here that you'd be mad to refuse.'

'Then I'd be mad,' she said calmly. 'Shall we have some pud?'

'Um, just coffee, I think.'

'The fruit salad here is out of this world – it's not your syrupy chopped up bits, but gorgeous slices, three kinds of melon . . .'

'Oh, go on then.' He looked round for the waiter, gave the order. 'But look, if you're still of the same mind by the end of summer, let me know. I can start preparing the ground. The work you've done here – specially if your paper's well received – should certainly command a seniorship. And on your terms.'

'Yeah?'

'Well dear, we both know teaching is not your forte. Research, on the other hand . . . Why are you grinning?'

She ducked her head. 'No reason.' In truth she was delighted. If this wasn't the old Laurie – politicking and scheming, gearing up to fight her corner – she had a sadly deficient memory. 'So – you wouldn't be put out by my moving back into 97?'

'Put out?' he asked incredulously. 'It's your own home! Just don't make any snap decisions for what you imagine to be my sake.'

'Of course not.'

'However, *if* that's what you want after mature reflection, I'm keen to see you get the best out of it. But bear in mind there may well be something of interest elsewhere in the UK. It doesn't have to be Thorpe.'

'But Thorpe is home.'

'We could always buy another place. I could change my job, come to that . . . Oh my!' he exclaimed, as an enormous plate of berries and sliced fruits was set before them.

'Fresh pineapple,' she pointed out, 'strawberries, raspberries, blueberries . . .'

The rain was over and it was a glorious evening by the time they left the restaurant. They linked arms and

357

strolled along the steaming pavement, stopping to peer in all the curious shop-windows – at displays of foreign bric-à-brac (items parted with for a song by Montreal's recent immigrants); at displays devoted to the occult, and to motorbike regalia; there were book shops, art shops, exotic underwear shops, carpentry shops, silversmith shops – many still open. Browsing, Claire was aware of being blissfully replete – and not just from her meal: Laurie wanted her back, she exulted.

He, as ever, was feeling partly one thing, partly another. He was thrilled – he couldn't help being – by her desire to come home, and energized by the rush of purpose it gave him. But he also dreaded encouraging her to take a wrong step, a step into a less than adequate future. 'It was a pity about Rob,' he murmured, as they studied items in the occult shop-window.

'Why was it? What do you mean? I'm over that now.'

'Because in one way, you and he were very well suited.'

She stared crossly at a fan of tarot cards. 'If you mean sexually, why don't you say so? And I haven't forgotten that we're not, I'm not planning to jump on you or anything.' (He had edged a little away from her.) 'What I've learned is, in this life you can't have everything in one package. So you have to decide on your priorities. Right?'

'It sounds . . . reasonable.'

'And I've decided mine are being with you. If that's OK?'

'There is no need to sound so aggressive about it.'

'But that is OK with you?' she persisted, her thin tone betraying a sudden ebbing of confidence.

Her wayward left eye wavering towards the bridge of her nose lent her the look of an urchin – a look that was familiar to him from childhood. It tugged at his heart. 'Come on.' He seized her arm, pulled her into his side. 'Of course it's OK,' he soothed, as they moved on and he leaned his head over hers. 'It couldn't be more so.'

The square was full of white gulls. They swarmed round the heads of the statues, swooped low over the grass. When the traffic was hushed – that brief moment between signal changes on Dorchester Boulevard – the air throbbed to their screeching. Perhaps the freshness of the day excited them, for after yesterday's rain, the sun's shining brought no oppressive heat or clamminess. On the corner of the Sun Life Building, a breeze billowed the skirt of Claire's Indian dress.

She looked over to the Cathedral. When the lights changed, took Laurie's hand and tugged him across. 'Let's go in,' she said, convinced all at once that in the lofty quiet the words she had been hunting for might come. He ran behind her up the steps – forty or fifty of them. When she opened the door, he took it from her, and together they entered the vestibule of Mary Queen Of The World.

The door into the basilica proper was fastened open; a service was taking place. Claire looked crestfallen. 'We can wait,' he said, and stood gazing down the central aisle at the baldachin beneath the cupola, and recalled his surprise at this sight on his first visit (for Mary Queen Of The World is an exact replica on a smaller scale of St Peter's in Rome, and the baldachin a copy of Bellini's).

A precentor began singing a canticle. 'Oh, listen,' Laurie murmured, reaching for her. She sank back against him, resting her hands on his crossed arms at her waist. As he closed his eyes and gave himself up to the sound, she examined the ranked portraits – of a succession of cardinals, she supposed – hanging on the vestibule wall. 'What a voice,' Laurie exclaimed at the canticle's end. What grim old codgers, she thought.

When the service was over, they stood back to allow the worshippers past – French-speaking matrons mostly, smart and stout – then went inside, Claire leading the way. She walked almost to the halfway point of the nave then turned into a pew on the left and edged along almost to the pillar before sitting down. He came and sat beside her, leaving a small space between.

He was going home the day after tomorrow. She had been reminding herself of this fact all day. For there was something she needed to say to him. Something . . . And to say it right, which, given her habit of abruptness – or even aggression when feeling nervous or pushed – was a lot to ask. She sat in the pew watching the flickering yellow and green votive candles. And after a time it no longer seemed to matter so much . . .

Not touching, not looking, they had lapsed into one of their easeful silences.

Laurie's eyes were exploring the baldachin: the crown beneath the ball and cross which seemed fashioned from octopus tentacles, and the stout, curvy lined columns which were like wonky elephant legs. The proud-breasted angels guarding the corners were more suited, he thought, to the prow of a boat; they were plump not ethereal, and might be buoyant but would never fly – in contrast to Claire just now, running up the steps in her breeze-filled dress; no, it didn't tax the imagination to picture *her* wafted aloft. Ah, Claire – who, in the spring, would be making her home with him again in Thorpe. He knew this for certain, knew no amount of objection on his part would prevent her. She had made up her mind. He viewed his helplessness in the face of her determination with a complacency akin to sinking into a warm and sudsy bath. Even the probability of trouble emanating from his association with Lydia (which he felt in his bones would come sooner or later) failed to agitate him or rouse even an echo of his former despair. If trouble came, he would have Claire. It was a profoundly reassuring thought, and resonant with memory. From her first steps, like the proverbial

360

duckling, she had fixatedly followed him. Or like his *shadow* – as one of the Foscote adults had rather derisively remarked. He focussed on the word, which seemed anchoring rather than insubstantial. He remembered reading once in some book of fantasy tales that it was always possible to tell a ghost because a dead man casts no shadow. It seemed apposite. Hadn't she twice now kept him alive?

Claire, raising her eyes from the candles and slightly turning her head leftwards, fixed on a picture hanging directly across the aisle. There was a caption beneath it in French. 'The blessed Margeurite Bourgeoys instructs the young savages', she translated – with disbelief. She was reminded of her one and only visit to an Indian reservation, not far from here. The guide's jocular commentary (full of warnings about flying arrows and not to give money to any importuning natives who would only use it to buy liquor) had so offended her, she had abandoned the tour and climbed back on the bus, and only managed to contain her indignation by recalling she was a guest in this State. And now here again. the same thick-headed assumptions. She supposed the picture was hung to be venerated, for it plainly lacked any artistic or decorative merit and could serve no other purpose. And this was the nineteen seventies! How long, she wondered, before a cleric or member of the congregation was prompted to take it down – or at least blank out the caption? Her certainty that one day it must come down was both cheering and frustrating – cheering to foresee an end to prejudice, frustrating to consider the millions who have suffered from it in the past and must do so meantime. And it suddenly struck her that were it not for prejudice of a different sort, Laurie would have been spared many agonies, and she her ignorance.

Turning her head from the picture, she stared again at the candles. Then, like a miracle, the words came to her effortlessly, as though she had not spent fruitless hours searching and straining for them. 'You know, Laurie,' she whispered, her eyes holding to the flickering flames, 'I wouldn't have you in the least bit different. All the bitterness I spouted that day in the kitchen – it wasn't due to disappointment in *you*; it was the waste of the years getting to me, years of striving after what I never could have. But now I know the score, I wouldn't want it. Because in order to have it, you'd have to be different, to not be you. What I'm trying to say is: to me you're perfect.'

He, too, had his eyes on the candles, and now saw all the green and yellow lights leap and melt and dissolve. 'It's what I always hoped,' he said quickly, 'but never dared test.' He waited a moment, then added more lightly, 'It's going to be novel, living together in full knowledge.'

'Yes,' she agreed happily. 'A brand new experience.'

He watched a verger emerge from the transept and begin laying out books in the front few pews. Some people trooped past from the back. 'They're very busy this afternoon.'

She laid a hand on his arm. 'Shall we go?'

'All right.' But he didn't get up; instead, turned to her, and for the first time since sitting down they exchanged looks. 'Thank you,' he said. 'And to me, *you*'re perfect.'

'I should hope so.'

'Hmm.'

At last he got to his feet, moved to the end of the pew.

Following him, she discovered she was giddy, perhaps from staring so long in such lofty space. Stumbling into the aisle, she banged her thigh on the pew end.

He caught her. 'Are you all right?'

She was, but cursed to think of the bruise that would develop. But then, as she hung on to his arm and set off, lurching rather, the idea of a bruise began to appeal: it would be a tender memento of this afternoon when, for once in her life, she had spoken up brilliantly; also it would remain with her for a while when Laurie had gone.

'Sure you're all right, pet?'

'Sure,' she smiled, and her elation as she went towards the west door of Mary Queen Of The World was as great as any bride's.

xii

Two years later, on the day of Monica and David's wedding, Claire was in Monica's bedroom helping her get ready.

'Just keep your hands off this husband,' Monica warned, brandishing a hairbrush.

At the ironing board, Claire very nearly scorched Monica's silver silk blouse. 'Whaah?' she choked.

'Didn't think I knew, eh?'

'Um, er . . . No.'

'Perhaps I should make it clear. When the matter was drawn to my attention you were in Canada and thus out of reach. Otherwise, you would most certainly have known about it.'

'Right. Bloody hell. I say, Monica, I'm really sorry. I never meant . . .'

'You mean to say you bedded my husband in a fit of absent mindedness?'

'No, of course not.' She bit her lip and bent over her task – with enormous care winkled the iron's nose in and out of a ruff on the front of the blouse – both to gain time and cover her confusion.

'Relax. The steam went out of the situation months and months ago as far as I'm concerned. All I'm saying is, try it on with David and you'll be very sorry.'

'Christ, Monica, what do you think I am? I wouldn't dream of it. And I didn't *try it on* with Paul, as you put it. It was the other way round, he was a perfect pest.'

'So I believe.'

'You see? I gave in once, when I was rock bottom –

utterly miserable. And afterwards I was so sick with myself I nearly threw up.'

'Yes, well, that's some consolation.' She squinted across at the ironing board. 'I'll put that on if you've finished with it.'

'Almost.' Claire completed the task and handed the blouse over, then busied herself by unplugging the iron and putting it to cool and folding away the ironing-board.

Monica put on the blouse and fastened the buttons, observing these actions and her immaculately made up face with much satisfaction in the dressing-table mirror. The warning she had given just now she knew to be entirely superfluous, for unlike Paul, David had eyes only for her. David had even confided that once Claire had horribly embarrassed him. They were in The Hesketh Arms having a friendly drink together, when it suddenly dawned that Claire was pro-positioning him – an unwelcome realization in view of Claire's lack, in his eyes, of the necessary sexual allure. He liked a woman of substance, a woman who *was* a woman. 'You mean like me,' Monica had purred, whereupon David had demonstrated that he meant like her exactly and in every particular. So she had no qualms whatever about her soon-to-be husband. Her sole purpose in raising the matter was to give Claire a jolt. If she had hesitated before to do so, it was because she remembered Claire's previous unhappiness – un-happiness to which she, Monica, may have inadvertently contributed with her mistaken assump-tions. She did not doubt that Paul had caught Claire at a very low ebb. However, Claire was no longer miserable. In fact, she was radiantly happy, and had been so for the past eighteen months, ever since her return from Montreal. Once or twice a rebuke had been on the tip of Monica's tongue – for instance, around the time of Claire's promotion to Senior Lecturer, or at the party last spring thrown by Laurie to celebrate the anniversary of Claire's return (at which Claire had pronounced the past year the best of her life). But Monica had delayed. It seemed more sporting to select her own occasion than to risk spoiling one of Claire's – though she had known the matter would have to be broached sooner or later if she and Claire were to continue as friends. Monica would never knowingly allow anyone to do her down and get away with it.

'I must say, sweetie, you've made a super job of this blouse. Pass me the skirt, will you?'

Claire removed it from a hanger and brought it over.

'Don't look so solemn. Better that I air the matter than let it fester, don't you agree?'

Claire, mumbling agreement, thought Monica had taken rather long to do so and then chosen an inappropriate time. However, she was hardly in a position to quibble. 'I'm truly sorry,' she offered again.

'I know you are,' Monica said, wriggling the skirt over her hips, smoothing it down, closing the zip. She turned, reached out and clasped her. 'There! Now we can forget it. Let's have a drink.'

'In here, or with the others?'

'Perhaps we'd better go and join them. I wonder: if I had met David's people before committing myself, would I have gone ahead?'

'Silly. You're marrying him, not them. Anyway, sounds as if he keeps them pretty much at arm's length.'

'And who can blame him? Is my hair OK?'

'It's terrific,' Claire confirmed, surveying the swinging burnished bob.

'So, go and pour out two large stiff ones.'

'Right,' she said, and gratefully made her escape.

In the sitting-room, David's parents, Mr and Mrs Guthrie, were ensconced on a sofa with Laurie. David, supported by an elbow propped on the mantelpiece, was engaging with Monica's sister, Audrey, and brother-in-law, Julian. Claire went to the sideboard and poured a strong gin and tonic for Monica (who had hung behind to do something or other) and a weak one for herself. Laurie and David, with looks and asides, both tried to draw her into their respective groups, but she merely smiled vaguely and took her drink to a distant armchair. She was still flustered by the exchange in the bedroom and needed to collect her thoughts.

This rather sedate affair was the pre-wedding party. Later, after the ceremony in the registry office, this same group would eat a meal together in the Paragon Hotel. And that would be that – Mrs Paul Cage changed to Mrs David Guthrie, and the bachelor state of Mr and Mrs Guthrie's only child (in which they had assumed he was nicely settled) changed to husbandhood.

Monica, David had confided to Laurie, had come as a shock and a disappointment to his parents. Throughout his seamlessly brilliant career – as grammar school boy, undergraduate, university teacher and historian – they had urged their son to beware women. Or rather empty-headed lasses, bound by nature to wreak disaster on the proper pursuit of a lad's studies. News that at age thirty-three (when they had thought the danger past) the lad had been caught by an older woman and a divorced one at that, was like learning the end of the world was to occur due to celestial oversight. Maternal pleadings arrived through the post. Mr Guthrie went so far as to stand in a call-box (one well distant from the family home and nosey neighbours), tears running down his cheeks as he begged his son to reconsider – 'Don't do it, lad, don't chuck yourself away.' Though he feared it would be a hard task getting disentangled – 'She won't give up easy. At her age she'll doubtless see you as her last chance – and she'll know all the wiles, with her practice.' David's protests – to the effect that his intended had nothing to gain by the alliance, for as well as owning a substantial house, she stood higher in the academic pecking order than he (Monica was a Reader while he was a Senior Lecturer) – failed to impress. It was doubtful whether, in the throes of his emotion, his father even took this in.

On their arrival here this morning, Monica in the flesh had rendered them speechless. But their greatest shock (soon converted to awed joy) was meeting Laurie, one of their favourite television personalities. 'Oo, we always watch *Natural World*. We love anything about nature, don't we Dad?' confided Mrs Guthrie as she and her husband sat and wondered at him. The feeling crept over that maybe their son had not done so badly after all. For here he was moving in celebrity circles. And this Monica had been on the radio, talking about some book she had written. Mrs Guthrie began composing the account she would give her next-door neighbour. ('That Laurie Stone off the telly were there – you know, does *Natural World*. He's a great chum of our David's. We chatted to him for hours. We were sat on the sofa with him, close as you and me now. A real charmer. And such a comic!') Mr Guthrie also was launched on a more cheerful train: one thing you could say for an older woman, she'd not likely be saddling the lad with kids. And this house of hers was right champion. Compared to the two up two down he and Mother shared in Macclesfield, it was a bloody mansion. Mind you, her relations were a disgrace . . .

On the other side of the room, David was having a tough time with Monica's sister. Audrey – a red-faced, rough-skinned version of Monica – and her hearty husband Julian were very noisily telling jokes against each other, bellowing denials and shouting embellishments, ostensibly for David's amusement.

The day stretched dauntingly ahead, separated into hours and minutes and thousands of seconds. Claire stifled a yawn behind her hand; reached for her drink. The real party had happened last night – at least for the female side of the equation. (David, she understood, had had a quiet dinner with Laurie and a couple of other colleagues.) The whole gang had been there –

Eleanor, Joyce, Yolande, Liz, plus Monica and herself. Monica's gang, was how she thought of the group, for it had been Monica who had brought them together, a cluster of young female academics prepared to stick their necks out if need be in the cause of fairer promotion. And with what excellent results! At last night's dinner in the Lotus Garden Restaurant there had been a great deal more to celebrate than Monica's forthcoming nuptials. Each member of the group – with the exception of Yolande – had risen higher up the academic ladder. 'And yew'll be next, gerl,' Joyce the Scouse had last night reassured Yolande, 'don't worry, we're werkin' on yer case.'

'Damn and blast,' Monica had growled at this, ducking her head and pointing with her eyes. Cautiously they peered in the indicated direction. 'I bet they didn't miss that. Wouldn't you just know it? The one occasion we dine out together . . .'

Sure enough, at a table in a corner, three of the more ghastly Senior Common Room misogynists (two members of the Theology Department and a Philosophy don) were doing themselves well. The discovery threatened to put a blight on their evening, conscious as they were of certain forcefully expressed opinions (that a ridiculous number of awards had lately gone to women; that this had to be pandering to hysterical pressure, for as any sensible person knew, a woman by definition could never be worthy as the next fellow in line). Which seemed to the women more than a bit thick. There had been no convention of Buggin's Turn or the old school lobby at their disposal. Each promotion had been hard earned. Eleanor's was scandalously long overdue; Liz and Claire had needed to work abroad to earn recognition; an offer of a better job elsewhere had at last secured Joyce's Senior Lectureship, and the English Department had been moved to make Monica a Reader on the strength of her actually adding to the supply of raw material from which academic livings are got.

'That's torn it,' hissed Eleanor. 'Their worst fears are confirmed.'

'Yep,' agreed Monica, 'they've seen it with their own eyes. We really do plot the downfall of Adam.'

'Silly pricks. Ignore 'em,' Joyce advised, topping up their glasses.

Then Liz – her eyes flicking between Monica and the dark-suited trio studiously ignoring the presence of their female colleagues – was struck by an aspect of their difficulty so far unconsidered. 'You know what's part of the problem? Women are just too visible. One woman in a roomful of blokes is a veritable blaze. So one of us getting promoted has a disproportionate impact. Five seems like caving in to an invading army.'

'I hope you're not proposing we become like them – wear hideous grey suits and let our stomachs hang over our belts. Because frankly I couldn't. If I met such a sight in my looking-glass, I'd give up – draw the curtains and go back to bed. I rely on my mirror to give me a boost.'

They looked at her and laughed: greyness and Monica were contradictory terms. And the men were promptly forgotten.

A marvellous, warm-hearted party it had been, Claire recalled, smiling to herself. And from all her friends, it was she, Claire, Monica had asked to support her today. So no need to worry, surely, over Monica's remarks just now. Monica wasn't two-faced, she couldn't have been bearing a grudge all this time. Simply, she had wanted to clear the decks now they were both happy and secure in their personal lives. Having settled this to her satisfaction, Claire smiled broadly when Monica at last came into the room. 'Your drink's on the sideboard,' she called.

'Ravishing, Mrs Cage!' cried Laurie. 'Every last minute, so well spent.'

'For heaven's sake, Laurie, stop calling her that,' urged Claire.

'No, no, I'm saddled with it, I'm afraid. *Monica Cage*

it says on my dust jackets, so Monica Cage I remain.'

'Never mind, dear. You kept the good bit and chucked back the rubbish. Cage does have a ring to it. But darling, shouldn't you be pacing yourself? That's an awfully large drink, and there's the whole day ahead of you. We don't want you collapsing before you've plighted your troth, not when we've all turned out to bear witness.' Laurie turned confidingly to Mrs Guthrie and said of her soon-to-be daughter-in-law: 'It's very sad. But she does battle against it. We must give her that.'

'Laurie!' cried Claire. But Mrs Guthrie had long since taken Laurie's measure. 'Isn't he awful?' she shrieked.

It was a cue for Audrey to loudly divulge the failings of yet another family member. Laurie smoothly detached himself from Mrs Guthrie and went to recharge Audrey's glass; and gradually, by soliciting more than he ever cared to know about fox-hunting and point-to-point meetings, brought down the volume. Then David remarked that it was very nearly time to go. At which Mrs Guthrie gulped, and Mr Guthrie debated with himself whether even at this late hour it was worth having another try at dissuasion. Catching renewed tension on the other side of the room, Laurie quickly returned to offer Mrs Guthrie his arm and suggest to Mr Guthrie that they travel together. Mrs Guthrie poked her husband eagerly. 'That'd be a big help, Dad, wouldn't it, seeing as we don't know Thorpe all that well?', and in her head enlarged on this further triumph to her next-door neighbour.

'Laurie is *so* dependable,' Monica breathed gratefully in Claire's ear as they followed the rest of the party to the door.

The words returned frequently to Claire. She recalled them in the car, then again when they were hanging about in the registry office, and later at table in the Paragon Hotel. She wondered – as Laurie skilfully knitted them into a jolly group – whether Monica's choice of supporter from among her women friends was informed by knowledge that one of them, Claire, came with Laurie attached – Laurie so indispensable to the awkward occasion, priceless Laurie of whom, given the limitless scope for social disaster in this petty world, there was simply not enough to go round.

But then after the meal, Monica inveigled Claire to accompany her to the Ladies. There, she felt into her bag and brought out a small box. 'I want you to have this brooch of my Aunt Harriet's. Blessed if I could find it earlier, which was why I was such ages coming out of the bedroom. It's just a thank you for being with me today – which I know cannot have been one of life's highlights . . .'

Claire stared at the tiny Victorian brooch. It was a reproach to her doubts. 'Hey, it's lovely, but I can't take it,' she said (meaning she didn't deserve to).

'Please. As a token of our friendship. I always meant you to have it, anyway. It's too dainty for me, much better on you.'

'Thanks,' she choked, stowing it into her bag. So she was definitely forgiven.

Later, when they were driving home from returning Mr and Mrs Guthrie to Monica's, Laurie asked in a casual way, 'Was something bothering you this morning? You seemed rather jumpy, I thought.'

'Did I? When?'

'While we were waiting for Monica.' He had a picture in his mind: Claire sitting on her own, chewing a side strand of hair and playing with her drink.

'Oh, then. Yeah, well, I was a bit worried, because Monica mentioned something I didn't even know she knew about. But I needn't have worried.' She felt into her bag for the brooch and held it up near the steering wheel. 'She gave me this – a token of our friendship, she said. Amethyst and seed pearls. Isn't it sweet?'

'Very pretty.' There was no need to ask her for

371

details, he could guess the sort of thing that had been said. He sighed, and thought of all the hurts glancing off people as they met and collided, like widening circles on a pond – he and Lydia hurting Claire, Paul and Claire hurting Monica, and so on – instances stretching beyond his knowledge but not his imagination.

'What's the matter?' she asked.

'Nothing. Just shattered. Such a trial of a day, I'm utterly exhausted.'

xiii

Number 97 was overrun by workmen again – builders and plumbers who were soon to be joined by Mr Hennage the decorator. The occupation was much in Claire's mind as she walked – none too quickly – along Devonshire Avenue. It was the reason for her leaving work rather later than usual. Let Laurie see them off the premises, she had thought to herself – she had done more than her fair share lately, and had done it alone, for Laurie had been away for three weeks, filming for *Natural World*. Now he was back, let him worry about coffee and tea breaks and one sugar or three, and remember to lay sheets over vulnerable carpets. Actually, she didn't really mind the builders, who were an amiable crew, nipping about the roof repairing the crumbling chimney pots, hauling up and hammering new beams; with their long hair and lithe bodies they were like an extra-athletic pop group, banging and sawing and singing the latest hits. But the two plumbers, a fat middle-aged greaser and his spotty assistant, were a different matter; both given to contemptuous staring, as if, when she brought them their mugs of tea she were also offering her body – and a poor one at that, a virtual insult to connoisseurs such as they (for they were avid tabloid readers, and left their newspapers behind at the end of the day folded open at the pin-up page). During Laurie's absence, she had decided to sack the plumbers on the spot should the friendly builders fail to arrive for any reason.

Ownership of such a large property was proving expensive. This second round of restoration – precipitated by Tim at last vacating the attic flat – would virtually wipe out the last of their Foscote money. Henceforth, any renovation would have to be paid for out of income. Fortunately, Laurie was earning lots from his television work. Even so, before embarking on this latest expense they had half-heartedly debated whether to sell up and move. They didn't *need* such an enormous place. On the other hand, they did love it. In the end, they decided to make a thorough job of turning the attic flat and the rear first floor rooms into self-contained accommodation for four students. That way the house would generate income as well as eat it.

With luck, Laurie's earnings from television would continue to rise. As a result of appearing in his own series, he was often asked to appear on chat shows and the like. It was lucky, she now conceded, that he had resigned from his position as Dean of Students (though when she returned from Canada to discover he had done so, she had been quite put out; it seemed he had relinquished the position on the spur of the moment, though he declined to discuss the matter with her). Lately, he had cut down even further on his commitments, had become a part-time rather than full-time Senior Lecturer. But this was a sensible decision. It meant Laurie could be open about the amount of time he spent on non-academic work; and the department could bask in glory reflected from owning a telly pundit, with no embarrassment about a member of staff pulling his weight. Thorpe was certainly keen to hang on to Laurie. It was thought that the frequently broadcast phrase *Dr Laurie Stone of Thorpe University* sounded well. Claire still grinned to herself hearing the title. It had never been challenged, even by the jealous cats of the SCR. It was as though Laurie had been tacitly granted an honorary doctorate in order to maintain Thorpe's *amour propre* – as if *Mr* Stone of Thorpe University might reflect poorly on the institution.

Having arrived at number 97, she turned into the drive. The plumbers' van was gone, though the builders' lorry remained. 'Good evening,' she called to one of the team who was loading it with tools.

'Evenin' Missus.'

Missus – if only! she thought. But she was grinning broadly as she stood before the hatstand unwinding her lacey green scarf. A second workman came running downstairs. 'See yer tomorrer,' he called.

'Right-oh. Bye-bye.' She closed the front door behind him and went towards the kitchen. 'I'm back and they've gone,' she called.

'Lovely. Martin's here. You're just in time for a cup of tea.'

Someone was bound to be here – always, always. But she wasn't too sad: floods of people coming and going was a sure sign of Laurie being on top of the world; it was when he became reclusive she needed to worry. Anyway, Martin was an old friend, a teacher at one of the city's schools. 'Hi,' she greeted him.

'Hello, Claire.'

Laurie poured her a cup of tea and fetched a clean plate. 'Have some of this delicious cake, and tell us all about your day.'

She and Martin grinned at one another. Anyone would think she and not Laurie led the glamorous life. 'Absolutely zilch to tell – oh, except they're trying to dragoon me on to the Assessment Committee.'

'Excellent. And of course you'll accept.'

'Oh hell, Laurie, you know I'm hopeless at that sort of stuff.'

'Nonsense. When I chaired the Sciences Co-ordinating Committee I was very impressed by your contribution.'

'Yeah? Well it was OK being on one of yours – you

know how to prod people, whip through an agenda. But Harry Welch, for Pete's sake, is the new chair of Assessment! It'll drive me potty sitting about while people gas and gas . . .'

'Look on it as a challenge. It's quite possible to hurry things along even under a weak chairman. The trick is to become his ally. When the voluble ones have had a fair crack and the argument starts going back on itself, look at your watch and say, "As the subject has been thoroughly aired, Mr Chairman – under your patient guidance – and as we seem unlikely to reach a consensus this morning, I move that we adjourn the matter to another occasion." I can guarantee it'll be carried.'

'You can?'

'Certainly. Every committee in my experience consists of two or three keeners – tenacious types with strong opinions; the rest are there reluctantly but hesitate to take the initiative for fear of exposing their total lack of interest. However, if someone sticks their neck out – with the greatest possible courtesy to the chair, of course – people'll back 'em, no fear.'

'Right. You'll have to coach me in some useful phrases.'

'Very well. But do accept with good grace. With your research record, you could make Professor by forty, but not if you shirk other responsibilities. And it's unfair to leave the chores to the diligent few. Don't you agree, Martin?'

'If I were in Claire's shoes, I bet I'd feel pretty much the same. But you're sure to be right, Laurie,' he said, with a wink at Claire.

'Sure to be,' she echoed, taking a second slice of cake.

'Steady on, don't ruin your appetite. We're eating at seven sharp.'

'Oh God yes, the programme,' Claire remembered, and returned the slice to the cake dish. 'Don't worry, I know which is mine, 'cos I've bitten a bit out. I'll have it later.' But Laurie slid a knife under the bitten slice and returned it to Claire's plate, then fetched a clean plate to cover it. 'Anyone'd think I'd got scurvy,' she spluttered – to which, looking pained, he failed to rise.

'I must go,' said Martin, 'but I shall be sure to watch *Natural World.*'

Claire went with Martin to the front door. They chatted for a while about a new production at the Playhouse, then Martin left and she went upstairs for her bath.

A delicious scent was wafting from the kitchen when she came downstairs.

'Can I do anything?'

'Wash the salad if you'd be so kind.'

She rinsed lettuce and chicory leaves, and thought how lucky she was – and how confused her stomach must be, indulged and pampered when Laurie was home doing the cooking and sent down any old thing to digest while he was away.

'Hurry up,' he cried, taking a bubbling gratin dish out of the oven.

'My God, I'm ravenous. What is it?'

'A vegetarian moussaka. I was inspired by some shiny aubergines in the supermarket.' (That was another thing, she thought. He always cooked without meat for her benefit, yet when eating out often chose dishes of chicken or beef.)

She helped herself generously. 'Mm, fantastic! You're a genius. What have I done to deserve you?' She often asked this, having frequent cause. Sometimes, when he was glum, he would protest there had to be some perks in putting up with him. But tonight he was in buoyant spirits.

'Mm, I agree, I've a natural talent. Maybe I should open a restaurant.'

They'd been through this before, too. Laurie fantasized endlessly about alternative careers.

'Don't you think all that standing over hot stoves,

mixing and stirring, would quickly pall? – and doing it night after night.'

'Mm,' he agreed regretfully. 'I suppose it might be a tie. Not much opportunity for all the other things in life.'

'Like playing piano for Miles Davis. Or making loads more TV. Or writing the book of the series,' she teased, but he quickly seized on her last suggestion.

'I've already thought of that. In fact, I had a chat last week with Steve. He's tremendously keen, and so, I might add, are a couple of publishers. Have you any idea of the sort of dosh to be made from telly spin-offs? Richard Osterly is seriously rich.'

'But his books are terribly lowbrow. That sort of thing might not go down too well at Thorpe. Telly's one thing, books are another.'

'There's nothing inherently to be despised in accessibility,' he snapped. 'Eat some more salad. It's good for you.'

She obediently took another heap of green stuff. 'Are the plumbers nearly finished?' she asked, changing the subject. But he hesitated, looked shifty. 'Oh hell, Laurie, you haven't! You promised when the first floor bathroom's finished, that'd be it.'

'I just thought, while they're here it made sense to ask them to put a shower in the downstairs cloakroom. Make it into a fully-functional bathroom. Then, when we have guests, they can stick to that, with no need for them to use either of the students' bathrooms, or either of ours. The bathroom question is always a nuisance.'

'Only to you. Honestly, the lengths you'll go to to prevent anyone spitting into your wash-basin or lowering their bum on to your lavatory seat. You ought to watch it, it's becoming a fetish.'

'Nonsense.'

'It's not nonsense. You made a terrible fuss about Jeanette's Jamie.'

This was true, but for an adequate reason: the

377

wretched boy had piddled copiously on the floor around the pedestal. However, he prefered not to defend himself than raise such a matter at the dinner table. He ate steadily in aggrieved silence.

'OK,' she sighed, 'keep 'em here as long as you like.' (She meant the plumbers.) 'Only I'm having no more to do with them. I hope that's clear?'

'Perfectly.'

'All right, then?' She tipped her face to show him a conciliatory grin. (We're becoming like an old married couple, niggled by each other's quirks, she thought with amusement.)

He acknowledged her grin and returned with relief to a pleasanter topic. 'Illustrated with shots from the film, of course.'

'Er? Oh, the book. Yeah. Great.'

Later, they carried their coffee into the sitting-room, and settled side by side on the settee – as was their habit – to wait for the start of *Natural World*.

As soon as it began, Laurie took Claire's hand and tucked her arm under his. He was claiming her fast attention, she knew, and if someone should now come in – as Phillip Grainger had two weeks ago – Laurie would hiss, 'Shh, sit down, we're watching the pro- gramme,' and her arm would be imprisoned even more tightly. She must attend to their viewing absolutely and with no let-up. Not that there was any hardship in this – she loved to please him, and had no intention of missing a single second. She sensed his deep satisfaction from her drinking it in.

He did not relinquish her until the programme's end, when he rose to switch off the set. Then he sat cautiously back down, and *she* caught *his* arm and squeezed it with pleasure. 'It was terrific! The best yet!'

Relieved, he was careful not to show it; he wanted her true opinion, not one prompted by pressure. 'It is the programme I had most hopes for – an attempt to get people to look at trees with new eyes. I think it came over – how remarkable they are, what treasures.

Though it can't have told *you* anything you didn't know.'

'Oh, but it did!' She jumped round, bringing her legs up, and turned to face him. 'Not in the technical sense, but . . .' her face knitted with the effort to explain – 'on another plane, another dimension. Like . . . it made me *identify* – with the tree, I mean. Specially when you were standing under that huge oak with your hands pressed to the trunk and looking out from it. I got this strong feeling of being solidly rooted – time passing slowly and the elements changing and all the different forms of life teeming . . .' She bounced on to her knees. 'What I mean is, say if I read a poem about a tree (which I admit I probably wouldn't) I might get the same sort of insight (if the poem was any good) a similar sort of feeling . . . Because what you do in these programmes isn't just put over the botanical stuff – which you do very well – but elicit the sort of response that an artist might. Yeah . . .' She seemed to have finished lamely, and sank doubtfully back on to her heels.

'I'm glad you feel like that,' he said seriously, 'because, now you mention it, it's precisely what I hope to do.' His face relaxed. He pulled her to him, gave her a long hard hug.

'Now dear,' he said briskly, putting her aside and standing up, 'we had better tackle that washing-up.'

'Not you, you cooked.'

'Let's do it together, then we can carry on with our lovely chat.'

And so, as she washed and he dried, they continued to go over the programme, recalling details that had particularly struck them; and with increasing excitement envisaged topics for further programmes.

'Where was it, that oak you were standing under?' she asked suddenly.

'In the Lake District. Just outside Keswick, as a matter of fact.'

'It's ages since we stayed in the Lakes. Can we

go there again soon, do you think? How about half term?'

'I should think I could manage a day or two. Depends on the weather, of course. Could be dodgy at that time of year.'

'We're usually lucky.' She let out the washing-up water and dreamily watched it fall away.

Laurie reached into a drawer for a dry cloth. 'Bother! We're out of clean ones. I'd better put a wash on.'

'I'll do that. You've done enough. Go and sit down.'

Leaving her to it, he returned to the sitting-room. He switched on the hi-fi system, then went to the cabinet to select a record. Perhaps because Claire's wry comment was lodged at the back of his mind, his hand went to a Miles Davis album.

When the record began playing, he stood listening intently. A measured tread from bass and piano had him braced for the trumpet's entry. When this came, he moved over to sit at the piano. He struck single notes only, softly and very sparingly, for Bill Evans was already providing the perfect piano part. Claire came into the room at the start of the second number. Matching the spry gait of 'Freddie Freeloader', her walk changed instantly to a lope – shoulders hunched and swaying, hips going neatly from side to side, exactly with the beat. He watched her appreciatively for a while, then rose to join in. They pranced over the carpet and pulled faces at one another. Two hip cats.

The next item, 'Blue in Green', was not to be sent up. To Laurie's mind, close attention, if not reverence, was in order. He flopped full length on the settee, pulling Claire down beside him. Cradling her head, he became a listening vessel; the plangent trumpet entered him, his breathing fell gently with the piano.

Claire listened, too, but with less dedication. She closed her eyes and imagined them back in the boxroom at Foscote, lying as they lay now, but on their battered old sofa, listening to jazz of a less sophisticated kind. At thirty-four years of age, she felt more akin to her twelve-year-old self than all the selves intervening. It was as if during their teens and twenties she and Laurie had repeatedly got lost, led astray by false expectations, by fears building, and disappointments. Thank God they had survived intact and were now safely returned to their natural state – together, but with no misunderstandings, no tensions. Together as they had used to be, as they were always intended to be. For ever and ever.

'Are you asleep?' he asked, mildly indignant that she seemed not to have noticed the music ending.

'Yes.'

'Then I'll try not to disturb you.' He gently dislodged his arm, hauled up and climbed over the settee's end. Then turned the disc over and stood waiting for the start of the next number.

She raised her head. 'Come back and I'll listen properly.'

'It's not compulsory. I thought you were enjoying it.'

'I was, I am,' she declared, shifting across to lie along the settee's back.

He returned and lay down and absently took her hand. With every beat, every note, the music claimed pre-eminence, pared Claire and all else away.

On the third and final day of their stay in Ambleside, they awoke to discover a freezing blanketing milk-white mist.

'And it has been so warm!' mourned Claire, staring disbelievingly out of the hotel window.

'Which accounts for the mist, I suppose – the sudden violent drop in temperature. Lucky we went to Keswick yesterday.'

Yesterday they had left the car on the edge of the town and walked up a lane to visit the field with the magnificent oaks. Then they had walked over Latrigg Fell and circled the Glenderaterra valley. The day before that they had walked and climbed from Little

Langdale. Claire told herself she ought to be satisfied. Two days out of three was fair going.

'We shan't get far afield today,' Laurie said. 'In fact we'd be mad to go anywhere by car.' Across the end of the drive, headlights were passing slowly.

After breakfast they put on weatherproof clothing and walked over the road to the lakeside. The visibility was down to a few yards, sufficient to put one foot in front of the other with safety, but inadequate for picking out a more extended route.

'But the sun's up there somewhere, trying to break through,' Claire persisted.

'I don't doubt it. Question is, how deep is this mist?'

'I'm certain the sun's not very far away. Look over there.' But when they had stared for a couple of seconds at the point she indicated, any hint of brightness had gone. 'I can still sense it,' she said stubbornly.

'All right. But we'll start out on foot. And we'll go somewhere we know.'

'Loughrigg Fell,' she said.

About halfway up, their heads broke through the mist and were bathed in light. It was an abrupt baptism, the mist so dense and white that the sun had merely frayed its outermost edge. A few steps further and they were standing clear in full warm sunlight, and everywhere, from the ground immediately under their feet to the mountainside way above their heads, etched in sharpest detail – the grass gleaming, rocks stark, stones glinting; all springing from a vast cotton-wool sea whose surface hovered a few feet below and stretched to infinity. Claire was triumphant – 'You see?'

They pushed on, stopping every few minutes to turn and gaze around. No stretches of water, no villages or traffic or roads to be seen; just endless, billowed, static mist – from which trees rose, and a house showed here and there on a fellside, and the familiar hills with their swathed footings seemed uncannily close. The fact that Loughrigg, a popular climb, was this morning deserted, sharpened Claire's victory. She thought of walkers going disconsolately about the town below in a very second-best way. They met only three other people. First a man making his descent: he'd been on the top for hours he said and was coming down reluctantly because he had a job to go to. 'You couldn't buy this!' he threw back over his shoulder as he dropped down. Then a couple, a man and a woman, walking one of the horizontal paths: he said he'd been walking the fells for twenty years without ever encountering such a sight; she flung out her arms and cast about with her praise – 'Beautiful! Out of this world! Magical!' Claire agreed politely and edged on upwards. Laurie hung back to talk for a while. It was touchingly human, he thought, to want to share the luck of this day.

At last they gained the triple peaked summit, and ran to each in turn, gallumping round dew pools and boulders. The familiar hills they identified promptly, and used a map to check those they were unsure of. Over and over they spoke the names of hills, like witches entranced by their own incantation. 'Lonscale, Dollywaggon, Great Rigg,' they said, 'Fairfield, Heron, Hart, Dove . . .'

Finally, on the north-facing peak they sank down. Laurie rested against a boulder. Claire lent back against Laurie – his legs along either side of her, his chin on her shoulder. Their silence lasted for the best part of an hour.

No-one came. Warm in the sun, they sat and gazed over their kingdom.

xiv

Claire it was who precipitated Laurie's mother coming to live with them. A stroke had left Margaret Stone clumsy, partially blind, and with a speech difficulty. The first of these was considered the worse tragedy, for she could no longer co-ordinate hand and foot, her fingers trembled, she dropped things: as a potter she was useless. But to Claire arriving with Laurie (summoned by a frail Kitty Gunn who herself would have retired months ago had not Margaret, still strong and vigorous, dissuaded her), the loss of effective speech seemed the most terrible outcome. Margaret was physically able to speak, but certain words, usually the key words of a sentence, would evade her tongue as they entered her head; they stood in her mind, looming larger and larger, yet could not be uttered. Conversation was reduced to a guessing game. To Claire, watching Margaret's facial contortions and furious frustration, it was like confronting, in a grotesque form, her own lack of verbal fluency. She became as agitated trying to guess the word as Margaret trying to produce it.

After an hour of excruciating dialogue over a scratch tea, Margaret, having lapsed tiredly into silence, suddenly gathered her strength to shout at Laurie, 'You must put me into a . . . Say, say,' she implored, jabbing at him with a forefinger.

'A home?' offered Laurie, the errant word seeming embarrassingly obvious.

Margaret nodded vigorously. 'That place, put me. I don't want to be a . . .'

'Nuisance? Bother?' he suggested, inspired, in spite of himself, by honesty. 'You're not a bother, Ma. I admit we'll have to work something out, but if we put our heads together . . .'

But Claire interrupted him. She hurled herself to the side of Margaret's chair and dropped on to her knees. 'We wouldn't dream of putting you in any such place, would we, Laurie?'

'Not a *home*,' he conceded, then spoilt it with a belated, 'exactly.' For it was obvious to Laurie that his mother could not remain in her cottage alone, not if this afternoon's performance were anything to go by – tripping over the rug, crashing into furniture, dropping and smashing the teapot and then howling like an animal when the proper release of an expletive deserted her. And certainly Kitty Gunn couldn't manage her.

'Only in *our* home,' Claire said triumphantly. 'It's the obvious solution. We'll turn the sitting-room into a bedsit.' (For they had no free bedrooms left; number 97 at long last had its full complement of lodgers.) 'What a blessing you had that shower installed in the downstairs cloaks, Laurie. It can be Aunt Margaret's bathroom. We'll just have to arrange our work commitments carefully. I expect Mrs Smethurst could come in more often. And there are always students about, and friends dropping in. You won't lack company, Aunt Margaret.'

Margaret Stone was watching her son.

'It's an excellent idea,' he said bravely.

Afterwards, washing up in the tiny scullery, Claire endeavoured to persuade him that it was. 'We can put a little telly in the dining-room, and we can take the hi-fi in there. Friends usually sit with us in the kitchen or dining-room. The only thing we can't have is big parties. But that won't hurt us. And in the summer we'll give a party in the garden.' When he said nothing, she added anxiously, 'After all, if it weren't for Aunt Margaret we wouldn't even *have* number 97.'

'That is true,' he conceded.

Jeanette promised to spend at least two school holidays a year with Aunt Margaret in the cottage which would one day come to her. So her leave taking of Kitty and St Ives would not be final, Margaret Stone was reassured. And Laurie and Claire could at least look forward to periods of respite. All in all it was a very sensible solution, Laurie told himself.

When his mother was installed and Claire continued to regard him anxiously and make timid little remarks, such as, 'It'd be a poor do, Laurie, if we couldn't take in Aunt Margaret, who was always so good to us', he felt impelled to voice his true feelings – so far as possible. 'It's not the tie, you know, or the upheaval or the inconvenience: I can put up with all that. What it is . . . Well, it feels peculiar. Slightly threatening.'

She looked at him intently.

'As if that old regime has reached after us – the Foscote regime. That it's wormed it's way under our roof. Into our privacy.'

'Then think of her as she's been for over a decade – Margaret Stone the potter. Not of Foscote, *of St Ives*.'

'Yes. Of course. And very glad I am that she's here. I really wouldn't have it any other way. In fact . . .' he reached for her and kissed her, 'thank you, darling.'

'Why thank me, you twit?'

He shrugged and smiled. 'For just being you, I suppose.'

Jeanette, as good as her word, the following August took her children to stay in the cottage in St Ives, while her husband (a member of a well-known orchestra) was on tour abroad. Laurie drove his mother down to Cornwall, and fetched her back to Thorpe at the end of the month. At Christmas the arrangement was repeated for a shorter time.

Margaret Stone had settled in well at number 97. The home help came four mornings instead of two, and several friends, particularly Monica Cage and Phillip Grainger, very sportingly popped in regularly to play the word guessing game.

On one of her lurching walks along Devonshire Avenue to the park, Margaret struck up a friendship of her own. Mrs Haines, a kind-hearted widow with time on her hands, lived quite close by. The two women began to call on one another. Claire, coming home early one afternoon, discovered Mrs Haines with an atlas on her knee. Margaret was endeavouring to name the various places in the world where her pots were on show, and had in mind a particular fan who was a collector in Denver. 'Somewhere in the United States?' asked Mrs Haines, turning to the page showing

North America. 'Yes!' shouted Margaret Stone – with excitement rather than frustration. And Claire silently applauded their turning a handicap into a pleasurable pastime.

One early morning in spring, Laurie discovered his mother collapsed on the cloakroom floor. He got her to bed and sent for the doctor. It was thought she had suffered a second and milder stroke, though with no obvious ill effects.

Afterwards, Mrs Haines's visits became less frequent and then ceased altogether. They assumed Margaret had discouraged her. For when questioned, she declared – in her laborious and roundabout way – that her erstwhile friend was really a tiresome sort of woman. Thinking the loss of companionship a shame, Claire tried to argue with this view and promote Mrs Haines's reinstatement. But Laurie silenced her. It did not follow, he thought, that because his mother was handicapped she was incapable of making up her mind about people.

But Claire detected – or wondered if she had – a subtle change in Aunt Margaret's manner. Wasn't there a suggestion of hostility sometimes, a hard glint in her eyes? Again, Laurie disagreed. So perhaps, after all, she imagined it.

It was sheet changing day. Claire, in the sitting-room, was removing the used linen from Aunt Margaret's bed. She had chosen this moment deliberately. Margaret was in the kitchen, occupied for a time with the washing-up. (It was useless trying to dissuade her when she took it into her head to tackle this chore. It was better to scoop up any precious pieces of china – though crumby, greasy or smeared – and stow them in a cupboard while her back was turned and just leave her the unbreakable or easily replaceable things to wash. Margaret was also put out if she caught either of them dealing with her laundry. 'Why,' she would shout, 'must you treat me like . . . ?' 'A famous potter? The Queen of England?' Laurie would suggest. 'Someone who has spent much of her life doing similar tasks for other people?' was Claire's usual tack: these and all the other variations with which they preferred to disguise the truth – that they did not want the trouble of calling out the plumber to unblock the washing machine again – merely serving to infuriate the complainant.) Claire had almost completed the task when the door burst open.

Margaret Stone took in what Claire was doing, then advanced into the room. 'You think you're so good,' she hissed – and her tone was startlingly unpleasant. 'But you're *not*. You're . . .' But as usual the crucial word evaded her.

Claire, somewhat stunned, sat down on the bed and gathered the sheets to her chest. 'Bad?' she hazarded automatically.

'More!'

'Terrible? Wicked?'

'*That!*' Margaret agreed. 'You play with. . . Bother!' her face trembled from her struggle. 'Those trouser people,' she got out as a compromise. 'Say!'

But Claire was no longer playing the game. She was engaged in a struggle of her own, against a wave of chokiness.

'Trouser people – say!' Aunt Margaret screamed.

'Men?' She shook her head in disbelief. 'You mean I play with *men*?'

'Take after your mother. Play. Hurt. Hurt Laurie . . .'

This was crazy. Evidently she had been right after all: that last stroke had affected Aunt Margaret's mind. 'Really, Aunt Margaret, you must know I wouldn't hurt Laurie.'

'You *have* hurt Laurie. Because you wouldn't . . . wouldn't . . . *do thing!*'

Claire stared. And suddenly, rather than tears, she was fighting back laughter. 'You mean I wouldn't get into the sack with him?' she gasped.

But to Margaret this unfamiliar phrase was evidence of guilty evasion. 'Wouldn't . . .' she persisted, jabbing at her wedding ring.

Light dawned. 'Dear God, you think I wouldn't marry him?'

Aunt Margaret lurched closer. 'Ought to go,' she advised. 'Leave. Let him find . . . *proper girl.*'

The words exploded wetly in Claire's face. She dodged to one side and scrambled up. 'Well, I'll certainly put it to him,' she said, retrieving the laundry.

But this was not what Margaret had hoped to achieve. 'No . . . no,' she stammered, clutching at a trailing corner of sheet.

Which Claire tugged from her. 'I'll be back later to make up your bed,' she promised, and hurried from the room.

Laurie, she knew, was getting ready to go to the television studios. She dumped the sheets in the hall and ran upstairs. 'OK if I come in?' she called, rapping on his door.

He opened it 'Of course,' – then saw her face. 'Something the matter with Ma?'

'No, no. Well, no more than I suspected. That stroke does seem to have had an effect. It must be that, I know you wouldn't have misled her.'

'Sit down,' he said, pushing her into a chair. He sat opposite her on the bed. 'Now tell me.'

'She's under the impression that I've ruined your life by refusing to marry you.'

'What?'

'She thinks I ought to vacate the field and allow you to bring on a "proper girl".'

'But she can't believe anything of the sort. I spelled it out for her in no uncertain terms.'

'You did? When?'

'When you were going to marry Rob. I knew she'd be upset. So I went down to see her. Made a clean breast of it.'

'I see,' Claire said, groping for a strand of hair to chew. 'And how did she take it?'

Laurie cast back. 'Evasively, I suppose. She turned rather pink, and said I was being ridiculous. Men, she had no doubt, got involved in all sorts of weird and wonderful practices, but nothing that the marriage bed couldn't put straight.'

They burst out laughing. 'Go on, she didn't say *straight*!'

'Cross my heart,' said Laurie solemnly. 'Furthermore, she advised me to write to you at once and admit I'd been a bit of a silly, but had now got it out of my system and was sterling husband material. This would bring you winging home like a sensible girl and, needless to say, we'd live happily ever after.'

'And so we do,' she said, still giggling.

'Poor Ma. I really did try. You never know whether she's truly other-worldly or just spinning a line. I suspect, deep down, she's known all along. You remember how she was always harping on about us settling down? I think you were supposed to be the saving of me – I think that was her plan. However,' he stood up, 'we can't have her attacking you like this. I'll go down and put her right.'

But Claire caught his hand. 'No leave it, Laurie. For one thing I'm sure her mind's been affected. For another . . . Well, maybe this is the version she prefers to believe.'

He thought about it. 'I see what you mean. But isn't that a bit hard on you?'

'Dear me, I can stand it,' she said.

The following summer, in her cottage in St Ives, Margaret Stone suffered a fatal stroke. They buried her down there. It was what she would have wished, they thought, to lie in the place where, during the latter part of her life, she had found success and satisfaction and friends of her own.

At the graveside, Claire, with her arm round a

sobbing Jeanette, reflected that the one parent figure she had truly loved was now beyond being persuaded to think well of her. They had passed their last months together uneasily, with barely suppressed venom on the part of Margaret Stone, studied forbearance on her own. Too late now, she thought, handing Jeanette a wad of clean tissues.

Laurie, on the far side of the grave, looked across at her seriously. And suddenly she was glad. Glad that however sharp the provocation, she had resisted the temptation to tamper with Aunt Margaret's illusions. It was a small thing, but she could take pride in it. It was something to set in the credit margin at last. Something to offset all those things she had done in her life and heartily wished she hadn't.

xv

'Oh, you can't take that droopy velour article,' Monica cried. 'Where's that smart cream jacket you bought with me?' She and Liz were helping Claire to pack. Monica scrambled up from the floor and went to the wardrobe. 'Here it is. Don't you agree with me, Liz? It'll look marvellous with everything. And it's terribly smart.'

Liz sank back on her heels to consider the garment. 'Very Professor Haddingham,' she pronounced.

'Only Visiting Professor,' Claire said. The correction was virtually automatic, she had made it so often. Her friends received it now with even less patience than formerly.

The letter inviting her to McGill for the summer semester as a Visiting Professor had arrived in her pigeon-hole at the university. Immediately she had telephoned Laurie – before sharing the news with her Head of Department or the colleagues she was currently working with, before carefully thinking the matter over herself. Predictably, he had been enthusiastic, foreseeing all kinds of opportunities arising, dismissing her fears that she was not up to ten weeks' solid teaching. 'Because that's what it'll mean, Laurie. They want to know about my extractions from pea roots.'

'Of course they do. I told you there'd be bags of interest. It'll be a doddle. They're not asking you over to supervise other people's projects, but to demonstrate your own. And don't tell me you can't do that. You had the Min of Ag people absolutely fascinated last week – now, didn't you?'

'I suppose so . . .'

'Mentioned it to Gordon yet?'

'No.'

'Well, do it straight away. Any difficulties, give me a ring. Oh, it'll be marvellous for you, darling. And it'll get you used to the title.'

'Title?'

'Professor, dear, *Professor*.'

'Only Visiting Professor,' she objected, and Laurie had made the same sort of impatient tutting noise now emanating from Monica and Liz.

'Anyway,' she told them, as Monica lined the cream jacket with tissue-paper prior to packing it, 'everyone's a Professor over there. Professors are two a penny.'

'But it'll make them sit up here at Thorpe,' frowned Liz. 'Every time they come across the printed words *Professor Claire Haddingham* they'll find the conjunction less improbable. Which'll be good for all of us.'

She meant good for the gang members, Claire understood, and demonstrated her submission to this proposition by refraining from further objection, even when Monica removed her floppy velour jacket from the suitcase to make room for the cream one.

'OK if I use your loo?' Liz asked, not waiting for an answer but going at once into the adjoining bathroom.

Outside, tyres squelched on the gravel. Monica rose. 'I'll go down and put the kettle on,' she offered.

'I'll wait for Liz and put some of this stuff away,' Claire said, gathering from the bed articles of clothing they had considered and rejected. She, too, had heard the car's arrival; it prompted her next remark. 'I hope Laurie will be all right while I'm away.'

'David and I will take a kindly interest,' Monica promised as she went out of the room.

She crossed over the landing. Sunlight streaming through a window was striking the wall over the stairs. Slim rectangles of darker magenta were revealed at the sides of paintings hanging there – like wrongly positioned shadows, thought Monica, disconcerted by the sight until she perceived these were less-faded patches of wallpaper and recalled that two pictures were missing, stolen some years ago by Lydia. Laurie had eliminated the resulting irregular gaps by jogging the remaining pictures. Perhaps these faint marks were evident only in powerful sunlight, nevertheless, Monica thought he would have done better to have repapered the wall. Unless, of course, he feared further thefts. But this was unlikely. Danger from that quarter was surely past. Laurie's main worry – the missing letters and photograph – had never been spoken of again in her hearing. In any case, one had only to witness Laurie's wonderful good form to know he had long since ceased to be alarmed by the loss.

Laurie was at the sink with his back to her when she entered the kitchen. Without turning, he hailed her confidently by name (her heavy-footed stomp down the stairs and through the hall was unmistakable – like a minor rolling earth tremor, he thought). 'What luck – if it isn't the ravishing novelist, Monica Cage.'

It halted her in her tracks. 'It certainly is, but how do you know?'

He dried his hands and came over to her. 'I have a sixth sense where you are concerned, darling.' Before planting his kiss, he grasped her arms firmly to prevent closer proximity. Adorable though Monica was, such quivering flesh ought to be under constant control for perfect peace of mind.

'Claire told you I was coming, I bet.'

'No she didn't. Ask her if you don't believe me.'

'Mm. Well, I've come down to make tea.' She reached for the kettle.

He smacked away her hand. 'I've already put it on. If you want to be useful, get out the cups.'

'I don't,' she said, sitting abruptly down on a hard chair. 'I shall sit here and be ornamental while you fetch and carry.' And she crossed her shapely legs with a rustle and snap that sprang an image in his mind of a snake darting through twigs. He could visualize her attraction for men such as David, but quailed at the thought.

Upstairs, having removed the cream jacket from her case and returned it to the wardrobe, Claire was now enfolding in tissue her beloved floppy velour jacket. Its faded lavender colour might not 'go' with many things; it was certainly not professorial; but it was decidedly *her*, she told herself, fingering the plaited strips across the pockets, brushing uselessly at the flattened pile on the elbows and across the back. It was a dear, comfortable garment: the sort you could stuff into a bag when the weather turned unexpectedly warm; the sort which, though subtly cosseting, you were never conscious of wearing. And to Claire's eyes it was also flattering – the way it hung down at the back and rose up in the front and fell softly in gathers from a drop-shouldered yoke, and the way its sleeves drooped. She laid it tenderly in the case. Then quickly shut the suitcase because the bathroom door was opening.

Liz came out.

'Monica's gone down to make tea. Shall we join her?' Claire stood back to allow Liz to go first. As they crossed the landing, voices reached them from below.

'Laurie's back,' exclaimed Liz gladly, quickening her pace.

He had set the table for tea. Her friends sat down and helped themselves with gusto, laughing and joking noisily. Their increased animation was all due to Laurie. It was his special gift, she thought, an ability to spring a small slice of everyday life into instant party.

Halfway through her time at McGill, a letter arrived – not at her digs but care of the department.

Hi, Claire! How're you doing?
I read in *McGill News* you were over here for the summer semester. Congrats on being a professor, by the way. I knew you'd make it.
How about you and me having dinner together sometime? The firm does a fair bit of business in Montreal, so I'm often in town. If you like the idea, call me on this number. (After five-thirty is best.)
Yours, Rob

Not a word of news, she noted, scanning the letter a second time. Irritating yet intriguing. But better ignored, she decided, putting the letter into her case. She had not really missed Rob, as it turned out. She never gave him a thought – just very, very occasionally remembered how tender he was in bed. And if she did give him a call, bed was where they'd end up. Sure as eggs were eggs. So, yes, his suggestion was better ignored.

She spent a busy and engrossing day. Then at five-thirty sharp, went into her office and shut the door. Brought out the letter, picked up the phone.

'You look wonderful, marvellous,' he exclaimed. Then, across the restaurant table, passed her photographs of his glamorous wife, his pretty three-year-old daughter and podgy baby son. She stared at the wife and marvelled. Was there ever a sleeker blonde, a deeper *décolletage* or pearlier smile? And if this woman fitted the bill, what the hell had he been doing wasting time with her? No wonder his parents had greeted her with some bemusement, poor ducks. She made no comment. Just grinned broadly and handed back the portraits.

'How about you?' he wanted to know. 'You with someone?'

She was taken aback, but only momentarily. 'I'm with Laurie,' she said.

'Yeah? But I thought . . . Beg pardon, but you and Laurie are *together*?'

She nodded, her eyes steadily returning his gaze.

'Sure, well, I sensed there was a real charge between you two. So it finally worked out. I'm glad.'

No point in correcting his assumption. Like most people, he needed to believe a relationship was sexual in order to grant it significance. So the truth was better served this way.

Which was funny, really, she thought, munching her salad and only half-attending to his account of a charming domestic scene punctuated by a hectic social round and a thriving business career; funny that he should get it exactly the wrong way round. Because there was nothing particularly significant about people having sex – as he and she would no doubt demonstrate before the evening was over.

'Come in,' she invited, when he drew up outside the place she was renting.

'You sure?'

She raised her eyebrows and grinned.

The moment he closed the door of her flat, she turned to him. He put his hands on her shoulders, ran them down her back. As his head came down, she opened her mouth.

They just about made it to bed. The first time proved very good indeed, but insufficient. Their talking – sweeter and more intimate than in the restaurant – led inevitably to a second round of lovemaking.

After this he recalled the time. And possibly his wife, she guessed, from the way he became suddenly abstracted and a chilly distance grew between them.

She did not care for this sense of being hastened from, being finished with. She sat up in bed and watched him dress, and allowed his insincere remarks to wash over her. When he was ready to go, she got up and put on her robe.

'May I phone you?' he asked, falsely courteous.

'No, don't,' she smiled. 'Let's leave it at that, Rob. It was a shame we ended so bitterly before. But now we've put that right. Nice to end it on friendly terms.'

He made a show of hesitating, but, as she had calculated, soon acquiesced. Always easier to give something up when you're sated, she told herself, giving him one last comradely kiss.

She lay in the bath for a long time, frequently topping it up with hot water. When she finally got out to get dry and clean her teeth, the bathroom mirror was steamed over. She wrote with her finger *Laurie and Claire*, and remembered writing these words years ago on her dusty bedroom mirror at Foscote. 'I'm with Laurie,' she heard her voice telling Rob. How she had yearned to be in a position to declare as much during those faraway Foscote years. And now she was. 'I'm with Laurie,' she said out loud. Nothing and no-one could take that away. Nothing and no-one ever would.

What she had, she held.

xvi

It was summer again. A year ago to the day that Margaret Stone died. Laurie was lost in thoughts of his mother when the telephone rang. 'Double-two five four seven,' he intoned absently.

Silence – which summoned his full attention. He repeated the number in a brisker tone.

'Is Claire at home?' a quiet voice asked, very abruptly.

'No. Er, she's away.'

'When will she back?'

'Well, tomorrow, actually . . . Um, who's speaking? Would you care to leave a message?'

Dialling tone. Whoever it was had replaced the receiver.

He went slowly back into the kitchen, all thoughts of his mother flown. That had been a very strange enquiry – 'Is Claire at home?' Is Claire *there*? would have been more conventional. More usual still would have been, May I speak to Claire? Presumably, given the lack of title or surname, the caller had been one of her friends or colleagues. But if this were the case, it was strange the caller was unaware that Claire was in Canada. Maybe whoever it was assumed she had already arrived home.

Recalling that Claire would in fact be flying home tomorrow, and that he would be driving to the airport to collect her and therefore had a hundred and one things to do today in order to make her properly welcome, he pushed the mysterious call to the back of his mind, put on his jacket, collected his car keys.

But driving into town, it suddenly struck him what had been truly odd about that simple enquiry. 'Is Claire at home?' implied a concern with Claire's presence in, or absence from, the house *here and now*. As to what this in turn implied, he had no idea. Soon, he was judiciously filling a wire trolley in a supermarket and had forgotten the call altogether.

The more mundane shopping over, he walked to the High Street to visit some specialist shops – a patisserie, a fishmonger's, a bookstore. On entering this last, he was confronted by a face-on display of volume after volume of his own book – the one based on his television series. *The Magic Of Trees* by Laurie Stone, *The Magic Of Trees* by Laurie Stone, *The Magic Of Trees* by Laurie Stone . . . His eyes sped along the rack, then along the rack below, and along the rack below that. The repeated image, glossy and vivid, stuttered in his mind like a stuck record. He stood motionless with his heart quickening, and faintly nauseous panic rising. Then pulled himself together and looked round, trying to locate the central selling point – a circular well surrounded by a high counter – where he hoped to collect the copy of Monica's latest novel he had ordered (to be sure of it) as a home-coming present for Claire. A familiar figure was leaning sideways to the counter: Thorpe's famous poet – in the ubiquitous grubby mac and round wire-rimmed spectacles. Furthermore, the cold regard behind these spectacles was directed unwaveringly at Laurie. Cursing that he had been caught surveying his opus, Laurie nodded curtly and joined him at the counter, taking care to leave a fair-sized gap between.

They did not speak, but joined in fixed observation of the assistant flicking through reference cards. It was not the first time Laurie had found himself watched by those blank eyes. Sometimes, playing the piano in a jazz club, Laurie would glance round and there would be the poet – usually standing at the back of the room, tall, lank, lone – staring at him, taking him in. Yes, invariably alone and always unsmiling. It had struck him as strange that this cold fish should be a lover of such an extrovert expression as jazz. But this was what he purported to be. Indeed, Laurie had keenly read the verses written in honour of the great clarinetist, Sydney Bechet. Had he imagined it, or was the appreciation therein somewhat reluctant, grudging, sneering? Possibly, he *had* imagined it, prompted by paranoid dread of some sneering future verse referring to a telly pundit; and people on campus sniggering – 'Have you read this? – I bet he means Laurie Stone . . .'

This silent proximity was becoming embarrassing. Shifting his weight onto his other foot, Laurie racked his brain for something to say. Fortunately, the assistant saved him the trouble:

'I'm sorry, sir, but it hasn't come in. It should be here any day . . .'

The poet shoved himself into upright position and

without a word stalked away.

The girl stared after him. Then turned to Laurie. 'Can I help you? Oh! – it's Dr Laurie Stone, isn't it?'

'It certainly is,' Laurie acknowledged happily (his days of being embarrassed by the courtesy title long gone, now that, thanks to television, *Dr Laurie Stone* was a household term). 'I ordered *Profanities* by Monica Cage.'

'Ah, yes . . . Here we are.' She produced and wrapped the book, then took his money.

Laurie tucked the package under his arm, picked up his carrier bags, smiled thanks and farewell, and left the store.

The fact that Monica had dedicated *Profanities* to *him* made Laurie rather uneasy. Uneasy, that is, as to Claire's reaction. (Might she feel piqued that she had not been included?) At least Claire need not see the copy Monica had signed for him (and under the printed dedication *To Laurie Stone,* had added in ink *you intriguing and lovely man*). Laurie had read the novel nervously and carefully, but gained no clue as to Monica's motive. When he asked what he had done to deserve the honour, she replied, 'Just been yourself, my darling – a very good friend and a veritable muse.' He did not enquire further. No, Claire need not see what Monica had inscribed. However, as she could not be kept in ignorance of the printed dedication, it was better, he had decided, to take the bull by the horns. That way he could stage-manage her discovery. Driving home, he visualized the scene in the dining-room. 'A surprise for you, pet. A little present to say welcome home. Yes, it's Monica's latest. But do open it, turn over the page. . . There! Isn't that sweet of her? Can't imagine what I've done to deserve it. I know she and I have been mates ever since I arrived at Thorpe, and I suppose I did lend moral support over the Paul business – of course, you were in Canada when that blew up . . .' Yes, he would manage it impeccably. He always did.

Turning in at the entrance to number 97, Laurie was obliged to jump on the brake. One of their student lodgers, Angela, was cycling over the gravel, her head down, her mind evidently elsewhere. The noise of the tyres alerted her. She sprang down, feet astride, and hoiked her bike to one side. He grinned and drove past, and drew up near the front door.

With his hands full of carrier bags, he went to the porch; set the bags down, unlocked the door, then entered the house leaving the door open behind him because further shopping remained to be collected from the car. But first he must deal with the fish. He unwrapped it, slid it on to a plate and put a second covering plate over. As he might have known, there was no convenient space in the refrigerator. He rearrranged jars and packets, threw out some sad-looking lemon halves, and at last stowed the fish.

'Hello, Laurie,' someone said quietly, very close at hand.

He swung round. (He had neither heard nor noticed anyone who might have followed him into the house, so it was the speaker's closeness that was initially startling.) But as he stiffened, the room continued spinning. For standing by the table with a hand resting on the back of a chair was an outlandish-looking figure – tall and gangling, faded, like a clown in mufti.

'Long time, no see!'

The voice came to him like the only sensible part of a dream. He would be saved, he felt, if he focussed on it.

'All right if I sit down?'

Flat, brisk, low. Of course: Lydia's voice. But as he nodded and pulled out a chair for himself, he could detect nothing of Lydia in this person. Until a rueful smile appeared, and he recognized its shape. 'Lydia?' he said.

'That's right. It's me.'

'I'd never have known,' he confessed, casting over the crinkly bags under her eyes, her orange-peel skin, and the bizarre short frizz of dull fair hair through which pink scalp was plainly visible. There were half-hearted traces of make-up – orangy smears on the lips, smudges of green on the eyelids, and sparse mascara'd spikes. Despite this, he knew, if he were asked, he would come down on the side of masculinity (perhaps influenced by the mannish trousers and jacket). Yes, a decayed, spent, weed of a man. Yet presumably she was now less of a man than formerly.

'That's because I've been ill. I still am very poorly. Which is why I came back home. I needed to see Dr Lessing – remember, I used to work for him? He was always so good, so understanding. I've been properly messed about in Spain. D'you notice the tan?' she asked, pushing up a jacket sleeve to show off a leathery arm. 'That's four solid years' worth. Costa del Sol.' She said this with pride, but fortunately did not wait for any admiring comment. 'You couldn't manage a cup of tea, I suppose? I'd kill for a proper cuppa.'

He hesitated, as several reasons why he shouldn't afford hospitality to this particular visitor occurred to him. But after all he couldn't be churlish. She was ill, she had said, and certainly looked it. 'All right. I can spare ten minutes. But after that I'll have to get on. Claire's coming home tomorrow. She's been away . . .' His voice died. His hand fell still on the kettle. He felt a fool, for of course she already knew this; he had imparted the information earlier over the phone.

'So, where's she been?'

'Montreal,' he said shortly, and filled the kettle and switched it on.

'You mean all this time? Heavens, she must have liked it. How many years is it?'

'No, no. She came home as arranged at the end of two years. This was a second, much shorter visit.' Reaching down cups and saucers, he came to a decision. 'I believe you have some property of mine,' he said in a neutral voice as he brought the tray to the table.

She raised her hands to her head, clasped it in mock-horror. 'God Laurie, I *know*. How could I have? You must understand, I was desperate. I'd have done anything to pay for that op. And boy, have I suffered for it! – the after-effects, I mean – 'spose you'll say it serves me right; couldn't blame you. But I'm determined to try and pay you back. You see, I don't actually have them anymore – the clock and the pictures and stuff. I sold them. But soon as I sort myself out . . .'

'Sugar?'

'Er, yes please. Mm,' she inhaled the steam, 'this is nectar.'

'Um, I wasn't referring to those things you sold – though their theft was a serious betrayal – and they were Claire's property as much as mine. No, I was thinking of some letters, and, um, a photograph. They were wrapped together in a large envelope which I kept in the bureau.'

She took some sips of tea. 'I honestly have no recollection,' she said, eventually. 'But if you *say* I took them – well, the state I was in, I wouldn't argue. I know where they'll be if I *have* got them – with my bits and pieces in my big trunk. The moment it arrives, I'll have a thorough search,' she declared magnanimously.

'Where are you staying?'

'Ah.' She set down her cup, leaned over the table. 'Laurie, I'm here to ask you a gigantic favour.'

Urgently wishing to remain ignorant of its nature, Laurie drained his cup and put it with its saucer noisily back on the tray. Deflecting words, such as *I hardly think you're in a position to ask me a favour*, popped into his head, but struck him as too pompous to utter.

'Laurie, please listen, I'm desperate. Dr Lessing needs to see me regularly to assess my programme. Without it I could actually die – no kidding!' Her eyes beseeched him; her mouth settled in an agonized twist.

Against his better judgement, and because he

couldn't help himself, he asked, 'What's the matter, exactly?'

'After the operation – which went fine – well,' (she pulled a face) 'it was bloody painful, but I could deal with that, I had no regrets . . . But a day or so later I had a thrombosis. They said I had to come off the pills – you know, the hormones I'd been taking for ages. Stupid fool of a doctor took me off them cold turkey. It was a total nightmare – I mean, hot flushes weren't the half of it, I just couldn't stand it; besides, I was beginning to look haggish. So this friend of mine started supplying me. And a year later I had a massive heart attack. Apparently, it was a miracle I survived. Ever since I've been on one thing or another – blood thinning drugs, heart stimulants, stuff to calm me down . . . But look at me, Laurie; you can see I'm a wreck. I've got to the point, the only one I trust is Dr Lessing. Thing is, though, I'm skint.'

Relief flowed through him. If money was all . . . His hand went to his pocket.

'And shit scared,' she went on, watching him. 'And totally shagged out. I need somewhere safe and peaceful for a few days – just till my money comes through and I can get my head together . . . Please Laurie, I'm too frightened to be on my own. Let me have a room here for a few days.'

'Out of the question!' he cried, getting quickly to his feet. 'Claire wouldn't hear of it. Besides, we haven't any space. We're chockful of students, every spare room let.'

Very slowly her hands rose; she kept her eyes on him till the last moment when her head suddenly sank. 'Laurie,' she choked, 'I'm begging . . . You're my last shot.'

'I've told you, Lydia, there isn't room.'

But even as he said it, a picture sprang to his mind of the sitting-room with his mother's invalid bed in it. (The bed was now dismantled and stored away in a large cupboard).

She caught from the way his voice trailed that he had remembered something, and threw up her head, eyes blazing with hope.

He looked away from her to the floor, taking in breath and courage to repeat his refusal. Which after all he was obliged to make – it was the proper, the only thing to do in the circumstances. But even as he anticipated making it, he cringed from himself as a callous, a despicable person. And then the glimmer of a possibility dawned that he might not refuse her – because he was too humane, because it wasn't in him to turn his back on a desperate fellow being. This, too, failed to bring ease, for now he cursed himself for a weak and sentimental idiot. 'Let me give you a sub,' he offered. 'You could find a pleasant little guest house, a quiet room in a hotel . . .'

'You just don't get it, do you, Laurie? Fact is, till Dr Lessing's got me stable I'm terrified to be on my own. I need a friend, someone who'll let me squeeze in with them – not for long, just a few days.' She waited, then continued suggestively: 'And if I was here, one good thing would be, soon as my things came I could hunt out the letters and photo you're so worried about. Hand them over. Simple as that. There'd be no chance of a – you know – slip up.'

He stood swaying slightly. The noise in his ears was like the sound of the air-raid siren he would hear as a child snuggled under bedcovers, and his sense of dread like knowing that any second he would be wrenched from his cosy pit and borne away to the ice-cold shelter.

Her flat quick tone was definitely more confident. 'You're famous now, aren't you, Laurie? I mean, *really famous*.' (The threat behind her flattery was not lost on him.) 'I saw you on the telly when I was over at Christmas. And your book's in all the shops. It's marvellous. But you deserve it, you really do. It couldn't happen to a kinder person. You and Dr Lessing are the two people in the world I can honestly say – with my hand on my heart – are truly good. Laurie, I need someone good right now. I feel like I'm on my last gasp.'

He grasped a chair back. 'All right. There's the sitting-room. Before she died my mother had a bed in there, which I'll put up for you later. But it can only be for a few days.' He heard these words, but as if from a distance, and as if only a part of him (a part he was not wholly in touch with) were speaking.

Her eyes actually filled. She might be false, but surely she couldn't fake tears, he told himself, feeling almost vindicated. 'I'm sorry you're in such a bad way. Look, pour yourself another cup while I get in the rest of the shopping.'

But, having groped into the car for the purchases, it was as if he had also recovered Claire on whose behalf they were made. 'One thing,' he said, as he re-entered the kitchen: 'I really oughtn't to have agreed to you staying without first consulting Claire. I don't imagine she's going to be thrilled. So I must ask you to keep out of her way – stick to your room – there's a downstairs bathroom you can use – I'll have to think of something with regards to the kitchen . . .'

Lydia stretched hands towards him. (He noticed nails with chipped varnish and dirt under the rims.) 'Laurie, you needn't worry,' she promised throatily, 'she'll hardly know I'm here.'

A sense of appalled incredulity crept over him during the afternoon, as the memory of the extraordinariness awaiting him at home protruded like a dream into the ordinariness of conferring with colleagues. There was a vacant Lecturer's post to fill. Someone's curriculum vitae was passed to him. He took it and stared at the top page. But instead of a list of previous positions held, saw an odd, sad figure hunched over a cup of tea at his kitchen table (at this remove, harder still to connect with the person he thought of as Lydia). Odd, sad, and *male*, he reflected – those lean angular bones draped loosely in masculine attire, those traces of make-up coming across as a pathetic and hopeless statement (which had never been the case before). So much for surgery without chemical back up! The outcome was worse than he'd feared: he had foreseen a bewitching paradox lost in a conventional woman; in fact, Lydia had dwindled into diminished manhood. But never mind that, he admonished, gripping the sheets of paper like a life-raft. The point was he had allowed this unreliable and disruptive person back into his and Claire's home. Claire would very likely go into orbit. What a home-coming! What a mess! What was he going to *do*?

'You OK, Laurie?' Gordon was peering curiously over his half-moon spectacles.

'Will you excuse me for a minute? I need to make a phone call.'

He needed to phone Monica. She was the only one he could countenance turning to for advice. Maybe she could come up with something.

But Monica was neither in her office nor lecturing, according to her secretary, who had a feeling Monica was in London today. With scant hope, Laurie dialled Monica's home number. He let it ring and ring.

There was no answer.

Laurie felt obliged to offer an evening meal. Lydia did not appear grateful – took the offer as a matter of course, hummed and hawed as to what food she could manage with her ruined digestion. Fricassee of chicken, said Laurie, in a take it or leave it fashion. They ate in uncomfortable silence – at least, to Laurie it was uncomfortable; Lydia was preoccupied with new pills prescribed by Dr Lessing, studying the printed leaflet with directions and warnings about side-effects. Afterwards, she said she had to go out for a while.

Laurie felt a surge of anger. 'The door will be locked at eleven sharp,' he snapped, like an old-fashioned seaside landlady.

'Perhaps it would be better if I took a key.'

He was not having that. 'I'm surprised you're going out at all. I thought you were in need of a rest.'

'I am. I was only thinking of your convenience.'

Then Phillip Grainger dropped in. Laurie was never more glad to see an old friend. And though Lydia returned from her outing soon after ten (and despite the fact that he needed to go to bed early in order to be up by five the next morning), Laurie kept Phillip talking until he was sure Lydia had retired for the night.

At last, secure in his own room, he prepared for sleep.

It eluded him. And he would not put on his traditional lullaby, the World Service, for fear of missing stealthy footsteps below. A sudden thump from above followed by stifled laughter was somehow reassuring. On another night the noise might have woken him up, in which case, thoroughly annoyed, he would have composed a stiff ticking off to deliver next morning. Now, he blessed Nigel, or perhaps John – or whichever student had knocked over whatever article – for the boisterous reminder of their proximity. And relaxed at last, he fell asleep.

By half-past five, Laurie had set off for London and the airport. He arrived there in time for a wash and a leisurely breakfast. When Claire's plane was registered on the screen, he went to the arrivals hall where he strolled to and fro, keeping a close eye on the customs tunnel beyond the barrier. He had decided to break the news about Lydia as soon as possible on the journey home (when Claire would at least be restrained by a seat belt). This would allow plenty of time for her initial reaction (he anticipated outbursts of incredulity and bitter recrimination) and then (as she was reassured by his promise that the visit would be fleeting) for her recovery.

At last she emerged – hair on end, pale, intermittently boss-eyed, grinning, animated. She had not slept on the plane. Her day, begun eighteen hours ago in Montreal, still carried on. Now she tried to draw Laurie into it. 'I had lunch at the Beaver Club today with the team. It was my goodbye treat. They're really pleased with my work – said I can go back anytime. I'm so glad you persuaded me I could manage the teaching, because, do y'know, I found I can. I even got to enjoy it . . .'

He couldn't very well interrupt her enthusiasm. 'How many did you teach at a time?' he asked, realizing they had missed their way, as usual, in the semi-detached wasteland of north-west London.

'It varied. At Guy's suggestion I divided them up. For lab work it was only five or six. But I held seminars for the whole group of twenty-four students. My knees were knocking first time. Guy sussed this, of course, and gave me some really good tips. He's in charge of the teacher training programme – the students were all practising science teachers needing to keep up with new techniques and so forth. Look, Laurie – *third exit.*' (Trust her to spot the right way, he thought. But she had less on her mind.) 'Anyway, Guy said I should constantly throw the seminar back at the students – not just by asking 'how' and 'why', but by getting them to speculate on outcomes and possible methods. That was really handy, because it worked like a dream. They got so engaged and argumentative, I ended up like a sort of ringmaster . . .'

They were now on the motorway. On and on she gabbled. He couldn't interrupt. Besides, he was glad to listen – even if hearing about Guy's useful tips was a trifle irritating; for there was nothing in his advice that Laurie couldn't have given if he had thought to analyse his own methods with students. It simply hadn't occurred to him to get down to such a basic level. Which just went to show: a few practical tips were worth any amount of bolstering exhortation . . . Heavens, wasn't that a sign for the halfway service station? 'Hungry?' he asked her.

'Yes. No. I'm not sure,' she frowned, feeling very distant from her body and its needs, as if she were all mind and voice. 'I've been stuffing all day – that enormous lunch, then dinner on the plane, and a bun thing just before we landed . . .'

'Most of that was yesterday.'

'So it was. I hadn't thought. OK, let's eat. Anyway, I expect you could do with a break. Did you come down last night?'

'Er, no. Early this morning.' Damnation. Trust the perfect opening to arrive just as they were about to get off the motorway. 'Look, if you're not really hungry . . .'

'Of course I am. Quick, here it is! Gosh, Laurie you must be shattered – all this way down, and now straight back. I'll take over the driving from here.'

'You certainly will not,' he snorted.

As they crossed the car park, he decided to break his news when they were seated in the self-service. With people about, she'd be obliged to keep her reactions muted.

'I saw Rob,' she blurted, as soon as they were settled. Laurie looked at her, startled.

'He wrote to me at the university, giving a phone number. I meant not to ring, but somehow I did. Hey, what do you think? – he's married with two kids! His wife is someone he went out with years before he met me. So clearly I was just a short excursion off life's main highway. But it was nice seeing him. And it was just the once.' Suddenly abandoning her knife and fork, she looked at him intently. 'Though maybe I shouldn't have . . .'

She wanted to get something off her chest, he saw. 'Tell me,' he invited.

Half an hour later they resumed their journey. After

a few miles, she began to yawn. 'Ah-haw-haaaw! Sorry, can't stop it.' She brought her feet up on to the seat, crouched and turned and dived head first into the back. 'I'll have to crash out. Sorry – ah-aaw . . .'

They had turned off the motorway and were driving east when she woke, with many groans and wails. Finally, she clambered back beside him.

'Urgh. I feel horrible.'

'Like to stop?'

'No, for heaven's sake. Just get me home.'

She sounded crotchety. Now she was going to be even less receptive than he'd envisaged. But it was now – or the never of allowing her to discover the deed for herself. 'I've got something to tell you – I'm very much afraid,' he added, with honest dread.

'Yeah?'

His knuckles whitened on the steering wheel. 'Lydia's back.'

Thirty seconds elapsed in total silence. Then, 'Back where?' she barked.

'Back from Spain,' he began gingerly. 'Back in Thorpe. Back, as a matter of fact, in number 97. But only temporarily. I must emphasize that; it's strictly for two or three days.'

A sharp intake of breath was the only further sound from his passenger. By the time he slowed and negotiated a roundabout a few miles from Thorpe, he had still heard nothing. Changing back into top gear, he stole a look at her. She seemed frozen in her seat – utterly rigid, frowning fiercely, staring ahead. It began to seem unlikely that she *would* speak, so he decided to enlarge. Told her virtually the whole thing – the sneaky way Lydia had got into the house, his shock at the sight of her, her sorry tale, her contrition over the theft of their paintings and ornaments. Finally, he dealt with the crux of the matter – Lydia's desperate plea for sanctuary, his inability to refuse her. He did not cite the most pressing reason for his inhibition – Lydia's veiled threat about a possible 'slip-up' in the return of the missing letters and photograph, for Claire was ignorant of this loss, indeed, was unaware that the envelope and its contents had ever existed. He merely explained that he'd felt unbearably moved, that he doubted whether he were capable of turning away a dog in such a pitiable state. And emphasized many times that the stay was temporary. He was saying this again, possibly for the sixth time, as they turned on to the Little Coates Road.

And never any response.

Now they were driving towards the avenues; first would come York, then Marlborough, then Northumberland, and finally Devonshire. They had passed York Avenue and were nearing Marlborough, when Claire suddenly blurted, 'Stop the car.'

'What?'

'Stop. I want to get out.'

'I can't, there's a bus behind . . .'

'Then turn into Marlborough. *Turn.*'

He braked, and swung left, and as the engine faltered, changed down. 'Why?'

'Drop me at Monica's.'

'Oh, Claire . . .'

'Please save me the trouble of walking back, because frankly I'm jiggered. And by the way, I won't be coming home till Lydia's gone.'

This he had not foreseen. But now she had thrown down the gauntlet, it seemed inevitable. Of course she wouldn't dream of living under the same roof with someone who had stolen from them and made their lives miserable – she had more sense, more judgement: how could he ever have expected her to? He drew up obediently outside Monica's house and glanced up at the windows. Someone was evidently home, for a soft light showed on the first floor, probably from a reading lamp. He closed his eyes for a second. 'This has all happened so swiftly, I can't take it in. If only *you* had been there, or Monica – or *anyone* . . .' But Lydia, he guessed, had made sure he was alone before she tackled him; had probably spied on the house, assessing coming and goings, had made that phone call when she failed to spot Claire. 'All I can say is, love, I'm truly sorry. I'm an utter fool. But I swear I'll get rid of her.'

Claire had got out and was reaching into the back for her overnight bag. 'Yeah, well, let me know when she's gone. Oh, and Laurie . . .' about to close the door, she pulled it wide and put in her head, 'watch out for yourself, and keep counting the silver – and the paintings – in fact anything that's not nailed down.' Then she swung the door shut and crossed the pavement, and went up the garden path.

He waited until the door was opened, then drove away.

'So you're back!' cried Monica, discovering Claire on her doorstep.

'Can you put me up? I can't go home.'

Monica took in this news, then reached for her arm and pulled her inside. Before closing the door, she peered into the avenue, and was in time to see the rear portion of Laurie's car glide out of view. She motioned Claire to the stairs, and then into the first floor sitting room. 'What's going on?' she asked, as Claire collapsed in a chair.

There was no immediate answer. ('I did wonder if she were having a fit,' Monica confided afterwards to David. 'She was gulping like a fish, and that rogue eye of her's darting back and forth . . .') 'Can I get you something? Glass of water, cup of tea? Or something stronger?'

Claire shook her head.

'Well, we're quite alone. David's at the university.'

But it was weariness, not delicacy, causing Claire to hesitate. The enormity of what had happened overwhelmed her; words could not be summoned to express it. In the end, she fell back on Laurie's bald announcement. 'Lydia's back.'

Now it was Monica's turn to fall into a chair. 'You can't mean it,' she gasped, gripping its arms.

'Laurie's just broken the news – he waited till we were almost home. Apparently, he's put her up in the sitting-room, on Aunt Margaret's old bed.'

'Then his head needs examining. He must be mad. After the trouble and misery he suffered at that ones' hands, I simply can't believe it.'

'Well, unfortunately, it's true. I told him I couldn't come home while she's still there.'

'And quite right too!'

'He said she'll only be staying for two or three days. But when she came the first time it was supposed to be for just one weekend, and how long did that last?'

'But how . . . ? I mean, he surely didn't invite her? Did she just turn up?'

'Something like that. And was in such a terrible way, he felt sorry for her. He felt sorry for her the first time – remember? – because she was having trouble with her landlord. And if she does leave in a day or so, what's to stop her coming back and him feeling sorry for her all over again? I can't put up with it.'

'I'm not surprised. And of course you must stay. We need a drink.'

'Not for me, thanks. All I need is sleep.'

'Then have a bath while I sort out the spare room. A friend came to stay last week, and I haven't yet had a chance to change the bed . . . Claire?'

Claire's head lolled to one side; her eyes closed. Watching her, Monica thought, You've gone too far this time, Laurie Stone; much too far. Whatever possessed you? At which a more cogent explanation than his just feeling sorry for Lydia sprang to her mind. Of course! – the missing letters and photograph.

She had started in her chair. The sudden movement brought Claire from her doze. 'Uh?'

'Those letters she pinched! I bet she's using them as a lever. Yes, I'm sure that's the real explanation. But why the hell didn't he mention that to you? Oh – I see.' For blank bewilderment covered Claire's face.

'What letters?' she asked thickly.

Monica rapidly considered the matter. Plainly, Laurie preferred Claire to remain in ignorance – though why was a mystery; Claire's knowledge could do him no harm (for she was more robust, less equivocal, in his defence than he was capable of being on his own behalf); also, in Monica's judgement, Claire deserved a full explanation. And thus she came down on the side of enlightenment. 'I don't suppose for one moment he'd have confided in me. It just happened that I barged in on him at the crucial moment when he was in the process of hunting for some missing letters.'

'But why didn't he tell me about them? He mentioned all the other stuff she stole.'

'I imagine he didn't want to worry you. These letters – and a photograph, I believe – he implied were mildly incriminating. He didn't go into detail, but he was in a high old state. So I insisted on hearing the bare facts. I also suggested it was high time he got rid of Lydia, and sure enough, a day or so later I heard she'd vamoosed. He looked drawn and ill for some time after. But then you came home, and he began to pick up. And look at him now – full of the joys of spring. I'd presumed the danger was long past.'

'When you say *danger*,' Claire said slowly, 'I presume you're referring to the possibility of blackmail.'

'Well,' Monica shrugged, 'I suppose I am.'

Claire hunched forward and hugged her knees. Her eyes traced the pattern in the woven rug. 'I must go home,' she said at last.

'Tomorrow. You need a good night's sleep before facing that situation.'

'No, now. At once. By keeping away you see what I'm doing? – strengthening Lydia's position. Hell, it's bad enough that I didn't arrive home with him. I'll phone him straight away, say I'm coming right over. Is that OK?'

'Help yourself,' murmured Monica. 'And I do take your point. But frankly, you don't look very bright. Promise me you won't get into anything tonight – rows, or accusations. You'll keep out of her way? This thing needs to be played carefully.'

'Of course. Now, can I please use your phone?'

'Use the one in the study,' Monica suggested, and when Claire left the room, went to the sideboard to pour a drink.

Claire, waiting with impatience, at last heard Laurie answer. 'It's me, love,' she interrupted him. 'I'm sorry I stormed off. I'm coming straight home.'

'Yes?' he said cautiously. 'But you know I don't blame you for being upset. I should stay with Monica tonight . . .'

'No, I'm coming home *now*. You are an idiot, Laurie. Why ever didn't you tell me about her stealing those letters . . .'

'Ah. So Monica's blabbed.'

'You know we always face things together. Anyway, just make an excuse if Lydia's noticed I haven't shown up; say I called on Monica to give her a present.'

'Right. Er, Claire?'

'Yes?'

'You won't start anything? You'll let me handle this?'

'I don't intend to say a word. I'll probably go straight to bed. I just want it understood that we're in this together – this . . . whatever it is. OK?'

'Of course. Thanks, darling.'

'See you in a couple of shakes.' She put down the receiver, then ran back to the sitting-room to collect her bag. Her energy had returned with a vengeance.

'I'll drive you,' Monica said.

'Don't be daft. It's only a step.'

'I'll drive you,' Monica repeated in a commanding tone. 'Furthermore, I shall accompany you into the house – to show solidarity, give her a sense of opposing forces massing, of Laurie's supporters staking out the ground – symbols are so important.' Also, she wouldn't pass up a chance, if she could possibly help it, to sniff the atmosphere.

Claire frowned, then brightened. 'Yeah,' she said, 'see what you mean. Thanks Monica, you're a pal.'

In the event, there was no special atmosphere to sniff, and no Lydia to be impressed by the massing of forces. Laurie shouted to them from above, 'Be down in a second,' and Claire led Monica into the dining-room.

'Darling!' he cried, making a beeline for Claire and then taking his time over an embrace. (She'd had many an occasion to observe – and had done so with the greatest pleasure – how he always came to her first and would keep the most wonderful company waiting while he thoroughly kissed and hugged her.) Now, at last, he turned to Monica. 'Thank you,' he said, kissing her cheek and holding her at arm's length, 'for bringing Claire home.'

'Where's Lydia?' Monica asked, dispensing with ceremony.

'Retired to her room. She merely put her head round the door when I arrived, to say she felt unwell.'

'Well, one can certainly see where she's been – gnawing at your nerve ends, pumping up your blood pressure. You look frightful, dear boy.'

'I've had a very long day.'

'So you have. Well, I'll leave you both to catch up on some shut-eye. But don't forget, my dears: anything I can do, just ask.'

They knew she meant it. She had an offhand manner, an insatiable interest in life's little crises, but was a staunch and generous friend.

'Anything you'd like?' Laurie asked when Monica had gone.

'Not really. Glass of water, nice hot bath. Then sleep, sleep, and more sleep.'

'Same here.'

They filled a glass apiece with water then went to

the stairs, switching off lights. Outside the sitting-room door they paused a moment, studied its top and bottom checking for slits of light. None were visible, so they turned away, and Laurie followed Claire upstairs.

On the landing, he slipped an arm round her, drew her close, pressed his lips into her hair. 'Lock your door,' he whispered.

They parted then, went into their separate rooms.

xvii

Claire's first sight of Lydia came in the morning – and very shocking it was.

'Hello, Claire,' came the quick flat tone, preceded by no warning footfalls.

Claire, bent over a newspaper, looked up. Nothing Laurie had said prepared her for this weird, almost unrecognizable travesty of the former beauty. Her heart thumped. Aware that she was gaping, she looked away. 'What do you want?'

'To make a cup of tea, if it's not too much to ask.'

Claire picked up her own cup, drained it, then set it back on its saucer and got to her feet. 'Laurie,' she called, needlessly loudly, as she went upstairs. 'I'd like a kettle and tea things put in the sitting-room as soon as possible.'

His door was ajar. Very soon, he came bustling out. 'Yes, all right,' he muttered, throwing her a warning look, and hurried down to the kitchen.

'I'll get a kettle and tea things for your room,' he began saying to Lydia, but she cut him off.

'I heard.'

'Right.' She had her back to him, was making toast. Her shape reminded him of one of those stringy old men you see hunched over the bar in pubs – the rounded shallow back, the unfilled trouser seat. 'How are you this morning?' he was moved to ask.

'Not too bad. I slept well. Best night for ages. Must be these tablets. Which reminds me: I'm seeing Dr

Lessing this afternoon. Wouldn't it be easier if I had a key?'

He hesitated. 'All right.' And went off to look for a spare one. 'I don't know what we're going to do about the eating arrangements,' he confessed when he returned. 'I haven't had a moment to think. I warned you Claire wouldn't be inclined to be sociable.'

Lydia buttered her toast and spread it with marmalade. She poured out a cup of tea. All without saying a word.

'You can't be surprised,' Laurie said, hoping, with this subtle reference to the fact that she had stolen from them, to focus Lydia's mind on a simple way to make amends. 'When did you say your trunk would arrive?'

She dashed a smile at him. 'I didn't. Because I'm not too sure myself. Maybe today, maybe tomorrow.'

'Ah. Well, help yourself to anything else you'd like – cereal, an egg . . .'

'This is quite sufficient, thanks. I'll take it to my room, out of the way.'

Mrs Smethurst's pleasure at Claire's return was ruined, she implied, by her discovery of Lydia's. Claire and she were in the kitchen – Mrs Smethurst at the ironing-board waiting for the iron to hot up, Claire sorting out the washed laundry. 'Lovely to see you back home again, duck, but you could have knocked me down with a feather when I saw her coming out of the downstairs lavvie. Not that I was positive it were her. Not straight off. What's she been doing to herself? Had one of them *operations* – you know, trying to change herself into a bloke?' Mrs Smethurst cackled at her wicked suggestion. Claire grinned, too, and looked forward to repeating it to Monica.

'I know it's not my place to ask,' Mrs Smethurst continued, as a preamble to going straight ahead, 'but did you know he'd gone and allowed her back, or did it come as a nasty shock?' Her sympathetic tone invited a confidence.

419

Claire, trying to disentangle a towel that did not require ironing from a sheet that did, made no bones about it. 'No I didn't, and yes it did.'

It took Mrs Smethurst as long to disentangle this as Claire the towel. 'Well, I don't know what he were thinking of, after what she got up to before. I'm keeping my shopper where I can see it,' she declared, nodding towards a tartan bag attached to a frame with wheels, which she usually stowed in the cupboard under the stairs.

I shouldn't think there's any need to go as far as that, Claire was about to say, when she changed her mind. The bag could be stuffed to the gills with desirable things for all she knew.

'Is he barmy, or what?'

'Lydia is an old friend of Laurie's and she's been very ill. One does have to be charitable.'

'Charity begins at home, I always say.'

'Exactly. This is his home, and he's being charitable with it.'

But her witticism was lost on Mrs Smethurst. 'Where's she billeted?'

'Eh? Oh, in the sitting-room.'

'You mean he's put her in his poor mother's old bed? She'd turn in her grave.'

'I rather doubt it, knowing Aunt Margaret. Right, that's got that sorted. Sorry there's such a lot of it. I must go down the road now,' (she meant to the university) 'and catch up with a few things.'

'*She* still about?'

'Yes, but so is Laurie. I'll tell him you'd rather he stayed within earshot, shall I?'

'If you don't mind,' Mrs Smethurst said delicately.

It was the end of term. Students everywhere were packing up, going home. At number 97 Devonshire Avenue, Laurie and Claire washed-up in the kitchen and watched, through the window, their two female lodgers, Angela and Pauline, stuff their belongings in

420

Angela's father's estate car. Inside the car, Angela wrestled to make space for her record player. A cardboard box toppled out, spilling a haphazard collection of student files and toiletries over the yard. Claire ran outside to help.

'Dad, we've got to get our bikes in yet,' wailed Angela, as her father and Pauline staggered on to the scene carrying an overweight case between them. Angela's father shook his head. 'Quart into pint pot won't go. Don't know why you're bringing half this stuff. That bike never leaves the shed from one end of the vac to the other.'

'I don't really use mine at home,' Pauline admitted.

'We couldn't leave them locked in our rooms, could we, Dr Haddingham?'

'I don't see why not.' Claire put her head through the back doorway. 'That's all right, isn't it, Laurie – if Angela and Pauline leave their bikes in their rooms?'

His reply came back eagerly, boomed out with unnecessary force. 'They can leave whatever they like up there. They've paid retainers; the rooms can't be used by anyone else.'

Well! No need to ask if they heard that. Claire walked casually past the kitchen window and glanced in. As she had guessed, there was Lydia. The chance to make that little speech had been seized on to prevent her getting ideas about moving upstairs. It annoyed Claire that this had even occurred to Laurie. Lydia was not supposed to be settling in. She was supposed to be on her way by now.

When the car started up, Laurie joined her outside. He put an arm round her shoulders as they waved their female lodgers goodbye. (Their male lodgers, Nigel and John, intended to remain, having both found holiday jobs in Thorpe.)

Angela wound down her window, Pauline leaned across. 'Bye,' they shouted. 'See you in October.'

'Have a lovely holiday,' Claire called.

'And open a book now and then,' added Laurie.

His arm was still resting on her as they sauntered inside. 'What was *she* doing in the kitchen?' Claire asked.

'Having a choking fit. She came rushing in, gasping for a glass of water – sputum spattering all over the place. Mercifully, I'd just cleared away the food. She was a horrid colour – blotchy puce.'

'Has she been through that trunk, yet?' (Yesterday, an outsize case had been delivered.)

'Please – I'm as anxious as you are,' Laurie hissed through his teeth.

'Yes. All right.' She said this pacifyingly, for the kitchen, she discovered, reeked of disinfectant, there were smears on the table, and a bowl of water with a cloth hanging over its side stood on a chair – all evidence of Laurie's real agitation.

'Anything I can do?' she asked, eyeing the bowl.

'Nothing, nothing. Out of the way,' he commanded, shooing her.

Because he didn't trust her to be thorough, she knew.

'I knew she'd be with us a damn sight longer than two or three days,' Claire grumbled to Monica. 'Two or three weeks more likely – if we're lucky.'

'Gin?'

'Thanks. If you ask me there's nothing but tat in that blasted trunk – she's just stringing Laurie on. She's had three whole days to make sure. If it were me I'd have it out with her. But the least remark and Laurie jumps out of his skin.'

Monica passed her the drink. They were in Monica's sitting room, studying details of the *gîte* Monica and David had taken for August. 'So,' Monica said. 'No sign yet of the missing letters and photograph.'

'Not as far as I know. I'm sure Laurie would have shown her the door by now, if there had been. Having her there is driving him mad. He's fussy as anything, always mopping and wiping things and insisting on personally doing the washing-up; terrified she's got something nasty and he might catch it.'

Having recently achieved a sighting of Lydia, Monica was inclined to sympathize. 'She doesn't present an entirely wholesome image, now you come to mention it.'

'Oh, Laurie was always a fusspot,' Claire said carelessly. 'But I hate seeing him so stressed.'

'It's not too stressful for you, then?'

'Of course it is. I ache to see the back of her. But it's not like the first time she was here, when he absolutely doted on her, and it was like – well – the bottom falling out of my world. Now it's the other way round – us two against *her*. And basically, so long as Laurie and I are OK, I can more or less put up with anything.'

'Yes,' said Monica, not needing to be told.

'Trouble is, Laurie is not OK. Far from it.'

Monica pushed her holiday details nearer. 'Do take a look. We'd love you and Laurie to come part of the time – not the first week – Yolande and Fred are coming then. But any time after. It might be a good move to set a date for a holiday, by which time Lydia would be obliged to clear out.'

Claire was doubtful. 'I know Laurie wants to get away, but he seems terrified of pushing her. He actually said if the worst comes to the worst and we can't go in August, we can always go to the Lakes in September.'

'Well, what a pity!' cried Monica. She sipped her drink thoughtfully. 'Perhaps you and I might hurry things on. Why don't we take a peek at Lydia's things? We could choose a day when she goes to see that doctor, then one of us keep a lookout while the other searches her trunk – and any other likely-looking receptacle.'

'But God, Monica, if she caught us . . . Or if Laurie found out . . .'

'We'd be very, very cautious.'

'I don't know. Anyway, she's bound to keep it locked.'

'Mm. Where would she keep a key, do you suppose? Handbag? Does she affect a handbag? — I've never noticed. Purse? Wallet?'

'How the hell would we rifle through those?'

'Presumably she takes a bath. Just a thought, dear. How about another small one?'

Because she had promised to be home in time for dinner at eight, Claire refused a second drink. (Laurie hated to have his efforts spoiled by tardy attention.) Armed with a folder containing alluring descriptions of the *gîte* and its environs, she set off, and by twenty to eight had turned into Devonshire Avenue.

Coming out of number 97 was Lydia, who paused suddenly, patting and feeling into her pockets. A gaunt, hunched figure — and minus a handbag, Claire registered, recalling Monica's remark. Evidently the contents of her pockets were satisfactory, for Lydia now advanced along the pavement.

They neared. Each closely and coldly regarded the other, and passed by without a word.

'I'm back,' Claire called, when she had closed the front door.

'Good. I was beginning to wonder. Dishing up in fifteen minutes.'

'Right-oh.' She stood in front of the hatstand, seeing in the mirror her shadowy image (for the light was fading), and beyond her head the door to the sitting-room. On an impulse, she crossed over and opened it. It was dark inside from closed curtains. She stepped in, shut the door behind her, switched on the light.

Lydia's mess was everywhere. The baby grand (pre-served under a dust sheet) had become a makeshift dressing table: jars of cream, a box of tissues, tubes and scissors and hairbrush and comb lay higgledy-piggledy in front of a mirror propped up against books. And an electric razor, noted Claire, with fascinated distaste. Chairs and settee were strewn with clothes. The trunk stood near the bed with its lid thrown back and draped over with under garments. The body of the trunk was mounded with stuff — scarves, towels, sheets, shoes, topped by a lidless shoebox full of glittery jewellery. The phrase *living out of a suitcase* sprang to mind. The whole scene cried a story — that of a drawn-out temporary stop-over.

As for the trunk (Claire shrank from actually putting her hands inside), its very openness declared lack of treasure, nothing worth hiding.

'You look shifty,' Laurie remarked, when they were eating. He had been trying to interest her in a telephone call he'd had earlier, from the producer of *Natural World*, requesting a further contribution — perhaps four or five episodes — and Laurie's thoughts on these set down on paper. Her response seemed to lack the customary enthusiasm. But this was a self-centred view. 'Look, if I can possibly fit it in, of course we'll go to France.' He pulled the folder containing the *gîte*'s particulars nearer to his plate. 'Sounds like excellent walking country.'

'I looked in her room,' Claire suddenly blurted. (Startled, Laurie looked up.) 'Just now. When I'd seen her go out. Do you know she leaves that precious trunk wide open? Anyone could poke around in it. All its contents are on show. Can't be a thing in it anyone'd want to get their hands on. Take a look yourself, if you don't believe me.'

He shook his head. 'I wish you wouldn't, Claire.'

'And I wish you *would*,' she retorted.

They completed their meal in edgy silence. Then both spoke at once.

'Love, I have got the matter in hand . . .'

'She mislaid those letters yonks ago, during her travels, if you ask me . . .'

'What?'

'It doesn't matter.'

They shrugged and smiled, and Laurie said,

'Does Monica want us to say definitely one way or the other?'

'I don't think so. Yolande and Fred are joining them for the first week. After that she's easy.'

'Well, so long as I've worked something out for the programme . . .'

And so long as Lydia has gone, she thought, but didn't say. Instead, referring to ideas for the programme, she said encouragingly, 'But you already have something worked out – in your head. Remember us talking about it? We had some great ideas.'

'You'll have to remind me. Truth is, I'm finding it hard to concentrate at the moment.'

'Oh dear, Laurie . . .' But ever practical, she began hunting for a solution. 'Why not get started by devoting an entire day to it? For instance, tomorrow. Shut out everything else. I'll shop and cook and answer the phone. Or you could go and work at the university.'

'And have people constantly putting their heads round the door? No thanks.'

'So use the dining-room. I'll put *Do Not Disturb* on the door, if you like.'

Claire was right; he must get a grip on himself. 'You're on,' he declared, and jumped to his feet. 'Now, I'll clear up in here, and you can relate some of our brilliant ideas.'

'That's the spirit. But it's my job to clear up.' She seized a cluttered tray she had just noticed on the sideboard, took it to the sink.

'Leave that!'

Ah, so it was Lydia's tray, and he alone could be trusted to deal with it. She had begun to suspect he was cooking for Lydia. For one thing, the other day he had complained she was slipshod in the kitchen.

'You mean, like me?' Claire had teased.

'Not like you in the least,' Laurie had retorted. 'She doesn't cook everything in the same saucepan and heap it all on to the same plate; it's not that she can't be bothered; just her stamina runs out. It costs her an effort to raise anything heavy above elbow height, I've noticed; her arms start trembling . . .'

'I'm not surprised with you watching, gimlet-eyed.'

'She starts off with good intentions then it all becomes too much, and she slops stuff on the cooker and down the side of the sink, desperate to be done with the job.'

'Have you asked her about this?' had scoffed Claire, 'or is it pure supposition?'

He'd said nothing. Practice makes perfect, he might have answered, but was too depressed. (To Laurie, it was not odd but perfectly natural to slip into another's shoes. Life might be a bit easier all round, he often thought, if it were more widely practiced.)

Now, faintly anxious about possible infection, he applied a nylon scourer to Lydia's cup and saucer. Lydia looked so awful she might have anything, he fretted to himself.

By his side, Claire was trying to think constructively about the TV programme. 'I remember one good angle we thought of,' she cried. 'Plants struggling for territory – you know, war between bracken and brambles, and the casualties left in their wake.'

'So we did,' he said delightedly. His hands fell still. 'Yes, it's beginning to come back.'

'Then tomorrow you can start writing it all down.'

On her return next day from shopping, Claire was most put out to discover the door to the dining-room open. And angry indeed to hear Lydia's voice within. Specially since, before going out, she had spoken to Lydia (a thing she could scarcely bare to do) expressly to warn her that Laurie had urgent work to do and must not be disturbed. Damnation, she cursed under her breath as she dumped carrier bags on the kitchen table. And marched off to have it out. But then hesitated. For what was now taking place might just possibly be the long anticipated hand over of the incriminating letters.

But no. From the hall, she caught all too clearly the drivel with which Laurie was being distracted.

'Just a quarter of the dose, Dr Lessing says, shouldn't do any harm. And if it boosts my morale it'll do me some good. Honestly, Laurie, it's an absolute pain looking so haggish. Mind you, I feel I'm improving already. What do you think? A bit fuller in the face?'

Having heard enough, Claire barged into the room. She ignored Lydia. 'Is this an important conversation, Laurie? Because I thought you had urgent work to attend to. I thought that was why I elected to hold the fort today.'

'Yes.' From frowning down at the papers covering the table, Laurie looked up and presented an apologetic face to Lydia. 'I am rather pushed . . .'

'Right,' Claire said, turning on her. 'Out, if you please!' And in an altered tone to Laurie, before closing the door, 'I'll bring you a cup of coffee in a minute.'

'Cow!' hissed Lydia to Claire, following close on her heels into the kitchen. 'Bitch!' Claire whirled in amazement. Lydia kept coming, craning and menacing, backing Claire against the kitchen unit. 'Don't treat *me* like dirt, you mean little tight-arse, you shrivelled up cunt. Can't get a bloke of your own, so you hang on to Laurie. Bet you'd breathe for the poor devil if you got the chance . . .'

'Get *off*,' Claire yelled, shoving her away with all her might. 'Get out of here!' as Lydia went spinning into the table.

Lydia doubled like a snapped stick. Sprawled onto the floor; choked, rasped, heaved onto her back; arched up, straining for air.

Laurie hurried in. 'Whatever's going on?'

'She . . . she . . .' Lydia gasped accusingly.

Laurie turned to Claire. 'Get her some water. Help me get her to her room.'

Claire filled a glass, but shrank from the second command. She stood holding it, as Laurie – his face twisted away and betraying the cost – hauled up Lydia and staggered with her out of the kitchen. Claire trailed after – through the hall, into the sitting-room.

At last Lydia was deposited on the bed where she lay writhing and rasping. Laurie stepped back and looked at her. 'I think we'd better get a doctor.'

'. . . Lessing,' Lydia breathlessly insisted.

'Right. Can you give me his number?' Lydia's hand pointed to an address book lying on top of the trunk. Laurie reached for it and turned to the L's, then went into the hall to phone. Claire stayed where she was, still clutching the glass of water, looking anywhere but at Lydia.

'He'll come as soon as he can,' Laurie reported. His eyes went to Claire's hands. Impatiently, he relieved her of the glass and bore it to the bed. 'Are you feeling any better? Try and sip this.'

Claire slipped out of the room.

Dr Lessing was a man of superior insight, wisdom and kindliness – at least in his own estimation. You could tell this, Claire explained to Monica, from his undentable confidence, his way of steadily smiling at obstreperousness while relentlessly pursuing his exposition. So far-seeing and knowing best for other people, in fact, that it was a miracle he contented himself with mere doctoring.

No, Lydia would *not* be better off in hospital; to suggest otherwise (as Laurie had) was to misunderstand the problem. The damage done to her system by hormonal abuse was too pervasive to be susceptible to surgery . . .

'And presumably he was the bastard who prescribed the stuff!' Monica now exclaimed.

'Mm. But you know how madly Lydia focussed on the sex change? Maybe she was reckless, tossed down more than the prescribed dose. Anyway, Laurie said while she was abroad she was still taking the stuff – against medical advice – *after* the first heart attack.

To get back to Dr Lessing . . . He said she'd had a pretty close shave, but had responded well to the stuff he'd given her. A sample of which he'd leave behind for us to administer in the event of another collapse.'

'He expects you to dose her?' Monica could scarcely believe her ears.

'He said what she needs is the support of under-standing and intelligent friends – in the short term to help her recover, in the long term (if she's to have any long term) to encourage her to live on a more stable and less excitable plane.'

'Friends indeed!' Monica spluttered. 'I hope you put him right on that score.'

'Certainly, I tried. But it was hopeless – like sticking your finger in rising dough. I said, "Look: this is our sitting-room – OK? It's very inconvenient. We've got lives to lead. Her sleeping in here was just a *temporary* arrangement." Had about as much impact as if I'd been clearing my throat. His eyes went right over me to Laurie. Hell, I know I'm on the short side, but he acted like I didn't officially exist. Started expounding to Laurie about people in Lydia's position being the subject of prejudice and so forth – and how she'd been exploited, and how lonely and friendless she'd become. He implied that putting her up in her hour of need shouldn't present insuperable problems to en-lightened folk of intellectual standing. Really got my goat, I can tell you. I'd have laid into him if it hadn't been for Laurie nearly wringing my arm off. I suppose Laurie did have a *try* – mentioned we were planning to go on holiday and so forth. But it was all smoothly glossed over: why, we should just go! – Lydia was perfectly capable of fending for herself for a while. "And *helping* herself," I said – at which his eyes sort of flickered. Then he was off again, graciously promising to investigate the lodgings situation himself, and take the matter up with the health people. But in the meantime, *no excitement*, he said, giving me, at last, a very definite look. I bet Lydia had told him I'd had a go at her.'

'But this is appalling! Laurie must put his foot down. Do you think it'd do any good if I spoke to him?'

'No, I don't,' Claire said hurriedly. Besides what she had forcefully put to him herself, Laurie was beset by too many conflicting points of view of his own to bear any further input.

Monica looked at the neat piles on the floor, of clothes, books and writing equipment, ready to be packed into cartons and cases.

'Look, I can see you're busy,' Claire said, getting out of her chair, going to the door. 'I'm sorry I barged in. I just had to get out of the house – needed to get away from Laurie, too; there was a bit of an atmosphere between us. I suspect he blames me to a certain extent. He'd witnessed the ticking off I gave Lydia, which obviously upset her. I admit I also gave her a hefty shove, but she was coming after me, mouthing some incredibly foul stuff. Next minute, there she was on the floor, apparently gasping her last.'

'Laurie has no business blaming you. I think you're a brick to put up with it. Stay longer if you want,' Monica invited, following Claire, nevertheless, downstairs. (The packing required concentration. Terrifying to be abroad for a month and discover something vital has been omitted – like a reference book, or refills for your favourite pen, or the only pair of scissors ever to understand the shape of your toenails.) 'Now,' – she pulled the front door open, 'go and put some backbone into that nuisance of a man. And brook no argument on the holiday front.'

'God, if Lydia makes us miss that . . . I'll be tempted to say, soddit, I'll go on my own.'

'*Don't let him get away with it!*' Monica admonished in her sternest tone. (Claire on her own did not conform with her picture of the holiday scene – the long table out of doors covered with fruits and cheese and sausage, with creamy tarts and sticks of bread and bottles and bottles of wine; the laughter and conversation among the friends from Thorpe and the expatriate friends from the next village; she presiding at one end of the table, David at the other, and Laurie being wonderful in the middle – droll, witty and outrageous, on top of his form: Claire was there as an embellishment, but Laurie was the prize.) 'Darling, this Lydia business is getting ridiculous. Those blasted letters are obviously lost. Why doesn't he forget about them?'

'Because,' Claire said slowly, 'it's not just the perceived threat. There's no chance whatever of Laurie showing her the door while she's in this pathetic state. Which is why this Lessing individual honed in on him, of course. He'd got Laurie's number; he could spot a soft touch when he saw one staring at him – all concerned-looking and grave and conceding the point.' She stepped over the threshold, letting out a sigh. 'I'm partly furious, partly exasperated, and partly . . . resigned. I mean, that's Laurie for you. Good at stiffening everybody else's sinews – bossy and domineering as can be – but so full of angst, he himself is a pushover.'

A little chastened, Monica laid a hand on her friend's arm. 'Strikes me,' she said, 'Laurie is a remarkably fortunate person.'

Claire frowned.

'Fortunate in that *you* happen to be the principle love of his life – staunch and unwavering. He's so hopelessly vulnerable, one shudders to think how he'd have fared if he'd picked on somebody otherwise. Now, sweetie, for his own good, do try and be persuasive. Both of you need a break.'

'I'll try,' Claire mumbled, and turned away before calling goodbye.

It was a blustery day, cold for the time of year. Claire lowered her head against the wind and set off home. Idiot, idiot, she scolded herself as she scurried along

432

the pavement – blubbing like a baby because someone makes you a present of a few kind words.

Gloom dropped over her as she entered the house. The sight of shopping still lying on the kitchen table made her head hurt. Recalling that she had volunteered to cook tonight's dinner, she cursed her ambitious plans of the morning and moved the loathsome items, one by one, from carrier bags to cupboard and fridge.

Laurie was in the dining-room, sitting at the table with his head propped on one hand, a pen in the other.

'Jacket spuds with cheese and salad OK?' she asked gruffly.

'Perfectly.'

She hesitated. 'Going all right, is it?' (She meant his work.)

He looked up, shrugged.

They eventually ate their meal an hour later than usual, in not altogether easy silence. When Claire caught his eye, he had a smile ready – of the polite and cautious sort. She looked quickly down at her plate. Yeah, he blames me all right, she thought.

That ferocious frown, marvelled Laurie. She'll have a permanent groove by the time she's forty. For which he would be not a little to blame . . . *Blame* – what a nasty little heart-sinker of a word – its explosive beginning, lingering end. And right now (and thoroughly deserved, he wouldn't deny it), *her* blaming *him* for this senseless spoiling of their lives, stood between them like a thick sheet of opaque glass.

They finished eating. He reached for their plates. She jumped up to forestall him.

'But you . . .' he began with the traditional objection, but she cut him off. 'Please,' she said sarcastically. 'It can hardly be said that I *cooked*.'

Useless to argue with her in this defensive mood, he knew; might as well let her get on with it. In any case, he was so weighed down by depression, inactivity seemed his best option. He studied the table and sighed deeply. 'Isn't it absolutely terrifying,' he mused (but it was as if his mind had sprung a leak, he did not consciously intend to share the thought), 'the way people can just sheer off downhill? One minute hale and hearty, the next a pathetic shadow . . .'

Her frown deepened. She marched to the bin and viciously scooted in their leavings.

He looked up, and understood she assumed his reference was to Lydia.

But his thoughts had gone way beyond Lydia's decline, to the human plight in general (and his own in particular); to invisible, unknowable pitfalls – germs and viruses lurking externally, witherings and growths occurring internally. They could strike any-one, any time – no matter how scrupulously one avoided contamination or stuck to a healthy mode of living. One had only to think of Gil Forster, that diet and exercise fanatic, who had dropped dead of a heart attack on the university playing field during a regular Saturday football game. And of poor Midge Arrow-smith of the French Department, taken off in her twenties by leukaemia. There was no need to deliber-ately sabotage one's system, as Lydia had. No-one was immune from arbitrary pitfalls. No-one.

Claire, squinting, ripped off a piece of cling film and smoothed it over the salad bowl.

'Have you got one your headaches?' he asked sharply.

'Yeah,' she said. 'Since you ask. A real pounder.'

It seemed to Laurie these ferocious headaches – or migraines – were becoming more frequent. He some-times wondered whether they were connected with her squint, though it was more than his life was worth to suggest consulting an ophthalmologist. Claire was adamant there was nothing wrong with her eyes (apart from needing spectacles for close work); she had this on the word of her optician. The fuss made at Foscote had been prompted by cosmetic considerations, she declared, which just went to demonstrate how shallow were those people's values. Folk who were hung up on regularity in the human form made her sick. At this, she had narrowed the eyes in question darkly at Laurie. No, he was certainly not going to risk any further reference to the subject. Of course, frequent headaches *could* be symptomatic of a truly hideous condition . . . He held his breath, and allowed the words *brain tumour* to stand in his mind. The shock they gave jolted him then and there to call a halt to his maunderings. Which, concerning Claire at least, were probably rubbish. What had happened this morning, and since, was enough to give anyone a headache. Which reminded him . . .

'Right.' He stood up. 'I'd better go and see if Lydia wants anything.'

Claire, who had moved to the sink, spun the hot tap, full jet.

xviii

Claire went briskly across the quad. August on campus, she thought. The desultoriness. Everything at half-cock.

But never mind that. Get into the lab, you idiot girl, and crack on with some respectable work.

In view of the miserable situation at home and the disintegration of their holiday plans – in other words, with Laurie giving trouble – she had fallen back on the second of her twin great loves: work. Cocking a snook at fate, she had begun a new project, one that could not in the nature of things be concluded before the elapse of four or five weeks. It was a way of accepting they would not go to France, of putting the possibility right out of her mind. (Though sometimes – walking to work on a dull morning – she enviously pictured Monica and Co sunning themselves). There was still the real possibility of a stay in the Lakes in September – as Laurie frequently reminded her. He'd mentioned it again last night. 'I'm beginning to suspect you were never too keen on the idea of Provence,' she'd said accusingly. 'Well,' he admitted, 'the way Monica told it, it did begin to sound like a scene from Sartre – you know, when you discover hell is an endless dinner party.' Yes, they were back to teasing one another. However bad things got, they could not be distant with one another for long. In fact, whether thanks to the work project taking her mind off Lydia, or Laurie's constant reassurances, her mood had taken a more optimistic turn.

In a cloakroom in the Biological Sciences Building, she went to her locker; put on an overall, scrubbed her hands. Then let herself into the darkened lab and flicked on the low strip lighting.

Dim greenish light glowed eerily on the seedling frame. She leaned over, and her heart lifted. The little darlings were shooting already. She pictured their developing roots, the intricate network of threads. Life, she marvelled.

The weather improved. By the middle of the month, Claire was no longer going to and fro the university in a mac and sensible shoes, but in a T-shirt, shorts and sandals. Afterwards, she relaxed in the garden with a cup of tea and a newspaper. Unfortunately, Lydia – now up and about – had similar ideas. This late afternoon for instance: while Claire was sitting on a garden seat, reading in the shade of the hornbeam, Lydia was lying on a rug some way off, bearing her leathery flesh to the sun.

But here came Laurie. 'Lydia,' he called. 'May I disturb you?'

Claire, peering over her reading spectacles, observed Lydia raise her top half a few inches and prop herself up on her elbows.

'I'm glad to see you're so well recovered. Perhaps this is the moment to ask you to make other arrangements. You see, we really do need our sitting-room back.'

Claire scrambled up, hurried across the lawn to the house. From the back porch, she caught Laurie's raised voice – and was so surprised by its tone that she hung back to listen: 'I don't give a hang whether you've got them or you haven't; or what you might or might not do with them. If you feel you have to try and harm me, then all I can say is, I'm sorry for you.' – now Lydia's voice intervening in a flat-toned volley of protest (Claire couldn't make out the words) – then Laurie again, 'Come off it! It's what you've implied all along with your hints and insinuations. But go ahead. I don't *care* anymore.'

She moved rapidly out of earshot. In the kitchen, closed the door behind her. 'Yippee,' she whooped under her breath. Suddenly, she was merry as a robin, high as a coot. She had an irrational feeling that by addressing Lydia forcefully like that, Laurie had half won the battle already.

She decided to give him a nice surprise. Cook something tasty, even exotic, if she could lay hands on some likely-looking ingredients. She pulled the fridge door open, peered inside.

When Laurie told Lydia he didn't care, he had spoken only the partial truth. He was inclined to agree with Claire that the letters no longer existed. But supposing Lydia did have them, then he certainly shrank from the prospect of having his private life made public, or being called upon to explain himself in any embarrassing way. However, during a sequence of sleepless nights (the World Service giving out, unattended to, beside him), he had sorted out his priorities. And first and foremost, he decided, he prized his happy home. Looking back over the past few years – those since Claire's return from her two-year stint in Montreal to be precise – he saw how amazingly happy it had been: damn near perfect – he and Claire living together as they wished, no longer feeling any compunction to explain themselves or maintain a pretence of being 'engaged'; the spacious house (worries about its upkeep overcome by letting rooms); good friends dropping in; Claire's work going brilliantly and more or less on the doorstep. He hadn't understood quite how marvellous a set-up it was, until Lydia invaded. So why, it then occurred to him to ask, put up with the invasion, since Lydia, who might conceivably have the power to harm him professionally, could not undermine what he valued most? It was amazing that he hadn't grasped this salient fact earlier. Now that he had, with the feeling of freedom it brought he could perceive any remaining threat as quite underwhelming. For what, when it came down to it, was so very terrible about a few love-letters (albeit passionately and explicitly expressed) from one man to another? The photograph on its own (that is, minus the correspondence), could appear wholly innocent – merely two men with their arms round one another. His memory of the letters' impact seemed dulled by the passing years – like time gently casting its veils of dust. Surely attitudes had softened? After all, congress between consenting adult males had been legal for the past decade. Why, he sometimes wondered, had he hung on to those sad mementos? There had been no affair with Angus (loving him had naturally ruled this out) despite Angus's clearly articulated wish to embark on one. Simply, he had been sufficiently touched to keep Angus's letters by him for a while; and then, when Angus was drowned in a boating accident, had felt compelled to keep them, together with the photograph. The more he reflected, the less he felt he would care if they did turn up one day on the Vice Chancellor's desk – or on the desk of the boss of Granada Television, come to that; or – and possibly more likely – on an editor's desk at some tabloid newspaper office. His employers could either sack him or keep him. (He could always earn money playing jazz piano in the clubs; he could write a book – not to do with the television series, a *proper* book;

he could become a counsellor – yes, he'd be rather good at that.) What he would *not* do was explain himself. Why the hell should he? It was not his nature to talk publicly of private matters; indeed, he shrank from the sort of person whose nature it was. This would be so whatever his status – hetero or homo, active or passive, practising or (as had been the case for the past three years) simply disinclined to bother. Fortunately, it was difficult to expose someone as celibate, he comforted himself grimly.

His resolve had hardened. As soon as Lydia was sufficiently recovered to move to another place, he would insist on her doing so. She could do her worst.

Late evening, a week later: Claire in the kitchen, Laurie running downstairs as the front door blew open, helped by a fierce wind.

'Ah, Lydia. Any success?'

'I don't know what you mean.'

'Stop fooling, for heaven's sake. You've been out all day – I presume looking for accommodation. So I repeat: any luck?'

'No,' she said shortly, and Claire, who had gone very still at the sink, jumped out of her skin as Lydia's voice sounded at her elbow: 'Mind if I get some water?'

Claire, stepping aside, thought she sounded vengeful.

Laurie had followed her. 'Look Lydia, I'd better warn you: this morning I went to see my solicitor.'

Having filled a glass, Lydia stood it on the draining board while she reached into her pocket for a bottle of pills. She unscrewed the lid, tipped out a tablet and placed it in her mouth. They waited tensely, watched closely, as she drank and swallowed. Even so, the abruptness of her banging down the empty glass and simultaneously turning, almost caught them on the hop.

But Laurie shot out his hand, seized her arm. 'You did hear? I've consulted a solicitor – put him entirely

439

in the picture. Because now you're recovered *we need that room.*'

'Do you mind?' she ground out, shaking him off. And marched out. A few moments later the sitting-room door was forcefully closed.

They looked at one another. Claire was quite awe-struck. 'Did you really do that?'

'Come outside,' he said.

They crossed the yard, walked over the grass till they were beyond the reach of the house lights.

'It's blowy,' she objected, clutching her bare arms.

'But the wind's warm.' He pulled her back against him, wrapped his arms around.

The wind shaking the willow and lilac, bending the hornbeam, singing through tall limes in the park beyond the garden, was also providing a spectacular show of light and shade. They stared up at the yellow three-quarter moon. Filmy gauze snaked over. Smoke streaked by. Then an immense patch of denseness loomed, closer, closer, till the light was abruptly smothered and was only visible at the extreme edge of the cloud – egg yolk showing through grey. Bright-ness returned as the wind drove the cloud and its trailing plumes onwards. And there again was the naked moon, throwing the faintest halo against a navy and indigo sky.

She was still gazing at the sight when she recollected her question and nudged her head into him. 'Well?'

'Mm, yes,' he said vaguely, unable quite to leave his sky-watching. 'Mm, I did.'

'How much did you tell him?' she demanded.

'Eh? Oh, the whole story.'

'You mean, all of it?'

'Every bit.'

She digested this for a moment. 'And?'

'He suggested sending her a stern letter threatening to apply for an injunction. I said I'd prefer a gentler approach. The last thing we want is her having another attack under our roof. So we compromised. Since it was the good Dr Lessing who persuaded us to put up with her while she recuperated, the solicitor's letter will be sent to *him* – setting out Lydia's history in our lives. Let's hope it gets things moving.'

'Let's hope,' she agreed fervently.

'Don't worry, pet; it'll soon be over.' He pulled her round to face him, gave her a rallying shake. 'September in the Lakes. I promise.'

The wind dropped, the temperature rose; a persistent heat-haze gathered. Claire was stifled both by lack of air and lack of unfettered sunlight. It was difficult to know where to put herself – so heavy outdoors, so clammy indoors. Thunder flies insinuated everywhere, even under the glass covering the watercolours. Claire stared with dismay at the besmirched paintings and despaired at the cost of reframing.

Menace filled the house. Claire felt this most surely. It emanated, she considered, from Lydia's air of malign purpose. She wondered whether Laurie noticed it. But he was all brisk confidence. She supposed he had to act this way in order to face out Lydia, and maybe to reassure *her*. Like a nun on the verge of losing faith in her vows, Claire struggled to be, and to remain, reassured.

Nevertheless, dragging her sticky body along the avenue to the bus stop, and then through the university quad to the Biological Sciences Block, the thought crept up again and again – that the impression she was getting from Lydia was of someone biding time.

That night the familiar dream broke her sleep, subtly altered. As usual, she was running through the Foscote woods, searching for Laurie. But the trees began to swell and twist, the sky lowered darkly, the moon bobbed crazily in the tree tops. Bramble stems tore her, protruding roots tripped her, her heart banged to her racing feet. Then from the floor of the wood a great wind rose up, sending a roar through the misshapen branches, driving clouds to cover the moon. In the blackness, a vast emptiness grew where her heart should be, and there was no pounding in her ears, only widening silence. And zooming into the void, the grim presence of Lydia.

She woke with a lurch. Sat up, wide-eyed. And then, in one of those awful moments of clear certainty, *knew they would never be free of her*.

So what if they succeeded in dislodging Lydia for the time being? Let another three or four years pass, and one mild and ordinary day, through a trustingly unlocked door, in she would slip with some new tale of woe, some renewed veiled threat. They were fools to believe they would ever finally see the back of her.

She sank back on her pillows. Resolve clenched her like a slowly closing steel clamp. 'It can't go on,' she growled in her throat.

In the morning there was blood in her mouth where her teeth had dug in. Her jaw ached. Dimly, she recognized the jagged pain behind her eyes. She was starting a migraine.

Laurie was reading some post when Claire came downstairs.

'Letter from Dr Lessing. He wants to see me. Thinks he's come up with somewhere for Lydia. Well, I can't manage it this morning – I've got to be in Manchester by half-ten. Maybe tonight – if he's available tonight. What's up? It's good news, isn't it?'

'Oh, yeah,' said Claire, trying to muster enthusiasm. But she could only feel hopeless, haunted by her clairvoyance during the small hours.

'Darling?'

The concern in his voice felt like a rebuke. Hell, he was doing *battle* on their behalf; the least she could do was pin her favour to his sleeve, give him some proper encouragement. And until this mood hit her, she had been doing just that. She'd been thrilled to bits by his new-found resolution. But the way Lydia had looked in the kitchen last night helping herself to a glass of water – mean, purposeful – had been enough to undermine her. It was easily done because there was so much at stake.

'Head hurt?' he asked, his hand smoothing her temple.

'Mm. Woke up with it. Might go off if I take something – nip it in the bud.'

'Stay at home,' he urged.

'You kidding? Me here on my own – with *her*?'

'I could change my appointment . . .'

'Don't. I really mean to go in; today's the optimum day for taking a root section. I'll probably feel better once I'm in the lab.'

'If you're sure . . . Look, why don't I give you a lift? And I'll be back in Thorpe by four or four-thirty. I'll drop by and collect you.'

'That would be lovely,' she conceded.

The headache did not go away. It got steadily worse. Maybe this was due to working under the green strip light. When she briefly closed her eyes, her blindness was shot with blood-red streaks.

At last, she gave up. Left the lab, and on her way to her office, collected a glass of water. The place was deserted. I could die here, she thought, and no-one would know. She practised some gentle breathing exercises for a minute or two, then sat in her chair and sipped her drink. If she could only empty her mind and relax her neck muscles it might help.

No good. Her head was full of darting needles. Whenever she closed her eyes, the red flashing persisted. She peered at her watch. Only half past twelve. Stupid to try and hang on till Laurie came. Better to go home now, and lock herself in her bedroom. Only bed would suffice when she was this ill.

She took a sheet of A4 paper, wrote on it in large scrawl with a black marker: *Sorry, gone home –*

migraine; and placed it, where he would find it, on her cleared desktop.

She had developed a special way of walking for when her head was bad – *conveying* herself, with only her legs moving and the rest of her body held still, with as little tension as possible. Luckily, a bus came almost at once. She climbed on to the nearest empty seat – a side-facing one near the platform – and concentrated on relaxed breathing. Along Devonshire Avenue she continued her gliding progress, and was certainly no worse, and possibly slightly improved (perhaps with relief) by the time she arrived at number 97.

She knew something was amiss the moment the door opened.

Hard on the noise she had made herself, came a rushed scrabbling sound, and a thud. Then silence – as she stood tensely on the threshold, and someone did likewise behind the dining-room door.

It was she who ended the suspense, flinging the front door shut behind her as she ran (for the first time in her life disregarding Laurie's strictures about safeguarding the precious glass panels) and skidded into the dining-room.

Lydia was in there, of course. She was over by the bureau, hanging onto it, one knee on the floor, clearly frozen in the act of rising. The bureau was a mess; one if its drawers was hanging out with its contents spilled, another drawer (obviously closed in haste) had papers protruding.

'Well, well,' said Claire, rapidly interpreting the situation. 'As I thought, you don't have those letters anymore, so you decided you'd try and lay hands on some other likely material.'

Lydia scrambled up. Then hesitated. Her mouth came open, her chest started working: free to breathe again, she evidently could not do so quickly enough.

She took a cautious step forward, keeping – Claire suddenly noticed – one hand behind her back.

'You found something!' Claire cried, shoving the door closed behind her. 'Well you're damn well not leaving till you've given it back.'

Quick as a flash, Lydia's hand swept round to her front and stuffed a folded piece of paper down the V of her shirt.

'You utter bitch! Well, I mean it – you're not leaving this room till you hand it over.'

Lydia's eyes darted. Her hands clenched and dropped to her sides. Otherwise, apart from the strenuous breathing, she made no move.

Not for a fleet second did Claire doubt her statement. Her headache was forgotten, as also was her inferior size. Lydia could have been at her physical peak, exuding the strength that had once given her pause for thought; it would have made no difference to her. She was power-packed with adrenalin, her entire will bent on retrieving Laurie's property. 'Why do you do it?' she asked, trying reasonableness in the first instance. 'Whatever's the point? Why not leave peaceably like a sensible person? We had a letter from Dr Lessing this morning; he's probably found you a place.'

The name galvanized Lydia. '*Lessing*,' she spat, and her body broke out in violent trembling. 'I wouldn't go anywhere he's found. It's all his fault, anyway. I'm going to sue him; he's going to be sorry.'

'Yeah, of course! Laurie's solicitor wrote to him, explaining a few things about you. I expect it shook him a bit, discovering what a lying thief he's been putting himself out for. Gave you a good talking to, did he?'

'You'll *all* be sorry!'

'That's right! 'Cos punishing and hurting really turns you on. Specially those who've been good to you.' (A light seemed to have come on in her head.) 'I reckon I've got you sussed: you're so dissatisfied with yourself, you despise anyone who takes an interest – you have to hurt them – like you're trying to hurt kind old Laurie; and now poor Dr Lessing had better look out. Well, hear this: as far as Laurie's concerned, you've me to reckon with. He's too innocent for you, always has been. But me – oh, I can be as hard as you any day of the week. So let's have it,' she demanded, putting out a hand.

Lydia, now shaking from head to foot, lunged for the door. Claire fell back against it to keep it shut, and at the same time reached for Lydia's shirt.

They struggled hard. At first, because she needed to keep her weight against the door, Claire was foiled by her adversary's height and jutting shoulder. Inevitably, the door came open. Lydia burst into the hall with Claire hanging on grimly. But now Claire was free to put everything into her objective – dodging kicks and jabbing elbows, she fought to break Lydia's grip of her shirt front. When Lydia swung out of reach, she lunged with passionate determination and brought her to the floor, where for the space of two minutes they wrestled remorselessly. Then, with curious suddenness, Lydia's grip loosened. Claire grabbed her prize, scrambled to her feet . . .

But Lydia did not rise up after her. She continued to flail about on the floor; her back arched, her chin thrust up, muscles and veins corded her neck. Staring down at her, Claire saw her colour change from leathery tan to deep puce, and heard, through apparently locked jaws, one forced out word: '*Pills!*'

Oh God, yes, she thought, running for the bottle which she knew to be still on the kitchen sideboard where Dr Lessing had left it. Two pills to be dissolved in a third of a tumbler of water, she remembered, dropping the paper she had retrieved on to the sideboard for a moment while she reached into a cupboard and seized a glass. She ran with it to the sink, turned on the cold tap; in her haste, overfilled it. Steadying herself, she emptied out water to the required amount, then turned . . . And was about to rush with the glass back to the pill bottle, when, for no conscious reason, her haste dissipated. Heaviness fell over her. She remained at the sink.

'Quick!' Lydia shrieked – but the sound came to Claire faintly, behind the loud ringing in her ears. Dizzily, she grasped the draining board. Closed her eyes – saw red blotches looming against blackness, throbbing like sliced open blood-vessels; opened them, and with relief viewed the greenery outside the window. Staring at the lawn, the willow tree, the seat under the hornbeam, she drank the water down herself. Then refilled the glass and drank some more. At last, set down the tumbler and went out of the kitchen, diverting only to collect the retrieved piece of paper.

On the hall floor, Lydia was still writhing and heaving, but her strained face wore an expectant look. Claire stepped over her. She went into the dining-room and dropped the paper behind the bureau desk lid. Apart from this one act of tidying, she left the room as it was.

Lydia had moved a small way when she returned to the hall. Like a stranded sea creature, she had flopped ineffectually about two feet nearer the kitchen. Seeing Claire observe her, she wasted her energy on a short venting of incredulous fury. 'Cow!' she choked.

The cry, and the strangled gargling which followed, came distantly to Claire on her way to the door. She let herself out, closed the door firmly, and set off down Devonshire Avenue, back to the university.

She threw up just inside the university gateway. It had taken all her will-power not to do so on the bus. It was her perfunctory breakfast, she supposed, though mostly bile. The worst part was when she retched emptily, clinging to a post for support, scared her guts would join the mess on the grass. When she could check the convulsions, she walked as composedly as possible through the quad to the Biological Sciences Block.

Still no-one about. She went straight to the cloak-room to wash and rinse out her mouth. Then to her room, where the message was just as she had left it. She tore the paper in tiny pieces, disposed of it under other clutter in the wastepaper basket. It was only two forty-five – Laurie would be ages yet: what to do with herself was the question. After some thought, she took a fresh piece of A4, and this time wrote, *Lying down in SCR – migraine.* Placed this on her desk, then left her room and the building; crossed over the tarmac, entered another building, and climbed some stairs to the Senior Common Room – and found it fortunately deserted. In a far corner, she drew a curtain over a window, laid a cushion strategically on the sofa beneath, and gingerly laid herself down.

When Laurie found her, she seemed to be sleeping. He knelt near her head. 'Claire? Darling?'

She was not asleep, but had a great fear of lifting her head.

'Can you hear me?'

Her mouth opened. 'Uh.'

'I'll go and back the car up to the door. Hang on, shan't be long.'

A terrible lurching, set off by the effort to speak, was going on behind her eyes. He needn't worry; she wasn't planning to go anywhere . . .

Oh God, he was back.

'Right, love. Do you think you can move?' He slid an arm under her shoulders, raised her a few inches.

'Nuh!' she squawked, as the lurching came again, and nausea like a dog making a nest turned and turned in her stomach.

'What then?' he asked, his voice sharpened by anxiety. 'Shall I get someone – a doctor?'

'Nuh-uh.'

'Um, ambulance?' he floundered. 'I know, shall I call one of the porters?'

'Nuh-uh-uh!' Terrible to think of people handling

448

her. Only one thing for it: she must discover her own method.

She leaned over the edge of the sofa, put her hands to the floor, then one foot, then the other. She felt his hands arrive in her armpits. 'Nnn,' she protested.

'Then how . . . ?'

There was no other way possible, she found, than on all fours. She could not countenance being vertical. Ponderously, she went over the carpet, changing to an eel-like movement on the hard, shiny surface of the corridor – Laurie all the time protesting and worrying. On the stairs, she found the only way she could descend was backwards on hands and knees. This upset him even more – 'Your poor knees!'

If they were all! she thought scathingly. Didn't he appreciate her *head* was threatening to explode? She took each step singly, keeping her head as near as possible to the ground. And it suddenly came to her that maybe gravity was the issue here. For her whole body craved contact with the horizontal; her head in particular reeled at the idea of being borne aloft. Had she hit on something? Maybe migraine was the result of some disturbance of the gravitational pull – or a misreading of it. She must investigate – not her field, of course – but, hell, her research could scarcely be empiricaller . . . empiricullar . . . empi . . . *Sod*. Now she'd lost it . . . ('Nearly there, pet. Can you manage through the door? I've got it open.') Caught up on some blasted word (like her knees were catching on this rough bit out here), she'd lost an important, possibly brilliant insight. Blast! she cried silently, as her legs and arms gave way. She lay with her cheek on the pavement. Tears rolled sideways out of her eyes.

'Love . . .' His hands were there at once, patting, stroking. 'You're almost at the car. I left the door open.'

She turned up her eyes. He'd left the *passenger* door open, the loon. '*Buhck*,' she blurted.

'Of course, you want to be in the back,' he tumbled, hastening to open the rear door.

449

She hauled herself onto her hands and knees. From under her brows, peered at the rear car seat. He was gearing himself to lift her. Desperate to forestall him, she launched herself, dived for it – hit the seat, rolled on to her back.

He looked at her with anxiety. Then went to the boot to collect a sweater, and made a pad of it to cradle her head. He could tell as he placed it under her that she'd passed out. She was unresisting.

Laurie drove carefully, aiming to make the journey a smooth one.

Claire was floating – not in the sea, for there was no regular forward roll: this was a lake, she decided, with fish swimming past sending ripples of water to nudge her, first in this direction, then in that. After a time, sudden choppiness made her think she had been mistaken, for a faint roaring entered her ears, like waves. Then Laurie said, 'I'll park as close to the front door as I can get.' And she knew exactly where she was, and how she had arrived, and why her heart had gone wild.

The car stopped, its engine died. Laurie got out and went away.

He was gone a very long time. She could hear birds calling, cars passing: no voices. She tried to picture the scene in the house – there were several alternatives, only one of them good. The bad ones were too dreadful to dwell on, but she could visualize an outcome: Laurie returning, his horror and incredulity plain on his face, his love for her utterly destroyed by what had been reported to him, by the callous depths he now knew her to be capable of.

This suspenseful waiting would kill her. Her heart's banging was now so loud it had drowned out even the birds. Her head must surely burst with blood pumping round it, double time. Be calm, *calm*, she pleaded, and tried to concentrate on her breathing. Shallow was the way – shallow, light, slow . . .

*   *   *

Laurie was back. He was sitting behind the steering wheel. 'Claire?' he said. And after a moment, 'Are you asleep?'

She couldn't manage a sound.

The engine started. The car moved – forward and back, forward and back, then steadily forward; swung off the gravel onto solid ground, and stopped.

She opened her eyes a crack. They were parked in the back yard. Laurie was leaning over to the passenger side, winding the window down an inch. Now he was getting out, and very carefully, very quietly – like a parent leaving a sleeping child for the night – shutting the car door, stealing away.

She breathed out lengthily. Slipped into unconsciousness.

People were snatching her, making off with her, pulling, jerking, man-handling. Perhaps they were bearing her off to jail – such gruff voices! – and one of them Laurie's. 'Never mind, just lift her onto it,' she heard him say.

Ah, but here was bliss . . . The smoothest softest ground imaginable.

Very far off the dream began playing. She knew she was dreaming; she could feel the bed beneath her. Her palms were flat on the bottom sheet; when she moved them, her fingers found mattress buttons. All she had to do was wake up.

But the dream's pull was irresistible. Against her will, she was drawn closer and closer into the trees, into the beautiful woods of Foscote. *Deceptively* beautiful: she knew better than to trust them. And sure enough, when she was totally surrounded, the trees – no longer benign – began to swell and twist, to encroach ominously. Now the dread wind rose up, snatching and propelling her . . . But just as she reached the heart-stopping moment, a supreme effort

451

allowed her to wrench her head to one side. To open her eyes. To find herself gazing – oh, the relief – at her own bedroom door.

But then, to her horror, the door very slowly opened. (It must have been the handle rattling that had wakened her.) And she knew with absolute certainty who was about to steal in. Lydia. Come to exact vengeance. She put out her hand to fend her off. 'No!' she cried weakly, out loud.

But it was Laurie who then swiftly came in and stood by her bedside and clasped her hand. 'Claire?'

The breath wobbled out of her. 'Oh Laurie, I thought you were Lydia,' she gabbled. 'I thought . . .'

'Lydia?' he cried. 'In here? Oh love, you have let her get to you! My fault; I should never have landed you in such an intractable mess. But how are you? Any better?'

She considered. 'Er, yes – think I am.'

'Thank goodness for that. Can I get you anything?'

'Mm. Glass of water.'

'Right.' He sped off.

She felt hopeful. He sounded very well disposed.

He came in with the glass and set it down on the bedside table. 'Would you like to sit up?'

'Yes, please.'

He found a second pillow to put behind her and helped her hitch up in the bed. Then gave her the water and watched her drink.

When she had finished, he put down the empty glass, and sat facing her on the edge of the bed. 'Love,' he said gravely, 'I've something to tell you.'

'Yeah?' she said hoarsely.

'Yesterday, Lydia died.'

'*Died?*' – the word erupted from her.

'Yes, quite a shock. When I came in yesterday, she was lying on the hall floor. I rang Dr Lessing. He came straight away, but there was nothing he could do, she'd been dead for some while. It was bound to have happened sooner or later, he said. Nevertheless, I could see the poor chap was upset. Apparently, Lydia had been to see him that morning; he'd had to be stern with her — he wondered whether he'd been *too* stern and got her seriously worked up. But as I pointed out, there was evidence she'd been up to her old tricks again — the bureau was all of a mess — a drawer pulled out, papers spilled. Maybe something disturbed her — the telephone ringing, or the doorbell — and the shock coupled with guilt just proved too much. Anyway, the theory comforted Dr Lessing. Pity it had to end like this, but there we are. At least I know I did my best for her. Thank heaven *you*'re brighter. I was so anxious last night I asked him to take a look at you. He agreed it was just a migraine, probably triggered by the strain of the Lydia business . . . And that close atmosphere yesterday didn't help. There was quite a downpour in the night. Did you hear it?'

'Nn-no.'

'It's cleared the air, made everything fresh. Shall I draw the curtains?'

'Just a little way,' she said nervously.

He went to part them. 'That far enough?'

'Mm, to begin with.'

He glanced over the front garden, over the rain-washed, sun-splashed trees and grass. 'It's a glorious day,' he said.

Coda:
AS IT WAS IN THE BEGINNING

Claire Haddingham stepping from a bus on the corner of Little Coates Road and Devonshire Avenue was a familiar sight to the greengrocer shutting shop on the opposite side of the main road, to the old lady sitting in the window bay of her ground floor flat at number 3, to the lad delivering the evening paper, and to others who returned to the area, like Claire, around five forty-five: a smart and daintily attractive figure, striding along purposely, carrying the inevitable brief-case. Tonight's outfit was a short dark tweed jacket with the collar turned up, draped grey trousers and black cuban-heeled boots; its severity relieved by a softly rolled jade green scarf looped round her shoulders.

In her late fifties, she looked a decade younger. And was possibly helped in this by a youthful haircut, and by her hair's dark colour being only sparsely invaded by grey. Facially she was much the same as ever, with none of the noticeable blurring of edges which had afflicted many of her more conventionally attractive contemporaries. Well aware of her late good fortune in the looks stakes, she sometimes – usually while surveying herself in the mirror – thought of her long dead mother. You see, Maman? she would point out. All that despair over a bit of squint, and in the end what does it signify? Such reflections brought not a jot of pain or regret; nor even triumph. She was no sentimentalist. For instance, it never occurred to her to wonder whether her promotion to Professor would have been a matter of pride to her father had he lived, or whether it would have altered Uncle Peter's pitying attitude. She was not specially proud of the achievement herself – glad to have won it, pleased with the enhanced salary it brought, but not gratified in any cumulative or self-vindicating fashion. Promotion, like other aspects of fortune, was just the way fate turned out. This was her gut feeling, and one shared, she suspected, by most of her friends. (Of the old gang, only she and Joyce had made it to Professor. Actually, Joyce had gone several steps higher, and was now Vice Chancellor of one of the new city universities – and still as Scouse as they come. Monica had retired from academia to become a full-time novelist; Liz had won a Readership; Eleanor, possibly because of her increased commitment to politics, had never progressed beyond Senior Lecturer. It was Yolande's death from cancer at age forty-three that had jolted their perspectives. Life was all at once revealed as a bit of a lottery.) Only Laurie (who had also taken early retirement to write – except that his books, unlike Monica's, were very slow coming) positively revelled in her success. The way he went on (she sometimes said to her friends), anyone'd think her professorial chair were the pinnacle of both their lives.

A cyclist overtook her, swung out round a parked car, and a little way ahead came to rest with a heavily booted foot propped on the pavement. It was one of their student lodgers, Lucy; looking like a layered pyramid, Claire thought – blond wavy hair flowing out over her shoulders, a long sweater widening over a long and full skirt: rather hazardous gear to be cycling in (specially with boots), but it was this term's indispensable uniform.

Claire was first to call a greeting. 'Good evening, Lucy.'

'Oh hi, I was hoping to catch you. It's about our cold bath tap. We can't turn it off. It's been dripping for days.'

'I see,' Claire said, with a sinking heart. 'Probably the washer needs replacing. We'll . . . um, get someone to look at it. When would be a good time?'

'We've both got lectures tomorrow morning.'

'Right. I'll see what can be done.'

'Cheers,' said Lucy. She continued pushing her bike by Claire's side, and racked her brain for a further topic. 'Quite nice at the moment, isn't it?'

'Yeah,' said Claire absently. Another sodding chore she was thinking; and never mind 'getting someone to look at it', it was one she and Laurie would have to tackle themselves. Life with students as lodgers was full of chores – someone's cooker or fridge packing up, or a radiator leaking, or a lavatory getting blocked, or one of them losing their key or smashing something. Which reminded her: 'Gary and Dave were pretty lively last night. Did they disturb you?'

'Oh, no,' Lucy replied with apparent surprise. 'They had a few people in, that's all. Me and Melanie went up there for a bit. It was great – music, a few drinks and that. It broke up at midnight. Didn't wake you and Dr Stone, did it?'

Not in a position to comment on Laurie's wakefulness or otherwise, Claire mumbled that perhaps it hadn't been too bad, and fell silent. After a few seconds, Lucy gave up. Repeating her thanks regarding the tap problem, she wheeled her bike onto the road and pedalled briskly away for the remaining few metres.

Students, like almost everything else, had changed. They were noisier, inclined to assume the right to do in their rooms anything that came into their heads, and more than ever strapped for cash. She and Laurie took rent from four students – two females on the first floor, two males on the second; but suspected that five or six were at times in residence. Also, items of food sometimes mysteriously walked from their fridge or a cupboard. Laurie preferred to turn a blind eye. Rent was paid more or less on time, and their suspicions about unofficial lodgers and pinched food were as nothing, he said, to some of the horror stories emanating from bedsit land.

We ought to have moved years ago, she told herself as she turned into the drive.

It was a thought she had frequently. They ought to have followed the example of most other senior academics and moved to one of the surrounding villages. Very few of the old crowd remained in the Avenues. Monica and David still had the house in Marlborough Avenue (and regularly escaped to their rural property in France); the Le Guinns (still fighting) had stuck it out in York Avenue, as had the Goodchilds in Northumberland Avenue. But the majority of the houses had been bought by absentee landlords and turned into flats. If only they had seized their chance during the eighties property boom when they had been approached by a company wanting to buy the house and turn it into a nursing home. (And which in the early nineties had probably gone bust, Laurie would point out, or else, to cut costs, was now packing in old ladies half a dozen to a room. 'But we'd still have the dosh,' Claire always retorted. And Laurie, raising an eyebrow, would agree with her facts but not with her dissociating from consequences.)

She was not really so hard. She shrank as much as he from the idea of their home turned into an intensive litter for grannies. But she did sometimes worry over how they would cope in this enormous house as they grew older. Such an appetite it had for cash. The fencing had blown down and had to be replaced last winter; the year before it had been roof tiles. While her salary had risen in recent years, Laurie's had taken a dip. He still received royalties from telly programme repeats and the spin-off books, but invitations to make fresh appearances were few and far between: there was now a new generation of telly pundits. It seemed to Claire that he spent more time at the university in his retirement than when he'd been paid to be there –

460

advising on this, acting as consultant on that, and generally being helpful around campus and boosting morale. No wonder the current book failed to materialize.

She reached into her pocket for the front door key. Here was another change: no-one in the Avenues ever left their door on the snib any more (a fact which, together with the general exodus, had limited the practice of dropping in); people were too wary of burglars. Laurie and Claire had lost a couple of paintings – and had promptly sold the rest, glad to bank the proceeds, glad of the resulting peace of mind. (And there had been a further bonus: the pleasure of touring Art School exhibitions together, and hanging paintings they had chosen – rather than Laurie's father – by artists trying to make a living now.)

As soon as she stepped into the house, her mood lifted. The dripping tap, which had led her into despondency, shrank to its proper size: a small blip in tomorrow morning. She closed the front door. Its glass panels reverberated slackly and threw tremulous patches of pink and pale green over the dark green carpet – an almost magical sight and sound, so dear they were, and familiar. 'I'm back,' she called, turning towards the hatstand.

She waited intently on his reply, which might indicate the presence of company – if, for instance, he called, 'At last! We thought you were lost,' or 'Well do make haste, darling, this pig, so and so, has nearly scoffed the cake.' He might be with any of several old friends – Phillip or Martin, or an ex-colleague, or Monica. Yes, Monica was often to be found in the kitchen with Laurie; she did love a little tête-à-tête. As Laurie reported it, she would phone him up around half-past three in the afternoon: 'I don't know about you, darling, but I've been stuck at this bloody word processor since half-past eight this morning. Isn't it time we authors took a break? – your place or mine?'

461

Sometimes Laurie would go round to Marlborough Avenue, but more generally Monica came here – this, because Laurie was conscious of his domestic responsibilities and would always leave after an hour, whereas Monica could sit gossiping for as long as she pleased at number 97, and was only shamed into leaving when Claire returned. 'My goodness, David will be home, poor lamb,' she would cry, kissing Claire and pausing to exchange a few words with her before finally departing. But tonight Claire was answered in the manner she preferred – with a signal that Laurie was alone, that she had him all to herself.

'Welcome home, pet. I've put the kettle on.'

Home, she thought. The nub of the matter. Unwinding and hanging up her scarf (opposite his shabby old hat), she thought how right Laurie had been to see all the snags and none of the benefits in moving house. If letting rooms became too much of a bother, why, they could simply desist; let the place crumble gently around them, as they themselves crumbled. Why not? – they had no-one to leave it to. It was unthinkable that they would ever leave. This slightly battered and faded home had been fashioned from dreams and ashes of their shared pasts. Once, she had literally fought to retain it, she remembered, going down the hall to the kitchen and stepping a little hesitantly over a certain place on the carpet.

'Hi,' she said, going to kiss him. 'What bliss to be back.'

'Grim meeting?' he asked, as he poured her tea.

'Tedious. Some blokes really get a charge out of the sound of their own voices.'

'I know, dear. But were you able to make your points?'

'Yes, and very glad we'd worked on them beforehand, specially when that sneaky bastard Doug Whitehead tried tripping me up. So thank you, darling.' (For the points had been more Laurie's than hers; his patient schooling still came in handy.)

'Nothing to do with me, I'm sure. But start at the beginning. Tell me all about it.'

He stood at the draining-board podding peas as he listened. She turned sideways in her chair to watch him. 'Well,' she began . . .

It could not be said that Laurie failed to show his years – the shock of white hair was a startling testament; also, his faced was lined, and his bearing a little stooped. The heedless speed of passing time left him deeply anxious, and much thought and care he expended on warding off the hour when it would finally run out – paid stricter attention than ever to diet, exercise and cleanliness, and set great store by vitamin and mineral supplements. In fact, it was in the back of his mind as he listened to Claire that very soon, an hour or so before dinner, was the recommended time to swallow a royal jelly capsule. Similarly, an hour or so after dinner was the very best time to take iron and zinc. There were so many little aids on the sideboard, in bottles and tubs and sachets and packets, all with differing instructions attached, that it was almost a life's work to keep up with them. Specially when it was prudent to do so discreetly. For yes, his coddling ways did rather get on Claire's nerves. She didn't exactly complain, but he could sense her impatience, and at times her irritation.

'That was a first class cuppa,' she declared, rising to her feet. 'Anything I can do before I fall into a bath?'

'Not a thing. Go and relax,' he ordered. And when it was safe, when the sound of her feet running upstairs had faded, went briskly to the sideboard and unscrewed the lid of the appropriate jar.

After dinner they went to sit in the dining-room (which functioned these days purely as Laurie's writing room; all eating, even with dinner guests, took place in the kitchen).

463

'Anything on the box?' asked Claire. (If there were, or if Laurie felt like playing the piano or listening to tapes, they would progress into the sitting-room.)

'Might be something worth watching at half-nine on Channel Four.'

'Right,' said Claire. Unless Laurie wanted to view, she herself wouldn't bother, not when it was just the two of them.

Over her newspaper, she covertly studied him. She didn't fool herself that he hadn't aged. But she was certain he was as attractive as ever. Indeed, had often been confirmed in her opinion by noting other people's reactions. She had only to watch from her office window as he crossed the quad to see how he still raised a flutter among the undergraduates. Freshers, she was sure, continued to send home the breathless news that they had seen, and even spoken with, Dr Laurie Stone of television fame. His arrival during union debates always raised the excitement level, just as his attendance at departmental meetings (in an advisory capacity) invariably boosted morale. Laurie was still a star. She still had to pinch herself sometimes to think she was the one (out of countless others over the years who would have jumped at the chance) he chose to spend his life with.

She sighed, as the moment approached to ruffle their cosiness – for if she didn't mention the dripping tap soon it might altogether slip her mind.

'I spoke to Lucy on the way home, by the way. Their cold bath tap needs fixing. Sounds like the washer.'

'Yes?' he said calmly – as if, she noted, it were not the most fearful nuisance and all down to them, but simply a matter of calling in a plumber and to hell with the expense.

'Well, I expect we can remember how to do it,' she said. 'And if not, there's always the book.' (*The Do-It-Yourself Guide to Home Maintenance* had been a frequent life-saver.) 'Tomorrow morning might be a good time, when both girls have lectures.' For neither

464

she nor Laurie had any desire to be caught groping with the lodgers' plumbing.

'I'll go to the shops first thing, call at the D.I.Y., then when I come back we'll give it a whirl.'

'Good,' she smiled, and kicked off her shoes and tucked her feet under her. Laurie opened a novel lent him by Monica.

Half an hour later the doorbell rang.

'Let 'em bugger off?' he suggested, to forestall any implication when he jumped up to answer the call that he was not blissfully content to be sitting alone with her.

She grinned, said nothing. He couldn't fool *her*, the fearful old fraud. As she had foreseen, when the bell rang again, he was up like lightning (never mind his tut of impatience). And two seconds later it was: 'Hell*o!* Come in! Don't be ridiculous, dear boy. Claire was just saying she was faint with boredom. You've arrived in the very nick. Claire, darling, it's Michael.'

'Lovely,' she called obligingly, but continued to read her newspaper.

Laurie drew up an extra chair, then fussed around getting drinks – brandy and ginger for the guest, neat brandy for Claire, mineral water for himself. At last sat down and crossed his long legs, and with an insouciant air, playing elegant fingers against the side of his tumbler, proceeded to tease, to flatter, to charm.

Michael, a young English don who had recently been involved in a student drama production, was duly charmed, flattered, thrilled; he constantly swept back his fall of flaxen hair, and in his chair gave eager little forward shuffles.

Not a chance, babe, Claire silently told him. He wouldn't touch Adonis himself with a bargepole; it might shorten his life by fifty seconds.

At nine twenty-five precisely, adroitly cutting into his guest's shy description of a play he had written, Laurie slapped his knees. 'There's a programme on now that you *must see*,' he cried, as if it were only

Michael's presence that made it required viewing. 'Come along.'

They picked up their drinks and trooped after him into the sitting-room to sit where he indicated – Claire and Michael at either end of the sofa, Laurie in a neighbouring chair. Throughout the programme – which was about newly discovered cave paintings in France – Michael watched avidly, as if alert for special meanings, deep clues.

'Amazing,' sighed Laurie contentedly when it was over. 'One can only wonder at the significance of those outlandishly exaggerated private parts.'

Michael had just opened his mouth to make his response (having delayed for a moment in order to form one that would cast him in an interesting light), when Laurie caught sight of the time. (Bedtime, garlic capsule time, and ditto of evening primrose.) 'My dear boy, lovely as it has been to see you, we old codgers do have to be getting our heads down.' He rose. Michael soon followed suit. 'But do come again – oh, and bring that script to show me, it sounds fascinating. Ah, but don't come next week,' he recollected, leading his guest to the sitting-room door, 'because Claire and I will be away. We're off on Saturday for our Whitsun jolly in the Lakes. We find a break now and then gives us some pep, don't we, darling?'

She nodded and called a meek 'Goodnight' – as befitted her understanding that the game had changed and they were now in their dotage. (Laurie might crave company, but she knew he could only stand it in small dollops.)

Having disposed of Michael, Laurie returned for their empty glasses. Claire rose to help. 'No, stay where you are,' he commanded, wanting time alone with the fortifying contents of his jars and packets.

'Bring me some water, then,' she said through a yawn, and pressed the ON switch of the remote control.

A quarter of an hour later he was back in the

doorway with her glass of water. 'Well, dear, I shall go up.'

She sprang to her feet, stabbed off the television. 'Me too. I'm bushed.'

They went upstairs, turning lights off behind them. Outside Claire's door, they paused. She held her glass of water to one side to save it being slopped by his bear-hug.

'Night, night, pet,' he said, pressing a kiss into her hair.

'Goodnight, Laurie love,' she answered.

With which they parted, each to their separate rooms.

In the morning, Laurie left early for the shops. As well as a washer for the dripping tap, he needed to collect food for this evening's meal. Normally when they were about to go away for a few days, they would make do with odds and ends. But tonight Monica and David were coming to dinner.

Claire put everything in readiness – a bowl, pair of rubber gloves, cleaning liquid and cloth, then occupied herself with a duster while listening for sounds heralding the girls' departure.

Here they came: great booted feet clomping downstairs. A pause as they collected their bikes (during which Claire moved to the window); then the back door banged open, and one after the other, in flowing layers, with rucksacks strapped to their shoulders, Lucy and Melanie emerged, wheeling their bikes.

The moment they disappeared round the side of the house, Claire sprang into action: gathered the bowl and cleaning equipment, ran up the back stairs to the girls' bathroom. For just as Laurie with his pre-meeting coaching armed *her* against the argumentative so-and-so's at work, so she sought to protect *him* from various aspects of room letting which she feared would be seriously upsetting. This morning she had in mind rings and stains in the bath and grubby articles of female underclothing left around.

Her fears proved justified. Knickers, bras, socks and towels lay scattered over the bathroom floor, a sweater had been left to soak in the basin, and the state of the bath made even her flinch. But first she would get rid of the clothes. The sweater she decided to leave, but gingerly hung the towels over a rail, then gathered up the smalls and took them to the nearest bedroom (Lucy's). She opened the door and tossed them inside (ownership to be disputed later); but then, finding one of the bras had caught under the closing door, she had to open it wider and scoot the whole bundle further into the room. Which brought to her attention the astounding mess within. Hell's bells! she thought, staring round. One of the curtains was hanging off the rail, half unhooked. It was a simple matter to rectify, but the wretched girl had been too idle to bother. She marched over to attend to it herself, annoyed to think of the poor impression of the house given to anyone looking up from next door's garden. Too short to reach the curtain trail, she pulled a chair over from the desk to stand on, and had the curtain hanging properly in seconds. Shaking her head at the indolence of youth, she climbed down and returned the chair.

But now the clutter on the desktop detained her. How in heaven's name was any work achieved on it? An open note pad with scrawled writing over the top page lay uppermost. As her eyes fell on it, her own name leapt at her. Taken aback, she leant over to scrutinize the relevant sentence. *Me and Melanie (the girl I share with) sort of assumed Haddingham was her professional name.* What could this be about? She began to read the entire page, which evidently formed part of an unfinished letter.

Remember me telling you about the landlord, Dr Laurie Stone, who used to be on that nature programme on telly and is *very* fanciable? Well, it turns out he and the landlady (who's a prof of Biology or something) aren't actually married. Me and Melanie (the girl I share with) sort of assumed Haddingham was her professional name. But someone Melanie knows in drama soc told her they've been together for years but can't get married because he's married already. And guess what? His wife lives in the next street! She's an invalid – lost a leg in a car accident, so it'd look sort of bad to divorce her. Someone actually saw him pushing her round the park in a wheelchair. It's funny because I only said to Melanie the other day that Stone and Haddingham act a bit lovey-dovey for a regular married couple. We were watching them from an upstairs window at the time. They were walking round the garden hand in hand, then she stopped to look at something and he put his arms round her. And they just stood like that for ages, like they were a couple of kids, not about a hundred years old.

Talking about Biology profs. There's a really weird old creep called Le Guinn. Years ago when his wife had a miscarriage, he actually pickled what came out and stuck it in the lab. No kidding! It's been there ever since. Anyone can go and look . . .

Fancy that old chestnut about the Le Guinns still going around, thought Claire. She turned rather dazedly aside, but remained so bemused by what had been written about herself and Laurie, that she sat down on the chair to read it again. And afterwards was unsure whether to be annoyed, amused or touched. Where the hell did they get such rubbish? What innocent little remark or occurrence had triggered off that fantasy? Then an image came to her – Zena in a wheelchair. Of course! About a decade ago, Laurie's old friend and colleague, Zena Turweston, broke her leg in a skiing accident, and Laurie, like many others – indeed, like Claire herself – had taken his turn to push her where she needed to go. Witnessed, no doubt, by some bright spark with an over-active imagination. And ever after, the story passing to the new crop of freshers, poor old Zena had provided the key to why Stone and Haddingham were 'together' but unmarried. Too bad that Zena no longer resided 'in the next street' but in Dublin with her husband of thirty-odd years! She was going to enjoy telling this one to Laurie. Though on seconds thoughts, maybe she wasn't. Laurie had scruples about reading other people's letters.

She got out of the chair. And as she did so, was struck by a further thought. The way rumour had accounted for her and Laurie was so incredibly old hat, so darned conventional. Being tragically unfree to marry was the sort of thing her own generation of undergrads might have come up with. So much for modern day sophistication!

But time was getting on. She had better put on a spurt.

Twenty minutes later, having seen through his eyes the squalor of bath, basin, lavatory, and floor, and dealt with all appropriately, she at last judged the room fit for Laurie's attentions.

It was with some trepidation that Laurie, armed with his tool box, pushed open the bathroom door. 'How reassuringly clean,' he cried in relief. 'I thought they seemed nice wholesome girls.' He knelt to investigate the problem, and Claire stood by with the D.I.Y. manual. In the event, the operation proved perfectly straightforward. 'That wasn't too difficult, was it?' he asked. As though the problems with letting rooms which she sometimes pointed out to him were grossly exaggerated, products of an overly pessimistic outlook.

That evening, Monica and David arrived promptly. They knew their host too well to delay; for at number 97, time was short however delightful. As they had laughingly reminded each other on the way over, by

470

eleven o'clock Laurie would have had quite enough of them to be going on with.

The dinner was delicious (even though the cook eschewed use of cream or butter), and Claire enjoyed it all the more for having had no hand in its preparation. No-one wanted coffee afterwards. They were content to linger at the table finishing their wine (or in Laurie's case mineral water). What, David asked, did they think of Thorpe's latest proposal for marking the turn of the century? But Laurie embargoed this line of chat. He was sick of the subject, and hoped when midnight came on the fateful eve to be allowed to ignore it. Monica, aware of how Laurie disliked to be reminded of time galloping by, quickly came up with a piece of gossip. Claire was filled with warmth for her. Totting up the years, she was staggered to calculate Monica's age as sixty-two. It seemed scarcely possible. She was still marvellous to look at, as vivid as ever, full of bounce and verve. David, several years her junior, was balding and a little paunchy; but he was still the same nice man with the same dry wit and the same endearing passion for Monica.

Having drained her glass, Monica insisted Laurie should play for her. She dragged him away to the sitting-room. Sharing the last inch of wine in the bottle between his glass and Claire's, David introduced the subject of the new Vice Chancellor. Claire related a tale she'd heard about this individual, and took a dish to soak in the sink. At which David started clearing the table, and eventually picked up a tea cloth. 'We may as well,' he said, when she paused and raised an eyebrow. 'Those two are well away.' (Gershwin was pouring from the baby grand.) They grinned, and got on with the chore and continued their gossip. Afterwards David excused himself and went off to the cloakroom. And Claire sauntered into the sitting-room.

At the piano, Laurie was now playing 'Night And Day'. It was not his usual kind of piece, and though Claire was no judge of musical style, she suspected he was camping it up a little. Monica was stretched full length on the sofa, her head thrown back, her eyes closed, in an attitude of ravished abandonment. Claire's suspicions regarding Laurie's performance were confirmed when he turned his head and winked at her.

And it suddenly came to her that Monica had always had a thing for Laurie. And that knowing this (for Laurie knew everything about everyone), and taking pity, Laurie had doled himself out to her over the years in tiny and infrequent consolatory measures – a bit of banter over a drink, sympathy over a meal, an exchange of books, little gifts, the odd confidence. Oh Laurie, she thought . . . Her eyes filled. Turning her head away, her misty gaze sweeping over the sofa misread Monica's shape lying there, and for a spilt second reported Lydia – as years ago, in the very same attitude, she had actually seen Lydia. Her legs went weak. She went quickly to a chair and sat down. So after all, Laurie did not know everything about everyone, she remembered. And for a moment, closed her eyes.

Lydia's death was not a memory she dwelt on. She was too ruthlessly honest to allow herself any truck with regretfulness or guilt. Only once had it seriously disturbed her. She and Laurie were guests at a dinner party given by Eleanor and Leon Goodchild. The talk turned to a case in the news, of a man who had refrained from helping an aunt taken suddenly ill because, he claimed, she had repeatedly declared she was weary of life. On the grounds of his omission he was charged with her murder. Some people at the table argued that he ought not to have been charged with anything, others that the charge was more properly manslaughter. But a lawyer present pronounced that in the eyes of the law, deliberate failure to take measures to prevent a death, did, in fact, constitute murder. Though Claire had remained outwardly calm, some hard and heavy object seemed to have crashed

472

on her head, jolting her into horrid clear-sightedness. What she had done was no longer ambiguous, but clean-cut.

David came into the room. He stole over to the sofa, leaned over his wife and tickled the soles of her stockinged feet. Monica squealed. Claire opened her eyes. Laurie took his hands from the keyboard.

'Are you all right, pet?' Laurie asked.

It frightened Claire a little to realize he had been watching her; but even Laurie could not see into minds.

'You look white as a sheet,' he continued. 'These people have tired you out.'

At which the people concerned collected themselves. 'Gosh yes, look at the time,' grinned David. Monica reached for her shoes.

'Don't go yet,' Claire protested. 'Ignore him. He's impossible.'

'No, no. You two have to make an early start tomorrow.'

'We do indeed,' Laurie shamelessly confirmed. 'Nine o'clock sharp.'

'Oh Laurie, so early?' Claire groaned, thinking of the packing she had to complete, of all the running round the house to be done in the morning, turning things off and leaving notes for people.

In the hall they took part in a four-way hug. Monica and David were off to the States in three days' time and would not be back for several months.

'Goodbye darlings. Have a lovely holiday.'

'Oh, we'll miss you. Take care. Write lots.'

'Bye Laurie. Bye Claire.'

'Try not to drink America dry, Mrs Cage.'

'I hate you, Laurie Stone – remember that.'

'Bye David. Bye Monica'

'Bye-ee!'

'Phew,' said Laurie when he had closed the front door. 'Nice evening?'

'Lovely.'

473

'Now, darling, do be ready on time tomorrow. It would be nice to walk round the lake before dinner.' (They were to stay in Buttermere, one of their favourite places.) 'And don't forget your boots. We lost an hour last time, having to come back for them.'

'They're already packed,' she lied.

They were almost ready to leave when the postman came down the drive. Laurie was at the back of the house, exchanging last minute words with one of the lodgers. Claire, on her way to the car, was handed two items of mail. One was a circular. On the second she recognized Jeanette's rolling hand and favoured green ink. It felt like a card inside. Oh my God – what was the betting the woman had remembered Laurie's birthday? – despite that for the past decade he had decreed it should be ignored. Claire ran with the mail upstairs to her room. She chucked the circular in the wastepaper basket, then ripped open Jeanette's envelope. As she had thought . . . Hell no, it was worse! The scatterbrain had only gone and anticipated the big Six-O by two whole years! In red on the front of the card, the message shrieked: *Congratulations! Sixty years young today!* And inside, in green: *This is one we just couldn't ignore! Love, Jeanette, Richard, and the boys. xxxx.*

She tore the card and its envelope into shreds and stuffed it under the circular in the wastepaper basket. Then galloped down to the hall where Laurie was standing looking impatient. 'Sorry, I forgot my lip salve,' she said, duplicitously patting her shoulder-bag.

'Have you forgotten anything else, do you think?'

'No, no.'

'Right. Then off we jolly well go.'

They stopped for a snack at Charnock Richard. By half-past three they had checked into the hotel, drunk tea in the sitting-room, unpacked in their respective rooms and changed into walking gear.

They set off along the farm track towards the lake. Their boots skidded off stones which stood proud in the compacted earth and were polished to a shine by the thousands of passing feet tramping by every year towards a lakeside walk or a stiff climb up Red Pike. Full of joy at being back in this place, Claire broke into a run.

Watching her dart ahead, Laurie had a sudden memory of chasing after her up the bank of the paddock as a child, and how comical she had looked plopping from side to side with her heels flying up. Then a white terrier shot towards and past them (soon followed by its fell-running master) and sprang a further memory: of the day they had strayed over the boundary in the woods and the forester had set his dog after them. So clearly did he recall details of the chase – twigs snapping beneath them, startled birds rising and calling, flashing greenery, sharp odours, that it was hard to believe half a century separated then and now.

She had reached the wooden bridge and now paused on it, waiting for him to catch up. The air was full of the noise of Sour Milk Gill, roaring and crashing down from Bleaberry Coomb. But the stream running beneath her feet flowed from the lake in stealthy silence; it was crystal clear; looking down, she could see its green silt bed heaped over with small pink rocks. She raised her eyes to scan the lake, and trace the long spine of Fleetwith Pike.

Approaching, he opened his mouth to share his recollection, to call, Remember when we were at Foscote? (a phrase which opened so many of their conversations nowadays). But decided against it. Don't hark back, he thought: look forward.

'Where shall we go tomorrow? The forecast is good.'

She turned to him. 'Haystacks is a nice one to start with.'

'So it is. Good. We'll do Haystacks.'

*   *   *

'I'm throwing caution to the winds this morning,' he said, tucking into a carton of low-fat yoghurt.

He was buoyed by a lucky feeling. Breakfast in this charming and familiar hotel dining-room on the first morning of their holiday – and the sun pouring in! (Invariably, on the journey up, they declared they didn't mind how the weather turned out, for it was abundant rainfall that made this the most beautiful place on earth; nevertheless, it was always gratifying to discover they had hit on a fine patch.) Any man in his position would count himself fortunate. But the miracle to Laurie was not knowing it, but *feeling* it. For once, optimism had overridden his besetting anxiety. Perhaps it was this that had emboldened him to select yoghurt from the buffet table, instead of following his usual procedure. (Which was to spoon dry oats, dry wheatflakes, dry nuts and raisins into a bowl and moisten them with a drop of orange juice; or call the waiter and ask for porridge, giving strict instructions that it be made with water, not milk – and should the waiter enquire 'Cream, sir?', bark 'No cream, no milk, just water!' – like some batty old colonel, Claire once hissed, hiding her embarrassment behind the breakfast menu.) Maybe optimism was part of it, but the real impetus behind his choice had been the sight of Claire helping herself to half a grapefruit, a Weetabix swimming in full-cream milk, while conveying to the waiter that she was dying for a pot of tea and could murder a kipper and a mountain of toast. So cheery and vigorous and top-of-the-morning she looked, moving through a shaft of sunlight in her navy walking trews and crisp white shirt. So dainty, going lightly over the carpet with her goodies to their table in the window. It had occurred to him just then to wonder how in God's name she managed to put up with him. He must drive her mad with his fussing and fretting, his squinting suspiciously at Nutritional Information on the side of packets, his frankly unattractive self-obsession. Poor little darling, he had thought. And full of remorse and fortified by his lucky feeling, had plucked up the carton of yoghurt.

Naturally, he rather hoped it would not escape her attention. Hence, as he began to eat it, that self-mocking remark. It was neat, he thought, the way it drew attention to his virtue and also acknowledged what a tedious old pain-in-the-neck he realized he'd become.

But all wasted, apparently. She didn't appear to have heard. She seemed taken up with something going on behind his shoulder, perhaps at another table. Now her gaze shifted to the sideboard where the waiter and waitress whispered together – maybe she was impatient for her kipper. Or maybe she *had* heard the remark but was not amused by it; simply fed-up to the back teeth with his pernickety ways and fast going off him altogether. In his heart of hearts he knew this couldn't be so (not Claire, not staunch, loyal, beloved Claire); he was just toying with the notion because it would serve him darn well right . . .

Ah, but her eyes had returned to the table. Indeed, were encountering the yoghurt pot. Now she was putting her head on one side, fixing on him that wry grin. (He was lucky indeed, life couldn't be finer.)

'There's *brave*,' she said.

OUTSIDE, LOOKING IN

KATHLEEN ROWNTREE

"SPARKLING . . . A DELIGHTFUL COMEDY'
Cosmopolitan

Aston Favell had many features of which it was justly proud –
the fact that it had come second in the Best Kept Village
Competition, its listed houses, and Mrs Bullivant's bring and
buy coffee mornings (there were, perhaps, too many of her
crocheted pot holders but no one ever had the courage to say
so). But now Aston Favell had something the inhabitants didn't
really want – a Peeping Tom. First spying on a courting couple
at Ellwood's farm, then on the ladies' exercise class in the
village hall, the Peeping Tom sends a frisson of unease round
the homes of Aston Favell.

To Kate Woolard the intruder meant more than unease. A young
widow, slowly recovering from her husband's death and fighting
against the trauma of loneliness-induced fear, the Peeping Tom
nearly shattered her growing equilibrium. Courageously she
tried to go about her normal life, part-time teaching at a local
school, and helping her friend, Will McLeod, with the tragic
problems of caring for his wife who has Alzheimer's. Will and
Kate, both emotionally wracked, do not need extra stress in their
lives.

Slowly, as the Peeping Tom – outside, looking in – observes the
everyday events of the village, many private and domestic
scenes are revealed, the most surprising being the finally
discovered identity of Aston Favell's spy.

Rich in hilarious, poignant, and eccentric characters, *Outside,
Looking In* captures all the tensions of contemporary village life
whilst at the same time telling a story of great emotional impact.

'SEETHES WITH EVERYDAY HUMAN CONCERNS . . .
POIGNANT COMEDY'
Madeline Kingsley, *She*

0 552 99606 8

BLACK SWAN

BETWEEN FRIENDS
KATHLEEN ROWNTREE

'THE FUNNIEST PORTRAIT OF VILLAGE TRIVA SINCE E.M.
DELAFIELD'S *DIARY OF A PROVINCIAL LADY*'
Cosmopolitan

Wychwood was a charming and enthusiastically organized
village. The women, with their pine-fitted kitchens and glowing
Agas, ran everything with tireless efficiency, from the W.I.
meetings (Dress a Wooden Spoon, and How to Decorate an Egg)
to Brasso-ing the church lectern and making mock-crab
sandwiches for the Christmas Bazaar. One hardly expected a
liasion to flourish in such exemplary surroundings.

But when Tessa Brierley discovered that her husband was
having an affair with Maddy Storr, she was doubly perturbed –
for Maddy was not only the life and soul of the village and
President of the W. I., but was also her very best friend, a friend
whom Tessa did not want to lose.

Stoically, resourcefully, observed by a community celebrating
crises, tragedies, and local festivities in its own eccentric
Wychwood way, Tessa began to plan how she would keep both
her husband and her friend.

'A HUMDINGER – SHARP AND DELIGHTFULLY
ENTERTAINING. A VILLAGE STORY IN THE SPLENDID
TRADITION OF JOANNA TROLLOPE'
Publishing News

'SPARKLING . . . A DELIGHTFUL SOCIAL COMEDY WITH
UNDERTONES OF REAL PAIN'
Cosmopolitan

0 552 99506 1

BLACK SWAN

A SELECTED LIST OF FINE WRITING AVAILABLE FROM BLACK SWAN

THE PRICES SHOWN BELOW WERE CORRECT AT THE TIME OF GOING TO PRESS. HOWEVER TRANSWORLD PUBLISHERS RESERVE THE RIGHT TO SHOW NEW PRICES ON COVERS WHICH MAY DIFFER FROM THOSE PREVIOUSLY ADVERTISED IN THE TEXT OR ELSEWHERE.

All Transworld titles are available by post from:

Book Service By Post, PO Box 29, Douglas, Isle of Man IM99 1BQ

Credit cards accepted. Please telephone 01624 675137, fax 01624 670923 or Internet http://www.bookpost.co.uk for details.

Please allow £0.75 per book for post and packing UK.
Overseas customers allow £1 per book for post and packing.